AND THE TRUTH SHALL BE TOLD

To Simone Aubry:
the explorer who repeats her
dreams— Life is an adventure!
affectionately

By *Mia de Laire*

Mia de Laire

authorHOUSE™

1663 LIBERTY DRIVE, SUITE 200
BLOOMINGTON, INDIANA 47403
(800) 839-8640
WWW.AUTHORHOUSE.COM

AuthorHouse™
1663 Liberty Drive, Suite 200
Bloomington, IN 47403
www.authorhouse.com
Phone: 1-800-839-8640

AuthorHouse™ UK Ltd.
500 Avebury Boulevard
Central Milton Keynes, MK9 2BE
www.authorhouse.co.uk
Phone: 08001974150

This novel is a fictional story rooted in history. In some places I have utilized the names of historical people who play a real part in the story. While their depictions are based on their characters and their place in history, this is a novel and no implication or conclusion of any kind should be drawn from it about real events in which they, or any other person might have participated.

First published by AuthorHouse 8/8/2007

ISBN: 1-4208-4770-8 (sc)

Printed in the United States of America
Bloomington, Indiana

This book is printed on acid-free paper.

Dedication

This book is dedicated to those who seek the truth and to my family.

Chapter One

The Agency had called him to the office — a small room at the back of the old brick post office on 69th St. and Third Ave. in New York City. The entrance was a nondescript door, glass reinforced with chicken wire and signs saying, "This Building is Protected by a Security System," "Do Not Enter," and "Trespassers Will be Prosecuted." A camera above the door followed what was happening in the street. The large brass buzzer, hardly noticeable to the left of the door, hadn't been cleaned in years. He pushed the buzzer, heard no noise, and pushed again while looking up into the camera.

How long will they make me wait this time; they know I have an appointment, he thought as he looked at his watch. Five thirty on the dot. It already had been a long, hot day. He had started work at six this morning, pumping gas at a station on 96th and the East River. At least there you had a breeze. Walking to the office, the hot air burned his throat and brought the humidity and exhaust fumes that shrouded the city deep into his lungs. While he waited he watched the heat rise in waves from the street and sidewalk and smelled the hot tires of the passing cars. *Soon,* he thought, *I'll be out of here. The heat in Africa will be different. At least my lungs won't burn.* The door popped open, letting out a thin stream of air-conditioned pleasure.

He stepped into the cool hall and headed for the stairs, ignoring the opened elevator door that waited for him. He saw no one as he walked up the two flights of stairs to a long, dimly lit hall and on to the office at the end. He knocked three times and again a camera surveyed him until his director opened the door.

"Come in, come in. Call me Aubrey. How's the service station training going?"

"Fine, just fine," Peter said while his thoughts raced, *The streets of New York are the best training I've been through. People who are supposed to be honest are dishonest and vice versa. To survive in this city I need an eye in the back of my head, antennae on all sides, a cat's night vision, and a highly developed sense of smell.*

Smell was important if you wanted something decent to eat. It also let you know if there were drugs around. He seldom smelled the sweet, acrid odor of grass in this area of town. Marijuana was found mostly in the Bowery, Greenwich Village, or on the West Side where most of the flower people lived. He'd tried it. The Agency had them "try" a lot of things and he had decided he enjoyed sex more than marijuana.

"I've asked you to come in today because we are looking at the Belgian Congo as an eventual assignment for you," Aubrey said. "Your French is obviously necessary. Your German will be helpful, too. There are a large number of Germans working in the area trying to get their hands on some of the mineral deposits in the Katanga. The British, as you know, have most of the holdings in the south and they are the ones who put the railroad through to the coast through Angola. So they know exactly what is being shipped out and where it's going. We'd like to keep it that way."

Tilting back in his comfortable chair, Aubrey was silent for a moment as he looked at the young man in front of him. Peter Landon was good-looking — photogenic, really. He had an easy smile, which showed a beautifully even row of teeth and expressive blue eyes that easily seduced all he came in contact with. His report had said he was born in 1930 of German parents (both Jewish) and became a naturalized American in 1955 after a stint with U.S. Army Intelligence.

Peter was about six feet tall with not an ounce of fat and in excellent physical condition. His shirt and tie, appropriate for this meeting, were perfectly tailored, ample enough so the hot night's sweat didn't completely soak him. He was an accomplished dresser and knew how to dress for any occasion — from working gas station pumps to black tie or tails. He always looked good. Right now, however, his dark, softly wavy hair drooped in the heat like a wilted flower on top of his head, and his face was covered with perspiration, which he wiped away with a linen handkerchief.

Peter had been given files on every French-speaking colony or country in Africa and probably had his own opinion on each. Since he didn't take up the subject, Aubrey continued. "We'll be sending you out some time next year. I suggest you find yourself a wife before you leave. Try to find one who speaks some French, who enjoys travel, and also who wouldn't mind leaving for some far-off country." With a smirk on his face he continued, "The adventurous kind, healthy, good-looking, if possible, and someone who can get along in a foreign culture. The other qualities I'll leave up to you. You'll be the one living with her."

"This is not what I had in mind," replied Peter. "You know I like women, I don't know if I can do this." Aubrey's one-sided smile irked Peter—and his dyed blond hair didn't go well with his deep brown eyes.

"Well, you have some time before we send you out. Try to find someone. Of course, she cannot know what you really do. It would put her in too much danger. You have to keep your mouth shut on that one. We still don't know what your cover will be."

"My God, Aubrey, I really don't want to get married." He started to squirm in his chair and his face was again covered in sweat; he wiped it off. He got up and paced the small room. Although it was air conditioned, he was suffocating. "I can't do this. I really can't do this — at least not right away." He paused, thought and said, "Oh, I'll look around, but if I don't find someone, will you send me anyway?"

"I don't know. They told me to strongly suggest that you find yourself a wife. She should be an American — easier for us to handle if you get into trouble. We're pushing for independence in certain African colonies and need to have maximum influence in the more wealthy ones. The Katanga is rich — diamonds, uranium, tin, cobalt and copper, some gold and silver. We're particularly interested in controlling the uranium so other countries won't have access to atomic energy."

"Is there anything else we need to talk about?"

"Give some serious thought to finding a wife. Eventually children — one or two — it would help as part of your cover. Take your time. She's out there somewhere. I had to do the same thing and I'm still married — two kids, just two. It's okay and it can make your life easier. Really."

Peter sat looking at the floor, stunned. What would he do with a wife? At this moment several women waited for him, even a married, blond, blue-eyed, all-American girl. He loved to run his fingers through her long, silky hair, to touch every inch of her beautiful body, to run his tongue around her hardened nipples and between her legs. She was great in bed, but he would have to give her up. She'd never marry him and go to Africa. She loved to travel, but not that far. Besides, that one was married.

"Shit," he finally said out loud. "Okay, Aubrey, I'm out of here unless you have some other good news for me." He stood up and would have

3

glared at Aubrey, but the short conversation had thrown him and all he wanted to do was get out.

"Sorry," Aubrey said with a smile. "Our next meeting is for November. You'll continue your training with Calder Oil. They're moving you into the office downtown sometime next month. And no screwing around with the secretaries."

"Don't worry, I have more than I can handle right now." He walked to the door, loosening his tie as he turned, "Anyway, you know where to find me if you need me." He opened the door and walked out, trying not to slam it.

"Married. Me married," he mumbled angrily as he walked rapidly down the hall. He pulled off his tie; shoved it into his pocket and undid the top four buttons of his shirt. He ran down the stairs and slammed the door behind him when he reached the street. The hot evening hit him full blast and penetrated every inch of his body. He slowed his pace as he rolled up his sleeves, thinking he'd have to change his shirt anyway before he picked up his date for the evening.

His life was now in total confusion and he needed to work it out. He increased his speed until his lungs burned and his heart didn't want to go on any more and reached his apartment at 96th and Park in no time at all. He ducked into the shower, unable to face his roommates. He planned to make love all night, four or five times, until all he could do was sleep. Tomorrow was his day off. *I'll go to Jones Beach, take in the sun, get battered by the waves and then think about my future.*

Chapter Two

The bitter cold New York wind swirled snow around the dirty streets picking up on its way a hat or two not held down with a steady hand. A hobo, happy to catch something new, covered his head in this February weather. As Peter approached the hobo called, "Hey, mister, could you spare a quarter for a cup of coffee?"

"It's too cold to wander the streets tonight," Peter answered. "Here's a dollar, go get yourself something to eat in a warm place." *Or you might freeze to death,* he said to himself.

"Thanks, mister, and bless you." The hobo turned around to approach another person hurrying home in the dim evening light.

Peter, arriving at an Upper East Side apartment building he knew well, shook off the snow from his overcoat and walked in.

"Good evening, John. How's it going? I see there's a crowd already. Any beauties?"

"Yes, sir, Mr. Landon. Lots of beautiful women and handsome young men, as usual." John knew most of his tenants' friends by now. For more than fifteen years he had been opening the door for these people. He knew them, and they knew him.

Peter shook the remaining snow off his brown felt hat and put it on the coat rack before handing his coat to the attendant.

"Good evening, Mary, and the top of the evening to you," he said with an Irish accent and a broad smile.

"And the bottom of the evenin' to you, sir," she answered with a laugh. "Now don't you be gettin' yourself into any trouble this evenin'. There's lots of pretty women there. I'll be lookin' to see who you're leavin' the party with." She was always happy to see him for he was not a snob and was a lot of fun for everyone.

He took the elevator to the tenth floor where the crowd had gathered. He smelled alcohol and cigarettes before he had even left the elevator and the chatter assaulted his cold ears, which he massaged gently before walking in to look for his hostess. He rapidly glanced across the room and then focused on a beauty surrounded by several men and women all in stitches over a story she was telling.

She was tall and slim with shiny chestnut hair piled into a French twist. The red baubles of her mobile earrings matched the color of her sensuous lips, which were in constant motion. Her simple black dress gave an illusion of a young athletic woman, which wasn't his criterion for being attractive.

"Hello, Peter. That's Lara. I'm surprised you two haven't met before. She skis every weekend in Vermont. Mad River Glen, I believe. Isn't that where you go?"

"Oh, hi, Pam. How'd you know who I was looking at?" He put his arm around her and embraced her.

"You've been standing there gawking for a few minutes. Come on, I'll introduce you." She took his arm and started towards the group. Peter was too surprised to say that wasn't what he had in mind and let himself be taken in hand. Actually their eyes had already met, and Lara who had noticed this handsome man as he had stood waiting, had smiled at him. *Ah, destiny,* she thought.

"Lara," Pam called out as she signaled her to leave the group she had been talking to. Lara excused herself and, with a smile and twinkling eyes, turned and walked over.

"Lara, I'd like you to meet Peter Landon. Both of you go skiing in Vermont. He's a Yalie. You probably know a lot of the same people. Peter, this is Lara Laughton. Oh, excuse me, there's the Ambassador," and she turned to greet a strikingly elegant man who had just arrived with his wife.

Peter took Lara's hand and kissed it European-style while looking into her eyes. "I'm so pleased to meet you." And all Lara could think of was his name, which had been crossed off the list of young men invited to her coming out party three years earlier. *Good looking, with charm, and a reputation for having a way with women. Funny how thoughts can flit through my mind at a time like this.* She was speechless, so Peter continued, "You have a lot of friends who went to Yale?"

Slowly she recovered her self-confidence and answered yes, she knew many men who had been or still were at Yale. "What year did you graduate?" she asked.

"I was class of '52. Did you know anyone in my class?"

Lara frowned as she thought, "Did you know Tim Russell? I think he was a '56?"

They had a wonderful time talking. Joking about places they had been, friends they had in common, a few laughs at different situations, and the usual questions about what are you doing in New York, your job, etc. The evening passed quickly.

They remained together moving from group to group and before everyone left the party he turned to her and said, "Let's go skiing next weekend, no," he paused, "actually what about the weekend after? I can't make next weekend." He had remembered he already had a date. *Just in time,* he thought.

"Great," was Lara's short answer. *Just as well I didn't meet him three years ago. I wouldn't have been ready, and his reputation is of little importance,* she thought. *Funny how much we've all grown up in three years.* They went their separate ways that evening. Peter had a late date and Lara's roommate was waiting for her for dinner.

A few days later she was chatting with some friends about her upcoming ski weekend with Peter. They all laughed and suggested she not count on it. He usually forgot about such engagements and if she wanted to go skiing she'd be better off with her usual group. There were five of them who drove up to Mad River Glen in Vermont on Friday evenings in a large station wagon, a fun and compatible group of three men and two women. Two would sleep on a mattress in the back with all their gear while three took turns driving. The two who slept on the way up would drive on the way home, usually stopping for dinner somewhere along the way. The three men considered the two women their dates, and whenever one showed up with an outsider the culprit would be hassled all weekend — sometimes Lara would be chased down the slopes by her wild friends, who were feeling very possessive.

Lara's friends knew what they were talking about. Peter did forget and she continued to ski just about every weekend until the snow was too heavy and had melted completely from the lower half of the mountain. After that she spent her weekends at school reunions, friends' weddings, or house parties. She didn't see Peter again until the beginning of June at his class reunion, and she was surprised that he even remembered her.

At the end of May Lara had moved from a two-room apartment she had shared with a friend into a huge apartment with seven other women.

She worked for Gruff Fabrics on East 52nd Street and Lara was looking for a wider circle of friends, more fun, more energy, more companionship, but while her roommates provided this, her new digs were far from luxurious She got the last available room — the maid's room with a basin in one corner and a bathroom down the hall. At twenty-five dollars a month she could afford it. The apartment was up four flights in an old brick building on 60th between Madison and Park. The fire escape climbed up the front wall to the roof. Her room wasn't much — a bed, night table, and chair — and the window looked out on a small, enclosed area so a fan which she had brought with her provided the only air circulation. *This is the dumps,* she thought. *What am I doing here? This is no way to live.*

She went out on dates quite often and had gone out with Peter several times. He was also dating, and was sleeping with one of the other women in the apartment. Lara wondered why he even bothered with her.

Peter had now finished his training and was preparing to leave for Africa. Aubrey had been on his case about finding a wife since their November meeting. Peter had proposed to three women so far — or was it four? — He'd lost count. The gals loved to love him in bed, but none of them wanted to go off to Africa with him. Too far, too hot, too many natives, not enough family and friends.

Peter had been to a house party at Lara's, at Oak Hill, Long Island and had enjoyed himself playing capture the flag, baseball, soccer, swimming, and then going to a formal dinner dance at the Winston's. He'd cuddled and necked with her, but hadn't been successful in getting her to bed. *She's different; she's beautiful, intelligent and fun, doesn't dress very well, has a great figure, loves sports, comes from a good family, has spent a year abroad, speaks some French, has a potential for inheriting,* he thought. *Maybe I should pursue this a little further. Ask her to marry me.*

So, before leaving for New York, he took her aside one evening when they were at her mother's house and asked what she was doing over the Fourth of July weekend. That was next weekend — a long one.

"I'm going to an Island on the St. Lawrence with the family," she answered. "Want to come? Swimming, tennis, water-skiing — you and Mom seem to get along well. My little sister will be there with a friend. It's paradise." She rattled on, "We can come and pick you up in Clayton, New York – otherwise we go to Gananoque and you'd have to drive around to the Canadian side of the river. It's all on the map."

Peter was taken aback by the invitation and surprised himself with his answer. "Sure, I'd love to. How long does it take to drive there?"

"It's about 350 miles, six and a half to eight hours, depending on how fast you drive, and traffic." she answered.

"I'll see if I can get out of work early or I won't get there before dark."

"Oh, that's okay. We all know the river by day or by night. Let me go ask Mom if it's okay with her. Just a sec," she walked away to find her mother.

Peter was saying good-bye to his friends when Bill came over to him. "How'd it go with Lara? If I didn't know she was interested in you I'd be after her in no time."

"Only first base," he replied a little discouraged.

"For once you have to work a little harder. That's great. Suffer, boy, suffer! She's worth it. Lunch next week?"

"Yeah, sure. Tuesday okay with you? I'll let you know how it goes, if it goes. Ciao." Peter waved good-bye to him as Lara appeared at the door.

"I can't find Mom. Can I call you?"

"Okay, as soon as possible." His good-bye kiss was long and sensuous.

"I'll call tonight, or tomorrow morning in case you have a date tonight. Bye." She blew him a kiss, turned and walked back into the house.

The Fourth of July was a beautiful weekend in Canada. Peter's trip had been long, the boat ride to the island relaxing with enough daylight so he could see the outline of the islands. The boatman knew the river very well. He had lived in *Gananoque* all his life and had worked at the island since he was a little boy. Peter felt he could relax, he was in good hands. The air was crisp, clear, and should have been invigorating except that he had snuggled Lara against himself. Her smell was intoxicating and he fell asleep with her warmth infusing his body.

It was the smell of the boat's engine that woke him as they pulled into the boathouse. Bags and groceries were loaded onto a cart, which would be pulled up to the back steps. "You can find your bags in the front hall later," Jacques, the boat man said handing him a flash light, Lara took Peter's hand and led the way up to the house. The island had an electric generator, which produced barely enough power to light the house at night. It was turned off at eleven every night. Guests either had to leave before or be happy with candle or flashlight. This usually meant guests had a good night's sleep and that was just what Peter needed.

Lara's mother and stepfather greeted him at the door and asked if he'd like a drink and something to eat.

"That sounds great," he said, "if it's not too late for everyone. Thanks for waiting up for me." Lara took him by the hand and led him into the pantry where bottles of booze stood next to the sink.

"What would you like?"

"Whoa, let's have a look." He picked up bottle after bottle until he found a Chivas Regal, which he seldom was able to enjoy since it was beyond his budget. The "12 years old" gold and brown label was slightly worn by anticipating hands, and the bottle was almost empty. Peter uncorked it, smelled it, and poured himself a stiff one on the rocks. He threw the bottle into the trashcan under the sink and turned with a big smile.

"This is the kind of welcome I like," he said.

He put his arm around Lara's waist when she returned from the kitchen with his sandwich and they walked into the living room where Lara's mother, Tori and her stepfather, Allen were sitting. Lara's mother was in her late forties with premature white hair. A good-looking woman with almond shaped eyes balanced by bright red lips that moved easily into a charming smile. *She's a tall woman, a little overweight,* Peter thought, *but in good shape.* Peter also enjoyed her nickname, Tori, which made her seem more approachable.

Allen, Lara's stepfather looked to be in his mid-fifties, balding and heavyset. His light blue eyes sparkled with a sense of humor. *I can get along well with him,* Peter thought. Peter remembered they both played a good game of tennis — his wrist work particularly good.

"We've lit some candles for you. Did Lara tell you? We turn off the generator at around eleven or when we go to bed. Tori and I are heading upstairs now, so I'll be going down to turn off the electricity. Lara will show you to your room up in the tower. She'll explain it all." They rose to leave, saying their goodnights and sleep wells, and sweet dreams, which Lara always added.

Lara and Peter sat on the large bay window seat, their backs propped against an array of pillows. Neither felt like talking, each wondering what the other was thinking. Peter finished his sandwich and the last gulp of his whiskey. He turned to look at Lara.

"You know? You're beautiful. Candlelight always flatters a woman, but you don't need the candlelight. You're as beautiful by day as by night and I love you."

"I bet you say that to all the girls you date," came her quick reply.

He sat up hastily and gave her a quizzical look. "What are you saying? What do you mean?"

"Your reputation has gone before you," she answered. Not wanting to ruin a weekend which had just begun she moved closer to him and whispered in his ear, "I like your reputation and I think I love you, too." Soft and gentle kisses followed one after the other until Lara had to catch her breath.

"I'll take you up to the tower before I lose total control of myself. Come on." She rose, taking his hand, and pulled him up into her arms. Her head was spinning, her heart pounding, her legs weakening. She pulled herself away, picked up two candles and started into the front hall.

"There's your bag. Come on, don't just stand there."

Peter also was having a hard time pulling himself together. He wanted Lara more than anything else right now and this was new for him. It was his intention to ask Lara to marry him this weekend. They'd have to do it fast since he was to leave for the Congo in mid-August. He walked up the stairs behind her, carrying his suitcase with one hand and goosing her with the other.

"Peter, keep your hands where they belong," she said in a low voice hoping not to be heard by anyone else.

"They are where they belong. One is holding a suitcase, the other helping you up the stairs and into my room. Why aren't we sharing a room anyway?"

"Peter!" was all she could answer as they arrived at the top of the stairs. She smiled and lit two candles to give him the light he needed until he went to bed, quickly kissed him good night, and fled with her candle down the stairs to her room. Peter, surprised by her quick departure, looked around what was called the "Tower Room." Windows on three sides opened up to a fantastic view of the Thousand Islands and, although it was close to midnight, there was enough light to see the outline of the many nearby islands on the river.

How beautiful, he thought as he walked to the center window, taking in the view and looking at the stars, wondering where the moon was and wondering what he was doing here. *Yes, this looks just like paradise. This is where I'll propose to Lara. Maybe the setting will help. Let's see, I'm now used to asking someone to marry me, I've been turned down how many times? He counted — one, two, three — the fourth was kind of incomplete. Shit, Lara is the fifth woman I'm going to ask and I'm running out of time and women.* His stomach flipped at the thought of finding someone to marry him before he left for Africa. But, it was also true that his feelings for her were different from his previous affairs. Something about her affected him more deeply than in the past. He knew he could never be faithful to one woman and when it would be time to say goodbye, well, that wasn't now — now was still hello. He fell on the bunk bed, flipped off his shoes, turned off his mind while blowing out the candles and went right to sleep.

When he awoke the sun flooded his room. Could it be that late? The windows had no shades or curtains and when he saw the long shadows of the trees he realized it was still early morning. The view was unbelievable. The river flowed east forever, dotted by rocky, tree-covered islands only a few of which had houses. It was totally silent, and just one small boat with a fisherman rocked on the water, pulled along by the current. The room was hot, and since Lara had mentioned an early morning dip before breakfast, he pulled on his bathing suit, grabbed a shirt, towel and sneakers and went downstairs to wait for her.

Lara was surprised to find Peter gazing out at the sunlit river so early in the morning. She thought he'd still be asleep after his long day. Quietly she walked up behind him, "Indian-style" — rolling the outside of her foot from heel to toe as she had as a child. Slowly she put her arms around him, pressed her body against his, kissed his neck, shoulders and, after turning him around, his ears, eyes, nose and finally his mouth.

"That's a great way to say good morning. How about starting all over again?" he said as he turned his back to her. This time Lara ran her hands across his chest, down around his waist and hips as she kissed his back and shoulders. Peter turned, put his arms around her and held her as close as possible. Pushing her pelvis tightly to him she put her hands around his face and then his neck. They embraced tenderly as the rising sun warmed their bodies. Upstairs, a door opened and voices broke the morning silence.

"Hello and good morning," Lara called. "We're downstairs waiting for you." She took Peter's hand and headed for the terrace door grabbing their towels on the way. "We'll meet you at the swimming rock."

All of this was a little abrupt for Peter, who tried to clear his head while being pulled outside. The change of pace was fast and he wondered if it was always like that. The morning swim was delicious, and the sun warmed everyone after the cool water of the river. All conversation stopped when a flock of geese swam by not ten yards away. *Yes, this place is paradise*, they all thought.

By nine o'clock everyone was dressed and having breakfast. Lara's little sister, Josie, was upset to have missed the morning swim. She and her friend had talked and giggled into the early hours of the morning and only woke up when the sounds and smells of breakfast invaded their sleep.

Morning activities varied — sometimes guests wanted to go shopping in town, then there was tennis and water skiing before or after lunch. Quiet time after lunch was *de rigeur* because some liked to nap while others read, painted, or took possession of the new hammock recently installed between the pine trees close to the river. Peter and Lara headed there, where it was always shady and cool. Little did they know that a few minutes later Josie and Susie would arrive to discuss the evening cookout on the adjoining island. Peter's mind wandered. Their voices did not distract his thoughts — when would he get to pop the question. When, where, and even *if* he would get the opportunity was troubling him. Today was Saturday. Perhaps the best time would be the day before they all left. Or maybe even the day they left. Timing was important. Would Lara accept? If she said no he was in trouble. He didn't really want to fall in love with her, and yet that seemed to be what was happening. Most of the time it was purely physical, easier to control. With Lara, it was different. There was more than just the physical attraction. Was it because she was playing hard to get or was there something more profound? He couldn't figure it out. *Get married, don't get emotionally attached, it's just part of your cover. Job and family, they're just part of your cover.* The chattering around him receded and he focused on the smell of pine, the river and the lapping water against the rocks. He heard the hum of an insect, a cricket's chirp, and then again his stomach started to churn.

"Peter, where are you?" Lara asked as she watched him. "Did you hear anything? Josie and Susie want us to play tennis this afternoon before we go water skiing."

"I thought this was quiet hour," he replied with a smile on his face. "Sure, we'll take you on later. When does the court cool down?"

"Who cares? We can play anytime," Josie answered. She was an avid player, having inherited a talent from her father in the game.

"OK, it's a date, around four?"

"Why so late? Are you going to sleep out here until then?" Susie asked.

"Yeah, I'm going to take a nap while Lara keeps the bugs away for me. We'll see you later."

Feeling thoroughly dismissed, the girls walked back to the house. Peter closed his eyes, closed out the world, and fell asleep. Lara lay quietly by his side pushing the hammock back and forth with one foot on the ground until she, too, fell asleep.

Tennis with the girls turned out to be more of a challenge than Peter had expected. The little sister played a faster, stronger, and more precise game than Lara, so the teams were well matched and a lot of fun. Water-skiing followed and as soon as everyone was back at the house the picnic was put together and all hands carried it down to the boathouse. They went off to the island next to Aragain where the boatman had already prepared a fire. Tori, short for Victoria, started cooking her favorite potato, onion and carrot dish which always accompanied the huge sirloin steak roasted on the fire afterward. Drinks, wine, and cheese calmed their appetites until supper was ready. Stories and puns and good conversation made the evening pass quickly. Then the fire was extinguished and the area cleaned as if no one had been there. They all piled into the boat and returned to the island. Peter and Lara stayed at the boathouse to look at the stars and the rising moon, the others walked up to the house in silence, leaving everything in the kitchen before heading for bed.

Peter's brief goodnight surprised Lara as she watched him climb the stairs to the tower room. She wondered what he was thinking of, why he had seemed so distant most of the day. She would ask him tomorrow when she had some time alone with him.

Sunday was the Fourth of July, Monday they would all be going — No, only Peter would be returning to the heat of the city. He had made up his mind. Tomorrow — Sunday — he would ask Lara to marry him. Having made his decision, he fell asleep listening to the silence of the river.

It was a beautiful day again. Peter and Lara were alone and quiet as they watched the dappled sunlight float across the river after their sunrise swim. There were never any boats at this hour; there were hardly any boats during the day and when one did go by everyone would jump up to see who it was and wave a welcome. Sometimes it was a motorboat, more often a sailboat, and then peace would return. Lara was taking the rest of the week off from work and looking forward to time with just her family. Peter envied her and said so as they walked back to the house for breakfast, wondering why everyone hadn't shown up for the usual morning plunge. Fun and games kept them busy all morning and Peter realized he wasn't dressed for lunch so he excused himself and went up to wash and change.

Tori turned to Lara as they sat around the bay window. "So, how's it going?" All heads turned and four pairs of eyes were riveted on Lara, waiting for her answer.

"OK, I think … he's had a wonderful time, thanks to all of you. I think I'm in love. But then, when do you know you're in love? Anyway, he leaves tomorrow." And after a brief pause, "What do you think?"

Josie piped up, "I think he's sexy as _____" and didn't fill in the blank. "He likes you. His hands are all over you when you're close to each other. Too bad he leaves for Africa soon. Mom, what do you think?"

Being wise about love Tori didn't answer right away. "He certainly is attractive and … charming. If he were interested in you, as he appears to be, would you want to go off and live in Africa with him? And a good question to ask yourself is, do you want to bear his children? There's a lot to consider when you fall in love."

Allen was about to give his opinion when they heard Peter on the stairs. The silence that followed was embarrassing until Peter said, "I bet you've been talking about me. Right? I hope you haven't said 'What a nice guy he is.' Nice guys finish last, and I need to be a winner." He had graciously broken the silence and they all got up and headed for the terrace where lunch was waiting.

Most lunches were cold meat, fish, and salad, sliced tomatoes from the garden, cheese, fresh fruit, and cookies. Sometimes a bottle of wine would appear guaranteeing a long nap for the grownups. Today was one of those days; even Lara's little sister and friend had a glass, causing much merriment and such laughter that almost everyone had tears streaming down their face. The release of tension was marvelous and by quiet time everyone was relaxed and happy.

The family went to nap, leaving Peter and Lara alone on the terrace. It was sunny and hot, even in the shade. Peter stood, took Lara's hand, and pulled her to her feet. "Come on, let's go up to the tower room, we'll have more of a breeze there and I need to talk to you."

The quizzical look Lara gave him made him smile. She knew the tower room in early afternoon was always hot even with all the windows open. Perhaps the breeze today would make it better.

They climbed the stairs hand-in-hand. With so much family around, they couldn't make love so she tried to push away her longing with little success. *Keep it light,* she thought and with that she goosed him up the last few steps and then they fell into each other's arms. Tender kisses at first became more passionate and the ultimate French kisses took their breath away. Peter's shirt was opened and she tickled his nipples. Lara's bra was undone so Peter could caress her breasts, taking the nipples in his fingers.

Lara let a groan of pleasure rise from her throat, their lips parted. Totally absorbed in each other, neither of them noticed the heat of the day. Peter lifted off her shirt, slid the bra off her arms and laid her quietly on his bed. "Marry me, will you marry me?" He had said it, he wanted her so badly, she was beautiful and fun and life with her would be wonderful.

Lara sat up surprised at his proposal. He was taking out one of her apartment roommates and they had slept together, when was it, just ten days to two weeks ago.

"What about Abby? She told me you were lovers and asked me why I bothered to go out with you."

Peter's heart sank. *Women talk too much,* he thought. "Abby said she didn't want to be a virgin any more — I obliged. It really didn't mean much to either of us," Lara knew this wasn't true, for Abby had told her she would prefer that Lara not go out with him.

"Come on, Peter, that's not what Abby told me. She even asked me not to go out with you. She didn't want competition. I don't know, Peter, are you serious?" She looked at him quizzically. "Do you really want to get married? You want to marry me? Aren't you going off to Africa soon?"

To all these questions, Peter was silent. His reputation for screwing around had finally caught up with him. He held her close, rocking back, and forth and slowly his mind cleared. His heart pounding, he said, "Yes, I'm off to Africa the end of August. Come with me, marry me."

Lara pulled herself away, put on her bra and shirt, and stood up. "I have to think about all this. It's obvious, I'm mad about you. I think I love you. I don't know." With that she fled downstairs and out of the house.

Lara wandered the island looking for a place to sit and think, a place where no one would disturb her. Peter was full of constant surprises and she never knew when she should take him seriously. This was one of those times. Marriage isn't just love and a physical desire, it's a life of everyday cooking, cleaning, ironing shirts, eventually having and caring for children, financial responsibilities. And with Peter it would mean travel, moving, entertaining business associates and clients and a multitude of friends, golf, tennis, card games, everything necessary to meet and get to know the people who would help his career. Teas, coffees, community service. There were so many obligations it made her head spin. She also would probably have to redo her wardrobe, hair, maybe even her figure, learn to speak foreign languages and spend a lot of time alone. Thank goodness she only thought of a small part of what would be her future. Had she known what was really in store for her, she might have made another choice.

She heard voices calling in the distance and looked at her watch. It was time for supper and time to return to the family barbecue, which she could smell far away from the terrace.

"Lara, where have you been? We've been looking all over for you. Peter came down after quiet hour looking for you, too."

Lara's stomach was churning. She couldn't say anything about the proposal, was feeling ill at ease from the looks everyone was giving her, and said, "I went for a walk around the island, found a spot, and I must have fallen asleep. Sorry if I caused any worry." She went inside to get something to drink. When she returned so did her composure. She was proud of herself for being able to act as if nothing special had happened. Peter would be leaving in the morning and that suited her just fine. A time of separation, that was what she needed — time alone.

A few days later, back in New York, Peter stopped by the apartment to pick Lara up. To his discomfort, Abby opened the door. She put her arms around him and kissed him passionately on the lips for as long as she could. Peter had a hard time pulling away from her, and seeing Lara, he didn't know what to say. He whacked Abby on the behind saying, "Thanks for such a warm welcome. Lara, shall we go?" He wanted out of there as fast as possible and reaching for Lara's hand, he pulled her past Abby.

"Good night, Abby."

Silence followed silence as they walked through Central Park to 59th Street. They were going to Trader Vic's, a Hawaiian restaurant in the Plaza Hotel, and then on to the Stork Club — to dance. The scene at the apartment was an uncomfortable beginning for a romantic evening and Peter wondered how it was all going to turn out. As for Lara, she never really cared for Abby, who was not a friendly person, but then she really had a reason not to be very friendly. Lara was the one Peter had asked to marry. Abby was left in the dust.

They were seated in a quiet, dimly lit corner and ordered drinks. Lara loved a rum drink that had a gardenia floating in it. Peter ordered his favorite whiskey and they remained silent until the drinks came and loosened their tongues. Peter was sorry for what happened at the apartment. Lara so much as said I told you so.

Embarrassed, Peter changed the subject and started to tell Lara about Africa. He'd brought a small map to show her where he was going, hoping she would go with him. There was not enough light to see much of anything, even reading the menu was a challenge. "Put the map away. You can look at it another time." Lara folded it and put it in her purse for future reference. She thought, *I really didn't care about the map or the Congo or where you are going.* She had decided to go with him anyway, but she wasn't about to tell him after this evening's incident with Abby. He'd have to straighten things out with Abby before he was going to get an answer.

Dinner was delicious. The two gardenias in Lara's hair perfumed the air as Peter leaned over and kissed the nape of her neck, peeking down the front of her dress to make sure everything was in place. Reassured, he enjoyed every morsel he popped in his mouth, licking his fingers after each bite and watching Lara do the same.

They talked about their families and friends. Lara avoided Africa and marriage as best she could. She knew she couldn't wait too long to give Peter an answer, but tonight was too early. She'd have to keep things light. They finished their leisurely dinner and started walking the few blocks to the nightclub. Lara in her high heels took Peter's arm to steady herself so she could keep up with him. The street heat was oppressive after the cool restaurant, but neither seemed to care. It was still relatively early when they were shown to a table next to the dance floor opposite the band. They ordered their drinks and looked around to see if there was anyone they knew. The usual beautiful women were sitting around the bar chatting, either waiting for a friend or an eventual pick-up for the evening. Some were call girls holding their usual spot until a call came through for them; they'd pick up their bag and stole and be on their way.

"Let's dance," Peter said, standing and holding out his hand to Lara.

"Shouldn't we wait for our drinks? Besides, there's no one on the floor."

"Come on, we have the place to ourselves," he said, pulling her to her feet. *Dancing Cheek to Cheek* was the song and this was the way he held Lara to him.

"Marry me," he said as he flung her away, twirled her around and brought her back close to him, their bodies melting into each other. The warmth of his breath in her ear made her tingle as he asked her again, "Marry me, will you marry me?" His look was loving and tender as he searched her face for an answer. She thought it said, "I want to spend the rest of my life with you."

The following weekend they told their parents. Peter's mother lived in Paris. She didn't quite know how to reply to her son's announcement. She was too far away to check out the situation, and wondered what he was getting himself into. She knew she would not go to the wedding. She was planning her own wedding and she would tell Peter about that at another time.

Lara's mother was pleased, having been charmed by Peter during his weekend visits with the family. His traceable background was St. Paul's School, where Lara's father had gone, and Yale also. He knew all the "Right People." He was one of "Our Crowd."

Lara's father was summering on Nantucket with his fourth wife and plans were made to introduce Peter to him the next weekend. Many plans were made in great haste, for it was mid-July and Peter's departure for

Paris and then Leopoldville, capital of the Belgian Congo was scheduled for late August or early September.

A few days after the engagement was announced in the papers an anonymous letter arrived, addressed to Lara's mother. It told an interesting and surprising story. Peter's parents were from Holland and Jewish, his father's name was Mark Steinberg and Alexander Landon was his stepfather. Tori wondered who could have sent such a letter. The postmark was New York City.

She would have to talk to Lara about it and fast before things went any further. She would wait until Lara got home from work. In the meantime, she needed to talk it over with someone, so she walked out to the vegetable garden where Allen was picking his lima beans. He loved his organic vegetables, and he planted, picked, and froze enough for most of the winter. Tori showed him the letter. Their discussion was short, given the heat of the day, and they walked back to the house and phoned a friend in Amsterdam. They asked their friend to find a detective to look into the Steinberg-Landon family, and gave her information from the letters and from conversations they had had with Peter. They explained Lara's hasty marriage and departure for Africa and asked her to get the information as soon as possible. As Lara walked in the door her mother was by her side.

"Lara, I have to talk to you."

"Can it wait? I'm headed for the powder room. Train's too dirty." She dashed past her mother, noticing a strange look on her face. "Just a sec, Mom, I'll be right back."

Lara walked into the library, "What's up?"

"Do you know that Peter's parents are Jewish?" This surprised Lara, Peter hadn't mentioned this. Was he afraid she wouldn't marry him if she knew? And his friends, she wondered if even his friends knew — and if they did, why hadn't they told her? Astonished, Lara didn't answer except to shake her head no. Not only was she madly in love, she knew her life would never be boring with him and their sex was going to be ecstasy. So, what if he were Jewish? Their friends came from the same crowd, he had a good job and a promising career, he charmed everyone he met, had a great sense of humor, and was good-looking besides. It was important to Lara that he was a practicing Episcopalian. So, what if he was of Jewish descent. Would this make a difference in their life together?

We have so much in common and life is an adventure, she thought. *I'm moving off into the world and I feel ready for anything.* Little did she know how eventful her life would be!

Chapter Three

By the last week of July, the wedding invitations for Saturday, August 16 had gone out. Lara wore her grandmother's wedding gown. The veil was her mother's long lace veil that she had worn as a flapper so many years before. She had shopping to do for her trousseau. Going off to "Deep, Dark Africa" they needed everything for eighteen months. Lara quit her job with Gruff Fabrics at the end of July giving her two weeks to organize everything for her departure. Lara's mother took over organizing the wedding.

Lara needed clothing, medicines and household goods. She didn't know there was just about everything one could want in the European stores in Leopoldville.

The company would take care of shipping their belongings. They would wait to include most of the wedding presents, which were slowly arriving in Oak Hill.

The only time Lara saw her fiancé during the last weeks before the wedding were when they went into New York City to meet his boss at Calder Oil and his wife for dinner, when they went for their medical exams and then went for their marriage license. The weekend before they were married, the family conveniently left the house to them and Peter said to Lara, "You know, next weekend is going to be emotional and exhausting. Would you like to give up your virginity? I want to make love to you."

Surprised by his question, she looked at him without answering. The house was quiet. It was the couple's day off. They would be getting their own supper. She knew she would be giving herself to him. Was this the right time? Some of her friends had been enjoying sex for years and had already had several partners. She'd had the opportunity a few times and had chosen to wait for the man she was going to marry. He was standing in front of her holding both her hands and looking quizzically into her eyes. She felt pangs of desire. Peter let go of her hands and gently took her breasts in his hands caressing them in such a sensuous way that all of Lara's doubts and hesitation disappeared. She took his hands and moved them behind her, put her arms around him and with a gentle kiss, said, "Let's go upstairs."

She gave herself to him fully — going from gentle lovemaking to passionate pleasure. The early discomfort of the first penetrations was quickly forgotten as they moved in harmony, each to their own climax one after the other. Lara asked herself why she had waited so long to experience this thrill and hoped that lovemaking would be a successful and frequent part of her life.

Peter wondered what she was thinking as they lay together. He caressed her body slowly with tender kisses, his hands returning to places already explored knowing the agreeable sensation he could give her and soon she yearned again to feel him inside of her.

"What about a rubber?" she asked.

"Don't worry. I'll pull out in time," he answered.

Motion was slow and irregular creating new sensations for each of them until they no longer could control their movements as they rose to an excited orgasm. Peter quickly withdrew as he started to ejaculate and, although satisfied, Lara felt incomplete not having him rest on her as he had done before.

They were both out of breath and delightfully relaxed when they heard a car drive in and the front door open. It was time to get up, dress and get supper. Act as if nothing had happened.

Peter drove back to New York the next day. He still had to pack and get ready for the festivities which would start the following Friday with their bridal dinner. One of his friends would be bringing out his suitcases for Africa. All he needed for the wedding and a few days in New York he would take himself. His thoughts were not on his clothes and packing. They were on Lara and their lovemaking. He had been successful in satisfying her. She had been wonderful and inventive for a first-timer and he looked forward to a sexual playmate who could, and probably would, satisfy him, although he still felt that she wouldn't be enough to keep him faithful. He would say his vows on Saturday knowing they wouldn't mean much to him. It was all part of the job.

Lara spent the week preparing for her wedding and departure. She missed Peter terribly. Making love had all of a sudden become a very important part of her life and not having him near her made her body, mind and soul yearn for him. She knew she was not supposed to call him at the office and some evenings he wasn't at home. She wondered where he was and with whom. Probably better not to ask. She had a lot to think about and accomplish before next Friday. She spent hours with her mother seating family and friends where they thought they would enjoy themselves the most. She, too, had her packing to do. Wedding presents were taken care of by her maternal grandmother — opened, listed and numbered. Lara would write the thank you notes once she was settled in Leopoldville.

The bridesmaids put on their finishing touches in Lara's bedroom and stood watching as Melanie, Lara's older sister, and Josie finished attaching Lara's veil to her newly permed curls. Everyone was feeling nervous and excited as they walked down the stairs to the waiting family. It was time. Lara went over to her father who had agreed to come from Nantucket to give her away, put her arms around his neck and whispered, "I'm so thankful you're here, my tummy's running around in circles. You'll have to hold me going down the aisle. Otherwise, I'll never make it." He gave her a gentle hug, not wanting to muss her dress, stepped to the side and offered his arm. They walked out the door and got into the limo where they waited in silence while everyone else did the same. Their car was the last in line to leave for the church.

Peter wondered why his mother and new stepfather hadn't come. Just because they had been married a week earlier wasn't a satisfactory reason for them not to be there. He felt lonely and abandoned. Then again, this wasn't the first time he had felt abandoned. When his father had walked away from the boat that had brought them to America, when he was sent off to boarding school or dumped on his mother's friends for vacation. History was repeating itself. He was doing what he had been told to do — get married before you leave. Take a wife with you or she'll never follow. You might be lucky and fall in love. Be careful, you never know how long it will last. With a sigh he took a last look in the mirror as a single man. In an hour he'd be hitched, stuck with a wife having made vows he knew he'd never be able to keep. He walked out of the bathroom.

"Okay, John," he said to his best man, "Let's get it over with."

Everything went as expected. The church was full of family and friends. The bridesmaids paraded down the aisle followed by Lara and her father. She was properly handed over to Peter. Vows were said. He kissed the bride, and it was over. The happy couple smiled as they walked out of the church, got into the limo and headed for the house. The reception, dinner and dancing were all part of the program. Speeches were made, the bridal bouquet was thrown and the couple went off to change. Rice was tossed as they got into John's car and drove off to New York, where they would stay in a friend's empty apartment until they flew off on Tuesday for Paris.

With a broad smile, the doorman welcomed them with the keys and congratulations. He had known Lara for at least seven years, had seen her grow into a beautiful woman. Recently she had reminded him of Grace Kelly and now she was married to a handsome young man — and they were leaving for Africa. He wondered how safe that would be for Lara and hoped he'd have news from her friends when they returned to their apartment in New York in the late fall.

Both Lara and Peter were exhausted, even too tired to make love, leaving their overnight cases in the entrance, they headed for the kitchen, a glass of water and went off to bed happy just to lie in each other's arms and fall asleep. After breakfast the next morning they went back to bed and started making love. Again their hands wandered over each other's bodies, stopping on the hardened nipples to play a little longer before descending to the place between their legs, pulling lightly on the pubic hairs, then rubbing gently wherever they felt the other's pleasure. The anti-pregnancy cream Lara had used with her diaphragm reduced the friction and pleasure and it took longer than usual to reach a climax. Exhausted, they fell asleep. The rest of the day they talked and walked around Central Park and went to bed early. Monday would be a busy day.

Peter was shaved and showered by the time Lara had breakfast on the table. He was out the door headed for his first appointment and then on to the Calder Oil office by eight, leaving Lara to take care of last minute errands.

Peter took off his coat and tie, rolled up his sleeves, messed his hair, and put on sunglasses so no one would recognize him. He walked the twenty-odd blocks to 69th and Third Avenue, rang the buzzer, and, looking up at the camera, remembered he had to remove his sunglasses before they would open the door. The pop startled him, bringing him back to the fact that he was going on his first assignment. He needed full control. His memory, well-trained for names and places, would be most important this morning since he was to receive only verbal instructions, and would have to memorize some faces. This time he took the elevator to the third floor, enjoying the cool air and a few minutes of quiet before his meeting. To his surprise he passed a man who hid his face as much as he could getting into the elevator. It was true that Peter usually used the stairs and would not normally have encountered this man trying to look as if he wasn't there. Peter immediately put to memory what he could: just under six feet, slight, dark and somber complexion and hair, liked loose clothing,.

Interesting, he thought, *I wonder if I'll ever see him again* and continued down the hall to where Aubrey was standing by his office door.

"Did you two meet?"

"Meet who?" Peter answered.

"The guy who just left here, did you see him?"

"We crossed getting in and out of the elevator. I didn't get a look at him, I was thinking about Lara and the trip tomorrow. Was I supposed to meet him?"

"No, no, just wondered if you two knew each other."

"Don't think so." Peter took a close look around the office to see if he could pick up any clues. Two cigarettes were stubbed out in the ashtray — short meeting. The butts had a cork type of paper around the filter and were smoked to the last draw of tobacco. Other than that everything was as usual. The desk was clear, the floor dirty, and the place smelled of cigarettes.

"Have a seat, Peter," Aubrey said. He sat down, rolled his own chair away from the desk, opened the top desk drawer, and pulled out a large file, which he handed to Peter.

"As you can see you'll be meeting some people from the Agency in Paris before heading off. Five names, two pictures. The Chief is related to Lara's stepfather. You'll be dining with him and his wife. Lara is very attached to them — she stayed with them when she was an art student in Paris. You picked a winner for a wife, by the way. Congratulations on getting married so fast and so well. She should be a big help in your career with us *and* with Calder Oil."

He waited a few minutes while Peter checked the file. When he got to material about the Congo Aubrey continued, "Just read through that material and put to memory as much as you can. There is no head of station in Leopoldville yet, a traveling agent will be by to see you and give you further instructions." Aubrey stood up and walked around behind him to see where he was in the file. "For the time being, get to know the country as well as possible, make a place for yourself socially so you're invited by all levels of society, learn the lay of the land — you know what's expected of you."

Returning behind his desk again, Aubrey let him finish the file in silence. Most of it was information he had already seen in newspaper articles and recent books on Africa and African history. The Agency was not very well informed and he thought it was about time they started getting people in place if they wanted to control Africa's wealth as they had the oil of the Middle East.

"What time is Calder Oil expecting you this morning?"

"I'm supposed to be in around ten. Since I just got married they gave me a little leeway. We've done everything we need to for the company. Our belongings won't be sent for a while since they don't have proper housing for us." This annoyed Peter. "I don't know if that was the Agency's idea or just their inability to provide, but we'll be staying in some hotel."

"Yes, I heard they are looking for housing for you. They don't have anything available right now. We can't interfere without causing interest in your arrival, so just make the best of it. Do you think Lara can manage? She really should go down there with you — not wait for a house."

"Oh, we'll manage." Peter said. He had told Lara they would be staying in a hotel for a few days and then would move. He didn't know how long it would take or where they would be going. That seemed okay with her — she had seemed more concerned about whether there would be more than a ceiling fan to keep cool and that there were screens to keep out the bugs.

Peter finished scanning the file and handed it back to Aubrey who, in turn, put it back in the drawer. Looking at his watch Peter said, "It's time I was on my way — the file is in here," pointing to his head.

"Is there something else I need to know before taking off?" He got up to go. "I don't have any particular questions. They can wait until I see someone in Paris or the agent on his way through Leo."

"That's enough for today. I'll be seeing you on your first vacation — eighteen months, is it? Yes, we'll talk then."

Peter's thoughts raced through the basic instructions — *keep a low profile, out of trouble, no accidents* — he knew he didn't have to repeat them. They were the same for everyone, constantly repeated during training: don't get caught, if you do we will deny any association with you. That was for everyone under cover. Peter was off and running.

"Thanks for everything. It will go well. I'll see you when I get back to New York." They shook hands and Peter was out the door. He put his tie on while going down the stairs —the jacket would go on just before he arrived at the Calder Oil office.

The rest of the day flew by — no time for lunch — it was too hot to go outside and he had paperwork to finish before he could leave.

Lara's day went fast also. She had some last-minute shopping to do — shoes she knew she couldn't get in Africa, a bathing suit and a pretty cap to match. Everything else she would manage without. It didn't matter. There was no more room in their suitcases. She had what she needed for Paris including two beautiful evening dresses she had had made when she was an art student. She returned to the apartment to wait for Peter. Tired from all the activity, they spent a quiet evening at a local restaurant and went to bed early.

The next day Lara's mother picked them up to drive them to the airport. The large suitcases were already in her car's trunk, the rest of their baggage didn't fit in the trunk and filled the back seat, leaving just enough room for Peter to squeeze in. The ride was hot and muggy as New York can often be in August, and the opened windows made conversation difficult. Tori dropped them and the baggage off at the Pan Am terminal and went to park the car. She was nervous about Lara's adventure into the unknown. They stood with the other excited and anxious passengers, waiting for the flight to be called. It was an all first class flight, Pan Am's President's flight — sixteen hours with stops in Gander, Newfoundland, and Reykjavik. Lara looked around her and noticed that most passengers had a group of friends seeing them off. Their conversation was light, and laughter surrounded them. Tori was sad and there wasn't much conversation. The flight was called and since Peter and Lara were in the back of the plane they let everyone leave before them and asked if Tori could accompany them to the plane, if that would be all right. It was time to go. They walked out onto the tarmac — heat rising in waves all around them — to the stairs leading up to the plane.

Lara gave her mother one last hug and saw the tears streaming down her cheeks. She was losing a daughter to a man neither of them knew very well, to a foreign country very far away. Realizing these hugs would have to last for eighteen months, Lara, too, burst into tears as they climbed on board. The door shut on the lone figure of her mother walking back to the terminal.

Calder Oil had treated them well. It was a long flight, but the seats were comfortable. A five-course dinner was served, champagne, wine, anything they wanted. They talked and slept, read magazines and books, ate and drank and slept some more and then it was Paris, where Lara would meet Peter's mother, Ida, and his new stepfather.

They were waiting at the foot of the stairs planeside and Lara felt Ida's animosity right away.

So, I'm not the beautiful socialite model you expected. I'm a tired, rumpled, all-American, athletic young woman, and what you see is what you get.

Ida's greeting to Lara was cold and brief as she took her son's arm and started walking toward the terminal for customs and luggage. Lara was left with the new stepfather, whose name was Gregory and who didn't understand the situation any better than Lara. Ida was a small woman who took very good care of herself. Tinted blond hair was impeccable—her make-up perfect. The coldness of her eyes changed to a sparkle when she looked at her son. For her, Lara was an imposition. As for Gregory, he had an Armenian look about him. He was a large man who, Lara found out years later, had been a soldier with the Foreign Legion. He had a friendly face—easy smile, deep brown eyes shadowed by heavy eyebrows, a balding head of hair shaved short. Peter and Lara were dropped off at their hotel with an invitation for dinner at eight, and Lara wasn't looking forward to her next encounter with Ida. They would be in Paris for a week to ten days and then off to Leopoldville. She thought, she hoped to be able to handle that.

Dinner was uncomfortable for everyone. Peter asked his mother about the anonymous letter sent to Tori. Was he of Jewish descent and if so why hadn't she told him? Who was Mark Steinberg? Lara wondered how he had gotten his American citizenship without a birth certificate. It must have been there — the real name of his father. Both were confused, and Lara wondered who, if anyone, was telling the truth.

"Your father was Mark Steinberg. He was an officer in the German Army." Lara could see she felt uncomfortable with her first lie of the evening. "He died four months after you were born and we moved to Paris where I met Alexander Landon. At that time his name was Alexander Von Lagen. When Alexander put us on the boat to New York he put you on my new Dutch passport under the name of Peter and Ida Landon." It was that simple, a good story to satisfy her daughter-in-law. Dinner was over and so it seemed was the conversation for the evening, so Peter and Lara said good-bye and took a taxi back to the center of the city and got out far enough away from the hotel to have a good walk. They needed air and exercise before going to bed. The evening had been confusing, and to take Lara's mind off the unpleasant conversation Peter started in on French vocabulary.

Lara hated vocabulary, in English or in French, and was annoyed with Peter. She had hoped for something more appropriate for a honeymoon than a French lesson and was so angry that she told him to shut up. Back at the hotel and in bed she thought, *This has been a lousy evening.* Thank heavens she'd had years of French, although it hadn't helped much.

The next morning Peter first went to Calder Oil, then in the afternoon he was at the American Consulate, meeting his counterparts in the Agency. Dinner was with the Bureau Chief Jim Hunt and it was a relaxed and fun evening for both of them. Lara felt great affection for both Jim and his wife, Eleanor, and it was obvious that they appreciated her as well.

The rest of the week Peter was at the office learning what he needed to know about oil sales in Africa in general, and some specifics about Calder Oil. Lara saw some of her Parisian friends, and the family she had lived with a year earlier. She wandered the streets of Paris that she knew well, and was happy to be back where she felt so at home. Their other evenings were spent with Peter's family and friends. Lara had someone else to talk to besides her in-laws, which was a huge relief!

On the weekend they went to a chateau in Belgium with Peter's parents. They were met by the maitre d'hôtel and staff for the Baron and Baroness Van Teigen who were occupied and would greet them Friday evening at dinner. "It's a beautiful place," Lara exclaimed. "I'd hate to have to rake this long pebbled driveway leading up to the house." She admired the ornate façade of stone and brick — the light stone and dark brick giving it a well-defined pattern leading up to the different points of the roof.

There were formal gardens on both sides of the courtyard and a semi-circular staircase meeting at the front door. Off to the right was a shallow mirror garden pool with a row of boxwood squares filled with flowers. To the left were trees hiding the back entrance where the staff parked their cars and deliveries were made.

Two young men came to pick up their bags asking to whom each one belonged so they could put them in the proper room. The mâitre d'hotel who had greeted them at the door showed them to their rooms, saying the Baron and Baroness were resting, cocktails would be served around seven, dinner at eight — dress, "de ville." Once the door was closed behind the valet Lara said, "Wow, this is quite a place. Have you been here before?"

"No, this is my first time. It's rather original in comparison to the other châteaux I've seen in France. Ornate, definitely 19th Century and very Dutch, with the heaviness of all the woodwork. Look at our bed," he said as he sat on it. "Come here and lie down. It's a monster. Look up at the canopy."

Lara lay down beside Peter and was amazed at the small pleats of silk meeting in the middle where a small silk circle held them in place — getting larger as they reached the outer wooden frame. There were four columns holding up the canopy, sculpted with vines and clusters of grapes, an occasional butterfly, beetle or other insect breaking the monotony. Sitting up she looked at the rest of the room. It was large — very large, the size of a huge living room — all wood-paneled. Two heavy tapestries hung on the walls. The windowpanes were of light-colored glass of different colors in the shape of diamonds and held together with lead strips.

"I think they gave us the best guest room. I'm going to check out the bathroom." She got up, looked out the windows at the gardens below and opened a door. It was a closet where she found all their clothes unpacked and put away. The other door opened into a spacious circular bathroom with beautiful old-fashioned fixtures and a huge tub — no toilet — she then saw another door and opening it was happy to find what she was looking for. She didn't want to have to get dressed and walk down a hall to the "WC" during the night for she had learned that not all bathrooms had their own "WC." She was relieved. They took a nap in their new surroundings, happy to be together in such a welcoming place.

Two butlers and a maid served dinner for sixteen in the formal dining room. Heavy candelabras lit the room and gave a warm glow to everyone and everything. Excellent food and wine, light conversation and funny stories filled the evening, and all went to bed relatively early.

In the morning, breakfast started at eight-thirty and people slowly filled the dining room. It was an English-style buffet with smoked haddock, ham, bacon, sausage, eggs, hot cereal, muffins, many breads, juices, coffee and tea. Two chambermaids helped keep everyone's plate and cup full, since lunch wouldn't be served until after two.

By the time Peter and Lara had finished breakfast two out of three tables were playing cards. When they came back downstairs for a walk all three tables were occupied — gin, canasta, and bridge continued until lunch. Immediately after lunch everyone returned to the card tables and continued to gamble until dinner. Peter joined the group, cutting in and out of all three tables when someone wanted to take a break. Lara was tired and went to their room for a nap. She spent the rest of the afternoon alone reading and walking in the garden.

Dinner that night was black tie and when Peter came up to their room Lara was just about ready. She had done what she could to be beautiful and well dressed — a golden yellow organza strapless gown, with a full ankle-length skirt, a Paris fashion, and beautiful high-heeled golden evening slippers. She felt good about herself and hoped Peter would, too. He looked her over, smiled, gave her a kiss and rushed to change. No comment, no nothing, just a smile. When they went downstairs Lara understood why. The women were beautifully dressed in the latest fashion and Lara again felt out of place. After dinner they all returned to the living room to play cards. Lara really felt left out and was surprised and pleased when the Baron asked her if she played chess. Thrilled that she knew how to play and could give him a good game, they sat down at a small table in a corner already set up with a beautifully carved chess set from the 18th century. Lara admired the delicately carved ivory pieces before getting on with the game. It was well after midnight by the time they had finished two games and Lara excused herself saying she needed to say good night and retire.

"Thank you so much for inviting me to play chess with you. It was fun. I hope we can do it again sometime. The pieces are beautiful. Do they come from India?"

The Baron answered, "No, actually they were carved in China. My grandfather brought them back from his journey along the silk route." He picked up the King turning it between his fingers. "He sailed from Antwerp to China and came home traveling across the different countries. It's amazing that they are still in perfect condition with camel rides, fleeing from bandits and the rest. They are beautiful aren't they?" He looked up from the chessboard into a tired face. "Thank you for playing with me. I'm afraid you have lost Peter to a card game, which will probably last all night. That's what happens here. I hope you sleep well."

The Baron got up as Lara rose and walked over to Peter who glanced up, "You're off to bed?"

"Yes, I'm feeling a bit tired even with the nap this afternoon." It wasn't normal for her to be fatigued like this. Peter stood up, kissed her good night and sat back down to finish playing the hand. "Sleep tight, I'll be up later."

Later was the next morning when he walked through the bedroom and into the shower, barely waking Lara on this way through. He changed his clothes and tried to sneak out the door for breakfast without waking his sleeping beauty. He was out of luck.

"Good morning, Peter. How was the card game? Did you just finish now?" she said in a sleepy voice.

"It's not finished yet, we'll probably finish around lunch time. Everyone wanted breakfast so we stopped the game for a while. Do you want me to wait for you?" he asked standing patiently at the door.

"That's okay, I don't feel like having breakfast. You go on without me." She rolled over and went back to sleep.

Sunday traffic was slow on the way back to Paris and so was the conversation. Ida and Peter fell asleep after the twenty-four-hour card game. Lara tried to be company for Gregory. He had had a good night's sleep since he didn't play cards either.

Monday morning Peter took Lara to the American Hospital to find out why she was so tired. By the end of the appointment they knew she was pregnant and that it was normal for her to feel tired and nauseous. Peter couldn't wait to get out of there. He was furious.

"You said you had taken all the precautions needed not to get pregnant. What happened? We can't have a baby now. No way."

Chapter Four

The phone rang — four a.m. — time to get up. It seemed as if they had just gone to bed after an evening of dinner and an unpleasant conversation with Peter's mother and stepfather. Lara wasn't feeling very well. Nobody wanted her to have a baby, at least not now. After all, they had just gotten married and, most important, her mother-in-law said she was too young to be a grandmother. Peter was angry with her for not taking proper precautions. She had done what she had been told to do, had done everything correctly. She was angry because her gynecologist had not said that her husband could have taken some precautions, even if she was using a diaphragm. It wasn't entirely her fault and she had already, over the last five days, given herself shots in the behind — a do-it-yourself prescription where she stuck the needle into the upper part of her buttocks, then attached the syringe and plunged the liquid into herself. The shots to get rid of the child hadn't worked and now they were on their way to Africa and she was still pregnant. Her in-laws were cold and distant and insisted that she end the pregnancy as soon as possible. So did her husband. That evening Gregory said, "We have a surprise for you." Lara was too tired and upset to be interested. Although Gregory was a good man she knew something was up. "Lara come with me," he waited and added, "Please."

"Sure Gregory," Lara got up to follow him.

There was an animal carrying case with a little black puppy in it. He said softly so the others couldn't hear him, "I know this can't replace the baby. I'm so sorry." He gave her a hug and carried the puppy into the apartment.

Peter was in a foul mood the next morning as they got dressed, finished closing up their luggage and left the crowded, messy room banging the suitcases against the threshold on the way out the door. The puppy was in its carrying case and would have to wait for its walk. The bills had been taken care of the previous night. The taxi was waiting for them, the driver having a smoke as he waited for the concierge to open the door. The driver took two of the larger suitcases out to the car, put them in the trunk and proceeded to stuff the rest of the bags where he could, leaving Lara with her toilet kit and the puppy to squeeze in as best she could. The streets of Paris were wet with rain, which had changed into a heavy misty fog. The lights were still on and, shrouded in moisture, glowed like small moons in front of the houses and apartment buildings still hiding in the dark. Orly airport was only half an hour away and they had more than enough time to have a cup of coffee and walk the dog before getting on the plane. Breakfast would be served after take off.

UAT, a subsidiary of Air France, flew from Paris to Brazzaville, just across the Congo River from Leopoldville, stopping along the way for passengers, food and fuel. The first stop was Bangui, the Capital of Central African Republic. They took the dog for a walk and had a cup of coffee in the airport, a simple structure with a café. Many of the passengers met friends who came to see them or were flying out to other destinations.

It was early morning; the heat of the day was still to come. They boarded the plane and headed west to Douala on the Atlantic coast of French Cameroon. At Douala everyone was asked to leave the plane during refueling so they walked the puppy again, gave it some water and went to have a drink themselves in the small airport building. Again passengers met friends. This seemed to be a ritual all over Africa. Their flight into Brazzaville was relatively short. The sun had set and they could see the lights of a sprawling city dimmed by humidity and the smoke from villagers' fires. Dinner was cooking. Their arrival at Maya-Maya airport was a welcome end to a long trip — sixteen hours on the plane, plus several hours in stopovers.

The plane rolled to a stop near a small building. The control tower rising slightly above was hardly noticeable. Stairs were rolled up to the door of the plane and after three quick knocks a crewmember opened the door, letting in the heat and humidity. There was the smell of engines just shut down, the tarmac, sweat, and many different kinds of dinner crowded in together. Lara's senses were working overtime trying to figure it all out. Where were the flower fragrances, the greens, moss, wood and the river that was nearby? So much seemed to be missing, yet there was so much already there.

Everyone was happy and energized as they walked down the stairs. From a distance, people were greeting the friends who had come to pick them up. They all entered the customs hall where *douaniers* were ready to check passports and baggage at the same time. Airport management personnel were all Europeans, dressed in white shirts with a black tie and khaki pants. The men who brought in the bags were Africans dressed in khaki shirts and English-style Bermuda shorts. Droplets of moisture covered most of their bodies and Lara realized how hot and tired she was herself.

"This must be like a steam bath." She said to Peter. "I've never been in a steam bath before. I hope it's not like this all year long." He didn't bother to answer as he went off to pick out their bags and have one of the men put them on a heavy wooden table covered with metal for inspection.

"Lara, come here," he called. "We have everything and are next in line. Where's the dog? Are you totally out of it? He's slipped his leash." Yes, she was feeling light-headed and hadn't realized the dog was missing. Carrying her heavy toilet case she moved through the crowd calling the puppy, "Bollé, Bollé — here puppy, come here."

It was early September 1956, their first night in Africa. So many hours on a plane from Paris to Brazzaville with a puppy had been exhausting. At least they had been met at the airport, accompanied through customs to the *vedette* across the Congo River to Leopoldville and taken to the Memling Hotel. They were worn out by the heat and humidity and were dismayed to find only a ceiling fan to help keep them cool — day and night.

Having had more than enough to eat in first class on the plane, they took the dog for a duty walk near the hotel and went to bed leaving the puppy in the bathroom with newspapers spread all across the bathroom floor. He was a hot, unhappy puppy who cried a good part of the night and whose sorrow was successfully drowned out by earplugs. If hotel neighbors had knocked on their door, they hadn't heard.

Although a seven o'clock breakfast had been ordered the night before, the early morning banging on the door jolted them awake and into their new surroundings and to the fact that breakfast was served. Peter pulled on his shorts and opened the door to the smiling face of a "Boy" carrying a large tray with a Belgian breakfast for two. He placed the tray on an empty desk and asked if they wanted breakfast on the terrace. The dilapidated iron table sat as dignified as possible on a small terrace in the sun. It was accompanied by two metal folding chairs that had seen better days. Paint chips had been swept into a corner where they continued to disintegrate, leaving a mark of rusting iron. Above the paint chips a folded parasol tilted against the hotel window. This was where they thought they would have breakfast for the next three weeks — until other accommodations were ready for them. The terrace overlooked a busy street where trees had been forgotten and the sun beat down unpityingly on the passing crowd. The sun was not too hot and so he proceeded to put up the rickety parasol, cover the old table with a cloth and spread out breakfast.

The puppy would get his walk after they ate but before breakfast he was let out of the bathroom. The soaking wet newspaper and the odor of it all was wrapped up with more paper and shoved into the waste paper basket.

Hot café au lait in a white pot, which matched the hotel china, *pistolets* (rolls the shape of an American football but much smaller) butter, jam, and a platter of sliced processed cheese and cold cuts. The orange juice was out of a can and tasted like it. From then on they learned to ask for *orange pressé* , freshly squeezed orange juice. When they had finished, the sun was hot and they never had breakfast on the terrace again.

The day started early in Leopoldville. Wake up calls began at three a.m. and ended at eight a.m. If you wanted to be wakened after that the only thing to do was set an alarm clock. Peter's office hours were from seven until noon. and two to five. The two-hour lunch was supposed to leave time for a nap before returning to work — a custom Peter was not accustomed to. The air was hot and humid as he stepped into the street, and he noticed the steam rising from the asphalt. The streets had been hosed down very early in the morning to keep the European part of town relatively clean. *The odor of Africa,* he thought to himself — difficult to explain since everything except the smell of coffee was foreign to him. He walked along boulevard Albert I^{ier}, Leo's main artery, passing in front of a sidewalk café filled with Europeans conversing over a cup of coffee and a croissant or a plate of cold cuts and cheese with the miniature football-looking rolls, *pistolets*. He paused in front of a record store filled with high-fidelity equipment and records covering the walls. As he moved on up the street he passed several clothing stores, a shoe store — that was where he was supposed to turn right. The company building would be on his right next to the gas station — at least that's what the concierge had told him before he left the hotel. His clothes were as damp as the air by the time he pulled the lobby door open and the air conditioning gave him an agreeable chill.

"Bonjour, monsieur, que puis-je faire pour vous?" The receptionist said.

"Je suis Peter Landon. *J'ai rendez-vous avec Sam Holder. C'est mon premier jour avec Calder Oil Congo Belge."*

"Oh, It's nice to meet you, Mr. Landon. I'm Cecile. You'll find Mr. Holder on the fourth floor. The elevators are down the hall on your left. He's expecting you.'

"Thank you, Cecile." Peter preferred her Belgian accent in French to the accent in English. He walked down the hall and felt his clothes dry on his body as he cooled down from his walk. The ride up was slow, but then, the reputation of the Belgians, particularly the Flemish-speaking Belgians, was of being slow — even slower in Africa because of the heat. He wondered if their work habits were slow, too. That could be a problem for him.

A tall balding man came walking towards him with an outstretched hand.

"Good morning, Peter, welcome to Calder Oil Leo. I'm Sam Holder. Let me introduce you to some of the staff and then I'll show you to your office."

Mr. Holder was in charge of the line employees. They made the rounds of managers who were at the office that morning. Several were either out on a job or out of town. There was a pool of three secretaries for all managers except Mr. Holder, who had his own. It looked like Peter would be doing a lot of his own typing — his other job was only by word of mouth and technically no one in Leopoldville would know of his cover, so this would not be a problem. His office was small with one window overlooking the service station. *How appropriate,* he thought, *since that's what I'm going to be doing.* His boss left him to settle in, saying there would be a meeting that afternoon. The papers on his desk explained what was to be covered as well and he found some old five and ten-year marketing plans which were no longer pertinent, but which gave an idea of the expansion of service stations all through Central Africa that the company had hoped to realize. It would be a great way for him to travel — get to know the country, make sorties into neighboring countries. He would get a very clear picture of what was going on. *Good show, guys — the job's perfect.* He sat quietly for a few minutes reviewing the names and faces of his coworkers and then set to reading the paperwork left for him. The morning flew by. There was a knock and the door opened, and a loud American voice and accent said, "Hi, I'm Paul Jardin. I was sorry

36

not to be here to meet you earlier this morning. How's it going?" Without waiting for an answer he continued, "My wife and I would like you and Lara to come for dinner this evening, if that's okay with you."

Peter rose from behind the desk to shake hands with his new boss. "Nice to meet you, Mr. Jardin. Lara and I will be happy to join you for dinner. Thank you."

"Good. I'll send the car for you. It's the easiest way for you to get to us — we live out of town. Park Acacia — it's a Calder Oil compound. You'll be moving there eventually — when a house becomes available. Let's say the car will be by at quarter to seven. Dinner at seven, dress casual." Jardin moved towards the door.

"Casual? Sir?"

"Yes, oh right, that means, sport shirt — no tie and jacket; nothing dressy for your wife. People usually dress for dinner parties. We'll only be six, as the Holders will be joining us. I'll see you this evening." His hand was on the doorknob and he left the room heading for lunch. Jardin was the General manager of Calder Oil. He was a big man. Peter remembered he had been a star football player at college — he had been asked to become a pro, refused, and decided to do something else with his life.

Peter was perplexed. He knew Lara would be tired and not feeling well. The invitation would have been better a few days after their arrival, but there was nothing he could do about it. Command performance.

It was well after noon when Peter left the office and headed for the hotel to lunch with Lara. One lonely secretary was sitting at her desk covering the lunch hour, taking calls, finishing up the morning's work.

"You don't get lunch today?" Peter asked.

"One of us has to stay, we take turns covering the office at lunch time and in the evening — sometimes — we stay until seven, getting calls from New York. It's part of our schedule."

"Can I bring you something when I come back?"

"Oh, no, thank you. I always bring my lunch with me when it's my turn to stay, and a snack, too." She opened a drawer to show him her lunch. "Thank you for asking. I'll see you later. Oh, by the way, Mr. Holder asked me to tell you, the meeting is at two thirty. Can you make it?"

"That won't be a problem. See you later."

He was late for his meeting with Lara, and annoyed that she was feeling sick so often and was always tired. He had hoped she would lose the baby — for now she was still pregnant. He walked fast, taking another route to the hotel staying in the shade of the trees, which lined the streets. He noticed some high-rise apartment buildings, maybe as high as 15 floors

— every apartment had a terrace and he could see it was part of a cross ventilation system, even though there were air conditioning units under many windows. The bottom floors were offices and shops — a supermarket, liquor and wine stores, more clothing and shoe shops — a great outlet for all the Belgian shoe factories. The butcher shop was closed, everything put away, the counters and floor were being hosed down, then wiped dry. Peter wondered where the meat came from and later learned that for the Europeans it came from Europe by boat in huge freezer lockers and for the locals it came from the countryside and was sold only in the native markets. The shop gave off an acrid smell of blood and rancid fat as Peter hurried by. He turned the corner to walk over to blvd. Albert and realized he had gone too far. The cafés on the boulevard were crowded with a mix of Europeans and locals chattering over the sound of jukeboxes playing loud music most of which was sung by American blacks. He recognized Harry Belafonte, but none of the others. He walked into the hotel out of breath and saw Lara sitting in a huge leather over-stuffed chair waiting for him.

"Sorry I'm late. I didn't see the time go by. Shall we?"

"Oh, don't worry, I'm not very hungry anyway. How was your morning?"

Peter told her about the office, and a few of his coworkers and remembered their dinner engagement for the evening.

"We're invited for dinner tonight at the Jardins' — a car will pick us up at quarter to seven. So you'll have to be ready at six thirty. I'm sorry. I know you're not feeling well. There's nothing I could do about it. Informal," he said, "no coat or tie for me. Something casual, you might get a dress ironed if it needs it."

He thought about what he knew of Lara's wardrobe and knew he would have to do something about it as soon as possible. Her good-looking clothes were stylish for work and play in New York in the winter and spring. Her summer outfits were definitely lacking and very country. And since they were married in such a hurry she hadn't had enough time and perhaps enough money to shop before they left. In Paris, because of her pregnancy, she was hopelessly tired and unable to even think about shopping and she needed to lose a few pounds, too. In fact he wanted to remake Lara into a smashing, sexy model who would attract people and help him with his career. They walked into the hotel restaurant and were seated on the terrace next to a swimming pool, where a few people were getting some exercise. They ordered a quick lunch — no salad because they didn't know if it had been washed with water and permanganate to kill the bacteria. Meat or fish and cooked vegetables luckily could be served cold with vinaigrette. Peter ordered a local beer. There were two beer companies in Leopoldville and one in Brazzaville, which made good beer, inexpensive and available to the local people. Africans were not allowed to buy hard liquor. They could buy only wine and beer. Knowing the hotel water hadn't been boiled, Lara asked for bottled mineral water — flat. All they had was carbonated water, which she had with a slice of lemon.

"What did you do this morning?" Peter asked, wondering if she had been able to get out at all.

"Went the wrong way. I went for a walk a few minutes after you left. I went behind the hotel into a street filled with shops, tiny shops with pieces of material hanging from everywhere as if the walls were made of them. Some were very beautiful. All the African women are draped in it. I wandered the street. There are trees on both sides and it stayed relatively cool. The food shops are awful," she said with a grimace. "There are flies on everything and bees on whatever is sweet. That's a mess. Those people must be full of worms and dysentery." Taking a long drink of her soda water she continued, "Anyway, a white man came up to me and told me I shouldn't be walking alone in that part of town, so I came back to the hotel and unpacked what I could. Got some reading done about this place, but you already know all that," she finished. For Lara that part of town would always be more interesting and she looked forward to being able to return to learn more about the local people, their art and their way of life, to see their market, try their food and to be able to talk with them. Her French needed much improvement before that could happen.

"What are you going to do this afternoon?"

"Probably take a nap, read, and take another walk on the other side of town. Have you a suggestion?" she answered.

"Not really. Just be in shape for this evening."

Chapter Five

Peter returned to the office, the long way around. He walked down the street behind the hotel where Lara had been that morning, only to find that a lot of the stalls were closed. Africans squatted on the sidewalk having lunch or stretched out for a nap wrapped in their *pagnes*, the colorful cloths they wore. He noticed a large number of men of Indian origin. Their skin was almost as black as the Africans and their eyes were black too, but their features were a lot finer — thinner lips, higher cheekbones, and wavy or straight fine hair. He was to learn later that there was a great jealousy between the local Africans and Indians, for the latter were tougher and better businessmen and therefore more successful and wealthy, taking business away from the local population. The shops would open after four, and they would once again be hustling and haggling in loud voices, with some kind of music to cover the agreed upon price for merchandise in hopes that the next client would pay more. Peter returned to the office arriving just in time for his meeting. The afternoon went by quickly. He had decided to stay late assuming that most of the employees would leave as fast as they could, giving him the chance to make a thorough tour of the building before he met up with Lara. And so it was. The only person on his floor was the secretary who stayed until seven. Her desk, along with the two other secretaries' desks, was in the central area in front of the door leading to the hall and elevators, restrooms, and a door to, he supposed, stairs. He had already checked out the restroom, now he walked up the stairs to the top floor to see what he could of the street.

He hoped to be lucky enough to get out onto the roof. The door to the roof was locked, which meant he'd need to get a key. In case of trouble the roof would be the best place to observe and transmit information from the office. Nothing particular in the street caught his eye so he started down the stairs stopping at each floor noting that the layout was very much the same as the fourth floor. He pushed the door open to the third floor and found a man sitting alone concentrating on pages of numbers. Both were surprised to see the other.

"Hi, Peter Landon. I've just joined Calder Oil, in sales. I'm sorry I disturbed you."

"Oh, that's okay. It's the only quiet time in the office. I have a lot of sorting out to do before the end of the year." He pushed his pile of papers aside. "I'm Mac Davies — accountant, as you can see. Have a seat," he replied, indicating the chair in front of his desk. Mac was a big man, with balding blond wavy hair and huge eye glasses, the metal frame cutting into the sides of his friendly face and easy smile.

"Thanks. Actually, I am on my way out and thought I'd stop by to see what the other offices looked like. My wife's waiting for me at the hotel." Looking at his watch, he said, "I have to go. I'd like to stop by tomorrow and ask you a few questions if that's okay. You'll be through with some of your paperwork and I won't be encroaching on your quiet time."

"Sure, that would be better," he paused, looking at the attractive young manager standing in front of him. "What about lunch tomorrow. I can fill you in on some of the characters here."

"Great," Peter answered. It was always interesting to learn about others from someone already in place. "What time?"

"Why don't you stop by around twelve fifteen. We'll head out to one of those air conditioned restaurants unless you really want to get used to the heat."

"Air conditioning is fine with me. I have plenty of time to get used to the heat. See you tomorrow." He thought of Mac on his walk home and of Sam and Paul. They were all large men — over six feet tall, all had blond hair, two with a receding hairline, blue eyes and a slight beer belly and yet appeared to be in good physical condition. Sam and Mac had quick intelligent minds; Paul was slower and more methodical, which was good for the big boss to be. The light was fading as he walked into the hotel and climbed the stairs. He noticed the run down condition of the hotel. He had hoped for better accommodations for Lara's sake, but the other "best" hotel in Leopoldville had no restaurant. At least they could eat here. Lara had spent the afternoon reading and resting up for the evening. She'd have plenty of time to visit the city. She wanted to be in good form for the dinner party.

They were waiting in the lobby when a chauffeur walked in, saw them and asked if they were the Landons.

"My name is Eugène. I work for Monsieur Jardin already two years," he said as he led them to a very large, comfortable black sedan and opened the back door for them. The engine had been left running, the car was cool as they drove off. Eugène, a tall lanky local, looking distinguished with his graying curly hair and soft voice, continued his conversation.

"They are good, nice people, the Jardins. Do you know them before? He says you are new with the company. He's a good boss," he babbled on in French as best he could, with Peter understanding most of it and Lara very little. "This is the main boulevard of Leopoldville named after the Belgian King Albert. Beautiful, isn't it?"

The boulevard was wide; that was as it should be. After all, it was the main artery of the city. Its main thoroughfare was in many ways a dividing line between European and Africans. It was six lanes wide separated by a divider of sidewalk and plants — bushes that never lost their leaves and Cana, which flowered all year. A few small trees had been planted here and there with no pattern, adding to the grandeur of the buildings on both sides where tall trees gave as much shade as they could. Some were palms, flamboyants or acacia, but it was difficult to tell the difference for the light had faded, the sun was down, and the streetlights, which ran along the center divider very high up, were not high enough to make a difference.

"That's the post office on the left, the building with the columns," which must have been four stories high. The lights were out in the building, the entrance, on the contrary, was brightly lit. They passed in front of one building after another — small shops under an arcade on the ground floor, offices or apartments above — all with a deep balcony or terrace to keep the sun's heat from penetrating the building. There were people walking in the street.

"Stores stay open until seven," he continued. All the Africans had left the European part of town except for a few who were either shopping or on their way home from the office.

"We're not supposed to be in this part of town after nine. It's not a curfew, but you get stopped by police and have to show your papers and a letter from your boss with a reason why you're still around. So most of us get home before nine."

"Do you get stopped, too?" Peter asked. "You'll be driving us back to the hotel later."

"Sometimes they stop us, if we go too slow and it looks like we shouldn't be looking around. Maybe to pick somebody up, like a taxi.

That's not allowed. If we have passengers in the car, it's okay. I'll go back to Parc Acacia and spend the night in the garage. I have to be back at work at seven."

"Do you do this often? I mean what are your hours like?" Peter was curious. Eugène certainly would get around, probably knew the area, the ins and outs of Leopoldville and eventually this could be a help for Peter. He really couldn't ask his boss to borrow the chauffeur. He'd have to work out something discreetly. This man had a certain education and a facility with people.

"How many languages do you speak? You do very well in French."

"Only Bakongo and French. I've taken some Swahili — it's the official East African government language in this area and good for doing business with people from neighboring countries — a little Kicongo Lingala, a reconstruction of the language by early Catholic missionaries, and some English since so many of the Americans who come here to see my boss don't speak any French. You speak very good French. Are you American?"

"Yes, my wife and I are both American. We both speak French."

"Well, this is Parc Acacia. All the houses work for the boss. Maybe one day you'll move here." The car pulled up to the largest house in the compound with a large covered terrace and all the lights ablaze. Lara had enjoyed the ride and she too had been impressed by their driver and wondered why Peter was asking so many questions. It was a way to learn about things seen from another perspective, and then again, Peter was always asking questions. She hadn't opened her mouth for the fifteen minutes it had taken them to get there and that was fine, too.

Meeting Peter's bosses and their wives was no big deal for Lara. She felt at ease with everyone and had worked very hard to get there. The courage for all of this had come when she was sixteen and sitting in front of a mirror getting ready for a party she really didn't want to go to. Jean, a woman friend of her stepfather, whom she didn't like at all, walked in and asked what was taking her so long? Her date was downstairs waiting.

"I'm shy," Lara answered. "I don't feel good about myself. I'm shy and I don't know what to say — talk about. I do better with older people. My date's no big deal. He can wait."

"You are a beautiful young girl. You have a sense of humor, know how to dance," she paused and looked in the mirror seeing an unhappy face and continued, "Look at yourself." Lara did. "Is everything in place? Have you put yourself together the best you can? Come on, get up, turn around, look at yourself and make sure everything is in place. The best you can do with yourself." Lara did and turned to look at this unfriendly, bossy woman. "Now turn around again and look at yourself in the mirror. And when you walk out of this room, forget yourself and think of others. Ask questions about their lives, what they like and don't like, where do they come from and where are they going. You'll be just fine. You'll see."

Yes, she thought as she walked in to be greeted by Peter's manager and his wife. *Jean changed my life. It's taken years and I'm doing just fine.*

Eleanor Jardin was a good-looking woman. Strawberry blonde hair tucked back in a chignon. Blue eyes well defined with just enough make-up drawing attention to her charming face. She was pudgy — well-rounded – and looked as if she loved life. And she did, Lara learned later, since she was the life of the party, loved to dance and laughed with everyone. Her gentleness, kindness, and intelligence made her the perfect Manager's' wife. She had been a showgirl in her younger years. She too was at ease with everyone, even the important people in Leopoldville's Belgian and foreign society, always carrying herself with grace and ease. And she was welcoming, as was Julia Holder who came right up to Lara to shake her hand. In contrast Julia was petite, dressed in the elegant style of a New Yorker. Her short curly dark hair suited her oval face, which glowed with inner beauty. Both these women looked like good prospects for friendship. Paul and Sam stood talking to Peter before they came over to introduce themselves. Their firm handshake and look in their eye told Lara who these men were. As Peter's superiors they would keep their distance until they knew the Landons better.

The houseboy served dinner. Light, simple food, easy to digest on a warm evening, with wine or beer. Lara noticed the American cooking style and wondered what kind of dinner she would be offering one day.

The men talked about the political turmoil — the Suez Canal crisis disrupting world trade, the Russians moving into Hungary. The women participated, then turned to Lara for more personal conversation. They could see she was tired and soon after coffee Eleanor said, "You've had a long trip. Would you like to return to your hotel?" Lara nodded.

"I guess I look a little tired. I'm sorry — next time I won't be a party pooper."

"How's the hotel for you?" Julia asked. "We all stayed there when we first got here. Not the greatest, but convenient."

"Oh, it's fine," Lara answered as she got up to leave. "It's got a swimming pool and restaurant — more than the other hotels I've stayed in." *I just hope it won't be for too long,* she thought.

Chapter Six

Ten days in a hotel was more than enough to break Lara into the heat of Africa. She had a bout of dysentery and lost the weight Peter had hoped she would. The model's figure he had wished for was already there. The problem of her pregnancy and morning sickness, which lasted all day, was still upsetting both of them and, of course, the heat with no air conditioning for Lara was debilitating. One week after their arrival, Peter had asked about other lodgings and had been told that one of the company apartments would be available within the next few days. Lara, packed and ready to move, waited patiently for another week before being taken to their new apartment. It was on the fifth floor of the company office building and she hoped to meet some other employees, because although she wasn't feeling in great shape, she missed company and was looking for new friends. Peter wasn't around much. Lara did not know that on weekends he would go off for the day. It was Eugène's day off and he would show Peter around the city and its outskirts constantly chatting, informing Peter of all kinds of things that would be useful to know. The *Vedette* for Brazzaville stopped at nine p.m. Eugène could find him an African who would take a person across the river at any time for a price. His outboard was located at a small dock upstream past the yacht club, and the huge docks for the river ships, which had tall standing cranes just like those in any large port engaged in international trade.

Eugène explained the difference between the many tribes living in Leopoldville, where they came from, the way they wore their clothes, their hair, the way they carried themselves and the language they spoke — who had schooling, who had little. Eugène knew the names of the

45

company compounds giving or renting housing to their employees, the ones who had a school for the employees' children, a medical dispensary, store privileges. Eugène was a man who knew a lot and he and Peter had reached an agreement as to their relationship, which in public was that of an employee of Peter's boss and in private a discreet informer with the appearance of friendship. Since Peter did not yet own a car they used the manager's wife's car. Eugène had permission to take the car for his day off if Eleanor didn't need it. When asked about the mileage he would say it was a family affair that had taken him so far out of town. They also used the car of Eugène's friends, which made their trips less noticeable. Peter was finally given a company car several weeks after their arrival. Lara was permitted to use it when necessary and this allowed her to get out of town and do some of her own exploring. She still wasn't feeling very well.

She had called her mother before she left Paris, saddened by the idea that no one wanted the baby she was expecting and angry that she needed to miscarry. She knew nothing about abortion and the shots she'd given herself in Paris had not produced results. Her mother sent her the name of a potent drug, which could bring back her periods and advice from the doctor to have the shots just three days before the third month's cycle. Also, she should find a doctor who was Jewish because Christian doctors would not be willing to prescribe this medication or to give the shots. In those days, ending a pregnancy was nobody's business except for the people directly involved. It just wasn't talked about. So that evening when Peter climbed the stairs to their apartment he found Lara in tears, sobbing while she sat on the floor, stroking the Dachshund puppy that had been given her for comfort. Peter hated Lara's tears. He thought by now she would have dealt with whatever problem was bothering her and get on with her life. Not so, he saw.

"What's wrong now?" he asked. He disliked complaining and wouldn't put up with it.

"I got a letter from Mummy today. It has the name of a medication which should bring back my periods." She sobbed hardly able to get the words out of her mouth. "Here, read it. It says to start the shots three days before my next cycle. I've calculated that's this coming Sunday." She thought to herself, *I hate you and your mother for this.* Lara got up, put the leash on the dog. "That leaves you three days to find a Jewish doctor and the medication."

"Have a good walk. It will be good for you."

Thanks a lot, Lara thought without answering. She walked out of the apartment.

46

The light was fading fast; the streetlights were already on. It was as if she didn't notice a thing. Her pain was so great. *What a mess I'm in and there's no one to talk to.*

Tears started to flow as she sat on a bench — one that was not directly under a lamppost — in hopes no one would notice her. She put the end of Bollé's leash under one foot and wrapped her arms around herself. She wished she had someone to hold her, to love her, to understand all this. *I can't leave — that's probably what Peter wants me to do.* She got up and started to walk again — into the night, into the darkness, into the light again. That was life, light, dark, light, dark. *Choose the light,* she thought, *leave the dark behind where it belongs. Shadows don't always come because of light or sun. They come from inside. Now you need only light and each day, each moment will take care of itself.*

She turned around and headed back to the apartment. She noticed the silence in the street, the rancid smell of people, food, cars, damp concrete and tar — a smell of Africa, which she hated already. She would survive — The baby, well, she'd see how that played out too.

She walked into a dark apartment, the only light coming from the street lamps. *He didn't even leave a light on for me,* she thought. Lara put the dog in the bathroom, covered the floor with newspapers, and went to bed. Peter didn't move.

When she woke up the next morning, she smelled the coffee and wondered if Peter had walked the dog before going to the office. To her surprise he was sitting at the kitchen table having his breakfast. It was earlier than she thought.

"Hi, how was your walk?"

"Good for me, just like you said," Lara answered with anger in her voice.

"Well, I've found a doctor in the States who will send the medication over with a Pan Am pilot he knows. It will be here Saturday. You can start your shots on Sunday, I'll have a doctor lined up for you by this evening." Peter was relieved to have been able to organize all this while Lara was out of the apartment. Her walk had given him the time he needed to get his thoughts in order and now that things were under control he could show a little sympathy.

"I know you're unhappy. I'm sorry about all this. You have to agree, it's best for all of us." He got up and put his arms around Lara who was in shock from the speed at which he had been able to organize everything. Tears started to flow as she pulled herself away.

"Leave me alone," she cried. "This is your fault as much as mine. Why

47

weren't you more careful? You and your Mutti are quite a pair. Have you walked the dog?"

"No, but the coffee's ready."

Lara poured herself a cup and walked back to the bedroom.

"Walk the dog. I'm going back to bed." She slammed the door. Yes, she was depressed and all she could do was cry. *So, the coffee will be cold,* she thought as she sobbed herself to sleep. *So what?*

A doctor was found, the shots given, the miscarriage provoked. Thanksgiving went by, they were moved to the Coq Hardy — a small inn near the oil company's compound. Bollé successfully chewed Lara's dressy shoes and one of Peter's sneakers and Lara was more exhausted and depressed. She had lost twins. One of the things she had hoped most to have in life was twins, and they were flushed down the toilet in a stream of blood which had continued for three weeks. The doctor had been unable to help. Little did she know the impact the death of these children would have on her and that she would carry it for the rest of her life.

In early December they finally moved into a house in the Calder Oil compound. Stairs up to a small covered terrace led to the front door. Two large opaque glass panels set in a metal frame opened onto a hall. Off to the right were two good-sized bedrooms with air conditioning and two bathrooms, one with a tub, the other with a shower. Stairs on the left went up to a large living room modestly furnished with two comfortable three-seat couches, a coffee table, two side tables and two arm chairs all made of the same light-colored wood. There was also a dining room table and six chairs that matched the other furniture. The previous occupants had worn the material thin just about everywhere, so Peter and Lara were able to choose patterns to their liking and get everything recovered at the company's expense. The fact that Lara had been to interior design school proved to be beneficial and even though their choice of material was quick it took three weeks for the fabric to arrive and another week for the furniture to be covered. It would not to be ready for Christmas.

Lara found Christmas in Africa strange! No Christmas tree, no snow, no cold. She had asked her mother to do some shopping for her in the States; things for Peter she couldn't find to her liking in Leopoldville — light-weight cotton pajamas with shorts instead of long pants, good cotton socks, a book or two in English that she also wanted to read. Cranberry jelly and plum pudding, turkey, champagne and all other trimmings she could get. Then one evening, three days before Christmas, Peter came home with a small evergreen tree.

"Oh, Peter! How wonderful! We have a Christmas tree! Where in the world did you get it?"

"A shipment arrived from Matadi day before yesterday. We only learned about it this morning. You should have seen all the Americans make a run for the door." He laughed. "They had a place set up by the railroad station. A large crowd — Europeans — I guess the Africans celebrate in some other way. People trying to bargain. I thought a small tree would be fine for our first Christmas. We can put it on a table. It'll look bigger that way. Next time we can order in advance. Anyway, next Christmas we'll be back home with your family." Yes, next Christmas would be different. Lara was watching his change of mood when he perked up, "Oh, I have something else in the car. I'll be right back." He carried in a box of tree ornaments and a bag of tinsel. They spent the evening decorating the tree and living room and listening to Christmas carols. Christmas was going to be okay.

By late January, the house was in order and Peter had bought a small Fiat for Lara. Since she couldn't have Peter's car all the time she had to hitch a ride into town to do her shopping or go to the coffee parties to which she was invited. This was how you met people in Leopoldville. Then there were the card games in the afternoon and sometimes they would play after dinner. There were always two or more tables of bridge with one extra person cutting in so the game wouldn't be interrupted. They both played a good game of bridge. Peter liked his poker, Lara canasta. Bridge was a great game in Africa. It kept one's memory working and created a challenge to see who could outsmart the other. In fact, Lara enjoyed it so much that she was playing three or four times a week until Peter suggested she keep it to two times a week and find something else to do.

Why am I such an obedient wife? Lara thought.

Golf took over several afternoons a week — always played after four, when the sun started dropping in the west and a breeze made the course a little cooler. Competitions were played on weekends — even for beginners. If you won, you would receive a demitasse silver spoon with the Royal Leopoldville Golf Club's initials RLGC engraved on it and a handicap of up to 36 for women, 24 for men. It took Lara over a year to get a handicap. Peter was at 18 by the end of the year. They met people of many professions at golf — the high society of Leopoldville — and Peter was amused to see Lara invited to play even as a beginner. The older men who could leave work when they wanted, at least more easily than the younger ones, would ask her to play, knowing they could flirt with her, have a wonderful time joking and get a kiss at the end of the game if they won, which they always did.

The clubhouse was a one-story brick building stretched out in a semicircle with a terrace bar and a single long table that ran the length of the terrace for light food and drink. It was at this table that they enlarged their circle of friends.

The 18 hole course had lots of sand traps and sand greens and the players were allowed to pick up the ball out of its dent and flatten the dent before replacing the ball. Then with the same wooden T-shape scraper they could make a straight line to the cup. Putting on sand was a challenge and usually caused a temper tantrum if you took the game seriously or loud bursts of laughter if you were playing for fun. Of course, in Leopoldville every game was played for something — money, drinks, dinner, kisses, a challenge which, depending on who lost, would be accomplished within a certain period of time. In the games between men and women it was often a case of seduction and therefore all the more fun to lose. Players always had caddies, most of whom had been on the course for years and one would reserve them for important games of chance or competitions. The course was rugged — it must have been part of the riverbed or pool before the river dug deeper into the land on its way to the sea, leaving the area dry. Mango and palm trees, many kinds of shrubs lined the fairways and roughs. One never went for a ball into deep rough or in the bushes — too many snakes or spiders and poisonous insects — only a caddy with shoes or high rubber boots would go after a ball, beating the ground with a club or stick to chase the vermin away. Lara remembered one afternoon hearing screams from a caddy. He had been bitten by a Mamba — a black snake that spreads a hood like a Cobra when ready to strike. Everyone stopped and many went to see if they could help. Lara being close by, went to do whatever she could, on her knees holding one arm of the caddy while two men were holding his leg with the bite. A tourniquet was already in place to keep the blood from going to the heart and one of the men began to cut a cross where the fangs had broken the skin. He then put his mouth to the cut and started to suck as much blood from the wound area as he could, spitting it out as fast as he could and sucking again. Someone arrived with a bucket of water and a syringe of serum in hopes to save the caddy's life. The antidote was given, but he began to shake violently and the other caddy had a hard time holding his head. Someone else had taken the other arm. The poor man was out of control and lost consciousness, all within three minutes of being bitten. Lara learned later that he died on the way to the hospital. The snake had been caught and killed. No one finished his round of golf and everyone stopped at the clubhouse bar for a drink before going home. Not Lara, who excused herself, got into her little light blue Fiat and started to drive home. She had to stop because she was shaking and had lost control and was in tears when she realized that it could have happened to her. She had walked past that spot a few minutes earlier, hit her ball and walked on. Peter was dressed to go out to dinner and sitting on the front steps waiting for her as she pulled into the driveway. He was sorry to hear the news and hurried Lara in to the house to change for dinner. She had fifteen minutes to make herself beautiful before heading back to town.

"It could have been me," she said.

"You're here, you're fine, come on, come on. We can't be late. I've put your dress out. Put some cold water on your face before you do your make up. Your eyes are all red. I'm sorry. You can take a breather on our way to town. The Jardins are picking us up. You can tell us what happened then."

It was rare for Peter and Lara to spend a night at home. They had met a great many people and were in constant demand, particularly at parties where both French and English were spoken — often seated between one language and the other, used as translators or interpreters as the case might be. Peter had sent Lara to night school to learn French, she needed to be fluent and was not when they arrived in Leopoldville. Fortunately she had had years of French in college, and during her stint at art school in Paris. The first few lessons at night school were old stuff and boring. She was the only European and woman in a class full of Africans whose accents were worse than hers. She said she wouldn't go back. Peter always found a solution to these situations and had the company pay for a private tutor, who, within six months, brought Lara up to par. Unfortunately, writing the *dictées* didn't help much. Although she couldn't spell in English; in French, she seemed to do better. It was cause for a good laugh since the constant criticism and corrections were no longer taken as an insult and given in good humor by everyone or anyone, even the "boys" who worked for them. However, often the correction or the Belgian slang word was incorrect and Lara would have to run it past Peter for confirmation. Lara loved learning a foreign language. She loved the sounds — like music to her ear whether in German, Swahili or Kicongo — and most Europeans living in Leopoldville spoke French.

It was during that time that Lara improved her cooking skills. Dinner parties were *de rigueur* and delicious food and wine a must. *The Joy of Cooking* was a beginning for just about anything she produced and improved upon, when possible, having participated in cooking lessons a family friend and gourmet chef had given Lara's older sister as an engagement present. Shopping was a challenge since Lara didn't know

51

the European counterparts for many American products used in cooking and baking in particular and often had to invent solutions. She had to learn the metric system — no more inches, feet or miles; no more ounces or pounds; no more cups, pints and quarts. Thank goodness spoon sizes were about the same, the "to taste" was still the best system for flavors, herbs and spices. The African marketplace had loads of these — many varieties of curry because of the large Indian population and new herbs and seeds from Africa increased one's creative talents. She had brought with her the usual herbs and spices one uses in the States and found that she could replenish the supply because most Europeans used them as well. There was an African market for Europeans where you could buy fresh fruits, vegetables, flowers and plants for the garden. There was European clothing, which had been made locally, mostly with local fabrics, and local art and drawings made for tourists. The Africans had stalls in this market — an oblong or rectangular table covered with a plastic or cloth, with four posts holding a metal corrugated plaque to keep out the sun or light rain. During the rainy season no one went shopping when it rained. It really poured then, a deluge that prevented seeing more than a meter or two in front of you. It was a great time to take a cold shower and rinse your hair in rainwater. It cleared the air, washed the plants and animals and cleaned the streets, but helped increase the insect population as well, so helicopters sprayed DDT over the whole city and most of the suburbs.

Lara loved the local market more than any other. There were rows of stalls here, too, and a covered part, somewhat like an open store for furniture and household supplies. Since one had to pay for a stall, most of the women laid out a *pagne* , a colorful cotton African print normally worn wrapped around the body, or a straw mat and placed their goods on it, usually without any order. In contrast, the Indian women would make a work of art out of their produce, giving the market a lot more character. You could find deep fried caterpillars and crickets, crunchy to the taste and like peanuts once you learned to enjoy them. There were also white worms that looked like small pieces of Jerusalem artichoke squished up into little pieces, which were boiled and served over cooked greens. Lara didn't ask what the greens were and chose not to try them, much to the delight of a crowd of African women who had gathered to listen to the explanation of African food and how it was prepared. Her contact with the locals was easy and they felt comfortable with her once they got used to her wanderings through the market, often with a friend, and when she was alone a few local women would follow behind her knowing that it was not always safe for a European to be alone in the market. They would come to her assistance when bartering became too passionate and they felt she was in danger. This often permitted Lara to walk away with a prize piece of art or food — whatever she had wanted to buy — at a very reasonable price.

Her new international European friends did not understand her fascination with the local market food and ambiance. The loud cries of the vendors could split your eardrums if you were caught unaware and passed in front of them at the moment they let out their cry. Lara had thought it might be a game. She was assured that was not so. There was also constant loud chatter because of the music played around the market. Sometimes the little children — little girls dressed in fancy, fluffy, pale dresses, sometimes in nothing, and boys with a flap of cloth tucked into a string that went between their legs front to back — would dance to the music. Mothers clapped hands to the rhythm, encouraging the children to let off steam. A basket would be knocked over, sending fruit rolling in all directions. Someone was always annoyed and everyone would rush to pick things up, put them back good naturedly, often with the little ones giggling, the guilty one hiding behind his or her mother. The men took care of the sales in the covered part of the market. Dressed in European-style shorts, some had African shirts, others sleeveless T-shirts, some bare-chested. Their talk was of the economy, the abuse or kindness of the Belgians, who were most frequently talked about since almost all commerce and industry was conducted by Belgian companies located in the city. From what Lara had seen, the Belgians had done more for the Africans than any other colonizing country in Africa. Peter had been informed of this on his weekend outings with Eugène. Lara had seen it for herself once she had a car. The African company compounds were noisy, as many family members moved in with the single person who was earning a living. The children could have schooling up through the equivalent of sixth grade. Since some parents and almost all grandparents could not read or write, the children often were seen in the evening light teaching other family members what they had learned that day in school.

There were also small clinics — lines of people waiting to see a doctor or nurse for minor injuries, colds, or just questions about their health. Hygiene was a problem in these crowded areas, with insufficient plumbing for the population and garbage spread over the sidewalks by scrounging dogs or because people thought they might find something useful in what others had thrown away. These compounds were like villages within the city. The streets were poorly lit, yet there was enough light to get around at night. In some compounds each house had electricity, in others only certain community buildings had it. A variety of trees studded the streets; some people had vegetable and flower gardens in front of their homes, and most had put up a low wall to claim their territory where they would sit during evening gatherings. The huge cockroaches, which crawled everywhere, came in from any vegetation no matter where one lived, be it in the native city or the European country compounds. Lara hated these huge cockroaches. They were the size of her thumb or bigger, the same color as the ones she had in the New York apartment, and faster. She didn't like to squish them because then she had to pick them up and wash the remains away. So it was usually the "Boy" who, upon arriving in the early morning, chased the cockroaches that had gotten in during the night or had been missed the night before and cleaned the floor when there were no more to be found. They were clever insects — one could see just the antennae peeping around a corner and by the time you got there or moved the object behind which it hid it would be gone. Then there were those who came in pairs and knew how to divide and therefore conquer for at least another twenty-four hours of feeding time in her home. They did not fascinate her the way the spiders and snakes did and since just about everything was poisonous, these had to be eliminated before they killed her. When she saw a spider web in the house she knew she had to find the spider before it found her. There were hardly any birds because of the lack of insects due to DDT spraying. Lara had been caught out once in her wanderings, had heard the helicopters and all of a sudden saw everyone run for cover. This she did too, darting into a covered stall in the market and covering as much of herself as she could with her full skirt, particularly her face and nose. To breathe it was poison and it could damage her sight. She had waited quietly until she heard people starting to move around before she even uncovered her eyes to see what had happened. The spray left a strong, unpleasant smell and stung her eyes. She was angry; the Africans were furious. She would talk to Peter about trying to warn the population sufficiently early so as not to be caught again under a misting of DDT. When she left the market she noticed a billboard with notices posted — one told of the day's spraying. Who had read it? There was nothing drawing your attention to the billboard. They needed verbal communication over the radio and cars with loud speakers.

Lara also wandered along the avenue de la Corniche, next to the river where the big, ugly, houses of the wealthy, well-established businessmen and diplomats were ostentatiously showing their wealth. It was close enough to the river for crocodiles to visit the gardens of these estates and gobble up a chicken or two before being chased back to the river or killed, depending on the mood of the mistress of the house. The wife of the British Ambassador would yell at her "boys" who would chase the crocodile with machetes. She would call out, "Don't harm the crocodile. Leave it alone, scare it back to the river." This was not so easy to do, with the crocodile focused on a meal in sight. The street was on the outskirts of town, about ten kilometers in the opposite direction from the river docks and airport. It was also where the Leopoldville Rapids started — the river leaving Stanley Pool and heading for the coast. The Congo is one of the fastest flowing rivers in the world and there were since the '50s, several hydroelectric power plants providing electricity for Leopoldville and Brazzaville as well as being able to sell the excess to distant customers. The beauty of the Pool and rapids provided an ideal spot for colonials. The farther out of town, the higher up the houses, the cooler the breeze. Peter and Lara had become close friends with an insurance broker whose house was just about the last one on this road overlooking the rapids. Matt's Sunday parties by his pool, where one could drink, eat and cool off at the same time, were a delight. There were always houseboys to serve anything one requested, a picnic or a barbecue and lots to drink. There was constant joking and laughter. It was there one New Year's Eve that Lara became intoxicated for the first time. She must have drunk at least an entire bottle of champagne before the end of the evening. Dancing had slowed to making love on the dance floor with whoever you danced with, changing partners, never really getting satisfied. It was so funny everyone finally gave up and went home. To Lara's shock, when she fell onto her bed the room started to spin, she felt awful.

"Peter, help me. I don't know what's happening," she cried. "The room is going around in circles."

"Do you feel sick?" he asked. "It's the whirly beds."

"No, just everything is twirling."

"Put a foot on the floor. That usually stops the spinning."

"How do you know? Has this ever happened to you?" she asked as she put her foot down and waited a few minutes. The room kept on spinning. Peter went over to her.

"Are you okay?"

"No, help me up. Can we go for a walk? When we were all dancing things were fine. Maybe that can help." He lifted her up, but instead of taking her for a walk he put her in the shower and turned on the cold water.

"Peter, that's my party dress. You're ruining it. Stop it, turn it off, please," she said as she started to cry and laugh at the same time. He took off his clothes and got into the shower with her, slowly undressing her and running his hands along her slim body.

"Maybe this will help take your mind off the spinning." And it did. Making love in a cold shower was new to both of them. Cooling their minds as the urge for pleasure mounted for them both. When Lara went to bed the room was no longer spinning — she was quite calm as they lay under the sheet since the air conditioning was going full blast. The New Year was well on its way.

Parties were a big part of life in Leopoldville. Once Peter and Lara were well settled in their new home, it was important to meet as many people as possible. To be a part of many groups in society and business was imperative for Peter. The more important the person, the more information he could obtain. The more Peter could help his friends, the more he could ask of others if need be. The fact that they now both spoke fluent French, were charming and amusing, intelligent and discreet, added to their popularity. The warm climate brought out strong physical desires in both men and women. Fidelity was too often absent in this moving population, and an occasion for a fling was rarely turned down. Lara was often jealous of Peter, with one too many under his belt, as he disappeared into the bushes with another woman, leaving Lara to the wolves. She had taken her vows and couldn't let herself go off with just anyone. No one was attractive to her. She loved her husband, never refused his sexual advances and couldn't understand this whole situation. She was living too far from home to leave, and she had already decided to stick it out at the time of her miscarriage.

Peter would return from one of his many trips with a gift for Lara. Once it was a red dress he had bought off a model in a fashion show in the Kivu. The trouble was the model was smaller in the bust and bigger in the hips than Lara. And Lara made him pay for his mistake. When the fashion show came to Leopoldville, Lara spotted a beautiful white lace dress with a low-cut neckline, long tight sleeves and a straight tight-fitting bodice and skirt. It fit her like a glove and cost twice as much as the red one Peter had brought home. She supposed there would be some exchange between Peter and the model. She didn't care — she loved the dress. Her only problem was learning how to walk in the tight skirt since there was no slit to give more room for a larger step.

And then there was Dado. He was a small Frenchman; his wife was also called Dado. He had been dying to teach Lara how to walk — not the American athletic walk, which was her style, but a sexy feminine walk to add to her charms. And so Lara asked for a lesson. The Dados loved to receive for Sunday lunch. They always served champagne — Moët et

Chandon, often pink — followed by a delicious light lunch. During coffee, Dado took Lara by the hand and led her into the garden where they would not be observed.

"*Et maintenant, ma petite*, this is what you must do. Exaggerate the movement so it becomes natural for you. Here, watch me." He put his hands on his buttocks and started to stride sliding each foot along the ground weaving his hips in motion with his shoulders. "*Serrez les fesses, les hanches en avant.* Tighten your buttocks, hips forward." His pelvis moved forward. "Lead with the pelvis, not with the chest. Keep your shoulders back, head up, glide instead of stride. Now you try." Lara put her hands on her buttocks and started to mimic Dado, burst into laughter, doubled over and sat on the ground laughing so hard tears came to her eyes. "*Allez, ma grande. Tout le monde va nous entendre.* Come on, little one, everyone is going to hear. They will want to know what we are doing alone in the garden, my reputation."

"You already have a wild reputation. I'm happy to add to it," she said as she was pulled to her feet and tried again to walk the slinky walk. This time they both ended up laughing. Dado mimicking Lara and vice versa. A crowd had gathered to watch the merriment and everyone joined in doing their best to imitate the "Dado Walk". The men were hysterical, the women very seriously trying to maintain a dignity impossible under the circumstances. Lara had learned not only how to walk in a tight skirt; she also learned how to curtsy to royalty should that become necessary. Again Dado had proven to be a treasure.

"Hook one knee behind the other, keep your chest up, always look the other person in the eye. It helps to keep your balance and bend only the knees. Try it." By that time Peter came up to Lara and gracefully held her hand. The curtsy was perfect, Dado was happy — applause for teacher and student.

The Landons brought the novelty of costume parties to Leopoldville with a toga party. Friends in the compound helped with decorations. Greek columns decorated the porch and living room. Drinks were served on rugs laid on the front lawn by the "boys," also dressed in costumes of short, white, belted tunics. Other rugs had been laid out for guests to lounge upon. The entrance hall was set for a buffet dinner and Lara's prize piece was a roast suckling pig with an apple in its mouth. The pig had to be cut in half to fit in the oven and was pieced back together as best she could, presented on a wooden plank covered with fresh leaves washed in water and permanganate in hopes of eliminating parasites. All vegetables were soaked in the same solution for at least a half hour, re-rinsed and either boiled or steamed — salad was rarely served. The buffet table was filled with dishes of curried rice and peanut salad, fried bananas, and several cooked vegetables and meats, and everything was accompanied by the appropriate red or white wine. Dessert was an assortment of pastries. Guests returned to the rugs on the lawn or sat on the steps or around a few small tables in the living room, which were removed for dancing after dinner. There were no DJs in those days, so the host, hostess or guests changed the records when the time came or the mood changed, depending on with whom they were dancing. Lara, by dancing time, was exhausted and had a headache. She slipped into the bedroom, turned on the air conditioner, which drowned out the sound of the party, lay down and fell asleep. When she awoke the sounds of the party were still very present. Feeling better, she got up to join in the fun. To her surprise, the lights were off all through the house and, not understanding why, she flipped the switch and caught everyone on the dance floor making out. Nobody was with their spouse — Peter included — and all were embarrassed. Peter left Michelle, came over to Lara and said, "It's okay, let me put the lights out. Everyone is having fun in the dark."

"Particularly you and Michelle," She felt like whacking him in the face as the lights went out. He put his arms around her to dance, but Lara was too upset. She left the house to see what was going on outside where she found more of the same. Why did Africa make everyone so horny? Several new romances started that night, provoking marital difficulties for many couples and one divorce. She went for a walk in the dark and then to a neighbor's house and sat on their steps until one of them came home and told her the party was over. Slowly she walked back to a quiet, messy, empty house. Peter had gone off with someone. She put a record on, danced alone in the dark, finally fell asleep on the couch, and woke up to Peter's return in the early morning.

"I looked for you last night. We went to Matt's for a swim."

And a screw, she thought.

"I missed you."

"I bet you did. Welcome home. Want to make love?" she asked.

"Come on, Lara. It's seven o'clock in the morning. I'm going to bed."

"You just came from bed somewhere. Too tired?" she said looking him in the eyes.

Peter didn't answer. He had a feeling this conversation would be best avoided. Anyway, he was leaving on Monday for Elizabethville. That meant he had less than 24 hours with Lara and would give her some cooling off time. He'd be away two to three weeks and it should be better by the time he got home. He shed his clothes in a pile and went to bed naked. Sex for Peter was the best tension reliever and sleeping pill. The air conditioning had cooled off his sweaty body and he was really feeling tired. *I have to be in shape when I leave on Monday,* he thought. *Pulling off two jobs at the same time is driving my brain and body crazy. Oil and service stations,* he looked at his left hand, *info and statistics,* as he looked at the right one. He noticed the shape of his hands — as if for the first time — square, short fingers, powerful, yet gentle with women, fine, strong wrists, hairy arms, hairy body. His eyes closed out the tension, mental as well as physical. He had a gift — he could turn off and tune out when not in a dangerous situation. He had learned his survival skills well, and knew how to use them. At least right now there were few trouble spots in the Congo. With the American government pushing for independence and wanting to take control of foreign policy and the mines, times were certainly going to change. That was why he was here — to gather information.

It was late afternoon when Peter woke up.

Chapter Seven

Monday morning Lara drove Peter to the airport for a five-thirty departure. There was less turbulence in the early morning. As the air heated up during the day, thunderstorms or high winds often made flying dangerous — better to get where you were going before noon if possible. As she kissed him good-bye, she wondered what kind of a gift he would bring her. Her heart ached as she watched the plane take off and, feeling hurt and teary-eyed, she drove home as the morning light filled the sky. She went back to bed fully dressed, hoping to fall asleep and forget her unhappiness. She had started to drink alone – gin and tonic. One went right to her head; she couldn't possibly have taken a second. She would turn on the record player and dance by herself in the dark until she could dance no more and then to bed, often waking in the morning with a migraine. She knew this was not helping, and was thankful when her aunt came through Leopoldville on her way to South Africa. Her aunt was very wise about jealousy, and she helped Lara learn how to deal with her degrading situation. Her aunt said that her uncle often had a mistress when he was off on a trip. But, when he was home he made her feel like she was the most important woman in his life. That seemed to be enough for her, although Lara wondered why. And besides, when Peter was home he played around right in front of Lara and everyone else for that matter. She knew that one day she would have to talk to Peter about it. But she was afraid he would suggest that they separate, that she could go home — and that for Lara was too much of a defeat. She was determined to learn to live with it.

Peter was fascinated by Katanga. Elizabethville, its capital, smaller in

60

size than Leopoldville, was a wealthy city because of the mineral deposits and industrial development. It, too, had a large military camp, a stadium, a zoo, separate hospitals for Europeans and Africans, and foreign consulates. Peter noticed a racecourse near the airport when his DC-6 flight landed around two in the afternoon. *The climate must be better than Leo if they can have racehorses here,* he thought. Happy to be off the plane, he understood why Elizabethville was a pleasant place to live. A thin layer of clouds diminished the sun's heat. It was the dry season, and the air was cool and fresher than Leopoldville. The 4,000 feet of altitude compared to Leopoldville's 1,000, made a big difference. As he walked down the stairs from the plane, he saw his Belgian counterpart from Calder Oil waving to him.

"Hello, Peter. Have a good flight?"

"Hello, Mathieu. It's good to put a face to someone I've talked to so often on the telephone. Yeah, it was a good flight, a little bumpy going over the mountains. What a view!" Peter looked Mathieu over — neatly dressed, even pleats in his pants. They were about the same size, same dark hair and blue eyes.

"I'm never bored flying here in Africa. The continent is so varied and beautiful, awesome; I get angry with myself when I fall asleep." Peter was not going to tell him that he had slept a good part of the trip, recuperating from his troubles with Lara.

The two men walked into the one story building to pick up his suitcase. "I see they have Customs here. Planes come in from Angola and South Africa?"

"Also from Brussels direct, and other countries. Everyone has to puddle-jump to get here. We have a larger percentage of Europeans here than in Leo." Mathieu looked around to see if he knew someone, waved to a friend. "It's a good life for me and my family — single sex schools, sports — pretty much like home except that I have a great house and my wife has two houseboys for the housework and one for the garden. I hope to stay here a long time. Not interested in going home soon. How about yourself? Like Leo? It takes a while to get used to it."

"We've been there about six months now. Made some friends — quite a social life — and I've traveled a lot. Tried to get down here a couple of months ago but with no luck. There's my suitcase." A porter rolled a trolley of bags into the waiting room and lined them up on the floor. No one was in a hurry; the midday heat always slowed everyone down. It was time for lunch and a siesta.

"Here, let me help you," Mathieu said as he reached half-heartedly for the bag.

"Oh, that's okay, I travel light. Where's the car? My secretary said I was at the Ambassador Hotel. Is that right?"

"Right," Mathieu answered. He called to the driver, "*Jean, viens avec la voiture.* I'll introduce you when he brings the car up. He'll be your driver for the rest of the week. We don't keep a driver on the weekends. Anyway, you might want to drive the car yourself. There are some beautiful places to visit not too far from town."

The car arrived shortly and introductions were made. With the suitcase thrown into the trunk they were off to the center of town — only five or six kilometers away.

"The hotel is on the avenue Royale, the most central location we could get for you. It has a relatively good restaurant. Would you like to have a late lunch?" Time was what one made of it.

"Sure," Peter answered. "I'll check in, go wash up and be right back, if that's okay with you."

"Good, I'll get us a table."

Hotel Ambassador was one of six three-star hotels in Elizabethville with a restaurant; hot and cold running water; and an internal phone, which meant that all of Peter's calls could be registered. The private calls he didn't want recorded would have to be made from the telephone and telegraph office. Those would be recorded too, but would be more difficult to trace directly to him. Some of the hotels had dancing at night, others had swimming pools. The Ambassador had neither. There were more good hotels in Elizabethville than in Leopoldville and more hotels and restaurants in general.

They had a quick lunch and Peter asked Mathieu if he had a meeting that afternoon and then excused himself and said he'd be at the office later to plan the next few days with him. He needed a shower and rest before facing a whole new group of people at the office. But as it turned out, by the time they finished their lunch it was starting to get dark. The office was closed and Peter had the evening to himself to wander or be driven around by Jean.

Peter had fallen into a routine during his travels around the Congo. The cities were planned mainly as a grid which adapted to countryside, river, or transportation; easy to get around, easy to know where you were. The streets were well marked and lighted and after Peter's visits to service stations and some clients, he soon knew his way around town. Hotels, restaurants, bars, nightclubs, newspaper offices, consulates, missions, schools, churches, hospitals, railroad stations, docks — all were of interest.

And here in Elizabethville were the central offices of Union Minière du Haut Katanga and other mining companies. The head offices were located in Brussels. Of course, what Peter most wanted was to be able to visit some mines. The Prince Leopold Copper Mines in Kipuski, the only underground mines in the Congo, were 58 miles away. They produced not only copper, but also zinc and sulfur. Other minerals found in the area were iron, tin, cobalt, manganese, zinc, radium, gold, diamonds — mostly industrial — and, of course, uranium. The U.S. Government, with its exclusive knowledge of atomic weapons, did not want this to fall into communists' hands.

Peter worked at Calder during the week, and on the two weekends drove out to whichever mines he could. During his travels he took in the scenery of the Kundelunger plateaus and its game, the Johnston Falls and Kaseng with its ruins of a 17th century fort. Before returning to Leopoldville, he stopped in Jadotville, north and slightly west of Elizabethville, to visit a cobalt factory for the refining of two different sorts of alloys, one rich in copper the other in cobalt, and then went on to Kamina, a trading and industrial center dealing in large amounts of cotton and other minerals. He continued on up to Luluabourg and Port Franqui, the end of the railroad from Elizabethville in the direction of Leopoldville. From there, river transport took over and ships brought the goods to Leopoldville. By the end of March, six months after their arrival, Peter knew the country inside out. He had been off traveling approximately two-thirds of the time and while work was going well, his marriage wasn't. The sales manager was going on home leave and Peter would have to stay put and cover for him for the next three months. That meant he had to work things out with Lara. A trip for her during this tour seemed out of the question, although Peter hoped to persuade his boss otherwise. He thought perhaps next term would be a good time to improve his cover by having a baby, and with a baby a trip to the parks would be impossible. He had made up his mind to be more careful in front of Lara, more discreet, more attentive to her. But Lara did not appreciate his attentions. What he really set out to do was a makeover — change her hair, improve her make-up. He gave 90% of the clothes she had brought with her to missionaries. They looked at fashion magazines, bought fabric, designed dresses, evening clothes, just about everything she wore. He even supervised her hairdresser. Lara hated to waste her time there, and yet felt obliged to be obedient. He took her to her fittings, and if she put on a few pounds, they had to come off before the next fitting. He knew about women's clothes. Dior, Givenchy, Guy Laroche, Jacques Fath, Jacques Heim, and Chanel — he knew them all personally. That is to say, his mother played cards with them and saw them socially. He would pick up some models' dresses when they went through Paris on vacation at below cost as a favor to a hard-working salesman. For now he reverted to his own knowledge of how to put a backless dress together or an overlapping skirt so when Lara danced her whole leg would be visible from time to time. Anything to catch the eye. Lara learned to design, too, and have her clothes made. The right place for a dart, a button or a zipper.

After several months of this attention, Lara put her foot down. Her hair had grown sufficiently to put it up in a French twist. No more hairdressers. And by then she had several groups of women friends with whom she loved to play cards. Mostly bridge — good for the memory in a hot climate, and she was becoming good at it. Duplicate tournaments proved her to be one of the better players. Peter then told her she could play no more than twice a week plus whenever they were invited to play in the evening at dinner parties. Peter played poker with the men while the women played bridge. With all the time she spent playing cards, he found that she had become a better player than he. He wanted her to spend more time improving her golf or tennis — less cards, he said. She had enough of being obedient.

Her art group didn't work out either. Instead of painting, everyone gossiped; Lara found gossip boring and mean. She wondered what they said about her and Peter behind their backs. She did love gardening though. Soon their house had a row of banana trees along the driveway, an avocado tree, started from a pit, growing by the garage door, a papaya tree just off the balcony, where she could pick a fruit for breakfast, and a pineapple plant just below the papaya. She found it odd that no one else planted fruit trees, only flowers. Then again the fruit trees were particularly for those who followed. Maybe that was the reason. In eighteen months things had grown a lot, but not enough to bear fruit. Lara was happy with the thought that those who had the house after her would have the fruit.

Peter had put a lot of work into remaking Lara, and he felt she was turning out pretty well, more like the model he needed and wanted as a wife; he knew his mother would be pleased with the change, too. Their relationship had grown easier on both of them, there was more tolerance, more understanding. Lara had changed inside as well as out.

Chapter Eight

Late one Sunday afternoon during the rainy season Peter and Lara had awakened from their usual Sunday afternoon siesta and were sitting quietly reading in the living room. Something in her book set Lara off on thoughts about her childhood and she realized she knew nothing about Peter's childhood, only that he had arrived in the U.S. at about the age of ten, that his parents were Jewish thanks to that anonymous letter and his mother's odd explanation and that Peter had gone to two different schools, both called St. Paul's, before going to Yale, all of which wasn't much of a history.

"Peter, can I bother you?" she asked.

"Sure. What's up?"

"I just realized that I know next to nothing about you and we've been married for over a year. What do you remember about being a little boy? Do you remember much of anything? Sometimes people can remember back to when they were three years old. I can't, but I do remember when I was four." She shifted in her chair. "Mummy sent me to take a bath. My older sister was in the room next to the bathroom listening to modern music and all I liked was classical, so I slammed the door to deaden the sound and got into my half-full, cool tub and the ceiling fell down on me." She remembered the scene well. "I screamed, nobody cared and I screamed some more and finally pulled myself out of the bathtub covered with plaster, wrapped a towel around me and went off looking for Mummy. Do you have any memories like that?"

Peter thought for a moment. His childhood was a blur. He remembered Schwester, his nanny. He had seen more of her than he had his mother. And then there was his father, Alexander Landon — or was he his stepfather? After their wedding and their arrival in Paris, Peter had called Landon to introduce Lara to him. Instead of being happy for Peter, he had yelled, "Who gave you permission to use my name? You're not my son and I don't want to see you!" and hung up. This had been a shock for Peter, and particularly hurt since he had handed the earphone to Lara so she could hear the conversation. Many phones in Europe had an eavesdropping device so a second party could hear the conversation. Peter had never expected this reaction from a man who had once asked him to call him "Papa." The man had been a loving father to him for so many years — at least until he and Peter's mother had gotten a divorce.

Confused, he started to tell his story. "I have some memories, not many. Some are from what Mutti told me and from pictures she has of me as a little boy. One is a time at the Lido — the beach just off Venice. I'm in a bathing suit, the kind you step into and pull up over the shoulders. The reason I know it was the Lido is that I have a life preserver over my shoulders with "Lido" on it. There's also one where I'm in *culottes courtes*, shirt and tie, very English with argyle socks and a dark blue sweater. I don't remember much about that time. I was maybe six or seven. Never saw much of Mutti. They were always off to parties or visiting wealthy friends. Schwester was my mother. Then, well, there was the news of the war and what they were doing to the Jews in Germany and Poland. This I do remember.

One night Mutti came and woke me, got me dressed, packed a few things in a satchel, and took my hand while putting a finger in front of her lips. We were leaving the house, and I wanted to say good-bye to Schwester. Mutti said no one could know we were leaving. We weren't safe. At the time I didn't understand the danger of being of Jewish descent. I didn't know we were Jewish. Papa wanted us out of Paris. He was a Polish diplomat and although we went to a Catholic church, since I was circumcised I supposed we'd be recognized as Jewish and we would probably never come back." He got up and started pacing. "We drove all night, I think it was Amsterdam. I was terrified and clung to Mutti. No one slept. As daylight started to appear I remember Mutti's eyes, tired, red, and swollen from crying — so full of fear. I think we both were wondering what we were going to do. Where would we go? There were several ships in the harbor, and Mutti and I waited in the car for hours. Many people were arriving, running from one place to another. They were looking for passage out of Holland, too, and probably most of them were Jewish, although nobody had those little black hats pinned to their heads."

A pause as his mind raced on. He turned to face her. "Anyway, Papa got us on a ship for New York. We stood in line for hours, the three of us. There were men sitting at tables. Their faces were stern and frightening. Papa handed over our papers, which were studied very carefully. The ordeal seemed to last forever, but finally it was our turn to go to the ship. To my horror, Papa kissed us good-bye, tears in his eyes. His hands shook as he hugged me. 'Take good care of your mother for me,' he said and turned to walk away." Peter remembered calling after his father, "Papa, Papa, please come with us," but he couldn't repeat the words for Lara.

Lara noticed the sadness in Peter's eyes as they filled with the tears, which he could no longer hold back. She got up and put her arms around him, sorry for having provoked the sad memories. "Can I get you something to drink? A gin and tonic?" Peter nodded, so Lara left him with his thoughts as she stifled her own tears and went to get Peter's drink. When she came back into the living room Peter had pulled himself together and immediately continued his story. "We walked up the gang plank. I was scared of losing Mutti. Papa was gone and I was with someone who had never really taken care of me. I squeezed her hand hard and I wouldn't let go. We got to our cabin. It was meant for two people, although there were five of us, another woman with her two small children. We had one bed; they slept in the other. The trip was awful. The sea was rough and almost everyone was seasick. It was cold and we couldn't go on deck. There was no room for us, people were in a lousy mood, and we weren't allowed to play in the room. Mutti played cards and made friends with some people in first class. She even got a job offer to sell hats at Macy's. I didn't see much of her during the crossing. There were plenty of people for me to talk to and some kids to play with. Hide and seek was the best game. No one knew that we were playing and I got to know the ship quite well." Peter sipped his drink remembering that time. Even when left to himself he felt he had done pretty well.

"Early one morning, everyone was wakened by the tooting of the ship's horn. We were approaching New York harbor. Everyone went on deck to see the skyline of the city and the Statue of Liberty. The Statue of Liberty!" He threw his arms up in the air. "She was something! And by then I understood what she stood for. Everyone, *everyone* was crying — joy, sadness, you name it." Peter was feeling excited. "There we were — free and safe from the Nazis." Peter stood up and started to pace — again. "You see, for us, we had a place to go — a small hotel on the Upper East Side. I don't remember the name." He was walking faster as he continued his story. "But a lot of the families on board didn't and for that matter, had hardly any money to get started. We were taken to Ellis Island, went through the immigration process, and since Mutti was the wife of a diplomat and knew people, we were checked through and were at our hotel before the day was over. Ellis Island was a mad house — such a crowd. Lines and lines of people standing in their overcoats tugging a suitcase along with them as the line moved forward. I wondered how they could sort everyone out and if there was enough room in New York City for everyone arriving. We had very little baggage — a suitcase each, a painting, a Reynolds I think, and a wooden carving of the Virgin holding baby Jesus. Two treasures from her family, her security. We settled in. Mutti went to work at Macy's. She had many friends in New York, and the women all went to her for their hats. She got a commission and within the first year there she became the buyer. She also made good money on the weekends playing cards — sometimes from Friday night to Sunday night, almost nonstop. I was sent to St. Paul's boarding school on Long Island — so she didn't have to bother with me. You know the rest."

Lara had a feeling there was a lot more about Peter's life that he wasn't going to tell — at least not now; maybe never.

Chapter Nine

Then, one evening, Peter came home with a story Lara had a hard time believing. He'd spent the afternoon with a safari hunter trying to get the company business and instead of selling gas, he was sold the idea of taking a safari. Lara had been invited to go on a photo safari and Peter wouldn't let her go, wondering if she'd come back to him or run off with one of the photographers. At the time, Lara had been annoyed. She loved to take pictures, had bought a Leica from her stepfather and had bought a 16-mm movie camera just to film the animals. Peter knew she didn't like to hunt, that she loved shooting targets fixed or flying, and that she probably wouldn't want to go on a hunting safari — leaving him to go with friends and leaving her behind again. She felt that if she couldn't go on a safari, he shouldn't go either. She listened carefully and in horror when he said a safari usually took a month, that some 1500 miles would be covered to find and kill all the animals allowed. In Kenya, for $40 you could bag 71 animals. In the Congo it was close to the same. If you wanted an elephant, that cost $210 more and a second one $280. For a white or black rhinoceros it was $56 per animal, $42 per giraffe, $28 for leopard or panther, $5.60 for an ostrich and $2.80 for different kinds of monkeys. That meant that Jackson's hartebeests with the horns sloping backwards, hippopotamuses and buffaloes (by far the most dangerous animal to hunt because they circle around and charge from behind), went for free. Once wounded the animals were always hunted to the kill. Old bull elephants are slow and become decrepit. Left out of the herd, they slowly die and are eaten by vultures and hyenas. Herds of sable or roan antelope, impalas, giant forest hogs, zebra, okapi, kudu, and muscle-deer could be hunted, two per license.

Chimpanzees, gorillas, several kinds of monkeys, baboons, wildcat, lynx, cheetah, wild dogs the size of wolves, jackal, lemur — many of these were limited hunting permits only for scientific study and carried a higher price tag. Peter was full of information and curiosity about the different possibilities to hunt, the different areas, which permitted hunting and the national parks and game preserves that were relatively small in comparison to the size of Africa and the boundaries of each country. A travel book he found did not say the same thing. From the book, Traveler's Guide to the Belgian Congo and Ruanda-Urundi, he read "Vermin, Schedule IV" and learned that the following animals could be killed at any time without a license. "Lion, leopard, hyena, wild dog, baboons, large birds of prey (with the exception of vulture, owl, and other night birds and secretary birds), crocodile, snakes, jackal, civet, wild cat and small felines, otter, warthog and bush pig."

"You know, one day I'd really like to go on a safari. It's too bad we can't afford it," Peter said.

"Remember the one I was invited on and you wouldn't let me go?"

"Yes, I'm sorry about that. I didn't trust the people you would be with," *and I didn't trust you,* he thought. "One day, we'll get to visit the Parc National Albert. It's on Lake Kivu. We'll fly to Bukavu in Ruanda —Burundi — way over on the east side of the Congo. The company is supposed to pay for one trip a term for you. I'll ask in the morning if we can do it this term." A term was 18 months in a hardship post and this was truly a hardship post for Lara. Often she had fungus growing on her skin, or dysentery, or an infection. Her miscarriage also had taken its mental and physical toll so a trip to a cooler, drier climate could do her a world of good. "We could also go to Kagera Park and maybe see the Watusi." The Watusi dancers were world renowned. Tall, supple, and handsome, even considered beautiful, they were the elite, sons of chiefs who paid homage to Mwami, monarch of the Kingdom of Ruanda. Their sons were trained and educated in choreography and the finer things in life such as proper social etiquette, eloquent diction, as well as military science, law, and politics. Peter would plan the trip to correspond with one of the days the group would be dancing for tourists — only twice a week, because the dancers had other chores to perform for their king. This kingdom with its traditions went back to ancient history, dating from the 15th or 16th century and wisely the Belgians took their time in altering the barbaric ways of the king into a documented justice system.

The first explorers through Ruanda to Lake Tanganyka were Burton and Spelee in 1857, followed by Stanley and Livingston in 1872; then

Baumann of Austria in 1892. Lake Kivu was discovered by a German, Count von Gotzen, in 1894. The first World War even found its way to the source of the Nile, when, in 1916, Belgian troops took over the German military post established shortly after von Gotzen's arrival in Ruanda. Burundi had found itself under Belgian rule ever since. The town is called Busumbura today.

With the hopes of getting out of Leopoldville, Lara started to read up on the Kivu, the mountainous area of the Congo where the 869-mile-long and 25-mile-wide central Rift Valley passed from north to south with an incredible abundance of wild life. Also, this area was known as the most beautiful area in all of Africa with several mountain ranges and large lakes. The Ruzizi, a fast flowing river, joined Lake Kivu to Lake Tanganyka. The northern range was the Ruwenzori or "Mountains of the Moon". Over sixteen thousand feet high, their peaks were covered with snow and glaciers the year around, even though they are on the equator. These mountains were said to produce the waters at the sources of the Nile. Lara was fascinated by the geological formations of central Africa and the creation of two such great rivers — one, the Nile, flowing north to the Mediterranean, the other, the Congo, flowing north, then west and finally southwest to the Atlantic. Because there was an active volcanic range, the Virunga, crossing the Rift Valley from east to west, it was thought that central Africa had once been an inland sea — If so, there would be fossils to prove it. She would have to content herself with the animals since their trip was to last only ten days and Peter would be working, except on weekends. There would be two weekends and two different parks to visit.

Their flight left at daybreak. The plane was not large — a twin-engine Cessna 310, with streamlined wing tiptanks and a leather interior that smelled luxurious. It was flown by their friend Cyril, who owned Air Brousse, a charter company flying planes to every corner of the Congo. The planes normally made refueling stops on the way to the more distant cities of Elizabethville and Bukavu, but the flight to Stanleyville would be non-stop. Peter had already flown to the Kivu via Stanleyville, which was their first and only stop before Bukavu. The plane flew low enough for Lara to see some detail of the very diverse country —dense tropical rain forests, savannahs, the relatively treeless grasslands where she could spot some animal life, small lakes and big ones, beautiful falls and streams flowing toward the impressive Congo, and villages of all sizes. And then there was Stanleyville, the end of the line for river transportation to and from Leopoldville. The city, although small, was on both sides of the river. They had an excellent view and since no one was in any particular hurry,

71

Cyril flew his passengers over the magnificent Tshopo Falls, the first with a drop of only about six feet and further on a larger falls of great height and width. Peter noticed construction under way a short distance from the second falls.

"Hey, Cyril, what are they building down there?" Peter hollered.

"They're putting in a hydro-electric plant and after that a water purification plant. I think they expect Stanleyville to grow over the next 10 years." He looked out the window to see if there were any changes. "Only thing is, there isn't that much trade going through in the way of minerals and raw materials — some cotton. They make beer here, too. There are a lot of offices — commercial center, fishing. You know, when you have time, it's interesting. There are four mango trees dating back to the 1880s on Kisangani Island. It's an historic town, quite impressive," Cyril said.

They were flying over the city on their approach to land. "What is this? The railroad is on one side, the airport on the other," Peter asked. He learned later that most of the Europeans lived on the north side and locals on the south side. Trains for Ponthierville, where merchandise was taken by river to Kindu, then by train to Kabalo, then river to Bukama, train to Fungurume and on to Elizabethville or to the west coast through Angola to Luanda. The complexity of delivering supplies in this part of the country with any speed was next to impossible except by plane. He knew it took five days by boat from Leopoldville to Stanleyville — too long in case of an emergency. He was happy to see a long runway at the airport, long enough for a DC-6 with good access. He had forgotten all this since his first trip out here. He'd traveled so much and all of it was supposed to be memorized. *Watch out, fella, you could get yourself into trouble for this,* he thought. Everyone left the plane — a law during refueling — and walked into the airport for refreshments, a visit to the washroom and a brief walk to stretch their legs. Looking over the departure and arrivals, Lara asked Peter if he had been able to get to Entebbe, Nairobi or Dar es Salaam, Ndola or Luanda. She knew he wouldn't have had time to fly down to Johannesburg. His answer was "no," his thought, *they're not in my territory.*

They were soon on their way again. Some passengers had left the flight and now all the seats were taken by tourists and the Cessna twin used most of the runway to take off. Cyril didn't like overloading his plane. The elevation at Bukavu was 5,700 feet and the runway was relatively short, on a peninsula of land extending into the lake. It was okay if the wind was from the southwest. If not, it wouldn't be the first time he'd had to push full throttle, pull up over the water and try it again. He really didn't like doing that.

Lara's eyes were fixed on the scenery below and a few hours later she saw the impressive snow capped Mountains of the Moon and Lake Edouard. She had asked Cyril if they could go a bit farther and fly over Victoria Falls — the most famous falls in Africa. Unfortunately, they were too far away and would have to fly over the Ruwenzori Mountains and across Lake Victoria's north end to get there. The plane was too heavy on this trip. He offered to take them up there on their own if his schedule worked out during their time in the area. Lara never got to see the falls, but Peter did on another trip to Ruanda-Burindi.

It was late afternoon when they started their descent into Bukavu, a small city spread out on five peninsulas like a hand reaching into the lake. There was a nasty crosswind and after circling twice, Cyril tried to land, only having to pull up at the last moment as the runway disappeared under the plane. Lara wondered if the plane could land on water and the general panic in the cabin was very disturbing to her. Cyril pulled up sharply, turned and lined up again with the runway, compensating adroitly for the wind blowing across the runway. The chirp of the tires as they landed safely set off applause from the cabin. Lara's heart was pounding; she had succeeded in not panicking and noticed Peter had been calm through the whole incident. *Nerves of steel,* she thought.

"How can you stay so calm?" she asked.

"Par for the course. It happened to me the last time I flew out here. I think it's kind of fun. Cyril is an excellent pilot. Don't know how many hours I've flown with him. No reason to panic. I'm sorry. I should have warned you. You did pretty well for the first time."

"There have been a lot of times when my life has been in danger," she said, her heartbeat slowing to normal. *I'm a survivor,* she thought. "Would you please let me know next time? A little warning would be helpful."

"Sorry, I didn't want you to worry for nothing."

"I'd rather know when there's a risk. I'm old enough to decide about worrying."

"Okay, I hear you. Next time, when there's a risk, I'll let you know."

They picked up their bags and took a taxi to their hotel. No one from the company was there to greet them since it was the weekend. The Landons were on their own. Saturday, they walked around the city enjoying the view and a game of golf in the afternoon. The course was placed on a ridge and was very difficult for Lara whose game was still that of a beginner. She lost a lot of balls in the rough and couldn't play the ones she found, her feet being two feet lower or higher than the ball or standing with one knee bent to such an extent it made her swing unmanageable. She gave up after the eighth hole and walked the rest of the course with Peter, having sent her caddie back to the clubhouse. It was on this walk that she saw her first active volcano in the distance, just a plume of smoke, no fire or lava. Everything looked a little fuzzy at this time of day because of the smoking volcanoes and humidity. Even the colors seemed softer. The atmosphere seemed very peaceful as they enjoyed the afternoon together. They went to bed early that evening. A car was coming to pick them up at four a.m. to drive them around the west side of Lake Kivu to the Kagera National Park near Kigali. It would take them about four hours to get there, a little late since the early morning was the best time to see the animals. A guide, free of charge and obligatory when visiting the park, would be waiting for them at the park entrance. The cost to visit this park would be around 200 Belgian Fr. — a reduction of 100 Fr. for residents of the Congo and including the fee of for Lara's 16mm movie camera. Peter had asked the driver to bring a picnic. Not wanting to leave the park for lunch, they'd eat and travel at the same time. Here they saw a large herd of black buffalo, zebra, roan antelope, some hippopotamus, a few giant wild hogs, hyenas and baboons; the list could go on. There was so much to see and taking pictures was holding Lara back from the full experience of just enjoying the animals. She handed Peter the movie camera and took fewer and fewer pictures as the day progressed. Her eye was her light meter and for almost every shot she needed to change the speed and aperture as well as the focus. When animals move, they can be slow or fast. It was difficult to work it all out. Their Jeep stopped at the top of a slight incline and they saw the animals approaching the water hole as dusk set in. It was a wonder to see the hunter and the hunted understand a truce, the time for an evening drink before heading into the plains for the night. The hunted had been killed and eaten during the sun's warmth, left to the hyenas and vultures, a protected species, to clean up the leftovers. It was a time of peace as the sun lowered onto the horizon. "This has been an incredible day," she said hugging Peter. "Thanks."

"It really was great, wasn't it?"

Peter and Lara headed for a guesthouse inside the park for the night. There they had a light supper of roast antelope and steamed vegetables before getting to bed. The hotel in Bukavu had loaned them sheets and blankets for the night. Guesthouses did not provide towels either. There was no running water. A pitcher of water with a basin and an "outhouse" were part of the experience.

That night Lara lay in bed visualizing what she had seen in the park.

Hippos swimming in the swamp with just their nostrils showing out of the water, then the eyes and ears twitching — a snort and everything disappeared only to reemerge meters away. Sometimes she could follow the direction by watching the floating plants move. Sometimes a baby hippo followed its mother. She was amazed that they could stay under so long and the speed at which they swam. They would climb out in an area where the land was relatively flat, their huge bodies, cumbersome and slow, covered with mud and plants. The drying mud kept off the insects, and birds perched on their backs to eat the insects that landed there or the marine animals that were caught in the mud on their way out of the water. They walked ponderously and took some time to build up speed if they had to run. Peter had explained to Lara that rhinos run faster than hippos and that babies often are left behind. If the baby were in danger, the mother would swerve to return and protect her little one. That was as far as Lara got before falling asleep. The next morning they would go out again to see the animals and leave the park by nine o'clock. Peter had to be back in Bukavu for a two o'clock meeting.

The week went by quickly. Peter visited the surrounding countryside, looking to expand the number of service stations, learning what he could about the other towns and nearby countries. The area held little interest for his second employer — the Agency— since there was mostly agriculture, mountains with communications by air or road for long distances and by boat on the lakes. Here the wealth was the tourist. The coffee and tea plantations were owned and managed by Belgians who made a luxurious living. There was a hydroelectric plant on the Ruzizi River — very little industry. The tribal situation was under control because of the Belgian military presence. The Watusi, Bantu, and Hutu existed in relative peace. Lara spent most of her time painting or drawing views of the lake or plants and flowers and they were happy to leave for Park Albert early Friday afternoon. They would have two full days in the park, staying in a comfortable lodge with a restaurant — an early breakfast, picnic lunch and a copious dinner of local fish or meat, fruit and vegetables. This was the kind of place they had both dreamed about, with a large wood-burning fireplace for cool evenings. African art and trophies hung on the walls; animal skins were on the cold terrazzo floor; Congo drums as side tables, carved wooden furniture, ceiling fans and on the porch hanging panels of heavy cotton attached to a rope and pulled during dinner by a boy to keep the guests cool. What a great smile these people had when you were friendly with them! Their dark brown faces lit up, the eyes alive, with a white-toothed smile spreading from side to side. They were a beautiful people and they would be dancing Saturday afternoon, not far from the park. Peter and Lara were disappointed in their morning outing. They saw the usual herds of antelope, buffalo and wild pigs — no big cats anywhere to be seen. As they were heading back to camp they came across a few straggling elephants and Peter asked the guide to stop the Jeep so he could film the huge beasts. In those days the guides were a lot more lenient and Peter hopped out with his camera in hand and slowly started walking toward a large bull with magnificent tusks as a matador would walk toward his bull, waiting for it to charge.

"He's crazy, your man," the guide said quietly. "He wants the bull to charge? Or is he just trying to get closer. He has a telephoto lens? I can't call him back, that will frighten the bull and he's sure to charge."

"He wants to get closer for the picture," Lara whispered. "I'll go get him."

"No, no, don't do that. Then two of you are in danger and I'm responsible." The guide picked up his loaded rifle, slowly got out of the Jeep on the far side from the elephant and took aim — ready to shoot if he had to. This frightened Lara even more than Peter standing quietly in front of the elephant. The guide whispered back to Lara. "If the elephant's ears start to flap back and forth and he lifts his trunk and lets out a call, he is sure to feel in danger and will charge."

"Why didn't you tell us this before?" asked Lara as she too got out of the Jeep next to the guide. "I don't want you to shoot anything," she said. "You might hit my husband instead of the elephant. I'll walk very slowly over to Peter and tell him to back off." The guide tried to restrain her without success. As Lara turned, she saw him cross himself and start to murmur what she thought might be a prayer. She wondered *What's he praying for, himself and his responsibilities, the elephant or us?* She, too, was in silent prayer. How could Peter do something so stupid, dangerous and inconsiderate? She very slowly and quietly walked up behind Peter, unfortunately giving him a scare as he was filming. His concentration totally on the animal and his camera, he was unaware of Lara's presence until she slowly and lightly touched his side and whispered in his ear. "The guide is really worried, he wants us back in the Jeep. He propped his gun on the Jeep to shoot if necessary. He says if the ears start flapping the bull's getting ready to charge." And just then the ears started to move and so did Lara and Peter — very slowly backing toward the Jeep. They had to run the last few meters as the bull picked up speed and was heading for them. The guide, seeing what was happening, jumped into the Jeep, calling to his passengers to hurry. The car leaped forward just in time for the elephant to pass behind it, knocking Peter and Lara off their seats. Happy that they had escaped harm, they were shaken and still were shaking by the time they returned to the Lodge. The guide hoped he wouldn't have to take them out again. He would ask if someone else could. He was going home for the rest of the weekend.

The afternoon was hot and dry as they headed for the native dancing. The Watusi danced on dry earth, sending up little clouds of dust as their feet touched the ground. The area was not large — a clearing with trees for the tourists to stand under and at the other end trees and a bamboo fence behind which the dancers readied themselves and cooled down between dances. The dancing was unbelievable. The tall, supple bodies swaying, stamping, running and jumping. The flowing costumes had a hard time keeping up with the rhythm of the drums and voices singing and chanting the story of the dance. They danced with spears on sticks with artistic symbols, using shells and long white animal hair to decorate everything. The cloth was homespun red, white and black, with bold patterns —a tradition going back hundreds of years. They truly looked like the Royalty of Africa.

That evening they went back out in the Jeep, another guide — they understood why. The sunset was spectacular. The outline of wild animals silhouetted against the flaming African sky would remain unforgettable. With this extraordinary experience they asked if they could go out before sunrise the next morning. The guide agreed because of an extra tip offered in U.S. dollars. The morning sunrise was paler, perhaps because of the night's humidity still in the air. Everything seemed softer and so much more peaceful than in the evening. They spent the whole day out wandering the park, stopping under a tree from time to time to rest or picnic or watch a lion play with her cubs, a chase to the kill for the day's food then left to the hyenas or vultures — whichever came first. The day couldn't have been better. There were only a few people for dinner that night at the lodge. Most guests had moved on before nightfall. Peter and Lara would drive back to Bukavu for their flight to Leopoldville early on Monday morning. This would be Lara's only trip to the east. It had been a good one.

People had been irritable for weeks and then the rains came. The Landons wondered if it was like this with every seasonal cycle. They hadn't noticed it the first time they had waited for the rains. It felt like Africa was getting to them. With all of Lara's health problems her blood pressure had dropped too low to be healthy. The doctor put her on small doses of strychnine — a highly poisonous crystalline alkaloid often used in small amounts as a stimulant. She was out of pep, had a hard time getting out of bed, her head would spin and she'd have to sit down again. And although Peter was annoyed by her inability to recuperate, he understood there was nothing he could do but send her back to Paris early. The American Hospital had specialists in tropical diseases and should be able to get her back on her feet in time to go skiing. He knew his mother didn't particularly care for his wife. He'd work on that over the next few months via mail, saying how great she was and such a help for his job in hopes that would be a help to Lara. He knew she missed her family. Thank goodness she had made so many friends in Leopoldville and Brazzaville. She still could get out and around — no more golf or tennis for now — just the swimming in friends' pools seemed enough for her. She was able to fulfill her wifely duties. He recognized this and was thankful.

In four months they were going on leave. During their whole time in Leo Peter had met with no one from the Agency. A Head of Station had arrived several months ago. He knew who was Head of Station — Head of Station did not know him — and he liked it that way. Peter knew the country, its geography and its people, the wealth and why, one day, it would be important to the U.S. and too dangerous to lose control of such natural resources; the game of independence was going to be interesting. He wondered if he would be around to see it.

Chapter Ten

As Lara settled in for the long flight back to Paris, her memory bubbled with all the occasions she had arrived there. Her mother and stepfather had taken her across the Atlantic on the Queen Mary, the biggest and most luxurious ocean liner of the '50s. It was her graduation present. She was in First class, with a beautiful cabin all to herself, and meals in a wood-paneled, two-level dining room. There was an orchestra and dancing every evening except the last one because people would be packing and getting ready for their arrival the next morning. She had loved the ship, getting to know it within the first few hours on board. Her sense of direction was excellent. She spent most of her time outside, walking or sitting in a lounge chair, watching the sea go by, looking unsuccessfully for a whale or dolphins. She brought bread with her for the occasional seagull — mostly there was just sea and sky. There was a car waiting for them at Le Havre and they drove right to Paris. Lara missed a lot of the countryside because she slept most of the way, having gone to bed after three in the morning. They stayed in a small comfortable hotel on the Place Vendôme.

Her next trip over was on the Liberté — a French ship. She and Andrea had had a blast. Cabin class, mixing with tourist class, they were out dancing and partying all day and all night. That time she stayed with a French family on avenue Kléber for four months. Madame la Comtesse charged ten francs to take a bath and breakfast was a baguette left over from the day before, soggy and stale, with jam and a cup of coffee or tea. She went to art school – the Academie Jullien, rue de Berri – from nine in the morning until nine at night and loved every minute of it.

Her next arrival in Paris was as a married woman. The meeting with her in-laws was still vividly in her mind. The discord, unwanted pregnancy, the shots, the uneasiness and she wondered how it was going to be this time. Her flight was late and she knew no one was coming to pick her up. Just as well, she took a taxi to a new address Peter had given her. His parents had moved into a house with a large garden in Neuilly-sur-Seine. Her in-laws greeted her at the door, in their dressing gowns and ready for bed,.

"Thank you for waiting up for me. We had terrible weather and had to fly around a storm over the Mediterranean," Lara said as she embraced them. "I'm sorry to have kept you up."

"Don't worry, Lara, you know we usually go to bed after midnight. Would you like something to eat? After your long trip, you look tired. Would you rather just hop into bed? The couch in the library is already made up for you. You'll share my bathroom," Gregory said as he picked up one of the suitcases and led Lara through the entrance and into their apartment.

"I am exhausted and hungry. If you'll show me where the kitchen is, I'll fend for myself, if that's all right," she answered, taking off her raincoat and putting it on a hanger Ida was handing her.

"Let me show you where you can wash up first. You'll find us at the end of the hall on the left when you're ready," Ida said as she hung the coat in an overstuffed entrance closet and opened a door into the bathroom.

"It's a beautiful house," Lara exclaimed as she closed the door. She felt unwanted and wanted to disappear. "I'll be right there." When she emerged she found the dining room with a large round table set for her. There was a Camembert, bread and wine. "I hope this is enough for you," Ida said. "We're off to bed." Lara kissed them both with thanks and a *bonne nuit*.

Lara was wakened at nine a.m. as usual. She had heard church bells ringing in her light sleep and wondered where the ringing came from and learned later there was a church across the street from 6 boulevard Jean Mermoz in Neuilly. She would always know the time of day from seven a.m. to ten p.m. every quarter, half-hour and hour and wouldn't need a watch. The apartment was beautiful. Seeing the living room in bright sunlight with its three large window-doors giving onto a semi-circular terrace and a huge garden with trees was impressive. They had three sheep grazing on the lawn to keep the grass down. She saw a gardener trimming the boxwood hedge around the terrace, waved a 'good-morning' and went off in the direction of the kitchen. She found Ida and Gregory finishing breakfast in the dining room.

"Good morning," she said as she made the round of embracing them both — a custom in all of Europe. "I slept like a log. Thank you for getting everything ready for me."

"Good morning, Lara. Marie is in the kitchen. She will give you what you want. We have croissants for you. If you'd like something else, just ask Marie. We couldn't wait for you. Gregory has an early meeting and I'm going to the hairdresser. Peter told us you have appointments all day at the American Hospital, so we'll see you for dinner this evening?" Ida asked.

"Yes, thank you. I should be finished around four o'clock. Will there be someone here to let me in? I love your apartment. It's so beautiful and the garden…"

"It looks better in the spring. Perhaps you'll see it on your way back to Leo in April. And yes, Marie will be here all day, so just ring. We'll have to get another key." Ida said turning to Gregory who had gotten up to change.

"Yes, I'll take care of that today. Lara, do you need the bathroom before I go to wash?"

"No, thanks, I'm in no hurry. My first appointment is at ten-thirty and from what Peter told me, the American Hospital is not far away. He said within walking distance. Is that right?"

"Yes, about fifteen minutes, I'd say. There's a bus you can take if necessary. I'll see you this evening." And he disappeared down the hall.

Lara spent the week in and out of the hospital taking care of dysentery, the fungus growing all over her body and other tropical infections she had picked up in Africa. Her white and red blood cell counts were off, too, and the week's rest before Peter arrived was a great idea. Her in-laws left her at home evenings — only one obligation — an evening of bridge with the Rothschilds and some other friends.

Ida said she would cover her losses and take her winnings. Lara's bridge was more than adequate and she handed over several hundred francs at the end of the evening. Talk about controlling. Lara would have to get used to that. What was it going to be like when Peter arrived? Live and learn, she decided. She should be able to cope with any situation. It was awkward. Ida had a son and Lara had no husband and was ignored by her in-laws except for a kind word from Gregory from time to time. He, also, had noticed the difficulty and couldn't do much about it. Peter tried to include her as much as possible, but gave up after the first week. He shortened their stay in hopes that the next time things would go better. He was devoted to his mother and knew he had to do what was necessary to keep his wife.

Chapter Eleven

Their vacation plan was to spend one month in Paris, a month skiing to help thicken their blood, which had been dramatically thinned by the debilitating heat and humidity of the African tropics, and one month in the U.S. They stayed in Paris only two weeks, and were invited to numerous luncheons and dinners. Because of these social events Peter and his mother seized the opportunity to take Lara shopping for designer clothes. There was only haute couture and with no time for fittings, they had to buy the models' dresses from the fashion show. Thank goodness Lara was thin enough, as long as the model was tall enough. She had a dress from Dior made for her return to Africa as well as one from Givenchy. For a dinner with Ambassador and Mrs. Schooman at the Austrian embassy together with the Duke and Duchess of Windsor she wore an evening dress from Guy Laroche — a multi-colored sequined bodice with a scooped neckline and shocking pink raw silk skirt with a multitude of petticoats. She looked beautiful, and Peter had made her go to the hairdresser for a chignon. They were eighteen for dinner, and since Lara spoke very little German and was a less important guest, she was seated third to the right of the Duke. She had a good view of the Duchess and her beautiful jewelry: huge South Sea pearls closed around her neck, diamond and pearl drop earrings and several bracelets of diamonds and pearls on one wrist, and a beautiful diamond watch on the other. Lara was happy she had her grandmother's diamond feather pin placed in her chignon like a diadem and diamond earrings clipped to her ears. She would have felt naked without them. After the eight-course dinner a card table awaited anyone whom the Duke would invite to join him after coffee (cigars and liqueurs for the men in the drawing room and coffee for the ladies in the living room. Liqueurs were also offered to the ladies, but most graciously refused.) When the men joined the ladies, the Duke asked Ida to join him for a game of gin rummy instead of bridge. They went off to their game while the other guests conversed a great deal about President Coty, who was thinking about asking de Gaulle to form a new government. How would the General work with General Eisenhower and the Americans, who had become very anti-French? Difficulties were growing about who would control the Suez Canal. Both France and England were arguing; Egypt and Syria had formed the United Arab Republic, and Yemen had immediately joined in, creating a new power to deal with. Would the USSR or the U.S control it? Mao Tse-tung and Khrushchev were on again, off again, and the fear of a nuclear war loomed in the Middle East. The U.S. no longer exclusively controlled nuclear arms — France, the USSR, and China also held this power.

Peter wondered what role Central Africa would play, if any, in all of this. The Belgians, although part of NATO, had remained quiet and passive during this period. They had mines full of uranium in the Katanga. And from what he was hearing this evening he realized why he was in Africa.

He found his mother amazing. She knew everyone and those she didn't know and wanted to meet were soon in her *carnet d'addresses* and attending her parties. The card game with the Duke ended well after midnight. They rose from the table and Ida announced in a loud voice, "*J'ai gagné sept cent francs ce soir, n'est-ce pas, Altesse?* I won seven hundred francs this evening — isn't that so, your Highness?" It was her way of obliging the Duke to pay his debt, because part of the Duke's game was to see if he could avoid paying the winner when he lost. He always collected when he won and Ida knew his tricks. Once the Duke and Duchess had said their good-byes and thanks and all the women had curtsied to them both, the other guests were free to leave. Peter went over to his mother and quietly said, "I'm taking Lara dancing at Maxim's, want to join us?"

"No, thank you, dear, Gregory is tired. It's time we went home." She turned to her husband, "Shall we drop Peter and Lara off at Maxim's on our way home? The maître d'hotel can call them a taxi, if you prefer."

"It's on our way." He answered. They walked over to the Ambassador and his wife to say good night and extend their thanks for a profitable evening with the Duke.

"You were very clever to announce your winnings to everyone. Did he pay you?" asked the Ambassador.

"Well, actually, no. He said he'd put a check in the mail. It looks like he has won again." And they all laughed.

Peter gallantly kissed the hand of Mrs. Schooman. "Thank you so much for a delightful evening. The conversation after dinner was particularly interesting for me. A big difference with our dinner parties in Leopoldville."

"I hope you will come more often. Your mother is a very dear friend of days gone by. We were in class together in Frankfurt for a few years before we each got married. It was a pleasure having you and your beautiful wife."

Shortly after the dinner at the Austrian embassy, Peter and Lara went off skiing to Val d'Isère in the French Alps. They both were looking forward to being off on their own. In those days, Val d'Isère was renowned for its difficult skiing. The mountains were not yet fully developed and they were thrilled with the idea of going off with a guide into the deep powder — spending whole days out on the undeveloped slopes. They took a night train to Bourg-St-Maurice, the end of the line, then rented a Volkswagen beetle and drove the thirty-five kilometers to their hotel in Val d'Isère. They were there by nine thirty, hurriedly unpacked what they needed to go right out skiing and were on top of the Solaise by eleven. They took a fast run down one of the easier trails checking their equipment and their muscle tone after the short night of sleep on the train. Since they both felt fine, they decided on another run and went to wait in the lift line. As usual, Peter started to converse with their neighbors in German. It turned out that one, Helli Langlen, was a member of the Austrian ski team and the current winner of the Kandahar races, which had taken place there a few weeks earlier. He invited them to take a run with him down the Black trail and then join the group for lunch on top of the mountain. Lara was wary of the trail and the speed at which they were going to descend. She was feeling tired and intuitively knew this was not what she wanted to do.

"Peter, you and Helli go on ahead. I'm feeling a little tired. I think I'll go down the same one we did earlier."

"Oh, come on, Lara, you're in good shape. We won't be going that fast. You follow Helli and I'll bring up the rear."

"I really don't want to do this," she replied.

"Do this run with us. We'll have lunch and you can go take a nap and be ready to go dancing this evening. Okay?"

"Lara, follow me; we'll go at your pace," Helli said starting down the slope. Lara took a few deep breaths and followed at a decent rate. On the third turn her legs were trembling from fatigue and she fell, her left ski catching in the packed snow. She tried to get up and, feeling a sharp pain in her lower leg, flopped down again. Peter was by her side in seconds to help her up and realized she had probably broken her leg. Helli had stopped a short way below them seeing something had happened. He had already started to climb back up.

"Peter, wait here. I'll climb back up to the cable car station. They'll call for the *secouristes* (first aid). It won't take long. Maybe there are two already at the station," Helli said on his way by. "You okay, Lara? I'm sorry and this is your first day here. What a shame."

"I'm so sorry, Peter. I hope it's not broken," Lara said. *I should have listened to my intuition. Why can't I hold my own?*

"I'm sorry I insisted," he said, but he wondered if she had gone off alone who would have been there to get help. He put his parka under her head and saw she was trembling. It was cold in the snow but the air was warm and the sunshine hot. He had nothing to put under her except himself, so he lifted her up as far as he could and sat behind her holding her in his arms, trying to stop her trembling. It took fifteen minutes for the team to arrive with a stretcher, another fifteen to get her loaded, her leg put in a splint, and start down the mountain. The guides asked Helli which trail they should take. They could slide over to the smoother, easier slope but since that would take longer they decided to take her down the black. After all, there were four of them. Well, it wasn't that easy. She slid sideways and almost tipped off the stretcher until they tied her on, and every bump they went over jerked her leg, causing greater pain. She had lost control, was in tears, and couldn't control her trembling.

By the time they got her to the doctor's office, she was hysterical and when the doctor told her to stop trembling, she answered that she had lost control on the mountain and there was no way she could stop herself. She tried deep breathing, which usually helped when she was in pain, but that didn't work. Her pain threshold was very low and she asked for medication to calm her. The doctor realized that if he was going to manipulate her to get a decent x-ray he would have to sedate her, which he did with a tranquilizer and, so as not to have to wait a half hour for its effect, a small dose of laughing gas. The x-rays showed a clean break with everything in the right place. He put on a cast up to her groin, said it could be changed in ten days to a walking cast, and told her if she kept her foot up at all times for the next four days all would be well.

Unfortunately, there was no elevator in their hotel, so Lara had to have all her meals in bed; in fact, she would be obliged to stay in bed until they were able to leave. The cast was very uncomfortable for the muscle was torn and local hemorrhaging made her leg swell until the pressure became unbearable. The doctor came to visit the next afternoon with his saw, cut slits up the inside and outside of the cast, relieving the pain. He told Lara the bone would heal faster than the torn ligaments and that it might be wise to keep a small cast on longer than necessary for her bone to heal, and that she should be careful to follow physical therapy conscientiously for as long as necessary once the cast was off.

It was a bore for Lara who spent her time reading or writing post cards and sleeping. Peter brought her flowers; even candy found its way into his hands. He would leave in the morning to ski, return for lunch with her and be back on the slopes all afternoon. His rhythm was broken one afternoon by a knock on the door. "Come in," he called, thinking it would be the maid picking up their lunch trays. A tall, well-built American walked in.

"Hi. I'm Terry Scott. You're Peter and Lara Landon?" he asked.

"Yes, what's up? What can we do for you?" Peter replied, wondering why this man was coming up to their room in the middle of the day.

"I was told to look you up. You just came back from Africa, the Belgian Congo?"

"Yes, we've been there for a year and a half. I work for Calder Oil in Leopoldville."

"I'd like to spend some time with you, Peter. I'm with the CIA — overt not covert —" he smiled at his own statement "and they'd like me to debrief you. We do that kind of thing with businessmen who travel or work in foreign countries of interest. Could you take some time with me this afternoon? It shouldn't take long. I see you're dressed to go skiing. We could do a couple of runs together and talk along the way. What do you say?"

Peter's mind was racing. Lara didn't know he worked for the Agency, and he wondered if this man knew. If he did, Peter would be obliged to go along, if he didn't it would be the sensible thing to do anyway. Pass on whatever he could according to questions asked, never give out more information than asked for, be careful not to make a slip. A few seconds passed as he thought of his answer. Terry had an uninteresting face, one that could disappear in a crowd and he didn't look dangerous.

"Sure, I'd be happy to. I'll meet you downstairs in a few minutes."

Once Terry left the room he said, "This is the first time something like this has happened to me. It should be interesting. I'm sorry this all happened — breaking your leg. I'll find someone to help me carry you downstairs for dinner tonight. A change of scenery will be good for you."

"Peter, how do you know he's telling the truth?" Lara asked. "Showing up like that without any warning. It seems odd to me."

"It's okay. I'll be careful." He leaned over and kissed her. She reached gently for his balls and said, "Take care of these for me. See you later." They kissed again and he walked out into a new adventure.

Terry skied well, but couldn't keep up with Peter, who made friends with a couple from Portugal while waiting in the lift line for Terry. Elsy was a tall, thin redhead with a great sense of humor; her husband, Pelo, a slightly balding Latin, had a large dark mustache which changed its shape when he laughed. They agreed to meet for drinks that evening. Peter and Terry rode the lift together, Terry asking questions, Peter answering as best as he could. They talked about the political situation, the economy, the education and participation of Africans in government and business. Were there any particular undercurrents Peter had noticed of Africans wanting to share the wealth, to be more active in running the country? By four in the afternoon Terry had asked about everything he needed to. He had to be back in Geneva that night - a long drive alone and there was no tunnel through Mont Blanc and very little *autostrade*. Peter didn't envy him. He went off to take another run with his recently met Portuguese friends who were already at the head of the lift line. He was in luck. Jostled by the crowd, he found himself next to a beautiful blonde whose husband was with another friend in the lift just in front of them. They all skied down together, decided to meet for dinner at the Landons' hotel, and agreed to help carry Lara down to dinner. Peter decided that Terry didn't know that he was already working for the Agency and that it was better that way.

That evening four men arrived and tried to figure out how to get Lara and her cast down from their room. It was finally decided that two of them would grasp each other's wrists and make a chair for Lara to sit in. One would hold her back; the other would carry her cast. The pushing and shoving, the hustle was so funny that they had to stop several times to control their laughter before they continued down the narrow staircase. A crowd had gathered at the foot of the stairs to see what was going on and a loud cheer went up when everyone reached the bottom without injury. The evening went well until Pelo asked Peter how he had met Lara.

"Oh, well," he hesitated, "I was in this striptease joint in Boston and one of the acts was this fabulous tassel twister. They were glued to her tits."

"Peter, you're not supposed to tell people that," Lara broke in, turning bright red with embarrassment.

"Come on, Sweetie — you were fabulous, still are."

Pelo leaned over and whispered in Peter's ear, "Does she still perform?" The answer was a smile and they changed the subject.

87

The train ride back to Paris was awkward and uncomfortable for Lara on her crutches. Two days later the old cast came off and a walking cast was put on — a square piece of wood being added to the instep so the cast would stay dry and not touch the ground. They were off to New York and Oak Hill to visit Lara's mother and stepfather. Peter would spend a few days at the office in New York and seeing friends while Lara recuperated at home.

Actually, Peter needed only a few hours at the Calder offices. He had two meetings scheduled at East 69th Street, the first as soon as he reached New York, the second 48 hours before heading back to Europe and Africa. He had questions he wanted to ask, and he knew his instructions would be given at the second meeting.

It was a crisp spring day. The air had been cleansed by the rain, which had also washed the city streets before moving out to sea. That was one of the good things about New York. The wind either from the ocean or from any other direction blew away the clouds and pollution; the rain washed the city soot from the air and the streets. Peter in his dark blue winter coat and brown felt hat didn't notice the people he passed in the street. He concentrated on preparing for his meeting with Aubrey. He turned the corner from Third onto 69th Street, walked the few yards to the rear of the building and saw the camera pick up his arrival as he rang the bell. The door buzzed open immediately. He walked in and up the stairs to the third floor. The place hadn't changed — even the smell was the same. He wondered if the building was ever aired. If he worked here that would be a necessity. He saw Aubrey standing in the hall waiting for him. *That's new,* he thought, *to what do I owe this honor?*

"Hello, Peter, come in, please hurry. They're expecting someone else." Peter heard footsteps, two or three people, following him up the stairs as they disappeared into the office.

Someone's timing is off, Peter thought. "What's going on?" he asked. *Am I that covert that no one is supposed to see me,* he wondered.

"Well, Peter, it's good to see you." Aubrey sat down and indicated Peter should do the same. "I've not had much news about you. Only a brief word from Paris and then, of course, from Terry Scott, who saw you in Val-d'Isère. How did that go for you?" Aubrey asked.

Peter wondered if he would ever know Aubrey's real name. "I found it interesting. He didn't seem to know I worked for the Agency, so I left it that way. Told him just about everything I had picked up about the lay of the land, the control of the Belgians." He waved his hands, "economy, politics, foreign relations, the way they keep order between different tribes."

"I need a written report — the basics, with whatever you think is important, particularly about foreign interests and influences in the Katanga." He reached for a pad of paper, took a handful of pens, and pushed them toward Peter. "How present is the USSR? What kind of aid is needed? Do the Belgians still invest?"

"Actually, the Belgians are very much in control. They own just about everything except for some small businesses; the oil companies all work through Belgium, too, as you know. Power companies, transportation, education, religion, beer and alcohol — all are run and owned by the Belgians. The Africans, although there are a few with an excellent education, tend to stay and work in Belgium — better pay and they mix with the whites. Some marry white women. In general, no African gets very high in business. They're kept where they can be controlled and can't create problems." The office was so stuffy that he got up and took off his jacket. "Some day this will change, particularly if the U.S. pushes the Belgians for independence — giving up the colony will cost them heavily."

"Yes, it will. We believe in independence, not in colonies: we're heading to push for Congo independence in the near future."

Peter wondered what exactly Alaska and Puerto Rico were to the States. After all the U.S. bought the Russian colony of Alaska in 1867 for somewhere around $7,200,000. It became a U.S. Territory in 1912. And Puerto Rico, under something called the "Jones Act" became a U.S. Territory in 1917. Territory or colony, what's the difference? Both are under the jurisdiction of and dependent on a ruling power, the U.S.

"So, tell me how it's going with your wife."

"We have our ups and downs. The climate doesn't agree with her." He wasn't going to mention Lara's miscarriage. *That is private business,* he thought. "She's had dysentery, fungus growing on her skin, different kinds of infections, lots of stuff. The doctor takes good care of her, can't complain. She has made friends, plays golf and cards and likes to cook, so we entertain a lot. That's really easy for her." He started to pace. "The company got her a tutor, so her French is almost fluent. That helps. We get invited a lot of places where I would have thought my boss and his wife should have been invited. I wondered if someone knew I was with the Agency, but when I asked around they told me it was because we both speak fluent French. No one knows I'm with the Agency. Once, Lara was seated between the Governor General and our Ambassador to Belgium at a black tie dinner at the Palace. She didn't get to eat much and spent the whole time interpreting. Anyway, we had to leave early, which isn't done under those circumstances. Lara had a roaring case of dysentery and the doctor had given her a shot to get through dinner. After coffee she really needed to get home. Not good, but then, what could I do? I was seated next to the governor's wife and the American military attaché. His counterpart was down the table. Our conversation didn't go anywhere. They talked after dinner. I had to leave. In any case, we're getting around. Lara is good at that. She likes adventure, goes exploring on her own in the local village and market. I'm lucky and I don't let her complain, so it's working out."

"You were smart to send her back to Paris early. Gives you time to do more than when she's around. I suggest when you return to a post you always bring her back with you or she might get other ideas, particularly if she doesn't like the climate. Have you thought about having a child?" He leaned back in his chair waiting for a reaction. "That will keep her busy. You're established now. If she doesn't feel well, you can still carry on your work. Once the child is born she'll have constant company and you'll be freer to move about."

Their conversation continued for more than two hours. Aubrey asked what he thought about going "deep cover." He'd heard the term before; knew this meant that the government would never admit that he worked for them or to any of his participation or actions if he was caught by a foreign power. He'd be on his own. Would Peter consider going "deep cover"? He was given the time to think about it. Aubrey wanted an answer at their next meeting. There were forms to fill out. The training he had been through was for an undercover agent. He would need a few days for further instructions. They'd work it out with Calder Oil. The pay? He'd get a slight raise and a guaranty that if something did happen to him his family would be cared for. Their conversation ended. "Here, take the paper and pens." Aubrey said, pushing them across the desk. "You can type if you prefer." Peter was shown to a small room across the hall with a desk, chair, typewriter, ceiling lamp and desk lamp. If he needed to wash his hands it was the last door on the left at the head of the stairs. He was to finish his report before leaving. "Do you want a cup of coffee and something to eat before starting?"

"Yes, and I need to make a phone call to cancel my poker game." He knew he wouldn't be finished before the game was over. He had to go back to Aubrey's office to make his phone call in front of him. He wouldn't have another chance to call before he was finished. He asked for a lot of coffee, several sandwiches and candy bars. That would be his lunch, supper and maybe even breakfast. There was a lot of information he hadn't included in his report to Terry. He sat down, closed his eyes and relaxed. Thank goodness he had an excellent memory; too bad his typing skills weren't as good. He heard Aubrey leave his office, lock the door and walk down the hall. He started to write; his facts were in order. His reference cards, stored in his memory, popped into place as he needed them. He lost the notion of time, he was back in Africa — page after page — a knock on the door brought him back to reality. What he was writing was reality, too. The knock was the present. The door opened, Aubrey brought a shopping bag of food, which Peter looked through. Several kinds of sandwiches, a large coffee, a couple of cans of Coke and lots of candy bars. Feeling hungry, he took out a sandwich and started munching.

"Want one?" he asked Aubrey, who had picked up the typewritten sheets and was browsing through them.

"No thanks, I've had my lunch. Can I take these next door?"

"Sure, I'd like them back to read through the report when I'm through." Peter wondered if he was to send the report or if Aubrey would take care of it. He also wondered if there would be any changes made to the report before it was sent on. He would ask when he handed in the full draft. The afternoon drifted into evening. Peter opened the window on a closed-in airshaft, stuck his head out only to find a small space. He looked up and saw a few stars, stretched, and went back to work. The thermos of coffee was empty. He started on a Coke and continued typing between bites of his last candy bar. Aubrey knocked once, entered, gave him back the pages, said he was going for a walk, would bring back more coffee and wait for Peter to finish his report.

"How much longer do you think you'll need to finish?" he asked Peter.

"Another couple of hours. I didn't realize there was so much to include. Do you want me to come back tomorrow?"

"Finish up tonight. I have a cot I can sleep on until you're done. Pretty impressive detail. They'll be interested in this. See you in an hour or so with some more coffee."

Peter left the office when night was slowly turning into day. It was raining. He headed for his friends' apartment and bed, hoping no one would notice his late arrival. He didn't want to make up some story about another woman, a late poker game he didn't get to play — whatever. He was tired and needed to sleep and was not looking forward to his next meeting on East 69th Street. He needed to decide about his career, his life, the dangers, thrills, excitement, but also his responsibilities to Lara now and a child if they had one. Taking risks with his own life was one thing, risking someone else's was another.

Chapter Twelve

A knock on the door brought him back to the city. He had been dreaming of violence and riots in Africa and realized he had slept poorly yet late into the morning. He needed to get up to make the luncheon date with a former girlfriend who had since married a sports newscaster. They had plans to spend the afternoon together in a hotel room and Peter wasn't feeling up to it. He wanted to be alone walking in the park, even if it was still raining, or to rent a car and drive out to Jones Beach. He'd buy a warm sweater, a heavy raincoat. He didn't care if he got wet. He needed time to think, to decide his future, and to consider Lara's future, too.

They had a quick lunch and when it was finished Peter excused himself saying he wasn't feeling well.

"Is this headache time?" Penny asked. "I thought it was the woman who pulled that trick."

He walked around the table, gave her a peck on the forehead. "I'll pay the bill on the way out. I'm really sorry. Can I call you when I get back to New York?"

"Don't bother, I don't want to be disappointed twice."

Peter walked out into the rain and headed for Central Park and the zoo. He strolled amid the animals, most of which came from Africa, and entered the monkey house and stood watching the gorillas swing around their cage, and the monkeys playing with each other. Was he going to be caged by Aubrey? Would he let them do that to him? He had no one he could talk to, no friend who knew his real identity and he knew he was caging himself in if he ever agreed to go "deep." Was his future worth the danger? He walked back out into the cold rain and wandered the city streets until he was soaking wet and the cold distracted his thoughts. Returning to his friends apartment, he changed and took the next train out to Long Island and Lara.

They spent their remaining time in the States visiting Lara's family in the country and Peter's grandmother and uncle in New York. The day before their flight to Brussels Peter went to the Calder Oil office for a few meetings and then on to 69th and Third where, understanding completely his future life, he signed on for whatever Uncle Sam needed him to do. He felt Lara could survive without him. She had survived so much already. It was in her blood. The Agency guaranteed financial support and he had a life insurance policy, which would cover expenses for a long period of time. He was comfortable with his decision.

In Brussels they visited the World's Fair of 1958. Peter was always running into friends: at the train station, the airport, everywhere. He pushed Lara around in a wheel chair since her mending leg was still bothering her. Then they took a helicopter from Brussels to Paris. Two and a half hours, flying over the fair grounds, recognizing the different exhibitions and seeing the colorful crowd of people before heading for Paris and a quick flight around the Eiffel Tower before landing at Issy-Les-Moulineaux. It was amazing how much one could see from a helicopter and they appreciated its utility. They had a few days in Paris to socialize with Ida and Gregory and to meet with diplomats, politicians, bankers and other Important people. Peter began to wonder if his mother was in the same business as he was and unable to talk about it. In any case, the people Peter met could and would be a great help to him and his career. They left Paris for a short stay in Madrid and Barcelona, where Peter met with other contacts. There he had asked Lara if she wanted a baby. Her answer was yes and was followed by constant love making, with pillows piled up under her buttocks to keep the sperm inside her as long as necessary to become pregnant.

They flew on to Lisbon where they were met by a photographer, who acted more like a journalist asking them lots of questions, and their Portuguese friends from Val d'Isère. The photographer turned out to be a friend of Elsy and Pelo, the fun-loving couple who loved to play practical jokes; made a repartee for the joke Peter and Lara had played on them about the tassel-twisting strip teaser. It was June and the weather warm and clear. They stayed for a week with their new friends, water-skiing, testing cows to see if they would produce courageous bulls, branding them with a hot iron. The smell of burning flesh made Lara feel quite ill.

They went out to dinner parties and dancing just about every night. They could rest when they got back to Leopoldville.

And this they tried to do because by then Lara was pregnant and not feeling too well. She needed a lot of rest to keep up with their social life. And, as usual, within four days of their return she had dysentery, lost twelve pounds, was back on antibiotics and rice, and never far from home. Her breasts had swollen while the rest of her curves became more prominent and she attracted many men's attention. She was embarrassed, Peter was amused. At times she wondered if he wanted her to have an affair, but he never said anything one way or the other. And if she did and he found out about it, he could feel less guilty, if he ever did feel guilty.

Chapter Thirteen

They returned to their old house and fell immediately into the old rhythm. Peter's office hours had changed. Instead of nine to six with time off for lunch, he was due in at six or seven and the office closed at two p.m., except for a skeleton staff to cover telephone, sales and emergencies. The Company had organized a snack service, which came around to the offices with coffee, tea, consommé, soft drinks, croissants, *pistolets*, sandwiches and fruit. Employees could take breaks without leaving the building and get their work done, allowing most of them the afternoon off. Lunch, siestas, card games, sports and, for people like Peter, a large slice of time to take care of other business. Since his stop at the office on 69th Street he understood that no one would be meeting with him because no one was to know he was there for the CIA. Being debriefed as a businessman had worked out very well. The Agency had decided to keep it that way.

Lara was totally unaware of his second job, had found it interesting that Peter had been debriefed in Val d'Isère, and hadn't given it a second thought. When he had gone off on his own for a walk in every city they had visited during their vacation, Lara thought either he was going for a walk or to a Calder office, doing a study of service stations or looking for ideas to improve the ones he was running in the Congo. Lara visited friends or family, and when she had no one to visit, she was happy reading a good book, visiting museums, learning how to put on make-up, particularly eye make-up for she liked looking into others' eyes and to do so meant they had to look into hers.

They were happy to be back in their own home. Lara's pregnancy was a difficult one because of the heat and morning sickness. She had a good doctor who tried everything he could to make her feel better. When intravenous shots of calcium and vitamin B didn't work he started treating her liver. That didn't work either. She stayed home while Peter went traveling and out to parties; she felt neglected and lonely even when friends came to visit or for a game of cards. During the last few months she felt better; her father came to visit and her life was more normal. The heat, the rainy season, and unease in Leopoldville made them wonder if Lara should return to the States to have the baby or stay. Peter and Lara had long heated discussions, which often included Lara's father. She finally decided to have the baby in Leopoldville. Dr. Pauley was trustworthy and he saw no complications for the birth. What was most troubling was the push for independence. The boys were becoming less obedient, talked back, were seldom on time, took to stealing things when the Europeans would not complain. The only problem Lara had with her boys was their tardiness. Meals were no longer on time and a craving for certain foods became a habit.

Peter was very busy with his promotion to district manager of an area of 650,000 square kilometers, giving him the opportunity for more travel and a better knowledge of what was happening in the bush, economically as well as politically. The Congo was still an area of exploration, as was most of central Africa. A group of German anthropologists came through Leopoldville to discuss their findings — discovery of the first Jews somewhere near the source of the Nile River. This was of interest to the Landons because of Peter's background.

To Peter's disappointment he found out later that much of the information he had given to Aubrey in New York, as well as his written reports from this period of time were included in a "white paper" to which the Agency and government paid little attention and therefore missed out on much of the future of the Congo.

The world was changing rapidly in 1958. Khrushchev was in power in Russia and meeting with Eisenhower and MacMillan. Eisenhower assured de Gaulle that he would not touch the subject of reunification of Germany until all Allies agreed. In September de Gaulle offered the French colonies the chance to join with France or become independent by plebiscite.

1958 and '59 also saw the succession of Pope Jean XXIII to Pope Pius XII, who had brought a huge increase of Catholics to the church. Mao Tse-Tung gave up the presidency of the Republic of China; Fidel Castro triumphed in Cuba; in some Arab countries Muslim women were given the right to vote for the first time and Khrushchev started putting pressure on the allies causing the Berlin Crisis.

Russia and China grew further apart. China took over Tibet, creating two Dalai Lamas — one pro-Tibet, the other pro-China. Early in 1959 the Russians launched a missile that flew only 6000 kilometers from the moon and went into orbit around the sun. They were also the first to hit the moon. So much was happening everywhere, it was hard to keep up with it all. Peter found he had to read four to five international newspapers in several languages to get a feeling for what was happening and he wondered where his work and the Congo would finally fit into the picture.

Chapter Fourteen

The Belgians were expecting trouble well before Independence. Lara's father had a thing about guns and had taught her to shoot when she was eight years old. Standing on a hill in the woods facing down toward a pond, he put a 12-gauge shotgun in her hands, having taught her before how to take it apart, put it back together, clean, load, aim and fire. She took the proper stance — left foot forward, knees bent because of the lay of the land, the gun hugged tight to her right shoulder. She laid her right cheek against the cold polished wood and took aim, lining up the sights on an object 20 yards away. She noticed how quiet, calm and welcoming the forest was and the stillness of the pond and to her horror all that changed when she pulled the trigger. The recoil threw her backward to the ground and her shoulder ached. Her hearing had been blown away with the blast. She was seeing stars and was in total shock. He laughed, but she didn't understand. He was drunk.

When they left for Africa there were two guns carefully wrapped in the baggage sent by Calder Oil along with their household goods to Leopoldville. When the shipment came across from Brazzaville the Belgian customs checked the guns. Sporting guns: a 12-gauge for Peter and a beautiful 16-gauge over and under for Lara. They would be going hunting, birds only; and Customs let them keep their guns.

Shortly before the push for independence and sensing trouble was in the wind Belgian Customs showed up and asked for their guns. The guns had been registered on arrival and again Lara fought to keep hers — a gift from her father. She still hoped to go hunting. (She hated to hunt but loved to shoot. As a youngster she'd gone out to the dump with friends for target practice. They set up bottles and with a .22 rifle would try to get three shots on a bottle — top, middle, bottom — and when there were no more bottles they'd go for the tin cans. In those days Coke and ginger ale came in bottles, fruit, vegetables, fish and meat came in cans.) Well, Customs went off with the guns.

They moved to another house in the compound and life went on with tensions growing as the U.S. pushed the Belgians and Congolese into independence.

Life in Leopoldville for them didn't change much even after their baby was born. She was not the most beautiful newborn baby — her nose flattened, eyes and hair black. However, they loved her and were lucky to have her. Lara had spent more than 18 hours in labor.

Peter drove her to the hospital early in the morning, stayed with her for a few hours, then headed to the office asking the nurse to give him a call when the birth was imminent.

"At the rate she's going with contractions it shouldn't be much before three this afternoon," the nurse answered, feeling Lara's belly.

"I'll be back before three," he said kissing her on the forehead. "I'll call Eleanor, she said she'd like to keep you company."

Lara felt dumbfounded. The very idea of being left alone at a time like this — abandoned. Another contraction. She started panting to ease the pain. *How can you do this to me? — it's your baby too,* she thought. She had to get used to the idea since he had often left her in strange situations. It wasn't the first time and probably not the last.

The doctor didn't show up for hours. It was five in the afternoon. The nuns who ran the hospital had gone to mass, leaving Lara and the baby in danger. Once the doctor arrived, he saw that the cord was around the baby's neck, the heartbeat was too fast and Lara was exhausted from pushing and getting nowhere.

He moved her into the operating room, leaving Peter and Eleanor in the room. "I'm going to have to make an incision and we don't have time to give you an anesthetic if we're going to save the baby," he said.

"Oh, Doctor Pauley, do what you have to do. Please, oh please save the baby," Lara cried.

"Nurse, call Mrs. Jardin in to help. Where are the nuns who usually take care of this anyway?"

"They're at mass, Doctor." The nurse ran to the operating room door and called down the hall, "Mrs. Jardin, we need you, please hurry. We really need you." She returned to help the doctor prepare the scalpel and suction instrument he would need once the incision was made.

Mrs. Jardin hurried in, was handed an oxygen tube. "Put it in front of Lara's mouth and nose. She's really tired." Lara let out a scream as the doctor cut a slit to permit him to attach the suction cup to the baby's head.

"Now push, take a deep breath and push until the baby comes out. Nurse push down on the belly" — as the nurse started to push too low down — "no, not there, start up by the rib cage and push down — yes. Come on, Lara, you can do it. That's it, take another deep breath — yes, now push as hard as you can."

Lara let out a primal scream as the baby's head finally broke through. The pain was excruciating and she felt the rest of the baby pass out rapidly. Once the cord was cut in haste, the nurse took the baby by the feet. "It's a girl," she said as she cleared the nostrils and mouth of liquid blocking the baby's breathing, slapped the baby's bottom and the newborn let out its first cry. The baby was alive, blue, but alive. She was going to be okay. She laid the wet baby naked on Lara's empty belly and went to assist the doctor.

"Lara, your baby is okay. I need to sew you up now. I'm going to give you a local anesthetic," the doctor said.

"Why bother, after all that pain, what's a little bit more?" Lara replied.

"It will lessen all the pain in that area for a few hours and you need to get some rest." He went to work for close to an hour trying to repair the incision as well as all the tears caused by the rapid delivery. Lara and the baby were taken back to her room where Peter had been waiting. He was white and scared as he embraced his wife and newborn. "Are you all right? I heard you scream. Everyone in the hospital must have heard you scream." He softly caressed Lara's tired face with a finger and continued to do so to his baby. With admiring eyes, he said, "We have a girl, she's alive and you're both going to be okay." Just then Eleanor Jardin walked in.

"Congratulations to both of you. It was a close call, Peter. Why don't we step outside and I'll tell you what happened." She took Peter's hand and led him toward the door. "Lara needs to sleep and so does the baby. Doctor Pauley had another operation, but he'll be by to see you when he's through." She paused, "By the way, what are you naming the baby?" Peter looked at Lara. "We thought, if it's a girl, Katrina. What do you think, Lara? Do you think she'll look like a 'Katrina'?" They all looked at the newborn and wondered what she'd look like later in life.

"Sounds fine with me, Dear, we can call her 'Tia' for short - Katrina sounds so formal." Lara looked at their friend, "Eleanor, thanks for being there for me and the baby. I don't know what would have happened without you." They embraced and Eleanor took Peter out the door. "Don't take him too far away. I need him by me for a while."

"Sleep, my dear, sleep. He'll be sitting beside the both of you when you wake up." She closed the door behind her.

The sun had gone down. Mass had ended and a silent stream of nuns came to visit the new arrival without disturbing either Lara or baby Tia. It was February 2, 1959.

Local European women who were friends or acquaintances supplied just about everything they needed for the baby. Since everyone came and left several years later, bed, pram, playpen and clothing remained for others. Dr. Spock was the baby Bible and whatever else was needed was available in the local pharmacy or department stores. Anything coming from the States still had to come through Delta in New York City, be brought in by friends flying through Europe, or by Pan Am directly delivered to the pilot at planeside. Things going back to the States had to be sent the same way. Pick up was at planeside on arrival, even if it was one a.m., both in the U.S. and the Congo. The Landons sometimes had to spend the night in Brazzaville to pick up what was delivered from France.

Their life returned to Peter's work, Lara and the baby were out and about, and they had parties galore thirteen days out of fifteen. Lara's father was paying for the babysitter who came in six days a week either morning or afternoon or evening giving Lara the freedom she needed to keep up with being a housewife and mother.

In June they had a package party — i.e., a cocktail party — and drew names for the people for whom one would put together a costume for the costume party one week later. Everyone, thirty-five of them, arrived with a package for their assignment. Packages were handed out and two dressing rooms — one for men, the other for women for all to emerge in costume with make-up. It was a fun evening — even the governor general and his wife came, unfortunately not in costume.

In July they had a party with a German theme, beer and sauerkraut for the Calder Oil employees, The boys, John, and André, the cook had created a huge stove outside and spent the day cooking sauerkraut, keeping it moist with beer and water when needed. Kegs of cold beer would be in place for the evening and the meat was added as the guests arrived. Many of the men came in Lederhosen and the women in dirndls and other Bavarian styles. But people started to talk and were concerned: the Landons were doing too much; their health and that of the baby would suffer in the long run.

Peter was traveling a lot. On a trip that should have taken twenty-four hours, he'd stay four days, telling Lara it would give her some time to take off the extra pounds she was still carrying since the baby was born. She thought he probably had a mistress, but he was actually gathering information for the oil company as well as for the Agency. Lara had the "Baby Blues," was more and more discouraged and couldn't wait to go home on leave. Again her blood pressure had dropped. The doctor had given her strychnine to make her heart beat. Lara wondered if it was normal, to give a poison, even if it came from a plant called vomica. Homeopathic? She didn't know. He told her to rest one hour in the morning, two in the afternoon and get eight hours of sleep at night. Her heart was still beating too slowly and she hoped they would not return to Leopoldville after their leave. She was unhappy and depressed.

Times were more and more troubled and by October they knew they were coming back. All Lara could think about was Christmas with her family and the eventual boat ride with Tia up the west coast of Africa on a ship owned by one of her mother-in-law's friends, skiing with their new friends from Portugal, and Tori's chalet in St. Anton or Lech. Peter headed out into the bush more and more often. Reports said that cars were being turned over to block roads. Different tribes were not only fighting with each other but also turning on Europeans. The Mau-Mau was at it again. Lara worried about Peter's safety. Although he was in good shape, he was tired and probably wouldn't have the stamina to get through a prolonged confrontation. Even with the strychnine she had become a nervous wreck. She was exhausted and disagreeable with everyone, even the baby. Her hands shook, her voice, too. She couldn't control her temper and was losing her memory. Her mind would wander.

Her thoughts returned to Christmas of 1958, the year before. They had been invited out for Christmas Eve dinner — the high society of Leopoldville was present. Twenty-four quail stuffed with *foie gras* and truffles followed by huge turkeys, which had been flown in from Brussels, with chestnuts, string beans, potato gratin, salad, Champagne, red wine and white. Yes, it had all come from Europe, even their Christmas tree which had been beautifully decorated in white and gold. The homemade ice cream and coffee were from the Congo. Just before midnight everyone left for midnight mass. The Landons, not being Catholic, went home to open the rest of their presents — they each had opened one before dinner. Christmas Day was again foie gras, turkey and Champagne with a *bûche de Noël* for dessert! They had shared it with friends, eaten too much, played some bridge, cooled off with a swim and went to bed. What a nice Christmas that was. This coming Christmas wouldn't be so gourmet, but it would be a family Christmas.

Almost all the gifts, which had arrived on time, were for the expected baby and they had spent the next few days preparing the departure for the hospital. They had to bring everything — sheets, pillowcases, towels, Lara's clothes and the baby's clothes, even the bands to wrap around the belly for the belly button. The reason they had done this was that Lara's father was arriving on December 31st for New Year's Eve. His first flight had been cancelled; the second arrived late at seven thirty a.m. They had organized a small cocktail party before the big New Year's Eve party for him to meet some of their friends. Unfortunately their dog ate a whole Camembert, which had been placed on a low coffee table and was very sick as their friends started to arrive. The evening was fun, food and dancing until two a.m. They were expecting twenty-four for brunch the next day and Lara tried to remember how much food disappeared in no time at all. Peter was the bartender and because one of their "boys" didn't show up (because he had had too much to drink the night before) Lara found herself running back and forth from the kitchen. It had been exhausting, but it was a great party.

"Thank heaven everyone's gone, my feet are killing me. I'm huge with child and need to take a nap." She looked at her watch. "Four hours of running, who says I'm not in good shape?" as she caressed her belly.

"Wonderful party, kids. If you don't mind, I think I won't stay up any longer. I can't keep my eyes open. Let me know when you all are up and about later. Think I'll sleep until then," her father said as he rose to go to his room.

"See you later, Anthony. Thanks for helping with the bar."

"It seems all you do is give and go to parties. What else is there to do around here?" he asked.

"There are beautiful places to visit out in the country and along the river. Lara will show you around. She's our guide for visiting firemen from the States, has it down to perfection — or at least the consulate thinks so." He got up and went over to Lara. "We play golf, tennis and bridge — nice golf course and a different tennis club. You'll see," Peter said with a yawn. "We'll go for a swim after the siesta, see you later." He pulled Lara to her feet and they all went for their nap.

That was January 1, 1959. On the 6th the riots began. Lara had sensed tension while touring with her father. They had been told everything was under control, that calm had returned to Leopoldville. It wasn't so. When

Peter went into the African part of the city on January 7, an obvious thing for an agent to do, his car was stoned. He came out unhurt and his comment was "It's the first time I ever got stoned by something besides liquor." All were informed that the Army, consisting of some Belgian officers, but mostly Congolese soldiers, would stick around until after the 13th when the Minister of Colonies was to speak on independence. Obviously, the Africans wanted the Europeans to leave, and the Europeans had too much to lose if they left.

All their letters home told of calm and security, because this is what they wanted to believe.

Peter's trips into the "bush" continued. Two had to be cancelled, one because a magneto in Cyril's Cessna 310 was out of service, the second because he had too much work to do. He was able to take Lara and the baby for a short trip to Luanda, Angola — a beautiful Mediterranean-style town built around an old fortress on the sea. There they spent most mornings boiling Tia's bottles and water, feeding her and sleeping. Afternoons were spent on the beach until Lara got sunstroke and the baby was sick. One day they went out fishing and just missed hooking a shark that Lara was happy got away. Sharks gave her nightmares, as did their return trip back down the river when the tide was coming in. A rip tide was causing huge waves for the small fishing boat and whirlpools that could suck the boat in if they got too close.

They made it back to port for a late lunch of lobster, huge shrimp, chicken, potato salad, ham, fruit salad, pink gin, beer and coffee. Food had become an important part of their lives. It had something to do with survival for all three of them. Their vacation was a gift from Lara's mother who couldn't imagine just what a wonderful gift it was to get away from Leopoldville and the tensions. It gave them courage to finish their term. Peter had asked Lara if she wanted to leave early. She didn't want to leave him, yet she did leave early. She took the vedette to Brazzaville, and then a thirteen-hour train ride to Pointe Noire, where she and the baby got on the *Jean Mermoz,* a passenger ship belonging to the French company, Fabra.

Chapter Fifteen

Lara was given one of the largest cabins on the ship with plenty of room for Tia, now nine months old, to play. During the day she and the baby strolled around the first class deck keeping pretty much to themselves. They would lunch and nap together. In the evening Lara was invited to sit at the Captain's table. He then proceeded to make a move on her. She made it clear she wasn't interested. The Captain always had first choice for a single woman passenger to join him in his cabin. By the end of the second day a young German beauty had succumbed to his charms leaving the field open to his officers' advances. Lara found this use of rank amusing and wondered if anyone would come her way. That evening, a tall, good-looking, young officer with dark hair and deep brown eyes asked her to join him for a dance in tourist class. She found him attractive and wanted to see what happened in tourist class. First class wasn't much fun.

"I'd like to, but I can't leave my daughter alone. Thanks anyway." Her heart sank and she hoped he'd find a solution.

"Let's go find your cabin steward," he said as he picked up the baby and headed for the bow of the ship and her cabin. Lara thought it interesting that he knew where her cabin was. *What else do you know about me? I know nothing about you except that you're charming and well practiced in the art of seduction.*

"There's Teddie," he waved a hand and called, "Teddie, I have a favor to ask you. Madame Landon is going to put - what's-her-name?" he asked Lara.

"Tia."

"Tia to bed. Could you keep an eye on her while we go dancing in tourist?"

"Of course, Lieutenant, I'd be happy to. I'll leave the cabin door open so I can hear her. My station is just down the hall. I leave my shift at midnight. I hope you'll be back by then."

Lara answered, "That's after my bewitching hour. I'll be back before midnight. Thanks." She took Tia in her arms and entered the cabin. "Please come and wait inside," she said, turning to the Lieutenant. "What's your name?"

"Jacques, what's your name — other than Mrs. Landon?"

"Lara," she said and turned her attention to preparing Tia for bed. He came and stood close to her as she kissed her baby goodnight. The warmth of his body was pleasant and exciting and she felt a longing twinge between her legs. It wasn't the first time she had been attracted to another man, but this could probably be the first time she would let herself go all the way. She looked at Tia, who was falling asleep, saw the crib wedged between the two bunks and wondered if something did happen, where it would happen. Her cabin wasn't suitable for an affair. He'd found a solution for a sitter; he'd find a solution for an appropriate place. He took her hand and led her out of the cabin leaving the door ajar.

"See you later, Teddie, thanks," he called as they headed for the sound of music and a party below. They danced everything together — Charleston, jive, samba, rumba, pasodoble, tango, even a waltz and then what the French call "a slow." He held her so close she thought she'd lose her breath. He took her arms and moved them up around his neck and bringing his hand down along her body passed his thumbs over her hardened nipples. He felt their bodies so close to each other he knew he didn't have to hold her to him and continued to caress her curves wherever his hands chose to travel. He looked at his watch behind her and said, "It's eleven-thirty. May I take you back to your cabin?" Lara wondered if that was going to be the end of the evening and felt a little disappointed since by now she really wanted to spend the night with him.

"I guess so. I didn't know it was so late." They separated, his arm around her waist and started up the stairs but instead of heading right for the cabin, he took her for a walk on the deck. *This is the kind of thing you see in the movies,* she thought as he slowly turned her to him, kissing her gently at first, more passionately after. "I want to make love to you," he whispered into her ear. They saw Teddie asleep in his chair, called to him, letting him know he could leave whenever he wanted to and entered the cabin. She went to check on the baby and saw Jacques standing by the open door between the two cabins. She smiled at him and said, "You had everything worked out, didn't you?"

"Yup, you're a beautiful, sensual woman whom I had hoped wouldn't end up in the Captain's bed so we could be together. I'm the lucky one."

"Let's see if I am, too," was her reply.

They made love several times during the course of the night and continued for the next ten days to Dakar. Even when she had her period they would make love: a first and delicious time for Lara. And then it was time to say good-bye. Should Lara give him a gratuity for being such a great lover? She gave Teddie a nice sum as well as the others who had helped with her baby, kept the two cabins clean and fresh and who would see her off the ship. She decided against giving him anything; she had given herself to him; she hoped that was enough. She left the ship in Dakar and went straight to the hotel.

Peter flew in the next day from Leopoldville and they flew on to Casablanca two days later having stayed at a beautiful hotel on Dakar's spectacular peninsula. She never let him know about Jacques, even when he told her he had won so much money at a poker game where his friends had teased him by saying Lara must be making out with some fantastic lover. For the number of times he had screwed around with other women she had no guilt feelings about her affair and he didn't need to know about it. The only way he might suspect something was if she tried something new on him, and she would not do that.

The flight to Casablanca was hard on the baby's ears. She cried all the way, disturbing the whole plane. Even the hostess tried to calm her, but nothing seemed to work. When they got off the plane she was still crying and made an awful first impression on her grandmother and grandfather. They were left at a hotel to be picked up at eight o'clock for dinner.

"Ask the hotel for a babysitter. We can't take a screaming child to a restaurant with us," Ida said. It was obvious this visit was going to be worse than their last.

"She should be asleep by the time you pick us up," Peter replied.

"All the more reason to leave her at the hotel. She won't bother anyone. Please, Dear, we've planned a very special evening with a few friends. We'll see you later. You have our phone number, right?"

"Yes, Mutti, we have your phone number. We'll be ready at eight," Peter said.

"How dressy?" Lara asked. Her mother-in-law turned to look at her as if she hadn't noticed her presence before.

"A dinner dress, of course," she answered. "You can get one ironed in no time by the maid at the hotel. We'll be back at eight. You even have time for a nap. Bye."

They went straight to their room, called for a babysitter, got Lara's dress and Peter's suit ironed, fed the baby and had time for a nap. The evening went well. Peter was charming and the center of attention. Lara spent most of her time with Gregory who spoke quietly and genteelly.

"Lara, my dear, you must have noticed Mutti's difficulty with you, particularly when Peter is around." Lara nodded and wondered what would come next. "I've thought a lot about this and wondered if I could be quite frank?"

"Of course, Gregory. I suppose it's difficult for you, too. What do you suggest?"

"Well, you and Peter are together for eighteen months. Mutti is with Peter for one month at the most when you come through Paris." Lara nodded again. "Is it possible for you to let Peter be with his mother, that is to say, let her have her son the time we're together? The rest of the time you have your husband."

Lara was shocked by what he said. Why should she even bother to be there if that was the way it was going to be? "Are you saying I should go right home to the States and leave Peter alone here with you?" Tension started to crawl up her neck — she didn't need the migraine that was starting to ache.

"Not exactly. I'm sorry to upset you so. That was not my intention. Just let Peter spend more time alone with his mother, find something else to do, see some friends."

"But our friends want to see both of us, not just me alone."

"You have the baby now, too, spend more time with the baby. I don't know," he said exasperated. He didn't know what he was getting himself into when he started the conversation and it wasn't going the way he had hoped it would. "I'm sorry about the way she treats you and I can't do anything about it. Think about trying to give them some time alone."

What all this meant to Lara was when the four of them were together Ida had her son; she didn't have her husband.

The next day was misery. Tia needed constant attention. Her grandmother scared her and the closer they were, the more she cried. Finally Ida slapped the child across the face, taking Tia's breath away, and Lara saw there was no way the two of them could get to know each other. Lara took Tia back to the hotel to the coolness of their room. In the evening, she took her for a walk and the two of them were asleep by the time Peter came back.

Early the next morning while Peter was still asleep, Lara snuck out to visit with Jacques. The *Jean Mermoz* was in port. They could have a few hours together. Peter could feed the baby if she woke. Lara left a note saying she had gone for a walk and they needed to talk.

When she returned they did talk without getting anywhere. They left the baby with friends of Ida and Gregory's in Casablanca and drove to a sumptuous villa in Marrakesh for the weekend. The Villa Taylor was where Churchill and Roosevelt had met to divide up the world before talking to Stalin after World War II. A walled garden of exotic plants and citrus trees surrounded a beautifully constructed Moroccan villa the color of reddish baked clay. The shutters were intricately designed to keep the dwelling cool during the hot day and still let in enough light for its inhabitants to get around. Some of the ceilings of the reception rooms were carved and painted domes leading the eye toward the sky and enjoyed only when the shutters were open in the early morning or at sundown. The furniture was typically Moroccan — carved wooden chairs and tables encrusted with mother of pearl and/or ivory, overstuffed couches, chairs and floor pillows covered in rich colors with silver or gold threads woven into the material. One could easily imagine a ruling pasha from *A Thousand and One Night*s lounging with his women or holding formal banquets and meetings with his courtesans. Huge brass trays made into tables covered with old wooden antique boxes and bowls left just enough space to circulate. They were moved outdoors to a terrace for any large reception that the Count and Countess would give. Peter and Lara were given the room that Churchill had used on his visit. It must have been ninety square meters with a huge wooden bed. The mosquito netting went from ceiling to floor around the bed and night tables. The sitting area was in front of an open fireplace. It was there they had breakfast and could take the time to talk or read if they were not running off somewhere — to the *souk,* which was a large open market where they could buy anything from livestock to household goods, or to see some beautiful palace, hotel or friends. The bathroom was at least thirty square meters with a gray sunken marble tub, gold plated fixtures and enough room for both of them at the same time. Fun and games. This was a vacation. A phone call Sunday morning changed all that.

The baby had cried constantly since they had left her in Casablanca. The family caring for her couldn't do anything about it. She wouldn't stop, wouldn't eat or sleep. Would they please come as quickly as possible? They were worried for the health of this ten-month old baby who needed her parents.

The fact that Lara and Peter felt they should leave right away put Ida into a rage. She yelled at Lara that she hadn't trained her baby and said too many disagreeable things for Lara to continue to listen. She walked out of her mother-in-law's room slamming the door on the way out.

She held her tears until she was alone in her room, then threw herself on the bed and cried. Why was Ida so mean to her? Tia was Peter's daughter, too. All the blame fell on her. It wasn't fair. Ida had her way. They left after lunch, drove directly to pick up Tia and on to the airport. She and Tia were put on an evening flight to Paris and *good riddance* Lara thought. *They got rid of me. She can't share her son and I can't change her way of thinking. So, she'll have her son a while, then I'll have my husband. She does not know how to share.*

Their flight arrived around nine p.m.; they were at *La Maison Rose* by eleven. Lara put Tia into the arms of Mademoiselle, an elderly woman with glasses perched on the end of her nose. It was instantaneous. They got along — no crying, a peaceful child in the arms of an older woman who knew how to love a child and the child could feel that love.

A huge relief overcame Lara. Worn to a frazzle, she burst into tears knowing she could let go of all the tension, which had accumulated over the last eighteen months. She would go to the American Hospital in Paris the next day and hoped the doctors she usually saw would give her what she needed to control her nervous system, rebuild her strength and again get rid of the fungus growing in patches all over her body, as well as the infections she still had from Africa. That night she fell into a deep and restful sleep and only woke to hear the church bells chime nine o'clock. She spent most of the day at the hospital, returned to *La Maison Rose* tired and satisfied with her doctors' care. The rest of the afternoon and early evening she played with Tia, bathed and fed her, all under the watchful eye of Mademoiselle who took over to put the child to bed. They dined together. Lara excused herself and also went to bed, still exhausted. The doctors told her it would take her a week to recuperate. She had five days before everyone returned to Paris. Five days to herself now that she had a wonderful person to take care of the baby. She could rest, wander the streets of Paris and see friends for lunch.

A few days after her in-laws' return, they were on their way back to the States for Christmas. With the new jet engine they only stopped once. It was a shorter flight, which made it easier on the baby's ears. And there was Mademoiselle, who was a large woman in her sixties. Short, white curly hair surrounded a very round, peaceful face with glasses that could not hide her sparkling eyes. She was a wise woman who had told Madame and Monsieur not to worry if their child loved her. She would be a part of their lives for a short time. Tia would always be a part of their lives. She taught both of them the art of trying to be good parents and when she saw them failing she would diplomatically help. Ida had chosen well.

The warmth of the family Christmas on the cold Christmas Eve was a dream for both of them. Peter had been taken into the family and felt like one of them. A few months earlier he had written Gramps for his birthday and expressed his gratitude for the affection Gramps had shown him. He had never had the full acceptance of one man for another; he had never had a family. The thoughts about his double life tweaked at the comfort he felt with this family and brought him back to the need to keep his distance. In moments like this he would turn to his sense of humor, which put him back on track. Most of the large immediate family loved to laugh and so gatherings were warm and fun. After the Bible reading, hymns and exchange of gifts, the typical German Christmas meal was served. Dessert was always minced meat pie and a flaming Christmas pudding with hard sauce laced with extra brandy, which the children didn't care for, leaving more for the grownups. "This is the best Christmas I have ever had. Thank you so much for everything. And I mean everything," Peter said, holding a Cuban cigar up in the air in admiration. "Gramps, you spoil me." They shared a bear hug. "Well, I'll be back for several visits when I'm not in New York."

"I thought you were on vacation. Why go to the city?" Gramps asked.

"We have some friends to catch up with and Tori has given us a couple of tickets for the theater. You know, we don't have that kind of civilization in West Africa, so we catch up when we're here and in Paris. But, don't worry. We'll be out here plenty. I'll come over for cocktails and a cigar. You'll see." Peter would be sure to return as often as he could. They had a special connection, which he was not willing to let go of. Peter hurried down the driveway, turned to wave good-by, "Don't catch cold standing out in the snow, Gramps. We'll be back soon," he called and disappeared. Peter thought he looked tired and wondered if he would still be there when they would return in 18 months. The party broke up before midnight with some heading to church, others to bed.

New Year's was spent in the city with one party after the other. The company had said, "Keep up your friendships" and that is just what they were doing. The nights Peter had poker games, Lara found friends for supper and a movie or skating in Central Park. She loved the winter and hated the heat. The cold winds of New York were just what the doctor had ordered. "Take as much as you can, you can't take the cold with you."

Peter also said he had to spend some time with Calder Oil. They wanted both of them in for a medical check-up. Lara said she had seen the doctors in Paris, but that was not good enough for the company. She thought, *they want to check on our mental health, too, after all the troubles. Maybe, if I faked it we wouldn't have to go back.* She wasn't very good at faking. That's why she hated to play poker. She couldn't get away with anything. It always showed in her face.

Peter also had to visit his other Boss, Aubrey. More than ever, he had to be discreet. He tried to get Lara to go back out to Long Island, but didn't succeed and knew he couldn't push it. She probably thought he wanted to see one of his old girlfriends and he was finding less and less time for this kind of play. Aubrey needed to spend some time with him. His reports brought back to the States by different airline pilots had been addressed to a list of "friends" so that no one would be suspicious. They needed to make sure none were missing and questions had been asked as to the validity of some of the information: Facts that the Agency didn't want to hear or acknowledge, facts they chose to ignore! *That was their problem,* Peter thought. *I'm doing my job. Damn good intelligence, if you ask me.* He might persuade Aubrey — the others, he'd never know. In the last few hours Peter could squeeze into his schedule he was given a list of people to contact on his trip through the Middle East on their way back to Leopoldville. Now he understood why he received a message saying take a trip. Make sure you get to Athens, Istanbul, Beirut, Damascus and Cairo. He had been given a bonus and turning in their first class airfare he had more than enough money and time to take Lara on a fabulous trip through the Middle East.

Leaving Tia and Mademoiselle with Tori in Oak Hill, they headed for the mountains of Switzerland in mid-January. Zermatt was a charming village at the foot of the Matterhorn, with access by train or foot only. A horse drawn sled picked them up at the station and took them to a small apartment they had rented for a week. Peter was out on the slopes immediately; Lara took a few days to get her act together. She enjoyed sitting in the sun, reading on the terrace or gazing at the mountains. She didn't want to go back to the tension, heat, and humidity of Africa and there was nothing she could do about it if she wanted to stay married to a man she loved so deeply. She knew Peter would find friends. He did that everywhere he went. He'd lunch on the slopes and they'd mostly have dinner at their apartment. One evening during dinner they heard a knock on the door and to their surprise and delight Lara's little sister was standing there with all her ski gear and a small suitcase. She'd come for the weekend from school in Gstaad. She was a hot skier and made perfect company for Peter. They spent both days skiing down the mountain at full speed. Lara couldn't keep up and went back to her book. Sunday evening Josie took the train back to Gstaad. The Landons had been invited to a cocktail party and Lara wondered how that had happened.

"Oh, just some folks I met on the slopes yesterday," he said. Lara found out later what had really happened. A group was skiing recklessly in deep powder. Peter had seen a man out of control and heading for a precipice. He was able to catch up with the man and make him fall away from the danger. The man came over to Lara to express his heartfelt thanks for Peter's having saved his life. She was often amazed at what Peter would and could do for others. He was a daredevil, loved adventure and thrived on danger. No wonder Lara felt they wouldn't be together for long.

They flew from Geneva to Athens, visited the ancient port of Pireus and then on to Corinth and Delphi. On their last night in Athens they made love laughing about the Corinthian morals of luxurious dissipation and trying to start another baby. Lara woke in the middle of the night to find the bed next to her empty. She didn't find Peter anywhere. She even had gotten dressed and gone out to look for him in the street. A man approached her. She thought he asked her "how much" which sent her running back to the hotel and locking herself into their room. She went and stood by the window for a while, hoping to see him return, found the air pollution so bad she closed the window and went back to bed. When they woke she asked, "Peter, where did you go last night? I went looking for you — even out in the street. Some man thought I was a prostitute and asked me how much. I came back here worried about you."

"Sorry, Sweetie, I couldn't sleep so I went for a walk, I should have left you a note," he answered, giving her an "I'm sorry" kiss. "It's late, let's pack up and have breakfast downstairs. We have to leave here by eleven for the airport. Lunch on the plane."

Lara didn't say anything more about his absence. She had used the same line when she had gone for a morning walk to see Jacques in Casablanca, but there, she had left a note.

Chapter Sixteen

The flight to Istanbul was just long enough for a simple lunch in tourist class and a wonderful view of the city, the Sea of Marmara and the Black Sea. They dined along the Bosporus, watching the ships go by, many more going toward the Mediterranean than going toward the USSR, Bulgaria, or Romania.

They visited the column of Théodore and the Galata and the Beyazit Towers, a new find of Christian Mosaics in an 11th century church that had been turned into a mosque and was now being returned to its original cult.

The crowded streets, noisy with vendors offering everything they wanted to sell, were an enchantment for Lara and her camera. Peter tried to hurry her along without success and said, "Lara, I have a business appointment this afternoon. I'll get you a guide. You can visit and photograph until we meet the Calder Oil people for dinner at the hotel." Lara looked at him. It was the first mention of his afternoon appointment and she was surprised.

"What are you talking about? You only told me about dinner tonight."

"Remember the note we got when we arrived at the hotel?"

"You pocketed it so fast I forgot all about it."

"I have to be in a company meeting at four. I guess I forgot to tell you."

"Sometimes I wonder if you haven't become absentminded. Are we having lunch together? I'll take that guide you offered me. We'll find him at the hotel?" she asked as she put away her camera and they headed back to the hotel. It also made Lara wonder how Peter always knew his way around a city he had never been to before. Sure they had a map once they got there, usually given to them by the concierge. *He must have a fantastic and quick memory. At least I have a good sense of direction, but nothing like his.* Peter stopped by the concierge on their way to lunch and asked for a guide to be there at two o'clock. They had a quick lunch and he headed out for the afternoon.

Lara spent the afternoon with a guide who took her to the Blue Mosque. She walked in and felt completely surrounded by blue. Looking up and around, the air took on a shape of its own — the air she breathed was blue. Was it blue dust particles lit by the row of small windows she saw in the cupola? The air was soft and pleasing, and felt like a blue caress on her skin and she felt she might walk out of there with a blue tint on her body. Looking at her bare feet, her toes scrunching into the deep pile of layered rugs, she saw a myriad of colors in the different designs and shapes. The writing on the walls was yellow, accentuating the blue. Small designs in red or green were also accentuated.

The flapping of pigeon wings high up distracted her. They, too, seemed blue. She saw metal bars that appeared to be holding the walls in place and long cables with candelabras floating between her and the ceiling. She turned to her guide. His face was blue, his smile a beautiful row of blue teeth. Lara began to laugh.

"You have a blue smile," she giggled.

"So do you," he replied.

"When was the mosque built?" she said stretching her neck to see up into the dome.

"The beginning of the seventeenth century," he answered. "Around 1616 I think it was finished. It needs a lot of repair."

"It's so beautiful."

After her leisurely visit they spent the rest of the afternoon walking the busy streets of the old city and a visit to Sainte Sophia.

Once Peter had left Lara in the hotel lobby, where the concierge had told him women on their own often ran into problems of having their behinds fondled or pinched and were mercilessly followed sometimes by a loud and noisy crowd of men, he knew where he was going and had decided to take some time to reconnoiter the area where he was to meet his contact. He hadn't had time to do this in Athens and it had taken him a lot longer to find his way back to the hotel in the poorly lit streets. He didn't want to repeat that experience. Lara had become too curious about his disappearing acts that lasted too long. In any case, he had to be more careful, more aware of what was going on around him. He had heard rumors about the Greek Army, about discontentment within the government and remembered the Baghdad agreement signed in 1955 with Turkey, Iran, Pakistan, Great Britain and, of course, the U.S. He knew the U.S. was backing the current President Alal Bayan, elected to office in 1950, and wondered about the reason for his meeting.

To his surprise his contact was a woman filling the brief description he had. He went by the table and addressed her with the standard phrase he had been given for his whole trip as a password only this time it was in French. *"Mais que faites-vous ici, chère amie, depuis notre derniere rencontre à Paris?"*

Slowly she looked up from her paper at him, saw an attractive, dark, blue-eyed man and answered, "You never know who's going to be around, I certainly didn't expect to see you." She folded her newspaper and added, *"Voulez-vous me joindre?"*

Their conversation continued in French. No names were used. She told Peter they were expecting more trouble. Laws passed to repress anti-government protests had worked for a while. They were expecting a coup d'état, probably from the Army. This was March 1960. In May General Gürsel would take over and dissolve the democratic parliament and relations with the U.S. would change dramatically. When the news reached Peter in Leopoldville after his return there, he asked himself what role, if any, the U.S. had played in the takeover?

They flew on to Beirut and visited the archeological site of Byblos. They drove over to Damascus via Ba'albek and back down to Tyre on the southern Coast of Lebanon. American troops, which had been requested for peace keeping in 1958, were still there. A coalition government had been formed and things were relatively peaceful. Peter's meetings in Beirut and Damascus were of little interest so they took a taxi, going south to the Israeli border. They had had a second passport issued in the States to be able to enter and leave — particularly leave — Israel for Egypt. A company car picked them up on the other side of the border and drove them further south to Jerusalem. It was a long drive for although it was only about 140 kilometers as the crow flies, the road along the coast and then inland up through the hills was a lot longer. They stopped from time to time to stretch, get something to eat and drink and to admire the countryside. What they didn't like seeing were the Palestinian refugee camps. People living in squalor behind barbed wire, with dust everywhere and the impression that there wasn't even enough water to drink, much less wash, and not enough food. Creating the State of Israel made prisoners of people living on their own land and being obliged to move while still remaining on their own land. These were the first refugee camps the Landons had experienced and they were embarrassed to be part of a world that had created this situation.

Jerusalem was a wonder for Lara. The Holy Land of Christ — visiting the sights she held in awe. The Mount of Olives, the Garden of Gethsemane with beautiful flowers, olive trees, and a path wandering through it; Golgotha (the Skull) covered by a dome where in full daylight Christ was crucified. A crypt below filled with gold and candlelight, a change of priests of different Christian religions at different times — *everyone gets their turn*, she thought; the rock from which He ascended enclosed in a tube of concrete painted dark green and covered with tourists names and dates scratched into it; a doorway in and a large hole in the ceiling so you could see the sky. *Disgraceful,* Lara thought and said, "Why do people desecrate places like this? A total lack of respect. I wonder if there are writings like this in Mecca."

"There's no one fighting for control in Mecca. Every pilgrim is a Moslem, only one religion. You're right, this is a mess. Let's go back to the hotel. Did you see the poster? Billy Graham is in town. We can have a rest and go and listen to him this evening."

Lara wasn't listening. "Don't you find it strange, the Christian side of town, the Moslem side? It's a funny way to cut up Palestine. Usually a river is a border. Guess they felt they couldn't take more land from Jordan and there's that strip which Egypt held on to. There's bound to be trouble," Lara said.

"Yes, this looks like future chaos; it's already chaos and it's all part of the peace process," he answered as they took a taxi back to their hotel.

The hotel was a charming two-story, white, stucco building around a courtyard with wisteria climbing over its walls helping to keep it relatively cool in the hot sun. It was a peaceful place and Lara was feeling particularly tired. She thought she might be pregnant again and after an early supper told Peter she wanted to go to bed. He could go to hear Billy Graham. She'd be sorry to miss him. That evening Peter met his contact, persuaded him to go and hear the Evangelist Billy Graham — a person unknown to his contact because he was a Moslem.

Their conversation was like two friends who hadn't seen each other for an age. At times heated discussion otherwise informative. Life was difficult for the Palestinians driven from their homes into camps that were

117

totally inadequate. "It looks peaceful now. That won't last."

"I see what you mean," Peter said as they said goodbye. "Please keep us informed, and good luck!" He entered the hotel closing the door quietly behind him and on the sadness he felt inside himself.

They were happy to leave the tension of Israel, didn't get to see Bethlehem, scooted by Jericho, crossed the Jordan River and flew out of Amman to Cairo.

Here they were met by Lady Boker's chauffeur. His name was Sobeké, a tall elegant Egyptian around Peter's age, who drove them to the Cairo Hilton — brand new and very Arabian. Air conditioning was a welcome surprise since Lara wasn't feeling well. She had not mentioned yet to Peter that she thought she was pregnant, wanting to keep up with their travels and give him the gift once they were back in Leopoldville. She always got dysentery the moment she stepped onto the continent of Africa and Egypt definitely was part of Africa. That night they dined at the home of Lady Boker's sister — a sumptuous meal which Lara couldn't enjoy, with fascinating Egyptians and diplomats. Sir Ian Boker was the British Ambassador to Egypt, a tall, distinguished man who had married a short, elegant Egyptian woman. They both had a wonderful sense of humor, were highly cultured and smart. Peter had one of the best evenings of his vacation and was sorry when he was told the car was waiting to take them back to the hotel.

The next day had been planned from breakfast through dinner. There was a visit to the museum, lunch at a private men's club for Peter, lunch with the ladies in the beautiful home of a private banker for Lara. In the afternoon she went for a visit to the Souk and shopping, two hours to rest and change before the car picked them up to drive them out into the desert for a large dinner under tents and a show by the Whirling Dervishes. After the show the dervish dancers asked members of the audience to dance with them. Lara graciously refused and turned to her hostess and said, "I hope I haven't offended you by refusing to dance."

"Not at all, my dear. I was afraid you might accept and ladies of our society don't get up to dance in public. Thank you for not accepting," she replied with a smile.

Ooof, thought Lara and she saw Peter with a huge happy grin on his face. This, too, had been a fabulous evening. The kind one might dream of and never get to see. Tomorrow they would fly to Luxor, the ancient city of Thebes, the Valley of the Kings and Peter wondered when he would be able to make contact and meet with his assignment before they left for Leopoldville. It was a short flight in a Fokker F-27 high wing plane with a gorgeous view of the Nile the entire way. It looked like most of the country's agriculture was along the Nile with places where the irrigation seemed to cut into the desert for miles and a pyramid or two popping out of the earth in the middle of nowhere. They were both fascinated with all the cities and little towns clustered along the river. It seemed to have changed little in four or five thousand years.

They visited one tourist spot after another. Ramses III Palace where a row of lions faced them on both sides as they walked up to the huge columned palace. They saw Tutankhamen's Tomb, which amazed them both. The guide explained the use of mirrors reflecting the sun off of each other for the light to reach far into the tomb. Ingenious — the whole tomb was ingeniously carved into the hillside.

"They must have had a lot of slave labor," Lara said. The guide didn't answer.

The next day they visited Karnak where Peter ran into a friend who said, "What are you doing here, my friend, since I last saw you in Paris?" Peter was taken by surprise. The roles had switched. He had been followed without even knowing it and he felt very uncomfortable.

He answered, "You never know who's going to be around. I certainly didn't expect to see you."

"If I'm not mistaken, I think we are staying at the same hotel. How about a drink? Around 6:30 or 7:00?", the stranger asked.

Lara watched the encounter evolve and wondered if Peter would introduce her to this slovenly looking character, whom she found rather unattractive. He was tall, had a long slim face partially covered by a beard and mustache. His eyes were deep-sunken and dark and he looked as if he hadn't had enough to eat.

"Good idea," Peter answered.

"Would your wife like to join us?" He held out his hand to Lara and said, "My name's Felix Raymon. We worked the service station together on 96th Street in New York."

She shook his hand and said, "Nice to meet you Mr. Raymon. I think I'll take a rain check and rest until dinner. If that's okay with you, Peter."

"Fine," he said to Lara and turned to Felix. "I'll meet you in the bar as close to six-thirty as I can get there, Felix. We're going for a camel ride at four and should be back in time."

Lara was too tired from the heat after their plane ride and walking in the sun to get up on a camel. She took pictures of the surrounding countryside and of Peter off on his run with the camel driver. She then went to sit under an awning of a shack, which served as an office for the camel rides and had a bottle of water. She looked down at her chest and realized her breasts had grown huge in the last few days and that she must be pregnant. Had Peter noticed? If he had, he hadn't said anything.

Lara went down to the bar at eight thinking it was time for dinner only to realize that Peter hadn't told her where and when to meet him and he wasn't there. Egyptians usually had dinner around nine or nine-thirty, but the man he was with — although he looked Arab — was an American, or at least so she thought. *Should I go back to the room, have a drink here? I'm hungry. Should I start dinner without him?* She found an empty stool at the bar and drank a cool bottle of sparkling mineral water with no ice. The water wouldn't be boiled in a small hotel like this. At the Cairo Hilton, she could have just about everything except raw vegetables and fruit. She'd come down with dysentery. That was Africa for her. She waited well over an hour, finally got up, told the man at the front desk to tell Peter she had gone in for dinner and that he could join her in the dining room. With no air conditioning, the ceiling fans reminded Lara of what hotels must have been like back in the twenties. The tables, waiters, dishes, glasses and cutlery all looked like the twenties — only the other guests looked like today.

It was after ten when he walked in looking absolutely exhausted. "Sorry, dear, I lost total notion of time. We had a drink at the bar and Felix suggested we have another with some Egyptians he had met." He sat down opposite her. "They were fascinating. I didn't see the time go by."

"I was worried and hungry, so I sat at the bar and had a drink. I don't know how many men offered me a drink, checking out my boobs," she said, hoping Peter would take notice of their size. "I got bored and came in for dinner without you. Do you want something to eat?"

"Yes, I'm hungry," he snapped his fingers three times looking for a waiter who came running over. "A chicken sandwich please and a beer, as soon as you can." He turned back to Lara, "Felix is a lot more interesting in Egypt than he was pumping gas in New York. I wonder how long he's been traveling around here. He knows a lot of locals, very interested in archeological digs. Doesn't work for Calder any more. Shit, I forgot to ask him who he works for." Peter's beer arrived and they sat in silence until he had about finished his sandwich. "Felix said we should get together in Cairo when we get back. I told him we were taking the train back and had a luncheon on the way there. Maybe we could see him in the evening. What do you think?" He looked at her quizzically, knowing she didn't think much of his newly found friend and noticed she was tired, that her décolleté was particularly attractive and larger than usual. "Are you okay?" he asked, "Are you pregnant again?" A smile covered his face.

"I think so. That's probably why I've been so tired the last couple of days — and not feeling very well. I hope that's okay with you," she said, looking him in the eye. She didn't want to lose another child because of timing, even if he had said he wanted another now and they had been exceedingly sexually active for this purpose. Peter got up, walked around the table, put his arms around her and kissed her tenderly.

"I'm so happy," he whispered into her ear. "So happy. Let's see, we'll have a baby in —" He counted on his fingers. "December." He counted on his fingers. He turned and signaled the waiter for the check. "Forget about tomorrow night. I don't need to see Felix. We'll have a quiet evening at the hotel. We have a busy next day with the pyramids and Sphinx. That will be enough for you."

"Peter, you can go out with him. We could have an early supper and you could meet him later. I'll probably want to go to bed and it's too bad to miss a good thing for you just because I'm tired." She looked at her watch, "It's late, let's go to bed," she said as she got up and started out of the dining room.

"I'll leave him a message. Be up in a minute."

Lara stripped, crawled into bed, and fell asleep. Eventually Peter came and lay down beside her. His hands started wandering over her naked body slowly feeling the fullness of her breasts, manipulating the nipples until they were hard and gently turning her on her back he started to cover her with kisses. He caressed her stomach feeling where his new child was growing inside her. The wonder of it all seemed overwhelming. His hand continued down between her legs, which she opened to his loving touch. He brought her to a climax knowing he would not penetrate her tonight. His baby was there. He just wanted to give her pleasure. Their bodies intertwined. They fell asleep only to be awakened in the darkness of early morning. The train left on time. They didn't see Felix get on board. He was probably taking a plane. There was no message waiting for Peter. He'd get one in Cairo.

The train was running three hours late because of animals and people on and along the track and a spot where the rails had shifted out of place. A conductor came by to find them. The train would make a special stop for them at a small station outside of Cairo, where their host's chauffeur would pick them up. This seemed a little out of the ordinary and the Landons wondered if it was wise to detrain early. However, Lara changed into her city dress. Peter changed his sweaty shirt and put on a tie. They would look to see if they recognized Sobeké or the car before getting off the train. Lady Boker was standing on the station platform and they waved to her as they went by a few yards before the train stopped. They thanked the conductor for his courtesy and started down the stairs, Peter calling to Lady Boker, "How did you work this out? We've never had a train stop somewhere just for us!"

"Oh, hello, Peter, Lara," she said waving. "Thank goodness they found you. Everyone is waiting lunch for you at Pasha Seidi's house." With a smirk, she added, "They've all had too much to drink, you'll never be able to catch up with them." They hurried to the car and sped away through a small town to a modest house in the country. Lara had never seen flowers so beautiful as these planted in front of the house. Two rugs of multi-colored flowers filled the area leading up to the door. It was magnificent and the sweet smell of tuberose, altered only slightly by delicious perfumes from the kitchen, gave Lara pangs of hunger. It was definitely time to eat.

They didn't get back to the hotel before dark and Peter felt nervous and anxious about the evening. His head was spinning with all he had learned over the last few days. Although Nasser had arrested the communists in Egypt in '59, the Soviets really had a foothold in there because they were financing the new dam at Aswân. Countries all over Africa were claiming, and many had been granted, their independence. The limited Arab Republic was gaining economic and political power in the world and all hell was brewing in the Belgian Congo — and that was just where they were headed.

Felix had left a message for Peter. Nine o'clock in the bar. That left him not even an hour to settle in and grab a bite to eat. Room service was going to have to be speedy. He was exhausted and wondered if the energy from excitement would carry him successfully through the evening.

Peter felt conspicuous in his European clothes. There was very little darkness to hide him as they drove through the center of Cairo. The streets were alive. Everyone appeared to be Arab. Men dressed in long, mostly white robes; the women in colorful long dresses, their heads covered by a shalla. They drove slowly through the busy streets filled with voices of every pitch, deafening to Peter's ears. He couldn't close the window — too hot for that — and the pollution filling his lungs made him cough. They passed brightly lit stores and movie houses, and the milling crowd seemed to reflect the light in every direction.

"You should have told me to bring my sunglasses," he said. "Now I know why you are wearing yours. Is it always like this? It's not even Saturday night."

Felix laughed, "Yes, every night the streets come alive. More happens at night than during the day. Only businesses with fancy offices work during the day — air-conditioned. We'll be out of this in a few minutes. Our meeting was for ten thirty, so we'll be a little late," he said looking at the dashboard clock. "Everyone is late here, that's part of life. At the Communist group I've been able to infiltrate, some wander in an hour and a half or more after we've begun. I put some clothes in the back seat." He turned to look at Peter studying his face. His blue eyes and dark wavy hair would look perfect in the coarse, washed-out blue robe. He could rub his feet on the car floor so they would be dirty enough in the sandals. He'd look like all of them, be one of them. Felix wasn't the least bit worried. He returned his attention to the street and continued, "Ever do anything like this before?"

"Like this?" Peter looked at Felix, his rueful smile to one side of his face. "Not exactly like this." He didn't want to tell Felix too much about his work. He had met a communist group in Leopoldville thanks to his boss's chauffeur, Eugène, and had gained a view of colonialism one evening that had given him a better understanding of what would happen in the Congo. "Do you have a signal for me if you see me getting into trouble — a safety net for both of us? I gather you'll be translating for us. You said some speak a little English otherwise it's all Arab?"

"Yup, let's see," a quizzical smile came over Felix's face and Peter wondered if he was in trouble. He didn't need a sense of humor right now; he needed a safety net. They were in a suburb he didn't recognize. Lighting was almost non-existent and he wondered how he would get back to the hotel if he had to run, if he had to separate from Felix. "Hey, Buddy, we're in this together." Felix glanced at Peter and saw he was worried. "Let's see, how about if I change from 'we' to 'I' you know you're out on a limb. How's that for an idea?" He pulled over to the curb and into darkness and continued, "Put the robe and sandals on now. Keep only your shirt and pants. We'll be there in a few minutes."

Peter looked around, saw there were no car lights headed their way, no lights in the windows of the surrounding buildings. He turned, pulled a heavy cloth garment from the back seat, noticed its dirty smell, and heard sandals fall to the floor behind him.

"Shit, Felix, this stinks."

"What did you think, I was going to put you into a sweet smelling robe fresh from the laundry? I wore that thing for two weeks getting it ready for you. Get your feet dirty, too, before you put on the sandals. You have to look the part," he said with a laugh trying to get Peter to relax, to get him to act as if everything was as it should be.

Peter took off his coat and tie, rolled them into a ball and shoved them under his seat, out of sight. He removed his socks and shoes and started to put them under Felix's seat, felt a gun, and pulled them out again.

"You carry a gun to these things?" he asked.

"No, it's kept there just in case. Put your shoes behind it. I want easy access, just in case."

Peter did as he was told. He slipped the robe over his head, opened the door and got out, rubbed his bare feet in the dirt of the gutter, and took the sandals from the floor. He sat knocking most of the dirt off his feet and wiped the bottoms as clean as he could before putting on the sandals. "A perfect fit," he said as he swung his legs back into the car and closed the door. The smell of the gutter added to the smell of the robe. "Do I smell the way you want me to? How do I look?"

"Perfect, you're going to have fun explaining this to your wife when you get back to the hotel," Felix said. "If the night porter asks what happened, have a story for him, too." They drove on to the meeting in silence.

An old truck stood alone in the street, and a donkey cart was on the other side a few blocks away. Felix parked the car facing back toward town, locked it, and the two men sauntered slowly toward what looked like an empty building. The only light was reflected from the city sky. Peter saw that Felix knew where he was going and what he was doing. *A good field agent,* he thought.

Dirt mixed with sand here. They were a long way from the city. The air was cleaner and cooler. Peter looked at the stars. Maybe tomorrow night he could figure out where they were, but then he realized how difficult that would be with the city lights. He didn't want to ask Felix. They walked behind the building, opened a side window and climbed in. After ten steps they came to a wall and walked to the left until they came to a door, which Felix opened. They went inside, and still very much in the dark, closed the door behind them. He opened another door on a room filled with light, smoke, and a stale smell. Obviously there was no ventilation. It was hot, worse than a sauna, and no one was sweating. Peter saw a small group of men, all poorly dressed. Perhaps they were poor, but they looked smart. As they introduced themselves with names which were not their own, he looked each one in the eye.

"This is my friend from Leopoldville," Felix introduced Peter. "We will call him 'Leo'. He comes with news from the Congo — Lumumba and what we are doing there." The meeting went well. Peter learned that the Russians were financing the Aswân Dam in Egypt and consequently would be involved in the construction and management of the dam and the future output of electricity. A huge foothold and influence, controlling such a large part of the country's electrical energy.

The return trip took a third of the time it had taken to get out of town. Peter walked in barefoot, holding his shoes and socks in one hand, his jacket in the other. He smelled strongly of smoke and alcohol, acted a little tipsy, asked for his key and walked to the elevators. No one said a word. He tiptoed into the room sometime after three a.m., took a long shower, left his smelly clothes in a plastic bag in the bathroom and fell into bed. It had been a long day and evening. He'd be lucky to get a few hours of sleep before leaving for the pyramids and Sphinx

The sun wasn't up when they got into Lady Boker's car. Sobeké climbed in and said, "This is Felix Raymon. He is your guide today."

Peter was shocked. Nothing had been said about them seeing each other again.

"Mrs. Boker's friend and usual guide couldn't make it. Mr. Raymon agreed to be his replacement."

"That's good of him. We had the pleasure of meeting Mr. Raymon in Luxor," Peter answered. He didn't care for the situation at all and wondered what was next. *Why was this happening?*

Lara was tempted to let out a groan to protest this intruder on their trip. She had generously let Peter go out with this man who had kept him out so late the night before. She didn't know what time Peter had returned, but it had been after two a.m. when someone knocking on her door had awakened her. She had forgotten to tell Peter about that in the rush to get dressed and have breakfast before their early departure. She had quietly gone to the door and looked through the peephole. There was a blond man, older than Peter, broad shoulders, dressed in jeans and a sports shirt. Lara saw him walk away when a staff security man walked down the hall. She needed to remind herself to tell Peter when no one could hear.

As they drove out of town, Felix started in as their guide. His voice was melodious to Lara's ears. She might fall asleep on their way out, but she didn't want to miss a thing. The size and shape of the pyramids didn't interest her very much. You could, and she had, read about them in guidebooks and mythology. She wanted something new. After the pyramids, he talked about the Sphinx. It was 70 meters long, 20 meters high, was built around 2500 BC, yet Christians claim the date to be between 5000 and 7000 BC. It has the bust and head of a woman, the body of a lion, and eagle's wings.

"What happened to its nose?" Lara asked. "Was it chopped off and stolen like so many personal parts of classic sculpture in Greece and Italy?"

Felix sensed the sarcasm in her voice. *She must be aggravated that I'm still here,* he thought. *But I have to speak with Peter before he leaves.* Someone from the consulate was trying to get to him and Felix didn't know on whose side the person was. "I believe it's the weather that stole her nose," he said. "There is a myth about her. Would you like to hear the story?"

"That would be a nice change," Lara replied.

Peter nudged her and said quietly, "Calm down. He knows the country very well. He could probably have been our guide in Luxor. Give the guy a chance."

"Yes, dear," came her sarcastic reply. She turned her head to watch the passing scenery and decided not to say another word.

Felix continued, "Sphinx was the daughter of Typhee and Echidna. She would pose unsolvable riddles to passers-by and when they could not answer she devoured them. One day Oedipus passed near Sphinx. He was given a riddle: What has four legs in the morning, two at noon, and three in the evening? Would you like to try and solve it, Lara?" he asked.

Lara, put to the challenge, said, "Yes, how much time did she give Oedipus to answer?"

"Take your time. No limit," he answered.

At least this was fun. She wasn't feeling very well with morning sickness and this was distracting. A riddle of the same type popped into her head, 'What's black and white and red all over?' A newspaper, of course. So what had or used four legs in the morning, two at noon and three in the evening? "Man," she exclaimed. "All four as a baby, a man walks with two in middle age and three when he is old with a cane."

"Right," Felix was amused. "You impress me. The story goes that Sphinx was so vexed to have someone solve her riddle she killed herself." They were back on speaking terms and the rest of the day flew by. They visited and did not climb the pyramids of Chéops, Kephren, and Myherinos. It was hot in the sun and the light reflecting off the light colored sand was hard on their eyes. They had a late lunch at an oasis restaurant and were back at the hotel before sundown — exhausted and happy.

"Lara, why don't you go up to the room and start packing. I'm going to have a quick drink with Felix. I'll be up right away," Peter said.

"Come on, Peter. You were out all night with Felix. Which reminds me, I have something I need to tell you."

"Can it wait?"

"It's waited all day. Just remind me when you get upstairs." She turned and entered the hotel, went for the key, and noticed the big blond in jeans and sports shirt talking to two men in the lobby. *That's strange,* she thought, and turned to find Peter to tell him they were there. She ran after Peter and Felix calling to them. They paid no attention, probably didn't hear her. Out of breath, she returned to the hotel. The men were gone. She went up to the room and locked the door. She fell on the bed and went to sleep only to be woken a few minutes later by the sound of the door opening against the chain, which blocked it.

"Lara, it's me, Peter. Open up," he said in a worried voice. "It's the first time you put the chain on. What's wrong?"

Lara pulled herself out of a deep sleep and went to the door. "Are you alone?"

"Of course, why wouldn't I be?"

She undid the chain, pulled him in and quickly closed the door, afraid that someone might push their way in behind him. "What's wrong?" he repeated.

"Remember I had something I wanted to tell you?" He nodded. "Well, last night around two o'clock a man knocked at our door. I got up to see who was there. You weren't home yet. I was very quiet, peeped through the hole and saw a blond man I didn't know standing outside, knocking softly — very insistent. The hotel security came by and he left. Then, when we got back this evening I saw him in the lobby with two other people. I ran after you and Felix, but you didn't hear me so I came back. I think he wants to see you. Why can't he leave a message? Do you know him?"

"Haven't the faintest," he answered and thought, *Felix just told me about a big blond from the consulate who wants to see me. Now they have me worried.* The phone rang. "Hello," Peter answered. He heard a deep voice on the other end.

"This is Tim Adams from the American consulate. We need to see you before you leave tomorrow."

"What about a cup of coffee in the café downstairs?"

"Not possible. Can't be seen in public with you. You went with Felix. They're following you now. Lady Boker's car will be downstairs waiting for you at nine a.m. Come down early with the bags. Ask your wife to wait a half an hour before coming down. Say you have an errand to do, shopping. I'll have something in a package for you."

"You called me about selling essential oils? You've got to be kidding," Peter laughed. "And forget it. We're checking out tomorrow, sorry."

127

"Get in the car, we'll drive around. You'll be back in time to leave for the airport. Be careful if Felix tries to see you again." They hung up. Of course Peter would do as he was told.

"That was a person who wants to see me. All this hiding. Maybe he wanted me to buy some drugs or stuff to take to Leopoldville. In any case, forget it. I won't be seeing those guys." He changed the subject. "You haven't started to pack?"

"I fell asleep. Can we have some supper? Packing won't take long since just about everything needs to be washed or cleaned when we get back."

They had a quick supper at the café and went straight to bed. They both needed a good night's sleep.

The next morning everything was packed and ready earlier than Lara had expected. Peter turned to her and said, "I'll take the bags down, check out, and get ready to go."

The phone rang. A deep voice said, "Your car is here."

"Thank you," he answered and hung up. "Lara, the car is here and I have some last minute shopping I'd like to do. Why don't you rest here until we leave for the airport? I know you're not feeling well." She was pale with circles under her eyes.

"If you don't mind, I'll lie down until you come back. We don't need to leave for the airport until ten. It's a bit before nine now. Call up when you get back. I'm sorry not to go with you."

"That's okay. I'll come up and get you."

He took the bags down, checked out, everything was put in the car, and Lady Boker's chauffeur opened the door for him. *I wonder whom he works for,* Peter thought. *He's seen everyone I have.* The window was up between the driver and passenger seat. That didn't mean the driver couldn't hear them. Tim had turned on the radio to cover their voices before even greeting Peter. Their conversation was short and to the point. Peter needed to be careful about his relationship with Felix. They wondered if he was a double agent. People he recommended could not be trusted. They had tried to warn Peter earlier but had been unsuccessful. "The people he took you to see — or someone else — has been following you all day. We know because we have, too. Felix is a loner, doesn't take orders very easily — never has worked with another agent until he was assigned to you." Tim leaned closer. He knew Lady Boker's chauffeur; didn't trust him, but this was the only way he could meet with Peter in private. "Did you notice the man who put your bags in the car? He was at the pyramids with you."

"That's where I saw him. He waited on us at lunch. If Felix knew him, it didn't show. *Was he at the meeting?"* Peter wondered.

"Word from Cairo will follow you to Leo. I hope all this won't blow your cover there. We're sorry not to have contacted you earlier. It's the first time he's brought someone to one of those meetings. Either you really got along or he's using you." Tim sat back. He had said all he had to.

"Question: How long has Felix been in Egypt and what's his cover?" Peter asked. "I didn't ask him where he worked. He never gave me a contact number; he found me, password and all. I thought he was one of us." Peter wondered also about Tim. Felix had told him the evening before that someone from the embassy might have or would contact him. "Don't trust him," Felix had said. "There's a mole somewhere in the embassy. Too much is being leaked. Be careful."

Tim leaned toward Peter. "Felix has been traveling around Egypt for several years now. He knows the country inside and out; works mostly with the underground. Don't know how he got to be your guide yesterday." He paused. "He must know some important people. He works for a magazine, *Encounters with the Past*, I think it's called. It has to do with ancient art and preservation, archeology. He meets a lot of scientists, spends a lot of time in the desert. He's very smart." Lowering his voice, he continued, "Personally, I don't like him at all. He's done a turn-about and still comes up clean." Tim tapped on the window and told the driver to continue fast around two turns. They passed the point he was to have left the car. If they had been followed, or if the chauffeur had said something to someone in passing, Tim had a better chance of getting out discreetly. He changed places with Peter and was out and behind a storefront before anyone could see him.

Good move, Peter thought. "Back to the hotel, please," he said. There was a small package on the floor. He opened it and laughed. Essential oils — how would he explain that one to Lara?

Peter saved his questions for Sobeké until they and the bags were out of the car at the airport. He wondered if the driver thought he was with the Agency, but couldn't ask that question. He left Lara by their luggage and went back to the driver to give him a tip and question him about Felix. It turned out that the driver had worked for a pharmaceutical company before working for the Bokers. Felix had dealings with the company. Peter let the subject drop. They were on their way back to Leopoldville and the dangers of the upcoming independence. He had had enough of Cairo and the Middle East. Things were going to be turbulent.

Chapter Seventeen

The riots started in January 1959. The Landons had left for home leave in December and returned in early March of 1960 to a country fraught with imbroglio. Tia and Bazi, the nanny, returned early in April. The Holders' old house was now the Landon's new one — at the entrance to the Calder Oil compound with a view of the whole compound and the city, which lay below. It was strategically located with two ways out in case of trouble. Lara's pregnancy was difficult. The pain was excruciating and the doctors couldn't figure out why. Lara thought it was a tubular pregnancy, but no one listened. She went through a battery of tests and x-rays and had exploratory surgery in mid-June, which showed an extra uterine pregnancy of about three months. She needed to be operated on as soon as possible, but after a previous general anesthesia she had to wait for at least two weeks. With all the troubles brewing her family and friends urged her to return to the States for the operation. They had all been forewarned that trouble was near. Independence was scheduled for June 30th.

April and May had been filled with social obligations, distracting them from the rising tension. The Landons gave two parties during this period — one of them was a 'Come as a Baby' costume party: all were dressed as babies or little children. Four came wrapped up in bed as a quartet, happy to be released after the photo. Peter was doing his usual traveling and Lara was asked to show visiting VIPs around the city. American businessmen and politicians were now interested in Africa and although Lara wasn't feeling well the tours kept her busy. Senator Soapy Williams came through and Dr. William Close showed up with Moral Rearmament. Dr. Ralph Bunche arrived at about the same time as the new

U.S. Ambassador, Timberlake, who took over from the Consulate General Bob McIlvaine. The Landons met everyone and found that Bunche was a great friend of Lara's aunt and uncle, which gave them a direct connection to the UN. Vice Governor General Cornelis, an outstanding economist, but unfortunately also a man of complete indecision, governed the Congo then. Perhaps this was understandable because all business and governmental decisions were made in Brussels. Cornelis — and Brussels — let the situation get completely out of hand. Congolese nationalism grew stronger as the Belgian government grew weaker. The U.S. and other governments were doing everything they could — discreetly or not so discreetly — to encourage independence. Unfortunately no Congolese had been trained to govern.

The situation was relatively calm the few days before independence. Lara's operation was scheduled for July Fourth after what was going to be a long weekend and much celebrating. She would be too weak to participate on Independence Day, even though they had been invited to many events.

"I don't like leaving you here with Tia and Mademoiselle. I asked the Boys if one of them could stay — taking turns even if I do get home to sleep. They both refused because they were going to be celebrating. Did they tell you they wouldn't be coming to work?" Peter asked.

"When did they tell you that? It's the first I've heard of it." Lara said with a shrug. "We'll manage,"

"The Kramers are going to be around. You can always call on them. Eugéne said he'd be working so he could stop by and check in on you. He'll be driving Paul and Eleanor to the various functions. In fact, I might ride with them. Traffic will be horrendous with all the visiting dignitaries and the crowd. He really knows his way around town." Peter got up from the floor where he had been playing with Tia. "Mademoiselle, could you take Tia? She needs a change." He handed over the child. "How do you feel being more or less alone out here with my wife and daughter?" he asked her. "I know things have really been tense and that you haven't had any time off since you got back. But it's better you both haven't been to town recently. The attitude toward whites is ugly."

"Monsieur, it is not the first time I have been caught in political chaos." She smiled. "I was caught in la Place de la Concorde during the Blum manifestations, an uprising in 1934. Bullets were flying, people running in every direction. I stay calm in those situations," she said with a smile, the twinkle of her eyes showing behind her smudged glasses, which she removed and cleaned. She left with the smelly child and turned, "We'll be all right, the three of us — just fine. You don't have to worry."

Peter turned to Lara. "I wonder if we are in trouble. In any case, Mademoiselle's great and I'm off. I really don't know how much I'll be home the next couple of days. I'll call often." He bent over to kiss her. "Take care of yourself. If you need to get to the hospital, I'll call an ambulance or you call one if it's urgent." He prepared his toilet kit and a change of clothes. He really didn't know when he would be coming home.

Independence Day, June 30, 1960. The sky was overcast, the air heavy with humidity. It would not rain that day, the rainy season was a few months away and tension was running high as it always did at that time of the year.

Early that morning, Peter had snuck out of bed, went to shower and shave, swallowed a quick cup of coffee and tried to leave for the city without waking Lara, who stuck her head out of the door

"You've got to be kidding. Thinking you could leave, particularly this morning, without saying good-bye." She put her arms around him. "Take care of yourself, the mob will be out." His arms held her tight. He knew he was going into dangerous territory. Even with all the *Forces de l'Ordre*, Belgian as well as Congolese, there was bound to be trouble.

"Don't worry, you know I'll be fine. Eugène will be taking care of me once he's left the Jardins off at their viewing point. Until then things should be calm. It's too early for trouble now." He kissed her good-bye, grabbed his jacket and walked out the door stuffing a tie into his pocket. "In case I get invited to join in the ceremony," he said, turning with a sly smile on his face. He had dressed carefully that morning, clean white shirt, sleeves rolled up just below the elbows, khakis clean and pressed, polished brown leather shoes and his usual navy blue ankle length socks. He could go anywhere, be noticed or melt into the crowd. He took Lara's light blue Fiat — small and easy to park on a side street. He had put his gun under the seat the night before. No one knew he had one and no one needed to know. He hoped he wouldn't need it. He drove quickly into town past the market and the bridge over the Gombe River, pulling off the main road away from the Congo River and the center of town. He left his car on the grounds of the riding club and walked via Avenue Prince de Liege to Boulevard Albert where the parade was to take place and hang around until there was action. He stopped at a café, had a croissant and coffee and watched the locals gather. The small number of Europeans in the street did not surprise him. They would all be over at the new Parliament building where troops were stationed every two or three meters along the road to keep the road clear for the dignitaries. He had Lara's Leica camera and also their 16-millimeter movie camera. He hoped he'd be able to get some good pictures of the total day. And he did, the parade of floats went right by him. Lever Brothers, Coca Cola, and IBM were among the biggest. The local beer companies and other Belgian companies had floats as well as the series of floats representing village life, slavery, hunting, and bringing home the game. There were African dancers and music blared from hyper-noisy loudspeakers, making Peter cup his ears. He then moved towards the government building to witness the dignitaries and to listen to the speeches given by King Baudouin and Lumumba for the passing of power.

At that same time the Kramers had gone over to Lara's to listen to the radio, which was closely covering the ceremony. The Kramers had returned to Leopoldville from the Kivu with their children. The Company felt it was too dangerous to leave its employees out in the bush and so most of them were in town. Only one or two men managing the branch offices were still out there. Because of the air conditioning, they were sitting in the bedroom glued to the radio and were astounded to hear the new Prime Minister, Patrice Lumumba lash out at King Baudouin and the Belgian Colonialists for taking so much out of the Congo and putting so little back. It was true that since the early 1870's Belgium had obtained great riches from this colony and committed barbaric atrocities against its people in the early part of its colonization, but this did not seem an appropriate time for such a statement. Lumumba was turning the Congolese population against its white settlers. Trouble was brewing.

"How can he talk like that, in front of the world?" Daphné said. "We've already had riots. What does he want anyway? He's in power now."

"He gives me goose pimples," Lara said, hugging herself. "The man sounds crazy and he's so charismatic he'll have the population on the move again. And to think he was only a postal worker." She turned to Tod and asked, "Did you have riots in the Kivu last year?" He put a finger to his lips.

"We'll talk after the speech."

Mesmerized, they listened to the speeches and the commentator all afternoon. It was getting dark by the time the Kramers left Lara. Peter had called to say he was staying in town with the Consul General. He'd be home for supper the following day.

The situation remained relatively calm and Lara went in for her surgery on July Fourth, leaving Tia and Mademoiselle in Parc Acacia.

Although the government, the Army — everything, — was unstable with independence, Lara knew that if something were to happen to her or to Peter, someone would take care of her daughter and get her back to the family in the States. Still, she was worried about Tia, and about her operation. It was an emotionally difficult time and fatigue and tension from the last year had accumulated. She chose to stay by her man, in spite of the feeling that their life together was not going to last long.

Lara's morale was low even though the operation went well. She had lost a baby boy. They had tried to reconnect the tube on her right side, had not been successful and she knew she no longer had a chance for twins. She was in pain, gas moving through her pelvis. It was hot and there were no painkillers. She didn't want visitors and the nuns were no help. Peter seldom stopped by, and when he did it was only for a very short visit. Too much was happening in town and Calder Oil needed him.

Then on July six the government fired certain Belgian officers and raised the salaries of the Ministers and Deputies to a level that the government could not afford. The *Force Publique,* the Congolese Army, started a wholesale mutiny. Lumumba upgraded everyone in the *Force Publique,* creating the only army in the world without a private. The leaders of the Congolese Army, overworked and underpaid, were not satisfied. They felt that they were more intelligent than the newly elected deputies and wanted the same salary of $10,000 per year. They took over in the Bas Congo, which was Peter's district, locked up the Belgian officers, raped their wives, and spread terror throughout the country. Peter got the news from his usual series of international newspapers, not from local journalists.

It happened so fast that many European settlers in the interior were caught by soldiers, tortured, and raped. He thought it was amazing that so few people were murdered. The Belgian authorities took advantage of the atrocities and were ready to immediately dispatch Belgian troops to the Congo. Lumumba took this opportunity to incite the Africans against the Belgians, claiming that the Belgian troops would slaughter — and had slaughtered — the Congolese by the thousands. Besides, Lumumba hoped to restore peace by bringing in Russian troops to throw the Belgians out.

Lumumba and President Kasavubu went to calm the forces in Thysville, Inkisi, and the seaports of Matadi, Coquilhatville, Madimba and Boma. Peter found himself driving Dr. Bunche and Ambassador Timberlake in a Calder Oil tank truck out to greet their plane upon their return. It was there at the airport that Bunche and Timberlake convinced the leaders to request UN troops.

At this same time panic took hold in Leopoldville. Riots had started anew. The Calder families in Park Acacia left the compound in a caravan accompanied by two U.S. Marines. Tia and Mademoiselle went with the others to the Ambassador's residence where U.S. Marines stood guard. That night Peter went to watch over Lara who was still unable to leave the hospital. While much of the electricity in the city had been cut off, the hospital had a generator, but the ceiling fan barely moved and it was hot. Peter sat uncomfortably in a chair tilted back against the wall trying to sleep. He was worried about Lara who was totally defenseless in the middle of an uprising. It was particularly hot, the rains had not arrived; the air was heavy and filled with smoke from burning cars and buildings. The noise of helicopters overhead brought him out of his daze. Daylight slowly moved over the city filled with confusion and Peter hoped to get Lara out of the hospital and over to Brazzaville as soon as possible.

The noise of the helicopter overhead also woke Lara and she saw Peter sitting there with a gun in his lap.

"Peter, what are you doing here at this hour?" she said slowly. "Where did you get that gun? We had to turn them all in, remember?"

"We'll talk about that later," he answered. "Right now all hell's broken loose. How you slept so well through the noise last night I'll never know." He got up from his chair. He looked awful, slipped the gun into his waistband under his shirt and went to talk quietly into her ear. The noise outside was horrendous.

"I need to get you out of here. Dr. Pauley will be here around eight. You need some breakfast and have to go to the toilet before he'll let you go. Can you manage that?"

"What's going on? I hurt like hell and I don't know if I can do that. I'll try. What's the rush?"

Peter didn't want to scare Lara anymore than necessary. "There's been rioting in the interior. Calder Oil's called all personnel and their families back to Leo. Things started popping here last night and I want to get you to Brazza before the border closes. Someone told me that's at noon today."

"You mean we're no longer safe here? Where are Tia and Mademoiselle?"

"I left them at the Kramers last night. They are being brought to town in a convoy with the others from Park Acacia. They're fine — installed at the ambassador's residence, Marine guards and all."

An orderly arrived with Lara's breakfast. "Do you want some coffee, sir?" he asked Peter.

"That would be great if it's not too much trouble."

"No trouble, sir. The hospital is almost empty. The nuns moved out as many people as they could. Their mass is later this morning because they couldn't get away earlier. I'll be right back, something to eat, too, sir?"

"Yes, please. What is your name?"

"Boniface, sir. I have worked for the nuns going on 12 years now. I won't leave them, never." He walked away quickly trying to hide his tears.

Five minutes later Boniface returned with a tray of rolls, butter, jam, ham and cheese, and café au lait. "Maybe you need to take something with you. Just wrap it up. There are extra napkins. Is there anything else I can do for you?" His expression was so sad that Lara started to cry.

"I'm so sorry," she said. "I think we have everything we need. *Que Dieu te benisse*, Boniface." Lara wasn't hungry. However, she understood she needed to make an effort. Things were not going well and she didn't want to complicate matters. They both sat silently eating what they could. Peter made several ham and cheese pistolets, reminding him of their first breakfast at the Memling Hotel so many years ago. So much had happened since then.

Dr. Pauley showed up a little after eight. He looked tired, his white doctor's coat was dirty, and underneath his brown plaid shirt was rumpled and had missing buttons. His khaki-colored cotton pants were torn in several places. His appearance was disconcerting.

"What happened to you?" Peter asked before even saying good morning.

"Hello, Peter, Lara. It's been a disastrous night — casualties in the Congolese hospital, pulling people out of burning cars. Who would have thought it would come to this?" He walked over to Lara, put his hand to her head. "No fever, that's good. Have you been to the toilet?" he asked.

"Yes and boy did it hurt, but I feel better now. Peter says you're putting me in an ambulance for the ferry - that the river might close. Is that true?" she asked.

"I don't know about the river. He's wise to try to get you out. You'll be going through crowded streets. Lots of people. Do you think you need medication? It's pretty hairy out there."

"I don't know," said Lara. "What kind of medication?"

"It's a new one called Valium, a tranquilizer. It helps to calm the nervous system." He was taking her pulse. "I think it's a good idea." Lara took a few seconds to consider the situation. She would be going into crowds, she was vulnerable and, all of a sudden, very uneasy.

"Yes, doctor. I don't need it right now, but it probably will be good

136

when they take me out of here."

"It takes a while to work and we're moving you out now."

Lara was surprised at the speed with which everything was happening. Peter and the doctor started dressing her with no consideration for her privacy. Obviously they were in a hurry. The doctor called down the hall and two Congolese orderlies came in with a stretcher.

"Lara, stand up." The orderlies put the stretcher on the bed. "Now get on the stretcher. Put the straps tight around her so she can't fall off," he said to the orderlies. They tied her arms down as well as the rest of her, picked her up and started out of the room followed by the doctor and Peter.

The ambulance was waiting for her in the shade, its back door open. She saw cartons under the space for the stretcher and she wondered what they were. Peter got in beside her. "You okay?" he asked as he took out the gun, making sure the safety was on and put it under her dress between her legs.

"Peter, what are you doing?" She had forgotten all about the gun.

"I can't carry it on me. If they frisk me I'll lose it. Is it too uncomfortable?"

"No, it's okay. I just don't like it."

"I'm going to ride with the driver," he said as he climbed out the back. "Everything's going to be okay." He hoped he was telling the truth.

The drive to the river took longer than it should have. They didn't put on the siren, not wanting to attract attention, and had taken several turns to avoid large crowds. Lara couldn't see much of what was going on. She could hear angry voices and chants. "Belgians go home." They finally turned down the ramp to the Ferry landing where a crowd had gathered. Peter and the driver got out, opened the back door, pulled out the stretcher and laid Lara on the ground. The crowd started to get angry. Lara panicked. She was lying, vulnerable as if naked, in the hot sun, surrounded by angry Congolese. All she wanted to do was pass out from the terror she felt. Her pelvis had been slit from top to bottom and her arms were tied down. If someone jumped on her, she would be torn open. "Please, Lord, get me out of here," she cried silently. "Or let me pass out so I don't know what's happening to me."

A Congolese in European dress stepped forward and said to Peter as quietly as he could, "Put her back in the ambulance and get her out of here." It was Eugène. What was he doing here?

Peter had not noticed him in the crowd. "Come to the embassy. Meet me there," Peter said. "I need your help. Can you make it?" Eugène

137

nodded. The driver and Peter slid Lara back in the ambulance and got in themselves. The crowd moved in and surrounded the ambulance.

"Put your foot on the gas," Peter said to the driver. "Push your way through the crowd. Do it now!" he yelled.

"I can't do that. I'll kill someone."

"You do it or we'll all be killed," he screamed over the noise of the crowd beating on the ambulance. Again, Lara only wanted to pass out. The tranquilizer was useless, she feared for their lives. She closed her eyes but the noise persisted, hurting her ears. Tears rolled down her face. She thought she was going to die.

Slowly the ambulance pushed through the crowd, up the ramp and onto the street as it picked up speed, the crowd ran after it. They took a turn, bumped into something and drove on. Lara opened her eyes. She was in shock. The driver must have been in greater shock, because his skin and hair had turned white in the time she had closed her eyes. Was it possible? She wondered if her hair had turned white too. She was trembling now, totally out of control and having a hard time breathing. Peter sat tensely giving instructions to the driver. He turned to look at Lara. "Are you okay?" he asked. "We'll be at the embassy in two minutes." He saw she was not well, but there was nothing he could do. They were out of the crowd and relatively safe. The gates of the embassy courtyard were in front of them. As they pulled up to the Marine guards Peter got out, showing his American passport.

"I need to get the ambulance inside. My wife's in there. Please open the gates." He turned and saw that on the other side of the street was a sidewalk filled with hostile faces. Panic returned to his face. Turning back to the Marines, he saw the gates open. The ambulance drove in and Peter walked hurriedly behind it. "We made it! We made it!" he called out. "Thank you."

The midday sun filtered through the smog that settled over the city and it was hot: at least 110° in the shade. Two men from the embassy greeted Peter. "What happened?" Philip asked. He was in charge of communications; coded or not, all correspondence via the wire system passed through his hands. He knew Peter well.

"It's a long story. I'll fill you all in later. Right now my wife is having a nervous breakdown. She's just out of surgery and I need to put her in a cool place."

"You can bring her in to the decoding room. It's cool and quiet," Philip said. "Here, let me give you a hand." They extracted Lara, still tightly tied to the stretcher, carried her up a few steps and into the cold. She began to shiver violently. She was speechless. She couldn't talk.

"It's okay, Lara," Peter said wiping her face with a dirty handkerchief. "It's okay, we're safe now." Someone took off their jacket and covered her. *Nitwit,* Lara thought. *I'm not cold, I'm in shock. Can't someone please untie my arms?* She still couldn't talk. The Consul General walked in and saw Lara lying on a stretcher on top of the decoding table. "You can't leave that poor woman here." He paused because the only place he could put her was in his apartment and he needed his privacy and rest. He'd work something out. Besides they were constantly in communication and only those who had top security status were allowed in the decoding room. "Take her up to my apartment. Who is she?"

Peter stepped forward. "She's my wife. Lara, this is Bob McIlvaine, Consul General. Bob, my wife, Lara."

When introductions were finished, Bob said, "Get her out of here. This place is top secret. No one should be in here except authorized personnel."

"Sorry, Boss," Philip continued. "It's my fault. She's had a rough time. Come on, guys, let's carry her up to Bob's apartment."

Four of them carried her up the steep stairs. Thank goodness she was still firmly attached to the stretcher for surely she would have slipped off given the tilt going up and around the corners. They carried her into the bedroom and finally she was untied and carefully laid on a bed.

"Before you guys go, let's move some furniture!" Bob said, "I want my bed in the living room. You can put the couch for Peter in the bedroom." When everything was the best it could be, they left Peter and Lara alone. They could hear gunfire from time to time but technically they were safe and as far as Peter knew, so were Tia and Mademoiselle.

"I'll stay next to you until you go to sleep," Peter told Lara. "Then I have to check on Tia and Mademoiselle and go back to work. You know the government has asked for UN troops. The sooner they get here, the better. So in the meantime, get some sleep. You're safe now."

Lara tried to talk but couldn't get anything out.

"Hush. Don't try to talk. Do you need the bathroom?" He remembered it had been a long morning. He got her on her feet and she almost passed out. He practically carried her there and back. She would be asleep in a few minutes and he could get on with his business knowing she would be better in the morning.

Peter went out to look for Eugène. He had been told not to leave the embassy because it was too dangerous, but he had work to do. He went out the small gate from the courtyard when he saw Eugène walk by. He headed in the same direction, not wanting to expose their relationship. He finally caught up with him. "Can you get me to the Calder offices?"

"The offices are empty —closed and your child is fine. There are more important things for you to do!" Eugène answered. "Your friends are trapped at the airport."

"That's a long way from here."

"Not so long if we cut corners. Maybe four and a half or five kilometers." They crossed the Belgika canal and the railroad tracks and although Congolese lived scattered throughout the area, no one seemed to be around. They stopped at the St. Paul mission to see how the fathers were doing, had a quick bite to eat with them, and continued in the dark to the airport. They found a group of soldiers in disarray, some so drunk, from alcohol probably stolen from the airport restaurant, that most were asleep. Eugène walked over to the few who were still conscious.

"What happened here? You all okay?" he asked.

"Sure, we're fine. What are you doing here? Not supposed to be anyone here."

"What about people inside?" he asked casually.

"Oh, they're there. We want to keep them there. No planes in, no planes out. Airport is closed," one said in a drunken slur.

"Why don't you take your friends home? I'll keep guard here for you. I haven't anything else to do. Hate the Belgians," he added for good measure.

"You trying to trick me? Think I'm stupid?"

"Hey, I'm a local. Can't you tell? I'm with you. You want to stay? You go ahead and stay. I'm moving on." Eugène turned and headed for the darkness around the side of the building. The electricity had been turned off here, too.

"Whoa! Come back here. You're not supposed to be wandering around. You okay here by yourself if we leave? We'd be back here after sunrise. What's your name?"

Eugène didn't want to give a name — certainly not a false one in case they checked his papers. "Ask your buddy. He knows my name."

The officer slapped a man sitting against the wall, "You know this guy?"

"Yeah, he's one of us," he said, his eyes half open, not even seeing who his officer was talking to.

"You wanta go home?"

"Yeah."

"Okay, let's all go home. We're going to have to help Pierre and

François. I think they're out cold. Come on guys. Let's get out of here." Those who could, stood up and helped the others to their feet or dragged them into the night. It was now safe to go in.

"Nice job, Eugène. How do we get in?" Peter said as he stepped in close to Eugène. They couldn't see very much. The electricity was out over most of the city and smog blocked the light from the first quarter moon. No stars were visible. They tried the doors where passengers entered and exited from the planes. All were locked. They walked around the building, which wasn't very large. No sign of life, no open door. They chanced a call, no answer. There was a noise. Peter knocked gently on the window. "It's Peter Landon. Cyril, are you there?" They listened for an answer. Then a flashlight beam headed their way. They did not hide and hoped whoever was inside didn't have a gun and that they wouldn't be shot. The light approached. They saw a Congolese Army officer and ducked out of sight.

"Who's there?" he called. Eugène moved to his left and stood up very slowly.

"I'm here, sir," he said.

"Who are you?"

"Eugène, sir. Your men asked me to tell you they were called back to town. More fighting there. They were needed."

"What are you talking about? They were drunk. Some of them could hardly stand."

Eugène started to move toward a door, the light followed him and so did Peter who had crouched low and remained invisible.

"If you'd like, sir, come and see for yourself. As you can see, I'm harmless, just a passer-by, curious to see what is going on after delivering a message."

The officer unlocked the door and stepped outside only to be hit from behind by Peter. They dragged him inside, took his flashlight, locked the door and went up to the control tower. They found Cyril and four other men bound and gagged.

"*Oh, mon pauvre vieux,*" Peter said to Cyril. Peter and Eugène started pulling out the cloth stuffed into their mouths. One man was already unconscious because he was unable to breathe. Then they untied the ropes. Cyril's face was covered with blood

"They beat you?" Eugène asked.

"They took a whack at all of us. I got the worst of it. God, am I glad to see you. How did you know we were in trouble?" Cyril spoke very slowly. His face was numb and swollen.

"Eugène heard some people talking. He said we had to come here. He got rid of the soldiers outside. We were surprised to find an officer inside. We took care of him," Peter said as he rubbed Cyril's wrists and ankles. Then they did the same for the other men. They had been tied up for over twelve hours. Some had urine-soaked pants and the place stunk. "Can we get you moving? We should head back to town. There's no electricity so you can't man the control tower. The place will be at a standstill well into tomorrow".

"And," Eugène added as he helped one man to his feet, "they have planned a general strike. The city will shut down and there will be dancing in the streets until the UN forces arrive."

"They've asked for help?" one of the men said.

"Yes," Peter spoke up. "Timberlake and Bunche met their plane yesterday. Were you here then, Cyril?" Cyril nodded. "Remember the Calder Oil tanker driving out to meet the plane. They were on it. That's when the decision was made, but it's going to take some time to get the troops here."

They moved slowly, first around the room to get the blood flowing, then down the stairs past the unconscious officer, and out the door. They took the keys with them. Since their cars had been stolen they were obliged to walk slowly back to town following Eugène. They dropped out of sight when a Congolese army jeep drove by, and continued when no lights were in view. They split up and Peter gave a strong handshake and grateful thanks to Eugène before he headed back to the embassy. He walked into the flashlight beam of a Marine, with his hands in the air, holding his passport. He was checked carefully and let through. "Where you been, man? Not good to be out alone so late in this mess. Have a good night's sleep."

Peter looked like he needed a good night's sleep; for nearly 48 hours he'd been running around. He climbed the stairs and opened the door as quietly as he could. Bob opened his eyes, saw Peter walk into the bedroom and close the door. He looked at his watch — 4:35 a.m. He wondered what Peter had been up to so early in the morning and went back to sleep.

It was the smell of coffee that woke both Peter and Lara. "What time is it?" she said. "I have my voice back." She burst into tears. Her nerves were worn to a frazzle but she was alive and she could speak again. They held each other tight for a long time and even Peter allowed himself to cry. It eased his tension, too. He was refreshed from four hours of sleep and ready to face the day.

On July 9 all communications were cut off with the outside world, but because Peter had connections at the embassy, he was able to send word by the embassy radio through Brazzaville to Lara's family Stateside saying all was well and there were no problems.

"No problems?" Lara said. "What do you mean? Look at what we've just lived through and you say 'no problems'. How can you say that?"

"I don't want your family to worry. You decided to stay here with Tia. All they need to know is that you are safe. You don't know, but there is a general strike. The Congolese are running wild in the streets, looting and fighting. I was told the new government has asked for all Belgian troops to be recalled to Belgium. All this mess, they say, is because of Belgian officers who want to renege on independence. I have to keep your family calm because somehow how all this news is getting out."

"What's happened to the Kramers? Were they able to get here from Bukavu with the girls? Is the airport open?" Lara stopped and thought a minute. "Sorry, it's only 8:30 and I'm asking all these questions. Let's have a cup of coffee. I suppose you need to go to work if you can brave the streets." She remembered she'd spent Independence Day with the Kramers — they must be here at the embassy too. There was a knock on the apartment door. Peter went to answer.

"Hi, Peter," Mac Davis was at the door with two large packages of food.

"I thought you all were at the residence. It's good to see you. Everyone okay?"

"We were at the residence. They moved us over here. Less places to guard. The Ambassador has moved into his office and all of Calder Oil is okay except our man in Luluabourg. We wonder if he's still alive. Oh, the food," Mac bent down, picked up the two bags and brought them into the kitchen. "Small, no room for two. How's Lara? We hope she's well enough to cook up a stew with everything here. Too many people tired of eating peanut butter and jelly sandwiches. Hey, Lara, how are you?" he called out.

"How do you think I am with my belly slit and all stitched up," she called back. She got out of bed to see Mac and Peter standing in the door of the kitchen. "You want me to cook? Look at me. I'm a wreck." She pushed them aside and smelled the fresh vegetables. It made her mouth water. "What the heck, I might as well peel and cook as lounge around feeling sorry for myself."

"Good sport, and thanks. I'll see you later, Peter." He turned to leave, "Oh, why don't you come with me. Your kid is there with the nanny. Maybe you can bring them over here. Mademoiselle could help make the stew. Come on."

They both ran down the stairs and a few minutes later there was a teary family reunion. Lara was overwhelmed with joy and held her baby so tight the child had a hard time breathing. Then she hugged Mademoiselle and kept saying, "Thank God you are well. Thank you for taking such good care of my baby — our baby. How are you?" No answer was necessary. They were happy to be back together again. The Consul General moved into the decoding room. There was so much going on he needed to be there anyway, leaving his apartment to the Landons.

On July 11 the doctor came by to remove the stitches and gave Lara permission to leave for Brazzaville as soon as the Beach for the Ferry was open. There had been a mass exodus of Europeans and Belgians from the airport. Cyril had gotten the airport open again. Sabena was doing most of the evacuations along with Pan Am planes painted white with "UN" marked on them. Streams of young families and older people left the country. Two days later the Beach was opened. They missed the first crossing, but plans were made to take Lara across on the second in an ambulance. The Calder Oil files would leave with her and again the gun was put between her legs under her dress and covered before she was attached to the stretcher, which she really didn't need anymore. Her arms were not tied down this time. Tia and Mademoiselle would follow later. Lara thought Peter would need his gun in Leopoldville, but he thought it wise to get it out of Leopoldville. He could always smuggle it back if he thought he needed it.

With the exodus all plantations closed down. The government-run transportation — OTRACO — that controlled all railroads and shipping closed down. Coffee, tea, and oil were ruined causing great economic instability and unemployment. Road maintenance and construction stopped. The country was paralyzed and Peter's messages home were a disgrace. Most went via Brazzaville, some with Pan Am pilots who were able to land and help in the evacuation, and even via Dakar where a friend owned a newspaper and could get information out. "Family doing well, no worries whatsoever, Peter." "Family at American embassy. Pay no attention whatsoever to newspapers. Safe and happy. Peter." Then the truth, "Everyone in Brazzaville in good health. Love, Peter."

The company finally sent word to the families of the skeleton staff. "Leopoldville advises political situation remains confusing but security for personnel remaining assured stop Lara still in Brazzaville" dated July 13.

On July 15 Peter was reading the International Herald Tribune headline during breakfast at the home of the Brazzaville Calder Oil manager who had taken in Lara and the baby — "Threat to act on Congo made by Khrushchev." Khrushchev charged western aggression: "If the states which are directly exercising imperialist aggression against the Congo Republic, and those which are instigating them, continue their criminal activity, the Soviet Union will [take] decisive measures to stop the aggression." The Soviet Union accused Belgium of aggression, which was strongly denied by Brussels. The Soviet Union asked for the withdrawal of Belgian troops so that the UN could do its job, saying that the Soviet Union would render necessary assistance to the Congo "for the victory of your just cause."

Peter read it aloud and then got up and said, "I have to get back to Leo. Can I leave Lara and Tia here for a few days? We're trying to rent a house in Pointe Noire for two months. I'll try to get it for August and September. That leaves two weeks. Okay?" He looked quizzically at his host.

It was settled and Peter returned to Leopoldville. Then the borders closed. The city was at a standstill. Lumumba's anti-white campaign took off. The Belgian troops refused to leave before the safety of the remaining settlers was guaranteed. The UN troops finally arrived. Peter had worked hard before their arrival. He approached Dr. Bunche and obtained the contract to supply the UN forces with gasoline and diesel fuel. He was asked to take the UN reconnaissance team around the Congo. The story he enjoyed telling the most when all of this was over, was his trip up around the Eastern Province of Stanleyville, where the river transportation ended and the rail line to the interior began. A hydroelectric plant and water purification plant had just been built at Tshopo Falls. They had taken a Citroën, one of those cars that adapted to the terrain of bumpy roads, and driven off into the bush... and ran out of gas. They had passed a small village about ten kilometers before, so the UN team left Peter, not in uniform, to guard the car while they went off looking for petrol. No food, no water, no gun. All he had was a machete. It was noon, the sun particularly hot and the humidity was high. Peter couldn't sit in the car because the open doors would wear down the battery. Then they'd never get out of there. So he perched under the overhanging trees to get as much shade as he could. He kept alert, looking around for animals, snakes, spiders, tsetse flies, and other hungry insects — and he was hungry. He got up and started walking looking as deep into the jungle as possible, hoping to find bananas, papaya, mangoes — anything he could eat. There were caterpillars, but he couldn't remember which ones were edible and besides they should be deep fried before eating. His mouth started to water when he remembered how like peanuts they were. Once you started, you couldn't stop. Lara had brought home a batch from the market and they quickly disappeared. He heard the noise of a car. Was it his group coming back with gas? Two, or was it three, cars passed, each slowing to look at the car when Peter waved them down. No one stopped; they were all Congolese and not at all interested in helping.

Peter pushed the car out of the afternoon sun, opened the windows and lay down for a nap. He wondered if he'd ever get out of there. He woke to the sounds of baboons screeching in the forest, got out of the car and walked down the road a ways to stretch his legs and to see what was going on. Large baboons flew out of the trees, and soon a huge family was on the road with him, noisy and aggressive. They started walking and then began to run at him. He ran toward them screaming, trying to frighten them. No good, so he turned and ran for the car. It was the fastest 200-meter dash he had ever run. He jumped into the car and was rolling up the windows when the clan started beating on the car. There must have been a hundred and fifty of them, maybe two hundred. The screeching and gibbering was so loud it hurt his ears. These faces surrounded him, watching him — hairy gray baboons with dark beady eyes and pink palms. The males had blue balls — he'd never seen these before, not even at the zoo. It was getting dark. He needed to open the windows a bit for air. A young baboon stuck in a skinny arm. Peter thought he wanted to play and gave him a finger. The baboon held tight, trying to pull the finger out the window to bite it. It became a tug of war. Peter did not intend to lose his finger to a baboon. And then the lights of another car approached and pulled up, keeping the baboon-covered car in its headlights. It blew its horn until the baboons returned to the forest and everyone could get out safely.

"You're lucky they didn't eat you alive. You know they're very aggressive animals," the Congolese driver said.

"Yes, I noticed," Peter answered. His team had finally returned with gas. They headed back to town to fill the tank and decided to take advantage of the town's hospitality and spend the night, hoping their throats wouldn't be slit. One of them kept guard all night.

The arrival of UN troops was difficult. The airport needed to be repaired and once the troops were on the ground the physical set up for camps, supplies and everything else an army needed still had to be organized. Cyril de Cloune had been running the control tower for over 72 hours before a member of the UN forces could take over. He and Peter had seen the flow of refugees from the interior into and then out of the city, and the arrival of UN troops. The last two weeks of July were exhausting and their trials had just begun.

During those last two weeks Peter was working three to four jobs every day. Lawrence Devlin, Chief of Station, and his team were covering most of the intelligence work. Peter was an unknown factor to the group, passing his information directly to his boss in New York by coded message through friends or pilots going back to the States.

Calder Oil work was overwhelming. There was no communication with the interior — that system had closed down a few days after Independence and most European personnel was either in Leopoldville or evacuated to another country. Service stations were ransacked and burned. Supplies were difficult to find and probably would be unavailable until the UN troops were organized. Somehow everything seemed to fall into place.

Although the compound in Park Acacia was guarded Peter needed to pack up their belongings and try to get them to safety. He had already taken care of the silver and Lara's jewelry; still remaining were the things that made their home personally theirs. It meant packing up everything that wasn't the company furniture — the linens, paintings, clothes, tableware and kitchen. And there was the dog — a boxer they had gotten to scare the Congolese away from the house. Her name was Togolita and they had taken the time to train her. The afternoon when the borders were open and the *vedette* was running Peter lost four suitcases and the dog. He was mad as hell, searched for hours, ran everywhere he thought they could be and finally gave up and went down to the dock on his way to Brazzaville. There they were waiting for him. That night he left everything in the car, the roof open, too tired to deal with anything except the dog.

"Dear," Lara asked, "are you sure you can leave our stuff in the car with the open roof?"

"It never rains at this time of year," Peter answered. "And it's perfectly safe with the gate closed and the house boy on guard with Togolita." Lara didn't think of it again until a loud clap of thunder and a heavy downpour at about four-thirty wakened her. She nudged Peter who couldn't wake up. She let him sleep and the next morning when he went out to get the bags he found them sitting in water. Everyone was watching from the porch — he opened the car door, was drenched by the flow of water and burst into laughter.

"Told you so," called Lara as everyone else doubled over in laughter.

His other job was with the State Department and Bob McIlvaine— the U.S. Consul General, which gave him access to the daily happenings in all of Africa as well as a better contact with the UN. Besides, with the Calder contract for fuel he soon found himself helping with all UN supplies. He knew he couldn't keep up this pace for a long period of time and decided to try to get to Pointe Noire as soon as his family was installed there. Leopoldville had become a bachelor's town with bullets flying. Fatigue and stress were getting to him. He had to be careful. And as for their belongings, Peter moved in with McIlvaine whose home was guarded by U.S. Marines and their crates stored in the garage. Then they were transferred to Brazzaville when the river opened up.

The UN Security Council ordered the withdrawal of Belgian troops on July 13; on the 15th troops from Ghana and Tunisia arrived in Leopoldville. In Elizabethville the local leader, Tschombé, kept his Belgian officers and blocked the airstrip so UN forces could not land. On July 11 he had declared the Katanga an independent state and he didn't want the UN to get involved. Between McIlvaine and Dr. Bunche, Peter was constantly informed of any change. A curfew was put into effect after the riots. No white man was allowed in the African town after 9 p.m.; no African could leave their town after 9 p.m. until 6 a.m. unless the "boy" had a special pass. Peter had gone several times to meet with Eugène his skin blackened by burnt cork, his clothes totally 'native'.

Lara, Tia, and Mademoiselle left Brazzaville by train — thirteen hours west to the Atlantic coast and Pointe Noire where Peter had found them a house. It was not a smooth ride. The train lurched from side to side, screeched to a stop in the middle of nowhere to pick up passengers as well as at the regular stations, and the smell and dirt from the coal-fed engine filled everyone's lungs. There was no air conditioning, no food or drinking water, and the sanitary conditions were minimal. Although there was a first, second, and third class, when third was full it spilled over into second and second to first so the corridors were full of people, with baggage and animals everywhere. Getting to the toilet was a challenging experience — crawling over sleeping children in a parent's arms, around a bunch of chickens whose feet were tied together so they couldn't run away, and sitting on or climbing over huge bundles of household goods or clothes. Everyone was hot and smelly in spite of the constant flow of outside air.

The trip was an ordeal for everyone and all were relieved when the train pulled into Pointe Noire. The Calder Oil agent was there to greet them and drive them to the house.

"What service," Lara said giving Theo a hug. "You don't know how much I appreciate your being here!" He was a big man with a smile on his face and a twinkle in his blue eyes. The Landons and Dumonts had met in Brazzaville months before the troubles had started and had found an immediate affinity.

"My pleasure," he replied. "Julie's at the house, she's made supper for you. We did some shopping for a couple of days." he said as he took their bags and put them in his car. "Peter called, said your car will be on the train as soon as he can get it across the river; said he didn't know when that would be."

Lara was speechless at the thought of being stuck in the middle of nowhere with a small child and no car.

Theo saw the sad look on her face as they got into the car, "Don't worry, Julie or I will be by every day to see how things are going and if it's nice we'll take you to the beach." He turned to her, "You know our house is on the water. You can spend your days with us if you like."

"Does anyone know when they're going to open the borders?" She quickly added, "Did Peter say when he'd get here for a weekend?" And Lara wondered if she'd ever see him again. "Life in Leo is horrendous," She started to cry again, "You know I've had a nervous breakdown. I cry all the time and Tia usually joins in too. I hope it's not contagious," she said with a teary smile on her face.

It was dark by the time they got to the house, which was just as well for Lara would have been all the more unhappy if she could see where she was. Julie was there to greet them and move them in. They left when dinner was on the table, knowing they had done all they could under the circumstances.

The house was small, three rooms made of whitewashed cinderblock. The largest room was the kitchen, dining and living room all in one; the two bedrooms were small and they had to pass through one to get to the other. Mosquito netting hung from the ceiling above the bed to the floor with instructions to spray the rooms with insecticide a half hour before bed. They were exhausted, thankful to find the beds made, and didn't bother to clean up the dishes or to see what time it was. They slept soundly late into the morning. It was then they saw where they were. A small garden on two sides of the house with empty grass fields all around. The port was visible, as was an Army base, otherwise nothing and no one. Two days later there was a knock on the door.

"*Bonjour, Madame,*" a young man in khakis said. "I'm your new 'Boy'. *Monsieur* sent me." Lara didn't expect anyone; this was the first she heard of having someone to cook and clean for her while she was there. She liked the idea, yet she wondered if this was really true or just some way for him to get into the house. He handed her an envelope. "This is for you. My references and a note from *Monsieur.*" Lara saw a bike, knew his transportation was taken care of, read the letters and asked him in. His name was Daniel, and he was a blessing. His presence meant that Lara and Mademoiselle would get a good rest before returning to Leopoldville. He kept the house clean and the car, once it arrived, spotless. The food was good, the laundry clean. There was only one unfortunate experience for Tia who had taken her nap outside on a sheet, which hadn't been ironed. Larva eggs had stuck to her forehead and although she had been well bathed, the eggs stuck, ate their way under her skin and thrived for several days before causing a high fever. A local doctor went over her from head to foot, found two worms just under the hairline of her forehead and said, "You're lucky. In twenty four hours the worms would have found their way into her circulatory system. The only time you can catch them before they get to the brain is when they show their head coming out of the tear duct of the eye." Lara felt nauseous as she looked at the worms. The hole they had left in Tia's forehead was full of puss.

"Is there anything that can be done then?" she asked.

"If you're patient, you catch the head and pull very gently and slowly. You wrap the worm around a pencil and keep pulling until you reach the tail. It's a very long worm. If it breaks, you wait, more will show, you start over again. It can take hours — and then the tear duct is irritated for weeks, the eye usually becomes infected. You want to avoid that at all costs." He finished cleaning the wound, put a bandage on and said, "Just make sure everything is ironed on both sides. Really hot and you won't have any more trouble." And they didn't.

It was the cool season, no need for air conditioning — there wasn't any anyway. They spent many days at the beach under cloudy skies, saw trains pass from the port on their way to Brazzaville and were amused to see the new French Ambassador Charpentier's large crates headed for Leopoldville, wondering how much of them were filled with wine and champagne. Nothing much happened in Pointe Noire except that the *Jean Mermoz* (the ship Lara and Tia had taken up the west coast of Africa) came into port while Lara was there. She called Jacques on the ship and made plans to see him again, tempted to have him as her lover while he was on leave. He invited her to his cabin discreetly when no one was around. It was three days of lovemaking and thinking about something other than the troubles in the Congo and the dangers Peter was living through. Lara missed Peter. He was unable to get to Pointe Noire as often as he had said he wanted to. And she felt guilty now about her affair with Jacques. The *Mermoz* sailed on Wednesday. Peter arrived on Friday. Lara decided she would never see Jacques again.

They were a family for four short days. Peter explained to them the difficulty he had in getting out of the country, hours spent waiting in the Minister of the Interior's office to get a pass out and back even just to be able to circulate around the country for his work.

"I got really angry. It was like getting permission to go from my bedroom to the bathroom."

"Do you see much of Ralph Bunche?" Lara asked, changing the subject.

"Oh, yes. I do a lot of work for the UN. Bob has even asked me to work for the State Department," he said slapping a mosquito, which attempted to feed on his neck. "What do you do about all these bugs anyway? I hope you all are taking your malaria pills. They've run out in Leo." He continued swatting the air around him. "Calder Oil has ordered a huge supply and medical supplies too. It looks like things are going to be rough for longer than expected." He got up and started to pace. Lara sensed his discomfort.

"You want a drink? It's almost cocktail hour."

"We've all been drinking too much. Life is so tense there. You know I don't even know if you all should come back when our rent is up here."

"Gin and tonic? And you, Mademoiselle, the same?" Lara got up, put out three glasses, poured the gin, taking very little for herself. "The ice cubes are made with boiled water so you don't need to worry about dysentery." She sat quietly with her drink, then added, "If you think we are going to live separate lives, think again."

Peter turned to Mademoiselle, "Will you come back with us or," he paused, "why don't you and Tia go back to the States until things clear up or we're transferred." He turned to Lara. "I've asked to be moved out of here. I'm even looking for another job but Calder doesn't know it. Russia is giving us a hard time and I want out before they come in and take over."

"Monsieur, votre femme est restée à vos côtés. Your daughter, too. You are a family — now I'm part of it — if Madame goes back to Leo, I go too, with Tia," Mademoiselle said firmly.

"Peter, I don't really know what's best for Tia. What's Leo going to be like? Will there be other children? — enough food, water? — bullets flying? — danger of kidnapping? — what the hell," she threw up her arms and knocked over her drink. "We all could be dead tomorrow, but at least we'll all be together." She knew she had another month to grow strong again; he'd probably not get back to see them in Pointe Noire before they returned to Leopoldville. "Try to find a house in town, close to Bob. See if you can get our old 'Boys' back. We'll manage. Anyway our tour is up

151

in February. We'll all leave then." Her hands were trembling and she was holding back her tears for once successfully. "I'm going to have another drink — anyone care to join me?"

Peter returned to a city in havoc — he had to fly across the river — those borders were closed, but the UN kept the airport open. Any kind of communication with the provinces was dangerous and close to impossible. Telephone lines were down, the post office on strike, the plantations left to rot, with the deterioration of the roads, bridges and boats the country was at a standstill. Food supplies were short in the cities and many of the locals were going hungry. Peter flew out several times with UN personnel on "Air Brousse," Cyril de Cloune's company. His area of service stations was nonexistent except for a well-guarded station under UN control. On September 2nd a Yale classmate stopped by to see Peter.

"Hey, Peter, I'm flying down to Matadi, want to join me? I hear the Russians have landed. McIlvaine will be interested to know what's going on." And to tempt Peter even more, "Aren't you expecting a tanker one of these days?" he said with a chuckle.

"Hey, Buddy. You men of the press know everything before anybody else. You know I'd love to. Can you wait a few minutes? I have to check with my leftover boss. Have a seat." He got up and headed for the door, returned to his desk, picked up some important papers, "Sorry, personal," he added.

Blaiser Johns was a tall, lanky, blue-eyed wonder. His dark curly hair had grown long — relatively long — during the last three months, still too short for a ponytail, which wasn't yet in style. He was unshaven and looked like a gangster in his dirty plaid shirt and jeans. If it wasn't for his camera and notebook no one would guess he worked for Time, Inc. He knew what he was doing and could blend in anywhere; go unnoticed alone or in a crowd. He also knew that if Peter went with him he'd have a better chance of survival. They met a group of Russians in a bar in Matadi, found one who spoke some English, asked the usual questions. The group was coming in as technicians for transportation, communications, and industry. They all looked like soldiers and Peter and Blaiser decided to fly back to Leopoldville as fast as possible.

Lara arrived a few days later to look for a house with Peter, knowing she would return with Tia at a later date.

Chapter Eighteen

They moved into a house in town with neighbors nearby: a Congolese family from Belgium on one side, an Indian family on the other. The Landons had a small garden in front and back and just enough room for shrubs and trees on either side for privacy. They tried to meet their neighbors but were turned down flat. The Congolese was one of twelve governing at the time, a dentist by profession, his income had dropped since his return to Leopoldville and Lara sensed they were embarrassed by their social standing. The Indian family — merchants who associated only with others from their country — were discreet and hardly ever at home.

Since there were few bilingual English-French people in Leopoldville, Lara was asked to work as an interpreter for the U.N. Indian Supply platoon. Although she felt inadequate, she accepted. Hours were from 7 a.m. to 5 p.m.. with two hours off for lunch, giving her time to be home with Tia for lunch and a nap.

Lara enjoyed the work. For her interpreteing meant translating what one person said to the other and if necessary, changing certain phrases in hopes of getting the best results for each. The dictionary says, "to clarify the meaning of" and this she did often because the Congolese had hated the Indians since their arrival a century before. She spent time translating documents and getting them typed by her boss, her spelling was miserable and her typing nonexistent. She also spent time running away from him. He would pull down the shades on both sides of the office and make a play for her. She knew the signs and would get up ready for action.

"You know, I could give you an orgasm just by kissing you," he said.

Lara wondered where he would be kissing her. People seemed to need more sex in a hot climate and there weren't many women around to ease the needs of the UN troops. She certainly wasn't going to become one of them. Her boss was a young man with a huge mustache and although Lara wondered what it was like to be kissed by a beautiful mustache, she wasn't going to play his game.

"I'm not interested," she said as she moved away keeping the desk between them.

"Do you find me unattractive?" he asked with a sad look on his face.

Lara hesitated. He was her boss. She wanted to keep her job. "You're an attractive man." Then she thought *he loves his mustache.* "It's your mustache. I don't like mustaches." He stopped short.

"You don't like my mustache?"

"No, I mean, yes I don't like your mustache."

"You know it's very soft, softer than the hair on my head or chest." Lara was wondering *what am I getting myself into?*

"I don't care. I'm a married woman and I'm not interested in a man who has a mustache." That ended the chase for the day. She was in shock when he came in the next morning without his beautiful mustache and the chase started all over again. She was sorry he'd cut off his mustache for nothing.

Life in Leopoldville was stressful. Every day seemed to be a struggle for survival. The *Force Publique* (Congolese Army) was still out of control. They set up road blocks wherever they wanted, stopping cars, searching them, stripping the occupants and sometimes raping the women in front of their husbands or the men who accompanied them. Anything to debase the whites. Peter and Lara were stopped almost every time they were out together after work hours. Curfew didn't start until 9 p.m. That didn't matter. The first time they were stopped Lara made Peter understand the calmer they remained and the more subservient their actions, the better their chance to survive unharmed.

"Get out of the car" one solder growled. They obeyed. "Your pass and identification cards," he barked. All were produced. Peter and Lara, once they had put the men's faces to memory, looked down. "Step over here," he said to Lara. A lower-graded soldier took Lara's arm and pulled her aside. Peter panicked and started to move to protect his wife.

"It's OK, Peter, don't move," Lara said with self-confidence. Her father had put her through a jujitsu course when she was a child living on an Army base; a class in self-defense meant to disable the attacker and even kill if necessary. Her intuition and survival skills were in high gear; she'd knee the soldier if necessary. She wasn't going to be raped. He passed his hands over her body, stopping on her breasts. She stood firm, not moving, ready to take action when necessary. He moved down one leg with both hands, then the other, then up to the crotch. *"Il y a rien là qui peut vous interésser* [There's nothing there to interest you]," Lara said in a firm voice. The soldier looked up to a calm face. Lara knew her anger would have excited him and then all hell would break loose. She was ready to knee his chin if he didn't take his hand away and jab both sides of his neck on the way up if need be. He could be out cold for hours, perhaps even dead. He seemed to understand it wasn't going to go any further.

"Bon, ça va" he said to his boss who gave Peter back their papers.

"Vous pouvez partir," the head soldier said, stepping away. They got into their car and drove to the safety of the embassy where Lara again burst into tears, trembling and out of control.

"That's the last time I'll wear a skirt," she cried. "Thank God you kept calm. I think it saved us both." Peter hugged her.

"You were great. I'm so sorry to put you through all this." *And it's not over yet,* he thought. He held her until she stopped crying and trembling. They went into the embassy where the Ambassador was receiving a small group of American businessmen with Bob and the commercial attaché.

In early November Peter was out checking the few remaining service stations still in operation thanks to UN troops guarding them twenty-four hours a day. He heard machine gun fire, parked his car, and ran into the closest building. Gunshots followed and then there was silence. He stuck his head out. The street was empty. He hugged the wall of the building, stopping in an empty doorway before rounding the corner and heading in the direction the shots had come from. He heard the click of running army boots and ducked into the darkened entrance of a store where he bumped into a local woman with a baby strapped to her back. "Don't worry," he said softly in her language, "I won't hurt you." The woman pulled deeper into the darkness. All Peter could see was the terror in the white of her eyes. "Please don't worry," he repeated. "Do you know what happened? The shooting, where was it?" She pointed towards the street and to the left. Peter went towards the doorway trying to look without being seen. Then he heard an ambulance siren, more running boots, and decided to brave a sortie. The ambulance meant that the shooting would not begin again — at least not right away. He walked out close to the wall, turned left at the end of the block and only then did he realize he was on Embassy Row. UN troops had been involved in the exchange of fire. He saw a few

UN soldiers, probably Tunisian, guarding the Ghanaian embassy. They were pulling bodies toward the embassy compound wall and back inside. There were also Congolese soldiers among the dead. It was the first time Peter had seen UN troops being attacked and killed and the killing of Congolese troops by the UN. He had seen enough. He headed for the American embassy to let them know and then headed home to a quieter part of town.

Because of this incident, a curfew was imposed on all UN personnel. The rest of the population was free to roam. Looting became a problem and violence in the African city went unpunished. The city was again in chaos and Lara wondered how long she, Mademoiselle, and Tia could survive under such stress. She thought the UN owed an apology to the Congolese, but what did she know about the situation. Their boxer puppy was now full grown. The Congolese didn't like angry watchdogs and Togolita saved them many times from roaming mobs, which — once they saw the dog — headed in another direction.

Peter came home one evening and asked Lara, "It looks like there's going to be trouble again with Lumumba. I could use your help."

"So what's next?" Lara replied as she watched him change his clothes.

"Where are my black pants?"

"In the laundry. The boys didn't show up this afternoon. I knew something was wrong."

"Could you get those pants for me? I need you to change into black too. If one of us gets hit, the other can probably get through."

"What the hell are you talking about?" Lara was shocked. She should probably have felt fear — fear can save your life — but she didn't. She felt excited by the adventure, and totally forgot her responsibility to Tia and her survival. Her husband needed her. She would go with him. He told her that the communication systems were out and that they would be running messages for the embassy between the different residences. There was a personnel shortage and they had asked Peter to help. As far as Lara was concerned they'd asked more than enough of Peter. She went to pick up his dirty black pants in the laundry and on the way stopped to talk to Mademoiselle.

"We're out again this evening. If you hear gunshots, please put your mattress on the floor and sleep there with Tia. The house will be locked up and lights out." Out of breath Lara continued, "Leave the dog to roam the house. She's a good watchdog. You and the baby try to get some sleep. I don't know what's going on; we'll soon find out." She wanted to say, "pray for us" but didn't dare.

She found Peter burning several wine corks. "Here," he said handing her a blackened one, "Rub it on your face, neck, hands — any part of you that will show." She had dressed in black pants and turtleneck, but her sneakers were white. "Here, put these on," he handed her his navy blue sneakers. He wore his regular black, everyday shoes. "and keep your mouth shut. I don't want to see anything of you except the white of your eyes. Anyway, if you need to say something you'll be whispering in my ear."

They spent the night in the deep drain ditches, running bent over, keeping their heads down. Bullets flew everywhere. The shooting was around Lumumba's residence and they wondered who was trying to kill him. By 6 a.m. it was growing light and it was too dangerous for them to be found out during curfew. They returned home exhausted.

In early December Peter was diagnosed with a liver problem, probably caused by the tension they were living under. "No more sun for you for at least two months" the doctor had said, giving him a medication for his digestive system and something else for his liver. "And no more food with sauces. You should get Lara and the baby and yourself out of here as soon as possible," Dr. Pauley said.

"You know that's not possible." he said. "There's only a skeleton staff now." Peter got up and headed for the door. "Thanks for the medications. If the UN wasn't here we probably wouldn't even have them." He put the packets in his pocket. "You take care of yourself too. Did your family arrive safely back in Belgium?"

"Yes, they're fine. Moved in with my parents until we decide what to do. I'll be going up for Christmas. I suppose, by then, you'll still be here."

"Yup." Peter walked out the door. *No more sun,* he thought. *Shit, the only time we get to relax is when we go out on the river to water ski or for a round of golf. No more exercise. It looks like I'll be taking more naps!* But the river had its dangers too. Bilharzia, a parasite picked up in stagnant water, which could age a person in six months to old age and death. Then there were the fish — large fish with seven rows of teeth, which could chop off an arm or a leg in one snap — and, of course, there were the crocodiles. No one was allowed to fall while water-skiing.

One Sunday afternoon during siesta time there was a banging on their front door. The dog barked wildly, Lara got up leaving Peter sound asleep, and went to the door. She looked out the window first to see who was there.

157

Three of their friends, friends whom they usually went water skiing and picnicking with on Sundays were at the door, and they looked worried. She unlocked the door, opened it, "What's the matter? You look awful."

"We need your help. The German Ambassador has been taken by a croc," Jon said. He was the Danish Ambassador to Zaire — a tall lanky Dane, slightly balding. His pale blue eyes seemed even paler given the circumstances. "Ambassador Goehring has disappeared. He was holding onto the towrope cooling off in the water. When we looked again his hat was floating down the river. We couldn't find him."

Jacqueline, the English wife of the Texaco manager said, "Hansie wanted her husband to see the progress she and her sons had made water skiing. He never wanted to go out on the river. Now he's gone." Her wiry body, partially covered by a dirty white shirt, exuded a nervous tension and she burst into tears.

"You know everyone at the UN," Mark said. He was the only Belgian in the group. He had lived in Leopoldville, which was now called Kinshasa, for most of his life selling insurance. A heavy set, fun loving man, Lara had never seen him look so serious. "We need helicopters to go out looking for him. Before he reaches the rapids. You know, the current is really fast when you move out from the river bank and islands." He was talking so fast it was hard for Lara to keep up with him.

She had just wakened from her nap and slowly realized Peter was standing by her side. He turned, went to the phone and called, "They'll be up in five minutes. Go back to the dock, they want one of you to go up with them to show them the starting point." He took Jacqueline in his arms. "You guys get going. I'll take her home or, would you like to stay with us for a while?"

"Oh, no thanks," she sobbed. "Could you take me to Hansie's? She needs company now. They all feel guilty about getting him out on the river; the boys are in a terrible state. I'll be all right. Can I freshen up first?"

Lara took her by the hand and led her to the bathroom. "I'll get you a clean shirt and pants, then Peter will take you wherever you want to go."

Both Peter and Lara went with Jacqueline to the German Ambassador's residence to wait for news. He was never found. Peter knew that once the crocodile had a carcass it would kill it and stick it under a log to rot until it could feed on it. They were told a few years later that the Ambassador's wedding band had been found in a crocodile a Congolese had killed.

They did get to play some golf — very early in the morning before the sun was too high and in the evening before sunset. The clubhouse was protected by the Blue Berets (UN soldiers), but the golf course was another matter. The *Force Publique* would drive by in a jeep next to an area far from the clubhouse and spray the course with machine-gun fire. The players usually saw or heard them coming and would dive into the nearest sand trap with bullets whizzing over their heads. Lara gave up golf. She went swimming instead in the large pool of a private tennis club, which had been taken over for UN personnel. Peter didn't have much time for either.

His job with Calder Oil was full time. He also had taken on supplying the UN with just about anything they needed. All information gleaned from the two jobs was passed to his Boss. At Christmas Lara's job with the UN paid off. They had *foie gras* and turkey; fresh fruit and vegetables; whiskey, gin, and champagne, which they happily shared with their friends. On Christmas Eve more than thirty people stopped by for supper. On Christmas day there was only the family with Bob McIlvaine and his young son, Steve. The 'Boys' came to work both days, knowing there would be leftovers for their Christmas, otherwise a large number living in the native part of the city were going hungry. No supplies for them had made it into Kinshasa. Peter had been out on the roads and knew most roads were too damaged to use; there were still no repair crews for anything and the railroad wasn't functioning. He told Lara to prepare three bags for the houseboys and the gardener. He gave them out Christmas afternoon, making sure that they'd return to work the next day.

It was at about this time that Peter heard that he was being transferred. Where to, they didn't know. Probably the CIA was finding it hard getting him a post that would give him and his family a calmer home where he could be useful. They knew they would be leaving Africa in March. Lara resigned from her job with the UN mid-February. Exhausted, she needed more time than usual to pack up. She was depressed again, often in tears and annoyed that she had so much to do. She kept crawling into bed for a nap, only to be called back into action. She organized and prepared dinner parties for the Consulate General, she returned several times to the supply depot trying to keep a good relationship between the Congolese and UN troops. American visiting dignitaries needed to be shown around. Their social life was busier than ever with the usual luncheons, dinners — she refused the afternoon card games. Then there were all the "goodbye" parties they could not refuse — a tradition for Europeans in Africa. They had been there for longer than most and there were more parties than usual even under the chaotic conditions they all were living in. They found a home for Togolita. She had been a great watchdog and would continue her good works for another family who had just arrived. Their belongings were being shipped back to the States and only the necessary clothes would go with them. They would travel light for once.

Peter drove them to the Beach and took the ferry across to Brazzaville, and put them on a plane for Paris. It was mother-in-law time for Lara, but this time she couldn't care less. Paris would be so much easier than what she had just lived through. Peter, as usual, would follow in a couple of weeks. And Mademoiselle was with her. That always was a blessing.

They climbed onto the plane, throwing kisses to Peter and settled in. Lara's last memory of Africa was the heat and humidity — a sauna-like air circulating in the plane, and she was so out of it she couldn't speak. Her thoughts were running as the plane took off. *We're alive, we're not sick — at least I don't think we're sick. We're tired, no exhausted. Even poor Tia is exhausted.* Lara clung to Tia, holding her tight in her arms. *She's my most precious belonging,* she said to herself. *We're alive and Peter will join us in Paris. He's like a cat except he has more than nine lives. We're alive, and I'm leaving Africa behind me.*

Chapter Nineteen

They were back skiing in the Austrian Alps: St. Anton, Lech, St. Christoph. The days were sunny, the snow getting heavier as the days were getting warmer. They always lunched on a restaurant terrace on top of a mountain, finding friends to talk, drink wine and end the day with. Lara felt comfortable here. She felt comfortable about herself, her body, and her husband — even if he *had* just been debriefed again by a passing CIA agent. She unbuttoned her shirt to the waist, pulled it down below her shoulders, rolled up her sleeves, and sat for as long as she could tanning her décolleté and making hilarious comments when men would stop to ogle her bared chest. Peter loved it and so did their friends.

"Okay guys, that's it for today," she said as she sat up and started to slowly bring her shirt and bra straps up over her shoulders, leaving almost a full view of her bosom to those who chose to watch. She started, one at a time, to do up the buttons from the bottom up. "Strip tease backwards — would you like me to start again?" She stood up to applause, did as graceful a curtsy as possible in ski boots and went to pick up her skis. She skied one run down with their friends and went back to their chalet next to the railroad crossing to rest for the evening party. It was fun seeing their friends and meeting new people. They got to know the Cassini brothers, Oleg and Gigi and, because of her bared chest, Oleg would become a good friend.

Their brief visit to Paris had been uneventful. Tia and Mademoiselle had been sent on to Lara's mother in Oak Hill — Ida still didn't care for little children. This gave Lara a good excuse to leave Paris early and return to New York. Peter would stay behind for a few days with his mother and

161

join them later. He had meetings planned with the company and Agency. It was always easier without Lara around.

Once Lara was home she realized she was pregnant again. No wonder men were ogling her breasts in the mountains. They had already filled out nicely, but Lara had not thought she could be pregnant again so soon. She decided not to tell Peter right away. "I don't know how he'll take it," she said to her mother one morning when she was already feeling morning sickness. "We are supposed to have a new assignment and if it's anything like when we arrived in the Congo he could be furious."

"You don't know where you're going yet?" her mother Tori asked. "When are they going to tell you? I would have thought you'd know before you left Africa."

"Maybe Peter knows, but I don't think so. He would have told me. I'm sure he would have told me."

"Lara, my dear, what kind of husband is he? Have you ever thought about the danger he put you through in Leopoldville? I mean, you could have been killed, and Tia too."

"I know, Mum. He's not been a good husband in terms of running around with other women, but he does love us, and we are home safely, and beside *I* decided to stay in Leo. I admit there were some very hairy moments and...yes, we were lucky to get out alive. And yes, I still don't know where we're going." She plopped down into a comfortable over-stuffed chair by the fire in the library and slowly sipped her coffee. "It's strange, taking marriage vows and knowing you won't be able to keep them. He must have known he wouldn't keep them. I feel I'm into this ''til death do us part' and don't know how it's going to work out." They gazed at the fire for a while. Then they heard Mademoiselle in the hall with Tia, who came running in, looked around, found her Mom and crawled into her lap. This was a happy moment for the three generations to share.

"Je peux vous laisser la petite? J'ai pas mal de choses à faire en haut? [Can I leave you the little one? I have a lot to do upstairs]" Mademoiselle inquired.

"Naturellement," Lara answered, hugging her child.

The days in the country passed comfortably for Lara. Peter came for two long weekends. Otherwise he was in New York and Lara reminded him that he was supposed to be on vacation with her. His answer was he needed some time with his buddies and he had to go to the office. The company was still trying to decide where to send him and it appeared to be taking time to find him a spot. The week Lara had spent in town with Peter was perplexing — he was off on his own more than he was with her. They didn't make love and Lara was sure he was with other women just about every night. He was distant and she couldn't understand why. Had she done something wrong? She was feeling sexy, her breasts were swollen and tender, her nipples hard. She longed for his caress. Frustrated, she returned to Long Island leaving Peter to his play.

Peter *was* preoccupied. He had been to see Aubrey on East 69th St. He had given his answer and now — they could place him since they knew he had gone "deep cover." He spent his days walking the city streets, thinking about his future work, his responsibilities to his country and to his family, how he would manage his time. It seemed overwhelming at times, exciting at others. The more he thought, the more exhilarated he became, the excitement of danger was difficult to resist. Again he rented a car and drove out to Jones Beach. It was a beautiful, clear day. Tomorrow he would start his new job. Today he would walk the beaches. Tonight he would make love to his long-time, blond girlfriend whose husband was out of town. He had finally made up his mind to something which had become a reality.

He didn't sleep much that night. He was overcome with feelings of passion. Lovemaking was constant and didn't leave him time to think. His sleep was fitful but he woke invigorated, and he was at East 69th St. at seven a.m. with a doughnut and hot coffee ready for his meeting. He ran up the stairs two at a time and got to the office before Aubrey had time to get to the door. He knocked and opened the door not waiting for an answer.

"Good morning, Aubrey."

"Come in, Peter." Peter was shocked to see Felix standing next to his boss. He noticed the smell of tobacco — the same cigarette butts in the ashtray the time he had passed a man in the hallway a few years ago. He was uncomfortable. What was Felix doing here?

"Hello, Felix. What are you doing here?" *A stupid question,* he thought showing the uneasiness he was feeling in his gut. He had work to do learning how to hide his feelings.

"What have you been up to since we last met in Cairo?" Felix asked, echoing the passwords of Peter's Middle East trip.

"Aubrey hasn't filled you in?" Peter said looking from one to the other — both shook their heads. "We lived through the riots in Leo, traveled through the Congo on reconnaissance with the UN, did quite a lot of work for the State Department. Anything else he needs to know, Boss?"

"That seems to cover it, except, tell Felix what the American consulate told you about him just before you left Cairo."

"Really want me to spill the beans?"

"Yeah."

Peter hedged a moment trying to soften the blow — then thought Aubrey was telling him what to do. He didn't like it, and felt he was being disloyal to his country. "They think you might be a double agent, working with and for the communists."

Felix let out a hoot of laughter.

"Please, Felix," Aubrey interrupted. "You have decided to accept our offer? This might be something we could ask you to do. Felix is not a double agent (*maybe not yet,* Peter thought) and not deep cover because they know of his existence in Egypt." This was getting complicated. He wanted a few minutes to sort things out. He asked a series of questions to which he already knew the answers, his thoughts raced on. He hoped he wouldn't be working with Felix, but then, why was he here if it wasn't for that?

"Aubrey, can we talk alone?"

"Felix will be one of the few people who will know you work for us. You seem reticent, Peter. You will have more training and will be well prepared for your work. You already are excellent with the basics. No one in Africa suspected you were working for the Agency. It's easy to keep it that way. What do you say?"

Both men sat down while Peter turned his back, trying to compose himself. He spun around and said, "My answer was 'I'll do it' earlier this morning. But it sounds more complex than I had expected and I will need more training. If I go for more training the guys will know who I am. Where and who will be training me?"

"Well, that's one of the reasons Felix is here. You seemed to get along well enough, but not well enough to become friends. That's the way we like it. He's an expert in the few things you need to learn. Now that this is settled we can tell you we'll keep you here for a few months, send you off to Sweden with your family and find you a new post later.

"Why Sweden?"

"Your wife has family there, she needs a change of climate and some downtime. She was perfect for you in the Congo, and we'd like to keep her that way. It's a good time for her to have another baby. Think about it. You still have ten days of vacation left," the boss said leaning back in his chair and looking hard at Peter. "Give some time to your family instead of your girlfriends. We'll have the company put you in a training program for a couple of months. Don't say a word until they tell you where you're going." It was an hour and a half before Peter could get out of there. He was anxious to get back to Lara and the baby. It was true; he had neglected them. It was time to go home.

During this quiet time with Lara, Peter seemed to fall in love with her again. He was happy that she was pregnant and looking forward to the new baby who would be born in Sweden. He had told Lara that he was to train for a few months in New York and that he would know their new assignment by the end of April. She could stay in Oak Hill, he'd come home on weekends and she could come to the city when she wanted. He knew he wouldn't have much time to play around and for once he was surprised to realize it didn't matter very much.

Lara finally was able to complete her dowry. The company agreed to ship some new things and furniture to Sweden for them, which would make their home warm and welcoming. After all, they had lost a lot during the troubles in Leopoldville. Things needed to be replaced. Peter was able to buy Lara a mink coat thanks to a friend of his stepfather's who owned a fur salon in New York.

Also, because of the two month extension they were home for parties and family gatherings, making them both happy. Peter renewed his friendship with Lara's grandfather, which made him feel as if he really had a family and slowly he became more attached to her and his new family. This was not recommended for his job. But it was irresistible for someone who had never experienced the joy of a loving family life. He knew he had to be careful. When they left for Sweden he would have to put them out of his mind until the situation changed.

Peter's training took place during his lunch hour (often extended to two) and in the evenings after work. He sharpened his observation skills, learned to notice people's clothes, the placement and shape of their ears, the shape of the head (with or without hair). He learned how to disguise himself and to notice if someone else was disguised with a wig, facial hair; changed skin, eye, or hair color. Body language was important. He learned how to spot a hidden weapon, how to use his own hidden weapon or his opponent's, how to walk into a public place and walk out as someone else, how and when to hide, how to see behind himself by using mirrors or his glasses, how to be aware of danger, how to control his nervous system — to tune out sound, light, smell, vibrations when he needed to rest and how to cope if he was caught. Sometimes Felix kept him so busy that he got no sleep. He didn't care. He knew he could catch up over the weekend in the country. Then one Friday evening Felix told him he wouldn't be going home.

165

"We're taking the train to Washington this evening. Give Lara a call. Tell her one of your buddies is having a rough time. You need to stay with him. If you can think of a better excuse, fine," he said, handing him his train ticket. "We'll meet at the taxi stand in Washington. We'll be going to the same place, 135 N Street in Georgetown."

"Shit, Felix. That's short notice for Lara. We had plans this weekend."

"You'll have to get used to this kind of thing. There are a couple of things I can't show you here. We have to go and Lara has to get used to your untimely disappearances," he said as he started to walk away, turned and added, "Has she questioned you yet or does she leave you alone? Leaves you alone, right?" Peter nodded

Peter wondered why Lara never — or almost never asked him. She probably sensed something and knew it was better not to ask.

Chapter Twenty

They left at the beginning of July, just as the heat and humidity settled in around Long Island. Lara was thrilled to be going north. They stopped in Copenhagen to visit Sam and Julia Harder on their way to Stockholm. Friends from Africa would probably remain friends forever and although Sam had been Peter's boss most of their time there, they had a strong friendship outside of work and the two women had also become very close. Africa had a way of connecting people. Far from their own country and culture, people clung to what they knew even as they ventured into new and different worlds.

Their new apartment outside of Stockholm was on the twelfth floor overlooking a golf course on one side, a Calder Oil service station on the other, and a forest beyond that. Lara was happy not to be in the city. Tia and Bazi could be out walking every day, strolling through the forest and enjoying the clean air. Peter could be at the office in twenty minutes either by bus or in their new Volvo. They had sold the two cars in Leopoldville for a good price, covering the cost of the new car. Unfortunately, morning sickness had settled in again and Lara was taken off food for ten days. The doctor had said it would change her body chemistry and after the first five days of just water and glucose she was allowed to add rice water with salt and a few days after that chicken consommé, then rice followed by a bit of chicken. She was cured of her vomiting and was ten pounds lighter.

Their social life took off when Lara's aunt gave several dinner parties and introduced them to the royal family and some of the most important young Swedish businessmen. They were also invited to the American embassy parties. One of Peter's Yale classmates was consul at the embassy and had married a beautiful Italian woman. They had twin girls and a younger boy. Everyone spoke at least four languages, which made Lara feel totally inadequate although she had become fluent in French and was rapidly learning Swedish.

Lara adapted immediately to Scandinavia's many customs and traditions. The first time she visited a new home she brought flowers — a rose or a mixed bouquet of three — it didn't matter. Another custom was to be on time. When they were invited for dinner they determined the number of expected guests by counting the people who sat in their cars waiting for the bewitching hour. Everyone got out of their car at the same time and walked toward the entrance. If they knew each other they said hello, otherwise they waited to be introduced by the host and hostess. One did not speak until introduced, so these arrivals were very quiet and formal. Usually the host and hostess greeted Lara and Peter last since they held no title and therefore would be last in line — titles came first, even if the party was given in their honor. The host and hostess left their usual seat at the table to the reigning royalty. For the first few months Peter and Lara found themselves sitting near the end of long tables at which the host and hostess were always in the middle, where conversation was livelier. Since Peter was good at telling jokes, he soon was moved closer to the hostess. Lara, who didn't like to drink wine, was constantly "skoaled" and would pick up her water glass instead. She learned that a woman was allowed to have a sip of wine only when a man looked her in the eye and said, "Skoal." This became a game for her, and she flirted from a distance, catching a man's eye even if he was at the other end of the table. She, too, found herself slowly moving toward the center.

The summer passed quickly: Lara made blueberry jam or pies with berries picked in the forest across the road, and applesauce from apples abandoned on the ground of an uninhabited house around the corner. Peter traveled north while it was still light and warm. He visited Östersund in the middle of Sweden, and then went to Rovaniemi on the Finnish border. There wasn't much for him to do up there either for the Agency, who had told him to take it easy, or for Calder, since oil was supplied pretty much by the government. The expansion of service stations in southern Sweden was already under way. He was there as a retail advisor only.

The days grew shorter and cooler. They no longer needed black curtains to block out the sunlight at night, and Lara began to wish she could warm herself by a fireplace in the cold evenings. She had been attending birthing classes at the local hospital. Peter had been with her several times and was to be present at the birth. This was not yet done in

America and they both liked the idea. She thought it would be good for Peter to see his wife suffering while giving birth to their child. He would have a better appreciation for what it took to put a child on this earth.

By December 13 the baby was already ten days late. "He doesn't want to be born yet," Lara said, caressing her belly. "I don't think he'll like the cold, so he's sticking it out inside me." They were on their way to the hospital. The doctor had decided to try to induce labor with an intravenous dialator, which lasted three hours —then into four, and then five, with poor results. Contractions were slow and weak so Lara was sent home to wait. Contractions came every once in a while, and she had been told to come back only when they were strong and regular, every five minutes. Peter went to the office the next day knowing that Lara could walk to the hospital if she needed to. *It was ten minutes through the woods no problem* he thought. She thought it was neglect–abandonment of her and the baby.

On December 16 friends from Africa came for dinner together with a young Swede. A few days later they learned that the Swede had committed suicide. It wasn't the first suicide they knew of. The morning after their arrival they heard sirens and looked out the window onto the service station below. The police arrived, opened the garage door to fumes and smoke and called, they supposed, an ambulance, waited for it to arrive, and brought out the body of a man. There were a lot of suicides in Sweden, not usually in the summer when there was sunlight. Still it wasn't a pleasant omen.

At around nine that evening, after dinner, Lara told Peter she needed to get back to the hospital. "I think it's time, Peter. I've been having contractions — strong ones — all afternoon. Now they're three minutes apart."

Peter turned to their guests, "I'm sorry, it looks like I have to get Lara to the hospital. Why don't you stay for a brandy or a slivovitz? I'll be back. It will probably take some time before the baby comes, but I do want to be there."

"Come on, Peter. You should be with Lara," Raoul said. "We'll drop you off on our way back to Stockholm."

"Thanks, but if you go I think we will walk over. It's just the other side of the woods."

"You can't do that to her. She's already exhausted, look at her," Marie-Louise answered. "Besides, if it's on a forest path covered with all that snow she might fall. Do you intend to pick her up and carry her?"

"Come on, Marie-Louise, she won't fall. The fresh air will do her good. It will help the baby along." Peter really believed this. They left together, Marie-Louise and Raoul grumbling, Lara finally feeling it was okay to do her panting when she had a contraction. She clung to Peter, weighing heavily on his arm. She thought it was mean of him to make her walk, but he wouldn't give in.

It was true, at the hospital time dragged. It was close to midnight and the doctor was annoyed that it was taking so long. Lara looked at the clock on the wall; it was finally December 17. This child didn't want to be born until then. The doctor, exasperated, said, "I'm going to give you a shot to help you push. It will speed up the birth." He turned and asked the midwife, "How far has she dilated?"

"She looks almost fully dilated," came the answer as the midwife worked to enlarge the opening of her cervix, which was very painful.

"Okay, Lara, I'm going to give you a shot to help us along. Be sure to control your breathing," the doctor added. Lara was exhausted with the pushing and panting and couldn't understand why it was taking so long. The shot made her push harder and the doctor panicked. "Stop! Breathe, don't push, breathe," he said.

"I can't stop. You gave me the shot," she yelled. "I can't control it." The baby came flying out so fast the midwife almost didn't catch it. Once she had a hold of the slippery child, she wouldn't let go. She jumped up and left her place to the doctor as she checked the clock for the time of birth, 2 a.m. on the dot. Lara was in tears, bleeding badly, her whole body shaking. "Is the baby all right? Can I see it? Where is it, what is it? Please, God, is my baby all right?"

"Yes, yes," the midwife answered in Swedish. "Your baby is fine." She walked over and presented a naked baby boy to his proud and worried parents. Lara could only cry for joy. Exhausted, she closed her eyes as she felt the passage of the afterbirth, and the doctor trying to slow the bleeding.

"I'm going to put you to sleep. I have a lot of stitching to do. You ripped badly. I need to sew you up."

"What's a little more pain?" Lara said. "I don't need to be put to sleep." It was the same story for Tia's birth.

"It will be easier for you and for me if you're put under. Besides you need rest and some relief from the pain for a while. Please, it really is the best thing for you. I'm sorry the shot caused such a strong reaction. I need to clean you up and stop the bleeding as soon as possible." *Or you might bleed to death,* he thought.

Peter came close to her, not knowing where to stand. He had been holding her hand, but after the shot all hell broke loose and he had to step aside. He stroked the hair off her forehead, bent down and kissed her there.

"It's okay. You were great. Thank you for our baby boy." She saw his pale face and wondered what he was feeling. She couldn't ask. He kissed her again. "If the doctor says it's best to be put under, please let him do it. You will rest, with no pain for hours. I'm sorry it was so hard. Do you want me to stay with you?"

"No, it's okay, if I'm asleep. But please be here when I come to, that's all." The nurse put the gas over her nose and she went out with two deep breaths. She always hated being put to sleep, wondering if she would wake again.

The doctor asked Peter to leave. He should come back around eight in the morning during visiting hours. Peter asked what time Lara would come out of her anesthetic and planned to be there at that time — whether or not it was visiting hours. He went home and sent telegrams by phone and returned at 6 a.m. to find Lara still asleep on a bed in the hallway. There was no room for her and probably wouldn't be before noon. Peter, annoyed, went to call Lara's doctor who had not been on duty the night of his son's birth. Their doctor was head of the hospital and if anyone could find her a room, he could. So Lara was comfortably installed before she came to, her husband and baby by her side.

They were all home for a family Christmas. Tia met her baby brother, Alexander, and was thrilled to hold him in her lap. He was better than the doll she had used for practice. Lara was happy to be able to nurse their baby and happy to have Bazi to take care of her and the children. What a blessing this woman was; she was always there when needed and always in good humor. The week between Christmas and New Year's Peter was told that they would be moving to Geneva, Switzerland. He would be working for Term Oil by the end of January. He felt lucky that they hadn't asked him to move before the baby was born. But how would he explain the fact he hadn't even been for an interview? They had left him in Sweden just enough time to have a baby — nine months.

Chapter Twenty-one

The move from Stockholm to Geneva was easy. The movers came, packed, and moved them out in two days. Since they had been living in what was called a furnished apartment, they would stay in Sweden until their belongings arrived in Geneva. That would take two weeks. Peter left for Switzerland ten days before the family to find an apartment. They would buy the furnishings they needed once Lara and the children arrived, but Peter planned to get the beds as soon as he had a place to put them. He found a three-bedroom apartment on route de Malagnou in the western part of the city. The building had three swimming pools on the roof and laundry facilities in the basement. It sounded perfect: a large living room, one end all glass sliding doors onto a narrow terrace, the other end a dining room niche, three bedrooms and two baths. The kitchen was small. They would have to buy the icebox, stove, dishwasher and whatever else they needed and fit it all into the small space. No room for an eat-in table and chairs or washing machine/dryer. Their meals would have to be in the dining niche.

Lara, Bazi, and the children moved in the first few days of February. Peter and Lara spent the next couple of days shopping during his lunch hour and, except for curtains, they had the apartment fully furnished within two days of their arrival. The pictures were hung and in the dining area all the masques, daggers, gunpowder horns, and African paraphernalia decorated the walls. The park was a five-minute walk from their new home and Lake Geneva was just ten minutes in the other direction. All was well.

It was Valentine's Day. Lara went to the hairdresser to make herself beautiful because they were having dinner with Peter's new boss and his wife. She loved looking at all the magazines she never had at home and she came across an article on palmistry, which she studied intensely. The idea of learning about one's life from the lines of the hand was fascinating. When Peter came to pick her up she asked, "Peter, I've been reading about the lines in our palms. Show me yours, will you?" He put out his two hands, palms up, so Lara could see them. A hot, then a cold sweat came over her.

"What's the matter?" Peter asked. "Good strong lines," he said as he looked at the lines of his hand.

"Yes, they're good strong lines," she agreed. She couldn't say to him *but your lifeline in both hands is so short.* She took his hands and kissed his palms. "Let's go home. It's getting late." She started to pray and the one phrase which stuck in her mind was, "Thy will be done." Even if he died at the age of 55 or 60 it would be too soon. She wondered what it all meant, and try as she could, it was impossible to put it out of her mind.

Their social life took off — cocktail parties, dinners, luncheons for Lara, gallery openings and visits with friends from her old prep school. Even her mother came for a visit on her way back to the States from skiing in Gstaad. It was a good time except for the foreboding thought of Peter's untimely death.

Chapter Twenty-two

Early Sunday morning Lara drove Peter to the station. It was a cold, damp March day and although the car had warmed up she felt a cold chill run through her — a feeling of ominous dread about Peter's visit to Berlin, a trip arranged a few days before by Felix when he stopped by to give Peter an envelope of cash in case of an emergency. Since she had learned of the trip she had noticed Peter had changed. He was more considerate about getting home in time to see the children before they went to bed. He spent more time with them, feeding his son his bottle (he didn't like to change diapers) and taking bubble baths and playing with his daughter. On weekends he would take Tia to the lake to feed the gulls. All old bread was put aside for this purpose. And on the warmer days he would take Alex out for a walk in the park in the old fashioned English pram with its huge wheels making it a smoother ride for his little boy.

He would even call if he was going to be late — a thing he rarely did except if he needed Lara to be dressed and ready for dinner and to meet him downstairs when he drove by to pick her up. He was changing and Lara wondered why. Had he finally really fallen in love with her? It seemed he was playing around less than in previous years and paying much more attention to her as well as the children. He'd packed his bag the night before, something else he rarely did. He seemed pensive, distant, preoccupied with preparations. He'd packed a turtleneck and sports pants, 'to relax in after work' he said, and for someone who was always impeccably dressed in city clothes, this was a change. He even put in his warm leather jacket, a scarf and a wool cap. Why would he need these things since he was wearing a warm herringbone overcoat and a black felt hat decorated with snappy Tyrolean feathers? He would take a Friday night train back to Geneva "if all goes well" he had said. What did that mean? At the station he got out, took his bag from the back seat and walked around to kiss Lara good-by. *God, I hope I come home from this trip,* he thought. Lara had jumped out of the car to kiss him good-bye. She felt one of the most loving kisses from her husband that she had ever had. She, too, was praying, *I hope he comes home from this trip.* The thought of February 14 and the short lifeline hit her in the stomach, she thought she was going to be sick when she heard him say "You're not pregnant again, already, yet, so soon are you?" He blew her a kiss and disappeared into the crowd. She drove home with tears streaming down her cheeks and the repetitious thought *Thy will be done.*

As the train pulled out of the station Peter sat back, closed his eyes and tried to tune out the chatter of an older couple also headed for Berlin hoping to see relatives trapped in the East, the voice of a German businessman dictating to his secretary who was accompanying him and another man who was quietly reading his newspaper. It would be a long trip through France into West Germany: Karlsruhe, on to Frankfurt and Hanover and into East Germany, controlled by the Russians, with long delays to clear formalities. There would be yet another checkpoint when they left East Germany and entered Berlin, making sure no one had left the train in between. He had been unable to catch a night train and make his first contact on time. He knew he had to be there the day before his meeting. Anyway he needed to rediscover the city and the changes that had occurred since he had been there with the U.S. Army in 1954. The wall had gone up. On August 13, 1961, barbed wire had closed off the Allied sector from East Berlin. It took twenty four hours. People were caught off guard. Families were separated and could not return — one direction or the other. On the 13th a GDR soldier helped a child who wanted to get back to his parents in East Berlin. He was reprimanded for it and moved to another post. People were jumping the wire fence, fleeing the East. Concrete reinforced slabs were put up creating a real barrier but before the concrete slabs were put in place, several GDR guards made their leap to freedom too. The houses along the wall became another escape route. Parents and children would jump from the sixth floor windows into sheets held tightly by West Berliners. The children managed to be caught; the older and heavier almost always had injuries. By October 1961 the bricklayers had closed off all windows facing the wall. Escape routes became more difficult. Peter had read in the newspapers about a tunnel being dug from West to East and another from East to West. They were to meet somewhere in the middle, but unfortunately they passed each other causing a weakness under a building. The building and the tunnels collapsed. The diggers in the East were executed and propaganda went out saying that those who helped others to escape were terrorists and the West was abducting East Berliners. Peter knew there were twenty-five kilometers of wall. Where the river Spree and the many canals roamed through the city, the Wall went under the water and above the water was barbed wire, making it impassable. Some wooden guard posts had been put up. Otherwise the wall was mostly guarded by military patrol on both sides. There was no more traffic from one side of the city to the other than there had been in 1954. Trolley lines stopped at the wall. No trains from East to West, no workers living on the opposite side from where they worked could get to their jobs, causing havoc in their lives and economic recession for most of the population. The U.S. was pouring money into West Berlin trying to keep it prosperous, and succeeding relatively well. Peter's official trip was to look into service station expansion in West Berlin and eventually move into East Berlin, which up until now no Allied oil company had been able to do. Peter had other thoughts on his mind. He didn't remember when he had been taken in as a double agent. Had it been his boss's idea? He couldn't even remember that. All he knew now was that he wanted out. His missions had become too dangerous, particularly this one. He had had feelings about this one from the moment he saw who was waiting for him on the street in Geneva to inform him about his mission. Of course he was perfectly suited for it. He'd spent a lot of time during his military service in this area. He spoke the language as well as any Berliner. He didn't understand, couldn't figure out why he was to cross at the Brandenburg Gate rather than Checkpoint Charlie where all Allied personnel and Allied visitors passed. He felt he was being set up, was being used and eventually would be eliminated. And then he knew that was all part of the job. He'd agreed to it all. That was before he had had to get married and now there were the children. What would happen to Lara and the children? They had said they'd be taken care of. Today, he loved them and wanted out. He dozed off and woke to the smell of food and wondered if the dining car was still serving. Food might settle his upset stomach and a couple of whiskeys calm his mind. He got up and staggered to the movement of the train, washed his hands on the way to the dining car and found it almost empty.

"Good afternoon," he said to the captain. "Am I too late to get a bite to eat?"

"The kitchen is closed until dinner. However, if you would be satisfied with cold meat, bread and salad, I think we can take care of you."

"Great, where would you like me to sit?"

"All the free tables have been set for dinner. Perhaps you could join someone," the Captain answered, pointing him in the direction of the occupied tables. Peter spotted an attractive woman sitting by herself at a table for two and headed for her with a smile on his face.

" May I join you? The Captain asked me to sit at a table already occupied. They want to set up the others for dinner."

She looked up from her book to see an attractive man dressed in a well-fitting dark gray business suit smiling at her. Caught unprepared, she answered, "Please." and returned to her reading. She had a hard time concentrating and finally gave in to her desire to know something about her new traveling companion. They chatted until the dining car was open for dinner, asked how late they could dine and said they would be back, thanking the captain with a large tip. Walking back to their seats Peter came up from behind, put his arms around her, turned her to him and gently moving a hand along her neck to the back of her head, started to kiss her at first slowly and softly, then with more passion as he felt her body melt into his. Pressing her back against the wall his hands held her buttocks, then caressed their firmness and slid up and around to her breasts. She let out a groan of pleasure as her hand wandered to his groin, fondling his hardened sex. They both wanted each other and knew the only private place would be the "WC" — tight quarters, but sufficient for their needs. They closed the door arranging themselves a bit awkwardly with the help of pushing, shoving and a lot of laughter. They took their pleasure, cleaned up and went back to their seats saying they would meet again for dinner, both hoping for a repeat performance. Sex was the best release for nervous tension and Peter needed all he could get. Obviously this woman enjoyed it, too. It wasn't the first time this had happened to her. A woman with a past, Peter thought. He would ask her about her past at dinner. She was sitting at a table for two sipping a whiskey when he arrived. "Good evening," he said in faltering German, still pretending a poor knowledge of the language. "May I join you?"

"Please," she answered with a warm smile. *Tonight is going to be fun. I wonder if he will come home with me when we get into Berlin?*

He ordered a whiskey and said, "Let's order right away so our conversation won't be interrupted. What would you like? Dinner is on me this evening." They ordered a sumptuous dinner of smoked salmon and Tournedos Rossini. They would choose a dessert later if they were still hungry. A half-bottle of Bordeaux and Evian. He said he was practicing

177

his German and would she mind correcting him if he made mistakes. That was fine for her. Their conversation continued in German with corrections on pronunciation and grammar.

"Your vocabulary is very good. Where did you learn your German?" she inquired.

"At University. They do a good job on vocabulary and reading — not enough on conversation and nothing on seducing women," he laughed.

"I think you have had a lot of practice on the latter. Are you really married or do you just wear a wedding band for safety's sake?" she asked, catching Peter off guard. He needed a few seconds for that was a question he was unprepared to answer. She saw she had put him in an awkward position. "Sorry, maybe that's a question better unanswered." If he answered the latter it would leave him wide open for an invitation he was not willing to accept. If he answered the former, he could be putting his family in danger if he were caught as a spy. He needed to prepare an answer in case there was someone else who would be interested to know.

"Thanks for taking me off the hook. I enjoy your company and wondered about you — you do not wear a wedding band. I'm curious, what kind of work are you in? Your home is in East Berlin? Or in the West? If all that's not too inquisitive."

"Actually, I ride the train quite often looking for spies," she said with a big smile. "What do you do? Am I lucky?"

"Sorry, wrong number," Peter answered. "I work for an oil company, nothing as glamorous as being a spy. I check out new locations for service stations, organize training for managers who train the man at the pump, write up projections of sales for five to ten years. Actually, I hope to get into East Berlin to look around for a few spots for my company. I believe there are no Allied oil companies selling gas in East Berlin and with the wall…" he paused, "I guess that won't be possible. Better to stay on the safe side." He wondered if she would pick up on East Berlin giving a hint of where she was coming from and he was pleased. He had remained calm at the mention of 'spy' and wondered where things would go from there. "Now you know what I do, tell me about your life in Berlin."

"I work for a newspaper, travel a lot, enjoy an attractive man from time to time. The job pays my bills and it's an interesting life. I hate the tension between East and West and can't see my friends who live on the other side as often as I'd like. Germany cannot go on being divided. People's mentality changes. The ones living in the East have become communist in their way of thinking and being. They're poor; we're rich. I get really annoyed," she said with a lot of emotion.

Peter, happy to change the subject, said, "Will you have something sweet to chase the bitterness away? Or would you like a cognac and a walk down the aisle of our weaving train?"

"Thanks, I'll have a crème de menthe and coffee. Then we can take a walk. We still have about two hours to go. Perhaps find a spot more comfortable than the last time?" she asked. She wanted him again even if he was a spy. What could she do about it? And for which side did he work? Forget the spy. Enjoy the man.

The train pulled into the ZooBahn late and everyone was in a hurry to go through the Russian and Allied formalities. It went pretty fast since Peter went through a different gate than his lady friend. When he got to the street she had disappeared and all the taxis had been taken. He asked for directions slightly off from where he was going in case someone might ask where he was headed. The night was cold and damp; he pulled up his collar, wrapped his scarf around his neck and headed off into the dimly lit streets he knew so well. He was not alone for the first fifteen minutes or so. He was aware of other people, the ones who had turned down another street, others who had appeared from nowhere. He stopped under a lamppost, looked up at the street signs, took a left and found himself alone. He walked another block, stopped, went into the shadow of the entrance to an office building, saw and heard nothing and started off to his rooming house. He had to walk fast to make up the time lost in wandering. The inn keeper would or could know what time the train got in and might wonder why it had taken him so long to get there. He had worked up a sweat so he undid his scarf. Then the bag became cumbersome and he changed hands and finally he saw the light of his rooming house two blocks away.

He was about to enter his rooming house when a voice pulled him back into the shadow of an already poorly lit street.

"Herr Landon."

"Yes."

"It is late for a stranger to be out on the street."

"Only if one is a stranger who tries to hide in the dark." Passwords exchanged, Peter followed the voice through an open door into greater darkness. Once inside, the door closed, the voice lit his small flashlight and pointed it to an envelope that he handed to Peter. "I will take your papers now until your mission is accomplished. I will be here every evening for the next three nights to make the exchange back to your documents. Your reservation is under this name. Leave the rooming house before returning the documents. You have all the other information you need in this package." The voice handed Peter the sealed envelope and a flashlight, which had been extinguished and left, closing the door behind him.

Peter thought to himself. *This is the closest I've been to cloak and dagger stuff* while he opened the envelope: *German passport, East German passport. What is this? I'm here as an East German?* He felt very uneasy. Who knew he was a double agent, did anyone know? His primary country was the U.S.A. They were the ones who had asked him to find a second job with the KGB through East Germany. The passport was under a new name — not even his code name in East Germany. Instructions for him to cross at the Brandenburg Gate were confirmed. He thought he should go through Checkpoint Charlie. Nobody from the Allied sector went through the Brandenburg Gate and he knew he had been set up for something — something he wasn't expecting. Yes, he wanted to see his superiors on the other side to tell them it was over. Could he now? Would that sign his death warrant? He felt haunted and hunted. He put to memory his new identity in a few minutes, put away his new documents as if they had always been a part of him, turned off the flashlight, popped it too into his pocket, opened the door, looked around, saw no one and walked back out into the cold night — into the light over the door of his rooming house and went in.

The warmth of the hall was welcome after his long walk from the station. He had chosen to walk so no one could follow without being noticed. Also it would familiarize him with the area, and even though there were few lights along his way at least the corners with street signs were readable.

"Herr Hermann? Is that Herr Hermann? Please come in to your left." Peter found the innkeeper seated comfortably in a lounge chair with a blanket over his legs. He must have been snoozing while waiting for his last guest.

"Yes, I'm Herr Hermann. I'm sorry if I have kept you waiting."

"No matter, your friend called to say the train was late and please to wait for you. Here is your key, room number four, up the stairs, around to the left. The place is small. You can't miss it. The WC is at the end of the hall, the shower next to it. Breakfast downstairs from seven to eight-thirty. I hope everything is satisfactory."

"Thank you, very much. I'm sure everything is fine." Peter took his key and headed for the stairs when he heard the innkeeper call out…

"Please, sir, could you lock the front door? I can't get around very easily — war injury. You're the last one in tonight. If you don't mind."

"Of course," Peter answered, went and noticed the lock, thought that he could probably open it if he had to, turned and walked up to his room

— number four. *Good or bad things always come in threes,* he thought, *what's the symbolism for number four? The four evangelists, or the four horsemen, one being Death.* He didn't like what he was thinking, opened the door into a small room with just a bed, chair, dresser with a lamp on it next to the bed and, of course, the usual ceiling light. There were hooks with a few hangers to hang his clothes on, an old framed print of what Berlin used to look like and a window with a shade. He lifted the shade and opened the window looking down on a courtyard with three other small buildings opening on to it. No view of the street. He couldn't stick his head out to see if someone could be watching the boarding house or if he had been followed. He thought of the woman on the train and knew he had to be more careful next time. He needed a sleeping pill and since the Company didn't permit sleeping pills, nor was he used to them, sex was the next best thing. And she was good at it. He had learned no new tricks from her — *too bad,* he thought, *it was good though, but it was good!*

He went to bed tired having looked through his new identity again, getting it all in place and burning the paper he was supposed to swallow. He'd empty the ashtray in the WC in the morning. He could hear someone snoring in the next room. The rhythm was so regular it helped put him to sleep.

He woke up in the dark, checked his watch and decided to nap until seven — another two hours of sleep would be helpful. He was amazed how he could sleep when under the tensions and threats of his mission. The ability to block out his thoughts was a blessing and he didn't need an alarm clock or wake up call under these circumstances. His body knew when it was time. His appointment was for eleven o'clock. There would be a car waiting for him a few blocks from the gate — he knew their plan; he had his own.

He woke at seven, washed and dressed in nondescript clothes, went down for breakfast and before returning to his room stopped by the desk to show his papers and fill out the usual hotel forms for the innkeeper. The innkeeper called out to him as he started up the stairs, "Herr Hermann will you be here this evening for supper or just the night?"

"Just the night, tonight, perhaps I'll have dinner tomorrow," Peter answered. He didn't know how long his meeting would last and if he could be back in time for dinner. Since he was from East Berlin he didn't have enough money to eat at a restaurant, therefore he needed to take his meals at the inn where they were included in the price of the room.

"Oh, you need your room for three nights? They didn't tell me how long you would be staying."

Peter turned and walked back to speak with the innkeeper. "How long did they say I would be staying?" he asked.

"They said two nights, maybe more. That you would let me know. It's not a problem. We're not a fancy hotel and often have people like you whose plans change at the last minute."

Peter wondered what the "like you" meant. "They are right. I have business to take care of and might even need a fourth night if that would be possible."

"Oh, that will be fine. Just let me know, particularly for the food. We are supposed to have a nice day, too."

It was a beautiful day and although the sun was warm the air was cold. He was happy to have his leather jacket on under his coat. He could have kept it in his bag, but then changing would be more difficult. He'd asked the innkeeper to have his suit pressed. It was a mess from the train ride and he wouldn't need it until the next morning. And for as much as it was a beautiful day the closer he got to the Brandenburg Gate, the more squeamish he felt. There was still a lot of rubble being cleared from the area. The monument had sand bags around its base and rolls of barbed wire between the gate and concrete barriers. From what he could see through the gate it was the same on the other side. A steady flow of cars and few people in the street did not distract him, for he felt very conspicuous in his good-looking tweed coat in comparison to the shabbiness of those around him and wondered if Berlin and Germany would ever be re-united.

He was thinking of Berlin, and the chic city it had been in the twenties and thirties. His thoughts returned to the present as he approached the gate with trepidation. Only one of the three arches was open to foot traffic. No cars went through this gate. He held up his East German passport to the Allied guard.

"What are you going back for?" was the only question he was asked.

"Business," he answered and proceeded to walk through the tunnel-like passage to the other side. There the East German guard took his passport and permit and went into the guard house to verify the papers, leaving Peter to be scrutinized by a group of guards. He looked for the car that was to pick him up at eleven. He was five minutes early and waited patiently for his papers to be returned and the car to appear. He ruminated about his East German boss, and how he could find a way to say that he had finished his work with them and was returning to Geneva and his family. He did not notice the car pulling up behind him. The guard came out of the guardhouse and handed Peter his papers.

"All is well, Herr Hermann. *Danke schön.*"

Peter had been caught daydreaming. *This is not good,* he thought.

"*Auf wiedersehen.*" He turned to face the car, signaled with his papers still in his hand and walked over. The driver opened the window and said, "It's too cold to be out on the street. Please get in." He started to open the front door. Peter went and opened the back door and slid in.

"Yes, it's cold", he replied, "and a fine day." The passwords correct, he continued, "Thanks, I prefer to ride in back if that's all right with you."

"Of course. Where would you like me to take you?"

"I'd like to drive around a bit. It's been a long time since I've been home." Peter discreetely looked around to make sure they were not being followed. The driver took him through the nicer part of the city where most of the rubble had been cleared and new buildings had been built. It still looked a lot poorer than West Berlin. Communism did not help the Germans here nearly as much as the Allies did in the western part of Berlin and the rest of Germany.

They passed a street corner, which Peter recognized as being close to where he was to meet his contact and asked the driver to stop. He looked around to make sure no one was watching and, without saying anything to the driver, got out of the car and hurried down a side street where it would have been difficult for the driver to follow.

The smell of freshly brewed coffee filled his nostrils. He turned in the direction he thought the smell was coming from and sure enough, it was the café where he was to make his first contact. He stopped to read the name of the street, noticed he was alone and darted down an alley on the same block — *don't change sidewalks, that puts you out in the open, dark doorway near the next corner* he jumped the two stairs and found himself completely hidden from anyone coming around the corner from either end. He slipped off his coat, which he rolled into a ball and shoved quickly into his satchel. He was now wearing a black leather suede jacket he had worn under the coat. A black wool cap covered his forehead and ears so when he returned to the empty street no one would recognize him as the well-dressed tourist he had appeared to be a few minutes ago. He continued his walk around the block, which was bigger than he had expected. He would be late for his rendez-vous — maybe five minutes. He didn't want to check his watch, inappropriate gesture for someone on his way for a casual cup of coffee. He looked around while turning the corner once on the street he would keep his eyes on the café, pick up his pace as if he was in a hurry to get warm inside.

"*Guten Tag,*" he greeted everyone as he entered, spotting his contact.

Several people grunted a reply. *"Wie geht's, Rudolf?"* he said as he sat down next to a man who was supposed to be an old friend. He turned out to be the same man he had crossed in the hall when he had been for his final meeting in New York. He was the same one who had called at his office in Geneva. Peter didn't like the coincidence. His heart was pounding, his gut in knots. He felt he was being cornered. He didn't like this mission, wanted it over with. *How did I get myself into this?* he wondered. *Merde!*

"Gut, sehr gut mein Freund," replied Rudolf.

"Kaffee mit Milch, bitte" Peter ordered. "How's your family?" he asked. This meant, what's up next? What the family was doing was what Peter would be doing for the next twenty-four hours.

"The family is fine, all are well. They will be having tea this afternoon, around five o'clock with Tante Fen. Do you want to join us?"

"Thanks, I can do without tea. Tante Fen was always on my case when I was growing up. 'Be a good boy' she would say. 'Try to stay out of trouble. You give your parents such a hard time.' They both laughed.

"In case you change your mind, here is the address," Rudolf handed Peter a small piece of paper with an address on it. Peter would quickly memorize it as if not even looking at the paper and put it in his jacket pocket. He would eat it when he left the café. *Great way to poison someone,* he thought. The two men chatted for another half hour or so and then, both left together. Rudolf handed Peter his satchel "Hey, don't forget this," he said. They went their separate ways. Rudolf had slipped a package to be delivered, into the satchel, unnoticed by all including Peter.

Peter had decided to head back to his rooming house to rest up for his afternoon sortie knowing it could go well into the night. The streets were more congested than he expected. People were on their way to lunch. It was a cold spring day and no one was dawdling. In comparison to Geneva or Paris at this time of the year, the streets were relatively empty, yet Peter felt unobserved and confident in his anonymity. He changed his mind and decided to wander around East Berlin.

Chapter Twenty-three

He walked for a while, enjoying the fresh air and trying to decide how to spend the afternoon. He passed a small pub, checked the menu in the window, and looked past it to a room filled with small tables, mostly occupied by men lunching with tall glasses of beer and a lot of smoke. He saw a row of newspapers hanging on wooden poles along the wall, *That's a good idea,* he thought. *Lunch, read a few newspapers — that should kill a few hours.* He opened the door and was engulfed by warm, smoky air mixed with odors from the kitchen and the beer everyone was drinking. The owner came out from behind the bar, wiping his hands on a dirty apron, "Lunch?"

"*Ja, Bitte.*" The owner pointed to an empty table against the back wall. There wasn't much light there to read a paper, but Peter decided it would be just fine. His back would be against the wall in the corner and he wouldn't be bothered by anyone. As he walked back many eyes followed him. He was a stranger; he didn't fit in, and he needed to act as if he didn't notice. He put his satchel on the floor next to the wall, fished out a package, which he slipped into his jacket pocket, and once he had ordered his lunch, walked over to pick up a paper. He wouldn't wait until it was time for coffee. Now he understood why spies so often were shown hiding behind newspapers. Not only could they hide behind the paper, it became a barrier between them and the public.

When he was served he had to relinquish the paper, hoping to get one back when he had his coffee. His mind started to wander, still looking for a way to free himself from this kind of work. He didn't even taste the food he was eating and by the time he was finished and had paid the bill, he felt he had outstayed his welcome. Two men had arrived after him. They had spotted him in the corner, and paid little attention to anything except their food until Peter got up to leave. They were in a hurry to pay their bill and the owner was taking his time. Peter felt uneasy again. He walked out calmly, noticing everything he could about the two customers who were trying to leave when he did. Once outside, he scooted off to the left and into a little mercantile shop.

"Good afternoon," he said to the shopkeeper. "I need a set of buttons for a tweed jacket. I've lost two of them and suppose I will need to change them all."

"It's hard to match a button unless, of course, you have one with you."

"No, I have left the jacket at home. I saw your store on my way to lunch next door, but you were closed then. So, I'm here now." He paused, watching two men in the street, who were looking for someone, probably him. "Nice man, the owner next door. He does a good business with regular clients. There aren't many inexpensive restaurants in the area serving such good food." He picked up a few buttons from the counter, looked at them and put them down.

"Usually I go home for lunch. Eating out is too expensive for me. Did you notice those two men who just walked by?"

The shopkeeper nodded.

"Are they regular customers at the *gasthaus*?" Peter asked as nonchalantly as possible.

"Not regular. They're Stasi. They are there from time to time, usually looking for someone. It's best to stay clear of them." He turned and pulled out a drawer of leather buttons appropriate for a tweed jacket and took out two different styles. "How many do you need and what size?"

Peter chose a style and started counting the number he would need, if ever he did need them. "Six large and four small for the cuffs." He paused, wanting to wait a little longer in hopes the two men would disappear. "Actually, these buttons look too bulky for my jacket. Do you have any brass ones? Even if they are old and used they could be more elegant."

"Just a minute, I'll check in back where I have more boxes. I'll be right back."

Peter followed as far as he could without being observed. He heard the shopkeeper pick up the phone and ask for a number. Peter thought he was calling the police about the man in his store who might be the man they were looking for and hoping for a reward. As soon as he had hung up, Peter stepped back into the shop and asked for the WC, which was always located in a courtyard giving on to the rear of many shops and probably the restaurant where Peter had had his lunch. The shopkeeper pointed him in the right direction and returned to the front of his shop to wait for the police.

"I'll be right back," Peter called over his shoulder as he walked out into the courtyard in the direction which had been indicated. He ducked through a shop on the other side and out onto a busy thoroughfare where he spotted an open movie house. He walked briskly up to the ticket window, bought a ticket and disappeared into the darkness. He hoped no one had noticed him. His heart was pounding. He did not know whom he was working for right now. It was better to steer clear of both sides until it was evident. He barely watched the movie. In fact, he had not noticed the storyline and he didn't care. All he knew was that he had to be at Tante Fen's by five o'clock. It wouldn't matter if he were a few minutes late. He shouldn't be a minute early and he wanted to take some time to check out the area, see how far it was for his return trip. He was worried and wondered if he would ever get back to Lara and the children. His lunch sat heavily on his stomach. He'd visit the men's room before leaving.

The sun was going down when he emerged. People filled the streets going home from work. It would be easy for Peter to find his way to his rendezvous. He had left his satchel in the restaurant, not wanting to run with it. If all went well, he'd pick it up on his way out and, if not, there were no clues as to where the coat came from nor to whom it belonged. The small package was tucked away on his inside left-hand chest pocket, his papers on the right. No bulges. He was a man who looked in good physical condition, although he knew he had room for improvement in that area. He crossed the Spree River on the Weidendammer Bridge and continued north to a fork of roads on the right. He walked quickly, stopping from time to time to use a store window as a mirror, looking around him to see if he was being followed. He took a right on Linden Strasse onto Oranienburger and a left at a church on Auguststrasse. He saw the building he was looking for with a small balcony the width of one window and five floors. Yes, it was number 80. He walked past the green metal and opaque glass doors, looked through a hole into a dirty, cluttered courtyard. He walked to the corner. Turning, he saw no reason not to proceed, and all he wanted to do was run away, toss the bottle in the river and go home. He opened the door into a space, which was large enough for several cars to park. The courtyard was empty. He found entrance C, walked up three flights of dimly lit stairs to a solitary door and knocked.

Within a few seconds the door opened wide, blocked by a large man in overalls and a turtleneck sweater. "Come in, Herr Hermann, I presume. We have been expecting you. Please." He signaled Peter into the next room. There still wasn't much electricity in East Berlin and both rooms had a single light bulb hanging at the end of a frayed electric wire from the center of the ceiling, enough to see his questioners. "My name is Wilhelm." He was over six feet tall, very heavy, fat blobs swelled around his small bulging eyes; he had a large nose and mouth. His face was full of pockmarks and a scar that went from his hairline above his left eye down to his left ear. Not a pretty picture to say the least, but he looked extremely fit. "This is Eddo." He put out his hand, European style. Everyday greeting was a handshake in the street, at the office, a store, restaurant — everywhere. Eddo was tall and thin. His clothes hung on him as if he didn't have enough money to eat well or have someone adjust them. He had long, dark hair and a mustache to match. His dark eyes danced as if they couldn't stand still. *Nervous,* thought Peter. The handshake was a limp, fishy fingertip kind. *Someone who needs to keep his distance,* Peter thought. The last person introduced was a doctor — no name, just the title. His blond crewcut sat on top of a ballooned face, and his ears stuck out. Peter felt very uncomfortable and it must have showed. He hoped he was in the right place since there had been no code given to him for the meeting. He was on his own and feeling scared.

"Can I offer you a whiskey? You look like you could use one," Wilhelm laughed.

"No, thanks. I had some trouble getting here. Sorry I'm late for tea."

"Do you have my package?" the doctor asked. "It's very potent stuff. May I have it, please?"

"Yes, of course." Peter opened his jacket and extracted a flask wrapped in brown paper and tied with a strong piece of string. He handed it to the doctor who proceeded to open it. He looked at it very carefully and tried to unscrew the top. It was on tight.

"Good. It hasn't been opened," he turned to face Peter with a very serious look. "You are in this now for life, whether you like it nor not. You must speak to no one, absolutely no one, about this meeting. I was told you work for the Stasi, but even they must not know about this. Do you understand?"

"You're not working for East Germany and the Russians?"

"It is none of your business, who I work for. You have never seen me. We have never met. Only the one who gave you the package knows where it was going and even then he probably doesn't know that either. This is top secret. Never speak to anyone about this," he said, shaking a finger at Peter. "If you are questioned by anyone — you met a few friends — heroin, black market, whatever. We will probably meet again. You will be the only courier — the only person I will deal with from now on." He wrapped the flask up in cotton and then the brown paper. He could not risk it being broken. "That is all for now. You may go. Wilhelm will show you out."

Peter felt dejected. What had he gotten himself into? He followed Wilhelm down the stairs and out to the door leading to the street. "I'll leave you here," he said putting out his hand and touching Peter's shoulder. "We are in this together. Take care, my friend, and be very careful." Peter opened the heavy door and walked out into the cold night air. He was happy to be out of there and didn't notice a car slowly following him. But Wilhelm had seen the car and knew Peter was in trouble.

Peter headed toward the river and the bridge he had taken to the meeting. Then he noticed the noise of a car engine somewhere behind him and turned to see what was happening. The headlights snapped on catching him in their beam of light. He felt cornered, no place to run, to hide. He stood watching the car. If it was going to try to run him over he could get out of its way. If they were there to pick him up, he was lost. The car pulled up alongside of him and two men in black trenchcoats, one with a black felt hat, got out of the car as soon as it stopped.

"Herr Peter, come with us," the black hat said as the other took Peter's arm and started leading him toward the open door. "We need to talk at the center. It shouldn't take long."

"Who needs to talk to me?" Peter asked angrily. "I have no one to see at your center." He tried to pull away, but was shoved into the back seat.

"Herr Schooler asked us to pick you up. He was not expecting you in Berlin at this time. You slipped through our fingers this afternoon, but this time we'll take you to him."

"So you were the ones trying to pick me up at the restaurant? You should have let me know it was Herr Schooler who wanted to see me." He hoped the panic didn't show on his face. They had called him by his real name and not the one that Schooler knew him by. His papers were under another name. *Too many names,* he thought. And now he was caught working for someone else — the CIA or who? — and he'd have to answer. He wondered what they knew and how had they known? He sat in silence until they got to the building. They took him to a back door. No one would see them go in. There was no light in the alley and he thought no one would see him come out. At least he could tell Schooler he didn't want to work for the East Germans anymore anyway. He had planned to make contact in the next few days, before he returned to Geneva. They walked down a dark hall, their footsteps echoing, through a door which banged shut behind them and up two flights of stairs to Schooler's office. *Toc, toc, silence, toc.*

"Come in," a loud voice replied. "Come in. Ah, Herr Peter, so good of you to join us," Schooler said in an exaggerated voice. He signaled to the two men to leave. "We weren't expecting you. I believe you know Fräulein Monica." Peter smiled at her.

"So you caught a spy — one who works for your side. And I thought I was home free," Peter said.

"You will be seeing Fräulein Monica again," Schooler said and toward her continued. "You may go now. Thank you for your good work. Please wait downstairs. The car will take you both back to your crossing points."

She disappeared out the door without even looking at Peter. He felt the noose tightening around his neck. How could he have been so stupid? They talked for well over an hour. Two other men were present. They sat in the shadows and did not speak. Peter could not see their faces and wondered what their presence signified. Peter told Schooler he didn't want to work for them anymore. Schooler accused him of being a double agent and gave him the choice, if you could call it that, of disappearing or working for them. He was being asked to turn against the country which had taken him in, a country he believed in. His family was in danger. His cover was blown. He wondered how he had been caught up in this mess. His life was over, and he knew it.

"It seems I have no choice but to work for you."

"That's right. You do have a family — a wife and two children I believe. Is that correct?"

"Yes, that's right. They know nothing about my work for you."

"Or the other two Agencies," Schooler filled in. "What other tricks do you have up your sleeve?" Schooler intended to make Peter squirm. "Your mother works, in a modest way, for MI5 and the French and, of course, for us, too. A very clever woman. Is her son the same?"

"I didn't know my mother worked for you or anyone else. We never spoke of her 'work' and she certainly doesn't know I work for anyone else except Term Oil. I guarantee you, she knows nothing about this." Peter had often wondered how his mother knew so many people. Now he understood.

"What were you doing here this afternoon? We went back to pick up your friends but they had already left."

190

"What friends? What are you talking about?"

"The people you went to see this afternoon. Where my men started to follow you. Did you think they had lost you? Who are those people?" his voice had risen in tone and volume. Anger showed on his face.

Don't squirm, Peter said to himself. He had an answer ready, having been forewarned that something like this might happen.

"Oh," he regretfully answered, "I sold them a few watches — black market." He reached into his pocket where he had an envelope of money — a good sum. And although he hadn't counted it, since he had to hand it over to Felix eventually, he hoped it was enough.

Schooler took the envelope, opened it and started counting. "A lot of money, the watches must have been very good quality. Are you sure they weren't drugs or was there microfilm in them?"

"They were watches I bought in the street, probably stolen. I was coming to see you and needed a little financial help."

"And your papers, Herr Hermann? Where did you get these?" he asked holding them up in his hand.

Peter reached for his pocket but obviously they weren't there. The black coat who pushed him into the car must have taken them. He hadn't even noticed.

"Your man in Geneva gave them to me," he said, hoping to find out if Felix was also a double agent and working both sides.

"What man in Geneva?"

"Felix, the tall thin guy. He said buy some watches and bring them to my friends. They'll give you a good price."

"We don't have a tall, thin Felix working in Geneva. Tell me another story." Schooler was getting angrier and louder. "What were you up to, Herr Hermann — Peter?"

"I have nothing more to say." He turned himself off the best he could to his surroundings. He still believed Felix worked with the East, Schooler's denial didn't mean much. It was the simplest way to protect Felix for future reference. He was sure they knew Felix, particularly because of his work with the Communists in Egypt.

Schooler instructed Peter about what had to change in his work for them. He could not drop out from either side. He was caught in the middle of a dangerous game.

The car dropped Fräulein Monica off at Check-Point Charlie and drove Peter over to the Brandenburg Gate so he would cross where he had come through in the morning. There was no curfew in the West and nightlife was active there until three or four in the morning. He walked back to his

Rooming house, reached into his pocket for his key, and found a paper, which had not been there before. He put the paper back, tried the different keys and let himself in.

"Herr Hermann, is that you?" the innkeeper called out.

"Yes, I'm sorry I woke you."

"No, no, please come in, but lock the door behind you. I hope you had an enjoyable evening. I understand some of the nightclubs are good fun," he said with envy in his voice.

"It was a good evening. They took me around to several places. I don't remember any names. Yes, a good evening. I'll be down late for breakfast."

"Oh, that's fine. Just be down before eight-thirty. Good-night."

When Peter returned to his room he reached into his pocket for the piece of paper. "Come to my home." An address, and "Monica." One thing he didn't want to do was see Monica again. He was exhausted, didn't understand why they let him go, and wondered how much longer he would be alive? That night's sleep was restless with nightmares. When he woke in the morning, he wondered how he had slept at all. It had been too late for him to pick up his papers and catch the night train. He would leave Berlin this evening after checking out the service station sites. He had no intention of returning to East Berlin to recover his coat.

Chapter Twenty-four

Wilhelm, sensing danger, told Eddo and the doctor they had to leave right away. It was a quick clean up, wiping fingerprints from everything they touched, leaving the clean dishes and glasses neatly on the table as if no one had been there. The window blocked slightly open to air out any left over odors of their presence. They left through a back window, climbed into an open one next door, hurried down the steps of another building and out onto Oranienburger Strasse. The street was empty when they reached their car, got in and drove off. Eddo made several turns to be sure no one had followed and headed for the airport. The doctor had an early morning flight for Frankfurt and another at noon for Tripoli in Libya. There he would spend the night and fly out again early in the morning on a military plane to a U.S. airstrip somewhere in the Sahara. In 1954, the U.S. had agreed to pay $46 million dollars over a period of twenty years for an air base at Wheelus Field. It was a convenient place to be dropped off and picked up. The man in charge was told he had not seen the small radial-engined Maxe Holste Broussard fly in and leave with an extra passenger who had just flown in from Tripoli the night before. Flying the plane was Sobeké, the Bokers' chauffeur, who had taken a few days off to help Felix who couldn't make Wheelus. Sobeké had been working on this project for years — first as an employee for a large international pharmaceutical company and then as a supplier of "volunteers" for medical research in the three hidden laboratories. He knew the countries and companies involved, the doctors and a great deal about the work and patients. He did not know who was boss. He was well paid and his conscience was clear. He helped people "disappear" for a worthy cause, and although he knew most of them suffered and would die — he also knew it was all for the greater cause of saving mankind.

"Hello, Herr Doctor. How was your flight?" Sobeké asked, greeting a tired rumpled man with bags under his eyes who looked very pale for a hot day.

"Fine, fine thank you. Your name?"

"Sobeké. I'm your pilot for the next few hours. Perhaps we can take some time to freshen up, grab a bite to eat." Sobeké said. He picked up the doctor's bag and walked off to the mess hall. "The toilet is to your right, if you need it."

He needed it, having spent the last three and a half hours on an uncomfortable military supply plane with no facilities. He took care of his needs, stripped off his shirt and washed the whole of his upper body. He felt better afterward but when he looked at himself in the mirror he knew he was tired. The strain of the last forty-eight hours had taken its toll. Coffee and food would help.

"You're looking better. Come have a seat. I ordered your steak, rare, that's how most Europeans like it, right? You can send it back if you want it cooked more." He took a bite of his grilled vegetables. "You'll get some of these with your steak. Everything comes from the States here."

"I'd like a cup of coffee, please, and yes most Europeans like their beef rare. Are you American?"

"No. I work for the man who hired you. Part time. You been on this project for a long time?" Each was trying to figure out the other without saying too much.

"Just a few months. It must be pretty important. I didn't realize the installation was so far away. Have you been there before?"

"Yup — several times. It's another two to three hours from here depending on the strength and direction of the winds. In any case, you look so tired you'll probably sleep the whole way. Excuse me," Sobeké said as he got up. "I'll get your coffee."

"Thanks," the doctor replied, looking around the mess hall. They were the only ones there. He counted six long wooden tables, ten stools to a table. *Sixty people,* he thought, *several sittings, I suppose. Not a very big base, probably not just for the lab, not far from the Middle East and oil. Too far from Russia.* There were windows on one side and doors on either end, ceiling fans and no cooling system. It was hot, and a constant stench of stale cooking oil came from the kitchen. He turned to Sobeké who put a hot cup of coffee down next to him and a bowl of sugar cubes and powdered milk.

"Sorry, they don't have any cows around here. No fresh milk. The powder's okay if you like milk in your coffee."

"Thanks." The doctor added a lot of sugar and milk and started to drink his coffee. "I'm looking forward to seeing the country." The steak arrived and he ate all he could before falling asleep.

Sobeké walked out to the kitchen. "Can one of you guys help me? My passenger's so tired he fell asleep on me and we need to take off. He's too big for me to carry out alone."

The soldier knew what had happened. He'd seen it all before. The coffee had been laced with an undetectable sleeping powder. He picked up the doctor, carried him out like a baby, installed him in the co-pilot's seat, put on the belt, and closed the door.

"He's all yours, Sobeké. Happy landing." And he went back to the mess. Sobeké stashed the baggage and some supplies in the baggage compartment of the plane and got in. He put a scarf around the doctor's eyes, hoping he wouldn't wake before they landed next to a small deserted town where a car and driver would pick up his passenger and the supplies and drive the last ten to fifteen miles to the lab. The doctor wasn't supposed to know where he was going. He'd be annoyed not to have seen the countryside, which was mostly sand dunes anyway, but that didn't matter. Sobeké had to fly back to Egypt before sundown and return the Broussard.

Chapter Twenty-five

It was still early morning as the three buses of workmen with their guards headed back toward the small Arab town where they had been living in solitude for the last three years with their families. They had been building a highly sophisticated underground complex and their work was finished. The buses, although air conditioned, were hot and oppressive for there were no windows to look out of or to open for fresh air. The lighting was too dim to read by so most of them dozed off after their long day or night of work, happy with the idea of returning home. No one knew exactly where they were. Perhaps near a mountain range — the walls of their compound were too high to see the surrounding countryside.

A few days ago they had been told that their families had been taken to a nearby airport and flown back to the cities where they had lived before being hired for this job. No one knew that they had been killed and buried in a mass grave in the middle of nowhere. The workers thought their pay was good: part of it was deposited directly to their bank accounts, part paid in cash for any extras they might need or want while living away on the job. There was a school for the children and a visiting doctor for health problems. People either got well or died — no one left the compound.

Only the bus drivers knew where they were going. The ride took between an hour and a half and two hours depending on wind and sand storms. Today was particularly hot and the heat waves rising from the sand were hypnotic. All three drivers were having difficulty staying awake. There was no road to follow, only a bump on the horizon if going back to the compound, a spot on the face of the mountain when headed for the complex. And today no one could see the landmark. It seemed to have disappeared. They had left the mountain behind them, had been driving for well over an hour when all of a sudden there was a blast. The three buses and all on board were blown to pieces.

If the explosion of the buses was picked up by a plane or satellite, it could be written off as terrorists practicing their training in the desert.

This was the third of three complexes built for medical research. All had been constructed under the sand, which was a perfect filter for the chemicals being used in the research. Actually, this complex was originally a natural cavern that had been discovered by speleologists in the late 1930s and it was relatively easy to transform it into a medical research facility. An underground river, fed perhaps by melting snow from the surrounding mountains, provided all they needed for water and was an excellent cooling system. Generators hidden in caves along the face of one of the mountains provided power transmitted underground. Trucks, navigating by compass or by the stars, brought diesel fuel in and deposited it in huge underground tanks during the night. There was no road and the trucks left no tracks. Since the sand was moved by the wind their route changed and was covered within a few hours. The generators ran only in the daytime when the heat of the sun on the mountainside masked the exhaust fumes. There was enough fuel to last for years.

Several doctors and their assistants worked at this facility. They had agreed to the conditions, understood their contracts, and knew they probably would never leave the complex alive. If they didn't catch one of the deadly illnesses they were working on, they would be shot or left to wander the desert until they died if they tried to escape. What was important to them was to save some of mankind from the dreaded chemical warfare. That was also part of the research. If a doctor died, one of the doctors already in the facility would take his place. Eventually, those who created this project might have to find others willing to commit their research and lives to the good of mankind. They also had to provide the guinea pigs for this project. They needed live, healthy — or relatively healthy — men and women of all ages to complete the work. People disappeared easily from the outskirts of desert towns but they also needed Eurasians, black Africans, and whites. This was one of Sobeké's tasks and so far no one had grown suspicious. After all, a few missing here and there weren't noticed. Sobeké removed the scarf from the doctor's eyes before he awoke and they approached for landing, taxiing toward what looked like a deserted town. The doctor noticed a high wall around the village, disintegrating, with scattered shards of glass glittering in the hot sun around its base.

"Did I sleep the whole way? I remember eating my steak. After that, nothing. What happened to me?" he asked, annoyed not to have seen the view of the country from the plane. "I wasn't that tired." He didn't dare ask if he had been drugged. He felt well rested, but something was wrong.

"You went out flat. I had to get one of the Marines to put you on the plane. It was a smooth ride. Did you know you snore?"

"So, that's why my throat's sore. I don't usually snore. I must have really been tired. Where are we?" he asked looking at the walled town and seeing no one.

"This is your drop off. Someone will be here in a few minutes to pick you up and drive you the rest of the way. You still have your bottle?"

The doctor panicked. He'd totally forgotten about the bottle. His hands went to his chest. He felt the bump, slid his hand under his shirt. Yes, the bottle was still there. "How did you know I was carrying a bottle?" He pulled it out, made sure it hadn't been opened and said, "You know a lot more about this place than I do. Tell me what's it like — you said you'd been there."

"There's your ride. You'll see for yourself in a couple of hours. It's quite amazing." Sobeké was happy he wasn't going back to the compound and suddenly realized he knew much too much to stay alive when they had finished with him. He would have to disappear before they wanted him to.

"Hey, Sobeké, how'd it go?" the driver asked.

"Very well, Lou. No turbulence. The doctor slept the whole way. Hope he keeps you better company." He handed over the supplies and the doctor's small bag. "I am on my way. Have a good ride. It's getting late — have to run."

Lou got the doctor into the car. "Wait here, please. Do not get out of the car. I have an errand to run in town."

"But there's no one there."

"Yes, it's supposed to look like no one's there. I'll be right back." Lou hurried into the town and out the other side. He had instructions to shoot a leak in the Broussard's fuel tank. That would be the end of Sobeké. *A good man,* Lou thought, *but orders are orders.* He screwed the silencer onto his Hechler & Koch 9 mm and got three good shots off into the tank as the plane was taking off.

Sobeké heard a pinging sound and knew something was wrong. He flew on until he found a suitable landing area and put down to see what had happened. He saw the holes in the tank, found some silver duct tape in his toolbox and stopped the leak. He had taken the precaution of putting three jerry cans of avgas into the plane at Wheelus, which he now emptied into the wing tanks. He had more than enough to get back to Egypt.

"So, they want to get rid of me already the same way they are going to get rid of Peter," he said out loud, talking to himself. "It's not going to be that easy, Felix, my friend. I'll get you before you get me."

He climbed into the plane, realizing he'd have to put down where no one would find the plane, and disappear. He had a plan. He'd spend the night next to Bzema or Rebiana oasis, fly east and put down close to Kharga oasis where he would hide the plane. He could get a ride to Qena and another south to Aswân. He'd heard there was work in Aswân. The Russians were building a huge dam. There was already a small one dating back to the 1900s. The new one was to be much bigger. He was sorry he wouldn't be working in luxury with the Bokers anymore. *All good things come to an end,* he thought. *But look out Felix, I'll find you somewhere."*

The doctor saw Lou reappear, sweating profusely. "Are you all right? The plane got off?"

"Yes, everything's fine. I didn't realize it was so late. I want to get back before sundown. I've lost my way more than once and had to wait for the stars to guide me. Come on, let's go," he panted as he started the jeep, ground the gears, and jumped forward knocking the doctor hard against the back of the seat. It took over two hours to get there. When they arrived it was still light enough for the doctor to see the complex, which looked as if it had been cut into the mountain — five stories of it. As he explored, he found two stories below ground and three above. What he didn't see were the ventilation outlets that went through long tunnels that came out at an angle between outcroppings of rocks, which hid them from view even from the air. Powerful fans pushed the air through filters and others pulled exhaust out into the open air. Lower down along the mountain's layers of rocks were the hidden filters which drew in the fresh air that was taken to each floor and distributed to the different area air conditioning systems. Air to and from the research area was particularly purified, so as not to contaminate other areas.

The doctor settled in, happy to have his own room. The showers and toilets were down the hall. Each room had its own sink. The accommodations were more than adequate, the food edible, and he had a clean smock every day hanging on a hook outside his door. The doctor was amazed because every morning he could tell who was up by the lack of the smock on the door.

On his first day he had twenty new patients to study before starting his research. Twelve men and eight women. He did not ask them their name or where they came from, only their age and how they felt. He had to remain impersonal. He was glad he didn't have any children in his group and glad there were more men than women. One woman was pregnant.

"How long have you been expecting?" he asked.

"Four, no a little more than four months," she answered, caressing her belly.

"Were you already here when you got pregnant?"

"I've only been here a few days. What is this place, anyway? I was knocked out — something he put in my drink, I think. It made me feel great. We had sex. I passed out and woke up here."

"Have you seen him since you've been here?" He wondered how the lab got its dispensable human guinea pigs.

"No, sir. I'd seen him in the bar a couple of times. Took him home more than once. He said he liked sex with a pregnant woman." She was starting to feel embarrassed and was pulling on her dress to hide her breasts.

"Are you a prostitute?"

"No, sir. Well, kind of. I enjoy a man's company from time to time. I had a part time job. It ended," she stopped to think, "about ten days ago."

"Do you know who the father of your child is?" he continued.

"Well," now she was beginning to squirm. "I was with two men then. One was like me; the other was a beautiful black man. I'd never had a black man before. We had a week together then he left. I'd hoped maybe he'd take me with him. The bastard just walked out and never came back," she finished with a pout.

"Let me see how your baby is doing. Please get undressed, put on the smock," he said as he walked out the door. "I'll be right back."

When he returned to study his patient, he gave her a name of Mary. He thought she was closer to six months along and didn't want to use her for his work. But he knew if he didn't, one of the other doctors would and he wanted to save the little one. He was already in trouble. He couldn't afford to care — only the research mattered.

When he had finished with his patients for the day, he found another doctor having tea, introduced himself as Herr Doctor and asked him if he had been there awhile. He repeated the same thing for his name. Herr Doctor asked if he could see the rest of the facility on his own.

"You haven't been shown around?"

"Not yet. Is everyone here called Herr Doctor?"

"No, just Doctor. You'll get used to it. I remember people's faces. You'll be 'crewcut' for me. I give everyone a name so I can keep us all in order."

"Thanks for the hint."

I'll use numbers, he said to himself. "How many of us are there? And nurses — are there no women?"

"Not here. It's better that way. We have to steer clear of the patients since they've all been contaminated. They didn't tell you?"

"It looks like they forgot to tell me a lot," he said. "Do I need permission to look around?"

"You're on your own. Better explore for yourself. Keep your emotions to yourself, too. There's no room for caring — at least not in front of anyone else." Doctor #1 walked out.

If we don't feel compassion, he thought to himself as he walked away, *what will drive us to find a vaccine for all these horrifying illnesses?* He went to explore what he had missed his first time around.

There was a group of children in a large playroom. They were all sickly. Some could hardly move; other children were taking care of them. He watched for a while and noticed that there was bonding between some and that others were loners. They were all dressed the same —gray, long-sleeved smocks. There were a lot of toys strewn around the floor, a round table with cups and cookies on it, which the children ignored, a few small chairs. There was no adult or doctor around. Children walked over to where he was standing and looked at the window as if looking at themselves — It was then he noticed that he stood behind a one-way mirror, and moved on.

He walked down a flight of steps and passed another lab. There were large dogs — mutts for the most part. Two Doberman Pinschers drooled and gnashed their teeth. He could see they were barking, but he couldn't hear a sound. The room was full of large, heavy-wired animal cages. Everything was clean. Then he saw a man dissecting one of two dead monkeys, making slides, which he quickly looked at under a microscope. Herr Doctor studied his face so he could recognize him if they should meet. He wanted to know what this doctor was looking for. Number 2 was tall and thin. He had a long thin face, high cheekbones, thin lips which he held very tightly closed, and huge eyes, which looked like they were coming out of their sockets. His only protection was rubber gloves and a rubberized apron covered with blood. Number 2 looked up at the stranger looking in on him, waved and walked toward the door.

"Hello, Doctor. What can I do for you?" he asked once the door was open. The noise was so loud that Herr Doctor didn't even try to answer. He mouthed, "I'll see you later," and walked away. He came to a set of doors where he needed to use a security pass. He punched in a set of numbers and letters and was admitted to a large area. White suits were hung along one wall, people's clothes on another. *This is where people suit up before going into a contaminated area,* he thought. He did just that. The suit was made of a heavy synthetic cloth — it didn't breathe. Then he saw a hood and an oxygen bottle and hose that had to be attached to the hood once it was on his head. The viewing area of the hood was 15 cm by 25 cm and made of thick plastic. He could see as far as he needed from side to side and top to bottom. The equipment not only protected him from the disease; it also helped to isolate him psychologically from the patients, to separate the staff from the pain and eventual death of their patients.

He walked through the next set of coded doors into a relatively long hall with cells on either side. Each door had a trap window, which was closed. When he had worked for a pharmaceutical company in Frankfurt, Germany he had learned he was doing work with the CIA. This hall reminded him of a prison he had visited looking for volunteers for his research projects. He opened the trap on a cell, leaned close to the glass pane and saw two women — one with gray hair cut very short, the other was about twenty years younger with light brown hair. They were both gaunt and their faces looked like skulls, the little bit of skin they had pulled tight around the bones. It was peeling off in plaques and was raw and oozing blood and puss. He felt nauseous as he closed the trap and thought the disease looked like "Yellow Rain," which burned the skin off humans. Or perhaps something called "Necrotizing Fascilitis" which had the same results.

He walked down the hall a bit farther and opened another trap. A man was seated on a toilet, doubled over in pain. The next five trap windows showed the same scene. Then he saw a note on the side of each door listing the product being tested and the antidote to be tried. The product was "Alimentary Toxic Aleucia" — a food protein used as a food contaminant. The remedies didn't look as if they were much good. He had seen enough and headed back to the staff quarters. He knew now that he had betrayed his Hippocratic oath, since most of the people here had been kidnapped or recruited by an emotional appeal to their patriotism. He ran into Doctor #2 while he was crossing through the mess hall. No one really paid any attention to the time of day — everything depended on the specific research group. Some would be having breakfast others lunch or dinner.

"Hello, Doctor. Weren't you working on some monkeys in your lab a while ago?" With an inquisitive look he continued, "I couldn't hear what you said with all those dogs barking. How can you work in there?"

"Oh, I use ear plugs. Sometimes I listen to music with earphones. I'm used to it now," he said rubbing his ears. "You new here? Haven't seen you before. I asked you if there was something I could do for you when you walked by my lab. Of course, you didn't hear. We get used to reading people's lips. You will, too," he smiled.

"I was just curious to know what you were working with on those two dead monkeys," feeling a little awkward, he hesitated, "Are we allowed to talk with each other about our projects?"

"Of course. That way we get input and pick up new ideas. Everyone knows what everyone else is doing. We'll probably never leave this place alive anyway, so who cares?" Number 2's face turned sad. "I'm working on something called the "Marburg virus" — green monkey disease. It's a fatal disease that causes internal bleeding, lasts a while, is difficult to detect for a few days. So the person administering the drug can be days away from where the drug was administered and not be associated to the illness.

"Some Romanian doctor working for the Allies used it against the Germans during World War II. I'm trying to perfect it. No remedy."

Herr Doctor wondered how long chemical warfare had been going on. Probably ever since man realized he had an enemy. Poisoned arrows were probably the first. The last was still to come.

Chapter Twenty-six

Peter found an empty sleeping compartment on the ten fifteen train out of Berlin. The routine checkpoints kept him up until well after midnight. His papers were in order. The East German identity left in the hands of a shadow only identified by code and he was on his way home. Yet, sleep was not easy to come by. The events of the last seventy-two hours, actually longer if he counted the train ride up to Berlin, had changed his life and probably his life expectancy. He'd seen Monica get on the train. At least she'd the discretion to leave him alone with his thoughts. He wondered when he would see her again. He knew he had to make contact with Felix or someone from the Agency, and it was not going to be easy. His mind rambled through the ways to shake a tail: disguise, disappearing around a corner, in the subway, a mass of people — certainly not a car chase. He knew they'd find him eventually. He only needed a few minutes and a safe phone. He slept fitfully until he woke to a knock on his door a half hour before arrival. Hot coffee and a croissant were what he needed and he gave the porter a good tip. He dashed for a taxi and headed home. His bag was lighter, his coat and satchel having been left behind in the restaurant. He wondered if Schooler had picked them up and if he would ever see them again.

He rang the buzzer and opened the door with his key. It was his way of announcing his arrival. Tia came running into his open arms. He felt the warmth of her as he held her tight and twirled her around. She giggled with joy as Lara came to embrace her husband, happy to have him home.

"I'd hoped you'd come home yesterday. We missed you. The office said they didn't know when you'd be coming back. I was worried. Was everything all right?" She babbled on nervously, unable to contain herself.

"Yes, everything's fine. I had some difficulty getting through the Brandenburg Gate into East Berlin to look for new service station locations. Other than that, everything's fine. How have things been here? Tia, did you take Alex to feed the gulls while I was gone?"

"No, Papa," she sighed. "It was too cold to take him out. He's coughing and his nose is all gooey. Can we go today, you and me?" she looked up at him, tugging his hand. "*Maman* can stay home with Alex and Bazi. Okay?"

"Not today, Sweetheart," he answered. "I have to go to the office. But tomorrow is Saturday. We can go then. What do you say?"

"Yes, Papa, yes!" she said with glee and ran back to her room to play. Lara followed Peter to their bedroom and started to unpack while he went to shower and shave.

"Peter," she called into the bathroom, "where's your coat?" His leather jacket lay on the bed. There was no coat on the stand in the entrance. "Did you forget it somewhere?"

"Oh, shit," she heard him exclaim. "I must have left it at the hotel. I'll give them a call from the office. Had to leave the hotel in a hurry to catch the train. My meeting went on much longer than I thought it would." He turned off the shower and stepped into the steamy bathroom reaching for a towel. "My raincoat, it must be in a closet somewhere. Can you find it for me? And that cashmere and silk scarf your mom gave me for Christmas." He wrapped the towel around his waist and went into the bedroom to dress. She had laid out his shorts and undershirt, navy blue socks, white shirt and a belt. The rest she knew he'd want to choose himself. He left the tee shirt folded on the bed thinking it was warm enough without it. Berlin had been chilly in more ways than one. Even his mind seemed frozen in time. He stepped out onto the balcony to see what was going on below. Four stories below he saw Monica leaning against a car, talking to a man twice her size. He stepped back quickly, hoping neither of them had seen him, went inside and slid the glass door closed slowly.

"Lara, do you need the car today?"

"I don't think so. I went shopping yesterday and am going to do the laundry today."

"Can't Bazi do the laundry so you can play with the kids?"

"She doesn't do laundry when I'm around. But she's great when she irons your shirts for me. It's okay, I don't mind. Take the car if you need it."

"Thanks, I think I will. Where is it? I didn't see it out front."

"Oh, sorry, I left it in the street headed toward town," she called as he headed out the door. "It's to the left outside the parking lot."

Peter ran down the stairs to the cellar and slipped out the back door. They knew which car was his. He couldn't take it and he didn't want Lara using it either. He looked calm as he walked through the garden to Rue de Contamines, turned down Rue de Florissant to Boulevard des Tranchées and caught a tram to the office. He was sure he hadn't been followed. Now he had to get into the office without being noticed. His phone was probably tapped, but there was one at the office he was sure was clean. He looked out the window of the tram as they crossed the Mont Blanc Bridge, watching his fellow passengers reflected in the window. He'd get off in front of the church and walk the rest of the way. It was at a time like this that Felix's training came in handy — His trip to Berlin was the first time he had had to use these skills.

He went through the back door of the adjoining building. He remembered that there was a crossover on the third floor that joined his office floor with that of the import/export company. He had made friends with the receptionist and had taken her to lunch a few times. It was part of his job. Know the ins and outs of where you're working; know the streets and people of your neighborhood, the public transportation routes in and out of the cities you visited. It was a lot to put to memory, but that was not a problem.

"Hello, Emma."

"Where'd you come from?" she said, surprised to see him appear behind her.

"I was out for a walk — errands — and thought I'd stop by and say hello on my way back to the office," he said with a broad smile on his face. "How's the baby?" He picked up the picture on her desk. "New picture. He must be a year old now." He held it in such a way he could see what was going on behind him. *I'm getting paranoid,* he thought, as he put the picture down.

"How's yours — any teeth yet?"

"Nope, he's only four — not even four months old. They don't start having teeth until they're six or seven months. Right?"

"Right," she laughed. "When are we going to have lunch — or what about a drink after work tonight? I have a baby sitter until eight."

"Sorry, I've been away and have a lot to catch up on. Maybe next week. We feed the gulls on Saturday morning by the water jet. Why don't you bring your son? I'd like you to meet my wife." He wanted her to know he didn't want to play with her.

She looked disappointed. "I'll see what our plans are. Maybe we'll get there." Some visitors arrived and Peter scooted off to his office. He stopped by his boss's secretary and asked if he was in, if there had been anyone looking for him. The answer to both was no.

"I have a private phone call to make. Where no one can listen in. Do you think I could use his phone?" he asked with a pleading look.

"Are you okay? You don't look too hot. Got problems at home? Actually, don't answer that. Go ahead. I'll warn you with a buzz if you need to get out."

"Thanks," he said brushing her cheek with a kiss. "You're an angel." He closed the office door quietly and went over to the phone. Neither of Felix's lines answered. He dialed New York. It was 5:45 in the morning and he hoped Aubrey was there.

"Hello, this is Wendy. How can I help you?"

"I'm looking for the man on extension 73 in New York." Peter never learned Aubrey's real name, didn't know whom to ask for.

"I'm sorry, we have no one on extension 73. What is your name, maybe I can pass you to someone else." Peter couldn't pull his code name out of his memory and didn't want to use his own name. He had no choice.

"This is Peter Landon."

"Just a minute, please," the minute turned to five, then six. Peter was feeling anxious. His palms were sweating, his heart racing.

There's no one there for me, he thought, *and I'm screwed.*

"Hello, Mr. Landon, I have Mr. Devlin on the phone for you."

"Thanks." Peter remembered Devlin was in Africa in the early 1960s. The line switched, "Hello, Lawrence?"

"Yeah, what's up Peter?"

It took ten minutes to tell the long and detailed story. It was all new to Devlin. He didn't even know Peter worked for the Company. The fact that he'd been caught as a secret agent, and a double besides, was a bit much for an early Friday morning.

"Peter, this is all news to me. What can I do for you?" Devlin's voice remained calm.

"Find out where Aubrey is now and let him know. He's no longer in New York. I never had his real name, only his code name. The only name I can give you is a guy named Felix Raymon. He's been running me."

"Never heard of Felix. I'll start checking to see if we can locate your man in New York. In any case, we know you feel cornered and you've been turned."

207

"Yeah, I feel I'm about to disappear." He sounded worried and sad. "Just make sure, if I do, that my family gets my life insurance and is protected from those bastards. The Agency promised they'd be taken care of when I went deep." Silence followed. "Did you get all that, Lawrence?"

"Yes, Peter. Where can we reach you if we need to?"

"Don't think that's possible. They'll know Felix. Maybe he's one of them. I don't know." Peter felt he was losing control. He panicked and was about to break down. "I have to go. My boss is coming back. It's his phone — secure. Don't know who or where to call if I get the chance. Send me a coded message to my office in Geneva. I'll figure it out. Where I can call again if I get the chance." He was repeating himself. "Thanks." He hung up and sat sobbing quietly. He was breaking down at the wrong time and he knew it. Pulling himself together, his face turned away, he walked out past the secretary. Calling back, "Thanks. I'll see you later," he disappeared around the corner.

The rest of the day was uneventful. He returned home the way he had left in the morning and didn't notice anyone following him. He tried to act as normal as possible and while he felt safe at home, as soon as he left the apartment he became worried and ill at ease. He loved his family, wished he'd never become involved in this mess and wanted out. There was nowhere to go. Lara noticed the change in her husband. Since she had never questioned him before, she thought she shouldn't start now. Their beds were still side-by-side but since his return from Berlin he had kept his distance. Weeks had gone by and they hadn't made love. She wondered what had gone wrong.

Tori came through Geneva on her way home from skiing in Gstaad. They went to parties and auctions where she bought several paintings — Vlaminck, Renoir, a Mani Katz — which she carried home with her on the plane. And during Lent they went to church every Sunday. When they lived in Africa and Sweden they had hardly ever gone to church. Here they found a small Episcopal church with a young priest and a lively group of parishioners. Church was becoming an agreeable Sunday event.

They went with Lorna and Josh who were friends from the States to a performance of Mozart's Requiem in the Protestant Cathedral of St. Pierre. Lara had been fascinated by this edifice, which had originated in the twelfth century and had been finished a century later. Actually the first church built on the site dated back to the mid-fourth century. The Romans then constructed a large cathedral in 1000 A.D. These walls were the foundation for the cathedral that stood there now. The interior was sober and perfect for music, and although the choir was not famous their concerts were. The Requiem started at two in the afternoon and was so long they had a two-hour break for dinner before returning. During dinner, Peter excused himself and headed for the men's room. He left the restaurant for some fresh air and ran into Monica who pulled him into the shadows of a doorway.

"You've been running away from me," she said as she put her arms around him and pulled him against her. She kissed his lips and moved hers slowly to his ear. "We need some information on three pharmaceutical companies. The doctor you saw in Berlin was working for one of them. They flew him to Tripoli and he's disappeared." She loosened her grip.

"You know I don't have anything to do with drugs or drug companies," he said, pulling away.

"You do now. One of them is in South Africa, another in the U.S. We think you can find the third one through these two. I'll be in touch next week. Otherwise you know where to call if you need to meet with me. Be careful, this one is bigger than both of us." She patted his behind and walked away, swinging her hips.

Peter walked back into the noise and smoky heat of the restaurant. He went to wash his hands and to make sure there was no lipstick on his face before returning to the table.

"You look pale, my friend. What happened to you in the men's room? Someone make a pass at you?" Lorna asked. Everyone laughed.

"How did you guess?" he laughed back. "You never know when someone's going to find you sexy." He reached for his glass of wine, fumbled and caught his water glass instead. His hands were shaking, his stomach churning. He couldn't finish his dinner and excused himself. "I'm going outside to get some fresh air. I'll see you all back in church." He handed Lara money to pay for dinner, drank the last of his wine, and left.

"What's wrong with him? Lara, I've never seen him like that," Josh asked. They had been classmates at Yale and knew each other pretty well.

"I don't know. Ever since he returned from Berlin he's been different — edgy. Maybe it's just his new job," she said looking at her watch. "We'd better pay and get back to the concert." Peter wasn't there. When Lorna and Josh dropped her home she found him asleep and crawled into bed next to him.

March turned into April. One day she stood in the parking lot looking down at her black polished shoes, which blended with the cold hard asphalt. Absentmindedly she looked up and remembered she was going to pick up Peter when he got out of the office. They were to drive into France to get some flowered material they had ordered for new bedroom curtains and bedspreads. Picking it up in France meant no customs tax and they had planned to return to Geneva by a small road with only one checkpoint. It was raining which meant also that they probably would not be stopped and the trunk of the car would remain unopened.

Lara pulled out of the parking lot, turned left heading for the center of town and Peter's office. She had to concentrate to remember the way since they had only been there six weeks. Usually Peter drove and she didn't know her way around. She found a parking place across from the entrance and turned to keep an eye out for his arrival.

Peter had been in his office that afternoon. His private line had rung only once and was a call he had been expecting. He listened carefully to the man's voice, which he knew well, answered with an "okay" and hung up. His mind started to race. So many thoughts. *Hugo was coming to see him. They had never met before. Head of Station was angry about the situation and Hugo was coming to give him orders.* Peter thought to himself. *It sounds like I've gotten mixed up in something where I don't belong* and he tried to think how he had been caught and about the information he had unknowingly received.

There was a knock on his door and a man of medium height and weight walked in not waiting for an answer to his knock. He was dressed in a dark beige suit which seemed to float around him, a dark brown shirt and black tie made him look somber and foreboding. "Hi, I'm Hugo, let's take a walk." Hugo knew Peter from pictures he had seen in his file and also from a brief passing in the hall by the elevator. Peter knew Hugo only by his voice, yet there was something familiar about him. Was this the same person in the hall in New York City? *He must be my boss—and he reminds me of Felix.* Without answering, Peter followed Hugo out of the room, down the hall to the stairwell that nobody used. They needed to get away from any possibility of being overheard.

"It looks like you've gotten in over your head, lover boy, and nobody is happy about it."

Peter did not understand what all the fuss was about and asked, "What are you talking about? I've been following instructions and fulfilling my work for Term Oil, maintaining my cover. What's wrong?"

"You've been meeting people who are out of your calling area. They've passed information on to you which you should never have seen or accepted. Now they're insisting you deliver it to the other side. Are you a double agent? We're wondering about that, too."

"You've got to be kidding," Peter replied trying to restrain his anger.

"No, I'm not kidding. Remember the Mozart concert you and your wife went to with Lorna and Josh? You stopped to talk to a woman outside before going to the men's room."

Peter remembered the woman, of course; Monica. Good looking, sexy dress plunging down the front to her waist, which was petite, the skirt short, tight and slit up the side, black stockings and high heels — she had a beautiful silhouette. She had stopped Peter, said a few words, kissed him and handed him her program asking him to call. Peter had stuffed the program into his jacket pocket, gone on to the men's room and returned to his friends and Lara for the rest of the concert. Except that since he wasn't feeling well he had skipped the rest of the concert and had gone home.

"Yes, I remember." He was annoyed. "Did you talk to Lawrence Devlin? He knows the situation."

"Yeah, Larry didn't know what you were talking about. You told him you were double, he couldn't confirm that." They were outside in the warm April sun. Had he made a slip? Aubrey was the one who told him to work with the East Germans. No one else knew. Peter's mind raced on. *They're letting me go, probably won't admit I work for them. Aubrey is getting rid of me.* "You must be kidding. I was with the Agency in Africa with Larry, and he doesn't know me?" *Have I been working on something that the CIA didn't even know about?*

Their conversation was going nowhere. "Anyway, I want out. You can tell them that back home." Peter turned and walked away.

They had made new friends, many of them *Genèvois* — not an easy thing to do because society in Geneva was usually closed to foreigners. There were too many of them around. One morning, Lara was dressing for a luncheon given by Addy, the wife of the CEO of Chase Manhattan Bank, so she could meet several Swiss women. There was a knock on the door. The bell rang several times. Lara went to open the door. A man from Western Union handed her a telegram and left. She opened it and read, "Grandpa died in his sleep last night. His funeral will be on Saturday. Don't think you should come home. Stop. Love, Mummy." Lara burst into tears. The last time they had seen her grandfather he was sitting in his upstairs study, smoking a cigar. Everyone knew he wasn't supposed to smoke, but he felt he could do what he wanted. After all, he was 96 years old and the only person he hid his cigar butts from was his wife, who would collect them after he had thrown them out the window. They always landed on the air conditioner below. She knew exactly what he was up to and never let him know that she knew. They had become Lara's ideal of the perfect couple, and now he was gone. It was too late for her to cancel the luncheon. She called Peter. "Mr. Landon, please. It's Mrs. Landon."

"I'm sorry, he's not in the office right now. Would you like to leave a message?" a sweet female voice said.

"Do you know when he'll be back? I need to talk to him," she sobbed.

"He said he'd be back before lunch. Would you like him to call you as soon as he gets in?"

"Yes, please, as soon as he gets in." She hung up the phone and looked at her watch. It seemed she was watching the time go by more and more often. She thought, *I should try spending a day without my watch or a clock.* For some reason she remembered reading a magazine about palmistry at the hairdresser's in February. Peter had come to pick her up. She asked to see his hands. She took them gently and lovingly and turned them over to look at his lines. His short lifeline hit her in the face. She had taken his palms and kissed them. A hot, and then a cold sweat rippled through her body. It was a sign for her. How long would she be a part of his life and he a part of hers? Peter had loved Grandpa as if he had been his own. He would be very sad, too. She wanted to share the news with him. Where was he? The phone rang.

"What's up, Lara? Missy said you were crying when you called," Peter said with a worried voice wondering what was next.

"Grandpa died last night. Mom doesn't think I should go home for the funeral and I have that luncheon I have to go to and all I want to do is cry."

"Cancel it."

"I can't. It's too late."

"I'll be home around three. You'll be home by then," Peter said with a sad voice. Grandpa was the first important death in his life and he needed time to deal with it. He left the office with tears in his eyes, saying he'd be back tomorrow. He went for a long walk along Lac Leman, past the casino to the jetty. It was a sunny day, cool, clear, with a very gentle wind that dried the tears on his cheeks. He reached the end of the pier and sat down with his back to the sun, trying to warm the coldness in his heart. He thought of his own death and wondered how soon? Grandpa's death was like a blow below the belt. He sat bent in half, his arms hugging his stomach. His gut ached, his heart ached and his head throbbed. He sat in a trance for hours, until he could no longer feel the sun on his back and got up and started to walk home. He heard the church bells chime four o'clock. Feeling guilty that he wasn't home for Lara, he went looking for a taxi.

"I'm sorry I wasn't here for you. I went for a walk," he held her tight in his arms, gently kissing her wet cheeks. "I couldn't believe it. I walked out to the jetty and lost track of time." He walked her into the living room, both of them crying.

"I had to go to that lunch. It was awful," she said in a staggering voice. "Everyone was so nice. At coffee, I excused myself and burst into tears; said my grandfather had just died. You should have seen the look on their faces. Addy got up and put her arms around me. I thanked her for lunch, said please forgive me and walked home." He handed her his handkerchief. "I was so embarrassed," she sobbed. "Thank goodness I had water-proof mascara. I'm a mess. I'm sorry."

"Do you want to go to the funeral?"

"I'd like to. The whole family will be there," she thought for a moment. "But I don't want to leave you and the children." She saw again the short lifeline in his palms. Lately when she had prayed it was still, "Thy will be done." There was no way she was going back to the States for her grandfather's funeral.

They made plans for Easter weekend. Tori had introduced them to Tina and Eric Windham-White who had a chalet in Verbier. Eric was head of GATT. They couldn't invite Peter and Lara to stay with them. Both their young daughters, Claudia and Mirabelle, would be with them and all they had left was a room with one bunk bed too small for both of them. Tina found a room in a small chalet on the way up to the cable car for them. It would be more private. They could have breakfast in their room. Easter was always a long weekend in Catholic countries. Businesses closed down on the evening of Maundy Thursday and opened on the Tuesday after Easter, giving them four full days to ski. The children would go off to Crans-sur-Sierre for a week of mountain air with Mademoiselle and her family. They would leave the day before Peter and Lara, returning two days after them. It seemed perfect.

Peter reported in to Monica the day before they left. She wanted to see him; he declined.

"I need to see you before you go anywhere. Those are my orders."

"I know what your orders are and I haven't got time. Tell me what you need to tell me. I'm in my boss's office. No one can hear." (He almost slipped and said it was a safe phone. Then they would know he had been able to warn his boss and Felix.) She asked him what he had been able to learn. Nothing. He hadn't met anyone who even knew the pharmaceutical business. He was sorry he couldn't oblige and hung up.

Chapter Twenty-seven

It was Palm Sunday. The church was half empty, parishioners making social contacts with friends — each with a bunch of boxwood branches held tight in their hand. The boxwood replaced the palms. Lara often wondered why for there is no similarity between the two. The church filled slowly as she sat, half in prayer, half watching what was going on, enjoying the warmth of Peter beside her. The sunlight now high enough to come through the upper windows just under the ceiling bathed the congregation in a golden glow. The lower stained glass windows were all much more modern.

The Mass began with a hymn — one she didn't know. The liturgy led to the Passion of St. John: Twenty-five minutes of the story of Christ arriving in Jerusalem, his betrayal and his ridicule, the crown of thorns. She felt as if the crown of thorns was on her head and there was no pain. She tasted the wine, which had turned to vinegar, and swallowed it since it wasn't bitter. She had never lived the passion of Christ so vividly and physically felt what was happening to him. Then she realized He had taken the pain away — but that was only after communion. She arrived home, removed her back strap put on that morning for her sore back. The pain was gone.

Thursday afternoon the office closed early. They were on their way, choosing the longer road north, around the lake, to avoid going through French customs. The highway was slow going because of the traffic. They stopped for a bite to eat, thinking it would clear out later, but that didn't happen. They got to Martigny, where the highway ended and started to climb on a narrow, winding road to Verbier. Lara slept part of the way on the highway but not on the twisting road that took them up the mountainside. She made constant conversation to keep Peter awake. It was a few minutes before midnight when they arrived and were shown to their room.

After sleeping well into the morning, they called for a quick *café complet* and headed for Mount Gelé and the cable car up to Atlas II, close to the summit. It would be a leisurely but difficult ski down to mid station for lunch. There they met the Windham-White family: Tina, impeccably dressed in the latest Bogner fashion, her short brown hair held in place by an Hermes scarf, a welcoming smile on her face; Eric, always the country gentleman, wore a tweed jacket with leather patches on the elbows and heavy corduroy knickers. His dark curly hair streaked with gray framed his round cheerful face. His professorial glasses could not hide the sparkle in his eyes. Wine flowed and all were happy eating out in the warm sun. Lara decided to ski back to town with Tina and the girls. Peter and Eric headed up to the top shouting "I'll bet you we beat you to the bottom!" Snow conditions on the bottom half were slow and slushy. The corn snow was heavy to turn in and tiring for Lara, who had a hard time keeping up. She was still recuperating from Alex's birth and she needed a nap. They were to meet for dinner and meet some of Tina's and Eric's friends who also had a chalet in Verbier. It was an early evening, good food, conversation and companionship with friends. The young couple was invited for drinks the next evening, and on Saturday would ski on their own.

Chapter Twenty-eight

It was Easter and late April. The *Foehn,* the warm west wind, was blowing up from the south. No one should have been skiing. Everyone knew it was too dangerous — yet Peter made it up the mountain. All of them were excellent skiers, strong and in good shape. Why did they go? Did he have a choice? He had met those people the night before at a cocktail party. To Peter and Lara the party felt hot, crowded, and noisy and the room smelled of alcohol and cigarettes. Peter was cornered by a couple speaking very seriously with him. She couldn't see his face and didn't know a soul, yet she made casual conversation with anyone who came by; just wanting to leave with Peter and go back to their room in the tiny chalet on the road leading up to the lifts. She remembered when they finally got away — out into the cold night — he put his arm around her shoulder as they walked up the road. He told her how wonderful life was. He had a loving and beautiful wife, a son and a daughter and his career was taking off. What more could a man ask for? And a ringing came to her ears. It brought back Folke Bernadotte's last words to Dr. Bunche in Jerusalem the evening before he was assassinated — "Eat, drink and be merry, for tomorrow I die." What did Peter know? Lara was scared, worried. What was going on? He'd made a date to go skiing with those strangers the next morning — did she want to go along? Maybe, she would see what the weather was like. As it was a beautiful night, it could be fun. Yet, something was wrong.

They climbed into bed, covered themselves with the down comforter, snuggled, and fell asleep. The next morning Lara woke up with a nightmare and a migraine. Peter wanted to make love and she wanted to be with him.

His gentle hands flowed over her body saying, "I love you." His lips were all over her, his tongue tickling where it was so accustomed to caressing her and they came together in joy and love. When it was over, Peter got up and asked if she was going with him. It was then that she said she had a headache, the *Foehn* was blowing, it was Easter and she thought she'd go to church. She would see him back in the room when he came off the mountain. She had a surprise for him and would give it to him then. On all fours with ski boots on, he crawled over the bed, gave her a passionate kiss and went out the door.

Peter left the room with trepidation. Is it today? *Is it Stanislas Masskoirlch and Ellie Courté? Shit, I'll never see Lara again, and Tia and Alex. What will become of them? Careful not to love — you never know when it's going to end. They warned me. I never thought it could be like this. Shit, shit, shit —* scenes of his life passed through his head, good times, bad times, dangerous times. He had always been lucky. His luck had run out and he knew it. *Time to get it over with. How can I think, say that. I can't even put up a fight. If I escape, they'll find me. Lara needs a body to lay to rest. If she does what I ask, has me cremated, there will be no proof to murder and that's what it's going to be. Me — murdered.* His thoughts continued in anger and fear. Could he escape? He could see no way out of this destiny and in panic he picked up his skis and poles and walked toward the lifts. What's it like when you know you're going to be killed — to die? This is what it's like.

He met the dashing Czech and his gorgeous blonde mistress at the foot of the mountain. They rode up together, just the three of them in silence. Very few people would be on the slope today — too dangerous. They all had the same thought. They knew today he was going to die. The two would work together — there was a plan. There must be a plan only Peter didn't know what the plan was — an accident surely. They skied all morning; stopped for lunch on top of the mountain and had lots of wine — it would ease the pain for everyone.

It was time; they skied down to the middle station and took the cable car to the top of the Tortin. There is a very narrow passage from the lift terminal to the slope. Perhaps they would push him there. Peter decided this was too easy for them. His skis were on and off he went. An expert skier — but then, all three were expert skiers. They'd have to catch him. His heart was pounding. He didn't want to die! *Please, God, don't let this happen to me! Please.* The air was warm and heavy. The corn snow could slow him down. He schussed down the narrow passage, the wind blowing his tears down his cheeks and into his hair cooling his head, which was

218

spinning with panic. When is he going to hit me? Wham — Stanislas' pole whacked across the back of his head knocking him to the ground. He rolled over and over, the snow was wet and cold, hard in places and he was losing consciousness. Fighting to remain alive, he found himself on his feet only to be hit again by this determined enemy. His legs were broken. "No," he called out to his Maker as he fell again to the ground. Stanislas kicked his face so hard he lost consciousness. The slopes were empty — no one had seen what had happened.

Stanislas and Ellie looked around. They needed time for his body to cool down and for Ellie to go back to where she was to start the snow slide while Stanislas pulled Peter into its path. Once the snow started to move, it moved so fast Stanislas was unable to move out of the way. It engulfed him as well as Peter. Tumbling over and over, deeper and deeper. It was hard to breathe. He wondered if he would get out alive. Ellie should have seen it happen — she would save him.

Ellie, watching what had happened, skied as fast as she could to the lift station to report the avalanche. The alarm was given that two people were caught in the avalanche and rescue teams were sent up the mountain. What she didn't know was that there were skiers who, seeing the avalanche, had skied down along it, seen a pair of goggles and had started digging. By the time she returned to the site the skiers were uncovering someone. *Thank heavens it's Stanislas,* she thought as she skied down to be with him when they were able to pull him out. He sat dazed, wanted to talk.

"Don't say where he is," she whispered into his ear. "Don't say where he is." Two members of the rescue team took him to the mid-station — he was on his way down the mountain to the doctor's office to be checked for any injuries. One of the team would remain with him until he was released. This guide had heard what Ellie had said to Stanislas and he wondered what was happening.

Little did Lara know that she would never see Peter alive again. Yes, she went to church. A concrete, modern church in the round, standing room only. It was warm outside and hot inside. She remembered the service — her head throbbing and people singing — light shining through the stained glass windows. After church and a brief walk around town she wasn't hungry and went back to bed trying to rid herself of an ominous feeling of disaster and the pain in her head. She felt sick to her stomach and the wet washcloth didn't help. She remembered the afternoon only too well.

She heard the sirens blow. The disaster had happened. She got up and went to the window, which overlooked the road leading up to the lifts. The road was shiny and wet from the heat of the sun — little rivulets trickled and gurgled down toward town and so did the people on their way back to their chalets. She saw friends and asked if they had seen Peter. "No," they replied. "There was an avalanche; two people were caught in it, but we're sure Peter is okay," they said and continued on down the road. Lara knew otherwise, dressed quickly, and ran up to the lift station. She tried to go up the mountain, telling them her husband was caught in the avalanche and she needed to help find him. "No one except the rescue team is allowed up the mountain."

"Please, I know I can help you find him."

Then the questions started. "What's your husband's name? Where are you from? What's his nationality? Where can we find you if we need you?" On and on and then, "Sorry, Madame, go back to your room and wait."

And so, in tears and prayer she walked back to the chalet, up the stairs to their room to lie down and cry. The huge chocolate Easter egg so beautifully wrapped up, that Peter would never see. She got up and started pacing — her head throbbing. All of a sudden she couldn't breathe any more, she fell to the floor gasping for air. It was about four thirty. Later, when she asked the doctor what time Peter died he said, "around four thirty." Other people passed on their way home. "Have they found anyone yet?" she called down.

"Yes," they answered.

"Where is he?" she asked.

"They have taken him down to the doctor's — he's all shook up." She dashed out of the room, slamming the door, and running down the stairs at least two at a time out onto the watery road leading down to town and the doctor's office. It was as if she knew where to go and she did.

She opened the door to the house and found a group of people talking, waiting. She asked, "Who did they bring down? What does he look like?" A young man came to her side and asked who she was. "Maybe it's my husband." When she realized it was not Peter, Lara panicked and the young man talked to her to calm her down.

"The avalanche dogs finally arrived: they will find the other person. You know," he said, "I don't understand. There was this woman. She said she'd stayed behind to go relieve herself behind a rock. That's what saved her. She's the one who skied down the mountain to tell us of the avalanche. When we found this man she told him not to talk, not to say where the other one was. The man, he was so confused — in shock — 'don't say where he is,' she repeated after a pause. Why don't you go back to your room? We'll let you know when we find the other person — maybe it's not your husband." Trembling and in tears, she walked back to the chalet to wait.

It was dark outside when the Windham-Whites came to pick her up. They asked her: "Why don't you come and wait with us. They've found Peter and taken him down to the hospital in Sion. They will call us with news at our chalet."

"Why didn't they call me here. They found Peter!" She was relieved and then she understood there was something wrong. "Is he OK?" she began to worry. "Can you drive me down to the hospital? I want — I need to be with him. Please," she begged.

"The hospital has asked us to wait at the chalet." Eric answered. "Come on, we'll go wait at home." He put an arm around her and led her out the door followed by Tina, a look of sadness on her face.

Lara really knew something was wrong when they told her to drink a brandy. She hated alcohol and the effect it had on her. She drank it anyway. The phone rang.

"We're on our way," was all that Eric answered. He drove fast down the curving mountain road, Lara was feeling sick from the brandy and had to ask them to stop while she got out to vomit. The car window remained open the rest of the way, and no one was talking.

They pulled up to the hospital door where Lara and Tina got out and were greeted by a doctor in a green shirt and pants, his white coat flying open as he walked rapidly to greet them.

"Is he all right?" Lara asked.

His face changed, "They didn't tell you?"

"Tell me what?"

"The guides dug him out of the avalanche; he was already dead. They tried to revive him." The doctor was surprised she didn't know. "They worked on him for over an hour on the slope — there was nothing they could do."

Lara went numb — in shock, her whole body was pins and needles. Realizing what had happened, the doctor took hold of her and slowly led her into the hospital. "I need to — no," he stopped. "I think you need medication — you're in shock. May I give you something?"

Dumbfounded, Lara was able to say, "Please." She wanted to cry and couldn't. "What am I going to do?" she whispered.

Tina was by her side. "I'm so sorry. We didn't have the courage to tell you. Eric only learned about it when the hospital called." She hugged Lara. "I am so very sorry."

"I have to call the children — oh no," she squirmed. "I have to call his mother. She's going to say it's all my fault." Lara felt light headed and sat down on a bench. The doctor arrived with a syringe and began rolling up her sleeve.

"May I?"

"Will it make it any easier? Will the pins and needles go away?"

"I hope so — just sit quietly for a few minutes while it takes effect." He gave her the shot and sat down beside her. "When you're ready, we need to have you identify the body." He wasn't feeling well about this either. *So young,* he thought.

"I need to call the children first and his mother — was — is he wearing the same kind of sweater I am?" she asked.

"Yes."

"Where is there a phone?"

She reached Mademoiselle. Ida wasn't home. She called Sasha, the French Consulate General in Geneva and a friend and asked him to let Ida know — that they could talk once she was back home. It was a relief. She didn't have to deal with her mother-in-law's shock. She had enough of her own.

"Can you come with me now?" the doctor asked.

"Yes." Slowly she got up holding onto the telephone booth for support. The doctor came forward to help her and led her to the room where Peter lay on a metal slab motionless. He held her tight and she nodded.

"Can you leave us alone?" she asked.

"Will you be all right? There's a bell you can ring next to the door if you need me," he said as he let go and took a step backwards.

"Thanks." He left the cold room and Lara walked over to her husband, caressed his face with both hands and tried to hug him. His body was cold and stiff; his clothes were dry. She kissed him and put her cheek against his lips, which parted. She needed a last kiss. She pushed them back together not wanting to spoil the two hours of labor the doctor had taken to push his face back into shape. "Good-bye, my love. I always will be true," she sang softly to him. "Good-bye." Totally numb she walked out. She still couldn't cry.

They drove home in silence — home? — their chalet. Tina tucked Lara in bed as she had her daughters a few hours before, turned out the light. "Sleep, my dear, the medication will help you sleep. I'll be here in the morning."

Chapter Twenty-nine

The next morning she woke up with cramps in her legs. Cramps whose pain she couldn't ease no matter what she did — massage, stretching, pulling. *How am I going to get out of bed and drive back to Geneva?* She thought. *I really want to be home when the children get there.* Then a reality came back — cramps in the legs were from the want to run up the mountain to find Peter. She knew she could have found him. After all, they had become one. She had lived his death, had suffocated at the same time he was suffocating. That's why she had the cramps. Somehow, knowing this gave her the courage to get out of bed and get on with it. Her mother-in-law had taught her self-discipline and that was what she needed now. She turned on the light and slowly slid her legs over the side of the bunk bed, looking around the small room where she had spent the night. A drugged sleep with an occasional nightmare had awakened her in tears. She noticed the knots in the walls of pine boards, which surrounded her and thought again of the knots in her legs. *I'm a knot today. Put your feet down, girl, and get up.* She opened the curtains and went out to find the bathroom taking her clothes with her. She could hear soft voices coming from downstairs and the smell of coffee made her wonder if she'd be able to eat. She also wondered what she would have done without Eric and Tina. They had taken her to the hospital and waited during the ordeal of informing everyone she could get in touch with and then drove her back to their chalet for the night. These were true friends.

She emerged a few minutes later still feeling dirty because all she had to put on were the clothes she had worn the day before and, for her, that was depressing. They held the feelings of yesterday's disaster. Her two hands holding firmly on the rail, she slowly walked down the stairs, a box of Kleenex tucked tightly under her arm. The box was something she could hold on to — like a child's security blanket — and she needed all the security she could get. Tina rushed over and gave her a hug. "Are you okay? You look pale."

"Good morning," she answered to all the concerned faces staring at her. "I have terrible cramps in my legs," and she burst into tears. "I can hardly walk and I want to drive back to Geneva — to be there for the children."

"Eric will drive you back. We've been talking about that this morning and that's all settled." He was nodding his head in agreement.

"We'll be driving back with Mummy so she won't be alone, Claudia and I will." Mirabelle said. "Mummy wants us home for lunch. We have to finish our homework and we can't ski today. The *Foehn* is still blowing. Mummy and Daddy don't want us to go." To Lara it sounded as if everything had been settled, unfortunately not the way she wanted.

"I need to drive back; it's something I need to do!" Lara said and the tears started to flow again. She wondered why she needed to drive home and decided not to question it.

"Tell you what, we'll drive you up to your chalet and pack your things and leave as soon as you like. We can decide at the last minute if you still want to drive or if you want me to drive. How does that sound?" Eric said.

"Fine."

"Now, how about some breakfast?" he said.

"I'm not hungry."

"Lara, at least have a cup of coffee or hot chocolate. The appetite comes with eating a bit." Tina said.

"Come sit by me," Mirabelle piped in moving to leave her room; a cheery welcome written on her face as her eyes said. *I'm sorry and I love you. You're like a big sister to me.*

Breakfast was eaten to the chatter of two little girls trying to help everyone through a difficult moment. When the table had been cleared, Eric ventured, "Shall we go?" and turning to his daughters, "Your mother will be right back. Why don't you pack up your things and make sure your room is neat and schoolbooks are in your satchels all ready to go."

"Oui, Papa," they chimed as their parents headed out the door with Lara. "Bye, Lara. We'll see you soon? Please don't cry. We love you!" They both came running for a huge hug, their cheeks dampened by Lara's tears. They stood at the door and waved as Lara rode away with their

parents.

Tina dropped her husband and Lara off at the little chalet, turned the car around and while driving back to her own, thought how different it all would have been if they hadn't found that room for them this weekend. She hoped Lara's mother would get there soon. Lara needed someone to love her, to care for her, not her mother-in-law who had always been difficult for her.

The chalet owner sadly expressed her condolences as she handed Lara the key and watched the two of them climb the stairs. Lara had difficulty walking up the stairs to the room where only the morning before she had made love with Peter, had wanted to give him a huge chocolate Easter egg, but had only wished him happy skiing instead. The reality that this would never happen again ate into her heart and the tears came streaming down her cheeks. With Lara unable to see, Eric had to put the key in the door to open it. Such deep sobbing made her short of breath and all she could do was sit down on the bed and cry. There wasn't much to pack so he did what was necessary to move things along. Lara seemed to calm down a bit. "I'm sorry, I just can't help it." She took the Easter egg in her arms and walked out the door. He followed with the suitcase and toilet kit.

"Who's driving?" he asked.

"I am. Since I can't drive and cry at the same time, at least that will do me good. Take a break from tears for a while."

When she went to pay the bill someone had already taken care of it. *Again,* Lara thought. "Eric, did you do that?"

"No, Peter must have paid it before he left for skiing."

That's strange, she thought. *Did he know he wouldn't come back?*

She turned to the owner and asked who had paid. They hadn't given a name and had paid in cash. She added that a guide had left Peter's skis outside the front door and that we should take them.

All weekend their car had been parked right next to the chalet so it was easy to put the baggage in the trunk, the skis on the ski rack and take off in a matter of minutes. Lara needed to concentrate on the winding road going down into the valley. This was the first but not the last time she would drive on this road because Peter had asked to be cremated when he died and for her to scatter his ashes up in the mountains. Then she realized why he had asked specifically about cremation and scattering ashes in his mountains. He must have known something was wrong. That would probably be the last time she'd take this road. The trip back to Geneva was uneventful. Her legs ached terribly and although her eyes filled with tears she could still see the road. Both were thankful for the silence.

She couldn't remember much after that except that she was happy to hold the children in her arms, the part of Peter that he left behind, – and to be in her own home.

The next morning Lara was at the airport with Gregory, Peter's stepfather, to meet her mother who had flown in from New York. Lara was dressed all in black, a veil covering her head. Tori's heart sank in grief as she hugged them both and set off to pick up her bags. The drive from the airport was a short one. Only the noise of the city filled the car until they reached the apartment. That afternoon Tina took Lara and her mother shopping for a proper black dress and hat for the funeral while Gregory and Ida went looking for flowers. They returned to the apartment late in the evening, both exhausted. Lara had sent a telegram to her mother who was vacationing in the Caribbean. The telegram had arrived by boat from Tortola. Reading it she had cried out in shock and said to Allen, "I have to go to her. She needs me." The thought of her daughter's pain was devastating. "Please get someone to take me to San Juan and get me on the next flight to New York. Give me an hour or two at Kennedy and put me on the next flight for Geneva." It had taken her eighteen hours to get to Geneva and Lara was thankful she had arrived.

That evening and the next, Lara, her mother, and mother- and father-in-law dined at Sascha's, the French Consulate General, leaving the children at home with the nanny. Gregory and Sascha took care of the mortuary and on Wednesday, they all went to visit the funeral home and put flowers — daisies and daffodils — around Peter's coffin. Someone had to go out to get more flowers for there weren't enough to go all the way around the coffin to cover the tin-like base on which it rested. There was water in the base to keep the flowers fresh for days. Ida asked to have the coffin opened. She wanted to see her son one last time before the funeral, but since the coffin had been sealed closed since Monday, the funeral director said it would be difficult. No one knew the funeral director had been told not to open the coffin under any circumstances. Lara didn't want the emotion of seeing Peter's dead face again, but then, she didn't have to be present if they opened it. She did not realize how important it was for Ida to see her son for the last time to say good-bye and this incident caused deep hurt and anger in her mother-in-law (who thought it was Lara's request not to open the coffin) and a greater dislike for her daughter-in-law whom she had never cared for in the first place. The cremation was put off until Saturday because Ida was hysterical at the thought of her son being cremated and would not have the cremation take place until she had left for Paris. She had allowed her terrible bereavement to show how difficult and awful she could be: selfish and out of control and yet so controlling. Lara seemed so dignified in her sorrow. It didn't matter to Ida that cremation was what Peter had wanted.

Lara and Peter had been to the American Church for Palm Sunday, had chatted with the young priest, Bill Bedford, whom Peter liked and enjoyed. Bill had come to visit Lara twice since Peter's death, sitting quietly in the living room listening to Lara sob and talk hesitantly, trying to catch her breath enough to speak. He was to perform the funeral service and needed to know more about Peter and his family to be able to give his eulogy. Often, during these two afternoons, Tia, who was now three years old, would climb onto her mother's lap, put her arms around as much as she could, kiss her mother's wet cheeks and tell her how much she loved her and that everything was going to be all right, only making Lara cry all the harder. The child's wish to make her mother happy was so strong that at times she succeeded in making everyone laugh. At those moments the look on her face was delightful. The child knew her father was no longer there. At her young age she didn't know what it meant; he had been away so much she would say, "Papa will come home! Won't he, *Maman*." Lara didn't know what to answer.

Thursday afternoon the church was crowded. Many people had come from Paris, Zurich and in fact, all over Europe, some with great difficulty as Air France ground crews had been on strike. There were so many beautiful flowers that the priest had to send some to the back of the church, reducing the space for people to stand. Lara and her mother had arrived at the church early, not wanting to have to talk to anyone. They were both dressed in black and Lara's veil, which was attached to her hat, was draped to one side instead of covering her face. She felt that if she showed sorrow that was normal and to even be able to get to the church she had to take a heavy dose of tranquilizers. The knots in her legs were ever present. Lara's mother-in-law sat in the front pew on the other side, showing how angry she was with her daughter-in-law. Lara thought, *it will take a long time to heal my relationship with Ida, particularly since there has never been any empathy between the two of us.* When Ida spoke to her friends about Lara it was always positive and complimentary, but she later learned her close friends witnessed the way she treated Lara— mean, calculating and controlling. The service went well. Hymns and music were beautiful thanks to the participation of the congregation and when all was finished, the casket was rolled out the front door followed by Lara who took Ida's arm to walk slowly out with her, leaving her mother to walk out with Gregory. It had been announced in church that the family would be receiving out of town guests at Lara's apartment after the ceremony.

Although it was a European custom, Lara had asked the funeral director not to receive at the church. Yet he lined them up on the steps at the church door and people started giving their condolences to Ida and Gregory first and then to Lara and her mother. Ida was in tears constantly wiping her face. Lara stood there stunned at what was happening over which she had no control. Tearless from the drugs she stood shaking hands, embracing friends and wondering what people were thinking of her not crying at Peter's funeral. She had wanted to be beautiful for him. Well-dressed, as he would always like her to be, even with no make-up her beauty shone through. Only her eyes showed her sadness as she remained dignified through the ordeal, which was not yet over.

There were so many flowers that they needed two hearses to carry them away from the church and back to the funeral home where Peter would be cremated. Again her thoughts wandered. They had taken him to the hospital from the mountain where they had found him buried under one meter of snow by an avalanche where he had suffocated and died in such pain. The doctor told Lara he had spent hours pushing and kneading his face into place so it would be presentable for her to see. The pain had been excruciating. Why? When you are cold you go into a peaceful sleep, but not when you suffocate. When your ankles have been broken and you're caught by the thundering, tumultuous torrent hurtling down the mountain, scaring the shit out of you. But that didn't happen either. The mountain should have been closed. Avalanche warnings were everywhere. How did Peter and his two companions ever get up the mountain again? She wondered. Did he know what was to be?

Once in her home, panic made it through the drugs and hit her in the gut. Her legs had still ached yet she could walk slowly, so at the end of the receiving line she was able to get into the waiting limo and be driven back to the apartment. Ida and Gregory drove to the apartment with the French Consul General, who had been kind enough to send his maid ahead with teacups and sandwiches. Mademoiselle had gone out to buy tea-cakes and cookies and nobody could have guessed there would be so many guests. Of course, food ran out before the reception was over.

The loss of Peter and all the activities attending the funeral left Lara worn to a frazzle. So when they arrived at the apartment, Tori said to the few who were already there, "Lara is exhausted, her legs are sore and she's not feeling well. She has to go lie down."

"Thanks, Mom," she said in an aside. "I really need to lie down for awhile. I'll come see everyone later." She kissed her children and went off to bed so that, when Ida and Gregory arrived Tori received them saying, "Lara's gone for a short rest and will be out later. Please come in and receive your friends with me."

"She can't do that! Not at a time like this. People will expect to see her here now," Ida said in an angry voice.

"The poor girl is at the end of her rope," Gregory said quietly, in hopes of calming Ida's anger. "Leave her be, you can see our friends in the meantime and Martha will take care of tea with Tori. Will you pour, Tori?" he asked reticently.

"Of course, with pleasure," she answered.

"I don't believe this. This is no way to act at a time like this. I'm going to see her," Ida said.

"No, that won't be necessary," Tori replied. "She's tired and with Tia, leave her alone."

"*Oui, Ida, laisse la. Elle est trop fatiguée. Viens, on va voir qui est déjà là*" he said, trying to arrange the situation. "*Viens. Je t'en prie.*" With that Ida burst into tears and went in to greet the guests as best she could, for she too was tired and overwrought with grief. Her tears would add to her grand entrance into the living room already crowded with her friends.

It was getting dark outside. Lara could feel the darkness taking hold of her, her moods those days were often affected by the rising and setting sun giving her a rhythm to her life and to the depression which was slowly taking possession of her body, mind and soul. She stood looking out the window and noticed as the light outside disappeared the more she saw of her image reflected in the window. She remembered she used to put on the records and practice the twist until she got it right. She loved to dance, it was great exercise and it gave her something to do when Peter was away. And Peter was away again. Forever! She turned around and went over to the phonograph, chose a record, not the twist, music by Lester Lanin and began to dance by herself — empty arms, a huge void. She heard the children. Tia was in the tub with bubble bath; she used to take bubble baths with her father, splashing and happily playing. Alexander was crying, she supposed he felt neglected and went to pick him up. He was an unhappy baby, just four months old with no father. Lara hugged him to her, returned to the living room and started dancing with him. Her arms were no longer empty. She clung to him as they moved, swayed, spun around. The baby stopped crying, Lara's tears took over and finally sobbing so hard she had to sit down trying to get control of herself, an impossible task at that time. Tia came in and saw her mother's tears, ran over and tried to climb into her lap, which was difficult with her little brother already there. Lara moved Alex to one side, making room for her and they sat for a long time together. Lara was finally calming down. The record had ended and the tuc-tuc-tuc of the record continued until Mademoiselle came in and turned it off. It was suppertime for the children.

Several days later the movers came. That was Thursday. The Monday before Ida and Gregory drove Mademoiselle and the children back to Paris, and that same afternoon a limousine picked up Tori and Lara to accompany Peter to the crematorium. Bill, the priest, was there, waiting for them. Lara was thankful she had asked him to be there — so was Tori — sharing the burden with him made it easier on all of them. They remained silent until the coffin was brought into a waiting area and placed on a table, part of a moving belt, which would slide the coffin into the furnace. The funeral director said, "Would you like a few minutes to say a prayer, Father?"

Bill turned to Lara who nodded, "Thank you, yes. We'll be a few minutes." He pulled out his Bible and read, "Let not your hearts be troubled: Believe in God, believe also in me. In my Father's house there are many mansions. If this were not so I would have told you." He read through verse 14 of St. John, Chapter 14, and then turned to The Book of Common Prayer, The Committal and read "And we commit Peter's body to the ground, earth to earth, ashes to ashes, dust to dust. The Lord bless him and keep him, the Lord make his face to shine upon him and be gracious unto him, the Lord lift up his countenance upon him and give him peace. Amen."

"Is there something else you'd like me to read, Lara?" She shook her head, her eyes were closed, most of her face hidden behind a wet handkerchief. "How about you, Tori?"

"No, thank you, Bill." She put her arm around Lara's waist and held her tightly, nodding to Bill to do the same.

"I'll get the director and tell him we're ready," he turned toward the door. "I'll be right back."

Lara and Tori stood waiting. Lara's whole body was shaking, an uncontrollable trembling, the way it had when she had broken her leg in Val d'Isère. She had gone into shock again. When Bill returned he saw the pain of two women whom he had grown to admire, "Are you sure you want to be here when the coffin goes? Why don't we wait outside? The director will be out to talk to us when it's all over."

"No, Bill," Lara sobbed. "I have to be here with him when he goes. I promised I would." She opened her eyes and looked around. She wanted to face what was happening. The room was draped in mauve satin, there was a small altar with a cross. There was no Christ on the cross. Of course, He had risen. Why couldn't Peter have risen, why was it Easter Sunday? Peter would never rise again. And she watched the coffin slide easily behind a set of curtains and a few minutes later heard the roar of the gas flames burning the body of her beloved husband. She wanted to faint and couldn't even collapse, for Bill and her mother were holding on to her so tightly that she felt she was their support instead of it being the other way around. The horror of it all was overwhelming and the spell the act had produced lasted until the Funeral Director came in to say it was finished.

"Thank you," they all said in unison, turned and walked out in silence. They got into the limousine, Bill joined them saying he'd come back for his car later. He thought they could use his company; he knew he needed theirs. This was a first for him too.

The movers arrived a few days later. Everything was to be finished by Friday evening, a night in a hotel and then they'd be on their way to Paris.

Lara watched their belongings disappear off the walls, out of the cupboards and closets, being wrapped and packed into cartons of all sizes. It was fascinating seeing her life with Peter put into boxes. All their memorabilia from Africa, which Peter had put on the walls around the dining room table — gone.

"You know, Miss," she heard one of the movers say, "I was caught in an avalanche, eight hours," he said as he packed a painting. "I was lucky. I poked a hole in the snow, in the right direction. I had air to breathe, they found me." He saw Lara was feeling distressed. " Miss, I'm sorry, they found your man too late." Lara moved away as far as she could get. She didn't want to hear any more.

Chapter Thirty

Heavily medicated, Lara helped Tori pack the car with their personal belongings for their stay in Paris and, carefully carrying Peter's urn, drove off to spend the night at the Hotel de la Poste in Beaune, feeling they deserved a good dinner and an excellent bottle of Burgundy. They planned to arrive the next afternoon in Paris, both hoping not to have a migraine on the way. Lara was glad the children had left for Paris with Bazi and Peter's mother. It would be easier for the children not to see their belongings being packed up, the apartment upside down, and their mother constantly in tears. The change of scenery would be good for them. They had a huge enclosed garden to play in. The sheep, originally bought to keep the lawn cut instead of needing a gardener, had been sold so the garden would be rid of the turds and totally theirs.

Lara wondered how all this was going to work out because she knew Ida hated little children and to have four extra people in her one bedroom apartment in *La Maison Rose* was going to be trying for everyone. As it turned out, by the time Lara and Tori arrived, Ida had procured the upstairs apartment for Lara, Bazi and the children. The occupants had gone away for the summer and the woman who was using the apartment was asked to find other lodgings for the month.

Ida had a constant flow of tears and friends every afternoon. Her tears came freely, easing her pain. Unfortunately it was not so for Lara who became *la jeune fille de la maison*, meaning she was there to serve tea and fetch whatever Ida asked for. She had little time with the children and even less for herself and her own grieving process. Every morning a pile of condolence notes arrived in the mail for Ida, who was surprised when she opened some to find the greeting addressed to Lara. She read them all and with annoyance put Lara's aside, saying to herself, why do people write to her here? This is my home, not hers. She was even more annoyed when Lara asked her not to open her mail and just put it aside for her later. They would go to the hairdressers together where Ida would answer her letters under the dryer, tears streaming down her cheeks, her handkerchief would be a dirty gray from the mascara and make up which got washed away by the tears and quickly replaced before leaving the salon. Lara just sat in a daze unable to do anything while the hairdresser worked on her hair. Returning to the apartment Lara would rush to find the children and some peace and quiet until the afternoon visits began.

One afternoon Peter's nanny, Schwester, and her husband arrived from Wiesbaden, Germany, the city where Peter was born. Schwester had come a long way to see Ida and Peter's children. She had already met Lara when Peter had brought her for a visit to Wiesbaden during one of their holidays away from Africa. Schwester had left her bedroom to the two young ones, the large, carved wooden bed piled high with the down comforter. The room wasn't large, but then the only thing they would do was sleep there. The house was small and hospitable, the living room, dining room and kitchen all in one space so family and friends would always be together. The young couple's visit had filled Schwester's heart with joy. Happy to see "her little boy" grown up, a handsome man with a beautiful wife and even though Lara spoke almost no German they still understood each other. Other guests who came calling for Ida that afternoon were asked to come back some other time.

On another afternoon Ida's friend Carla Riche came to take pictures of Ida and her grandchildren. Unfortunately, that morning Tia had taken her pink plastic scissors and cut holes in her little brother's hair. He was a mess and totally unpresentable. Ida was furious to see the mess Tia had made and scolded her and Lara with such a loud angry voice that both children wouldn't stop crying. Hours later with the situation under control, Carla placed the children in such a way that there were no signs of damage and pictures were taken that became part of a disagreeable memory for Lara.

Sunday before Lara's departure for the States, her mother-in-law had to get rid of Lara and sent her to the races at Longchamp where friends could take care of her in their box. She thought it would be fun for everyone since her friends' horses would be racing and Lara had loved going to the races. Going to an owner's box on a weekend, people dressed, men in morning suits, women in beautiful silk dresses with a warm jacket or stole and a beautiful hat usually large brimmed. Lara was wearing black since

233

Peter had died and she chose to remain in mourning to go to the races. This provoked her mother-in-law into making all kinds of uncalled for remarks about how she looked. Lara ended up saying, "If you want me to go to the races, this is what I'm wearing. It's a chic black dress from Dior, which Peter bought me this spring. He loved me in it and it's what I'm going to wear or I won't go to the races. Why aren't you coming to the races with me?"

"Oh, I can't do that," Ida answered. "It wouldn't be appropriate for me to be seen at the races only two months after my son died. Besides, I have Ambassador Charpentier, Couve de Murville and a few friends from England coming for tea this afternoon. Maria is coming to serve, so I don't need you and everything is all organized. Gregory will drive you to Longchamp and Freddy will drive you home."

"If it's inappropriate for you to go to the races, it's inappropriate for me to go," Lara said impertinently.

"Oh, it's not inappropriate for you, my dear, you need to get on with your life, meet new people, find yourself another man." Actually, people had bets on her being married before a year of mourning was over.

Lara was shocked by her statement. She thought, *you don't want to be financially responsible for me and your grandchildren, so the sooner I get remarried the better for you. Well, Grandma, it's not going to be that way. You can get rid of me for the afternoon and I'm out of here in four days so you can't boss me around any more. Your son didn't provide for our future, so you're going to have to help.* All she could say was "How can you say such a thing?" and Lara's thoughts went back to conversations she and Peter had had a few weeks before he died. He had told her what he wanted in case something happened to him. And again she wondered, *did he know he was going to die soon? Why did he want to be cremated right away, have his ashes blown and scattered in the wind on top of a mountain; did he know when he was going to die?* Her thoughts raced on in so many directions that she burst into tears and fled into the garden as far away as she could get from everyone.

The races were misery for her. Although she loved the feeling of the thundering hooves moving through her whole body, the noise of the crowd was too much and again finding herself in tears, she excused herself, said she would find a taxi home and went back to *La Maison Rose*.

Much to her surprise, the inner courtyard was filled with cars and chauffeurs. There must have been five different ambassadors' cars there, all from different countries. You could tell by the license plate numbers and there were two official French government cars plus one from Paris.

Lara said to herself, *this is something more than tea.* She was stopped at the door and asked who she was and where she was going.

"Who are you to ask me? I'm going into my own home," she said, pulling out her passport.

"Security, Ma'am. We were told you would be at the races." The guard said looking from her passport to her face. "The children have gone for a walk with the governess and will not return before 6 p.m. The house is closed until then."

"Well, I'm sorry. I have no other place to go. I have my own key for upstairs. Please excuse me. I need to rest."

"I'm sorry, Ma'am, that won't be possible. Why don't you go to the café across from the church and wait there?"

"I am not going to any café the way I'm dressed and the way I feel. You go in and check with my mother-in-law, or whoever you need to ask, if you have to. I'll wait here for a few minutes, then I'm going up." Lara was surprised at herself for being so assertive. She felt she had no other choice. She had had enough of being told what to do. She had decided to take more control of her life and prayed to have the strength and courage to do so. Lara sat on the steps and waited in the hot sun. Her black dress seemed to absorb all the heat it could pick up and her thoughts returned to the heat of Africa and how much she hated the heat. When the security guard returned her face was covered with droplets — hard to tell what was sweat and what was tears. She wiped her face with the wet handkerchief, stood up, walked past the guard and up to the apartment without saying a word in passing. The guard had started to open his mouth to say something. It was just as well nothing came out. Sullenly he returned to a spot in the shade where he could keep an eye on the door without roasting in the hot afternoon sun.

It must have been well after six when the children got home. Only a few cars remained in the courtyard and the security guard was gone. Fully dressed, Lara had fallen asleep on the couch in the dark living room. The shutters had been closed to keep out the sun and heat of the day and when Mademoiselle had started to open them to let in the evening light and coolness she awoke. Although her body and dress had dried off she felt sticky, smelly, and dirty as she hugged the children. "How about a bubble bath with *Maman*?" she asked Tia. "Mademoiselle, I think I will take a bath with Tia who needs one as badly as I do. Could you give Alex his bath in the kitchen sink? I'll be in to fix supper afterwards and I'll take care of the children while you wash up if you'd like."

"*Merci*, Madame, that will be perfect. How did you enjoy the races?"

"I couldn't stay — too much noise, too many people — I'm not up to that yet. I never should have gone. When I got home there was a guard at the door. He didn't want to let me in. I came upstairs anyway. I'm sorry they kept you out so long. What did you do all afternoon?"

"We took a taxi to the *Jardin d'Acclimatation*. There are always many children for Tia to play with. I met a friend there: she had two children with her. We had a lovely time. Alex spent the afternoon watching everything and playing with his feet. He loves to play with his feet."

"And the *goûter*?" Lara asked.

"Oh, I had cookies with me, but we stopped at the terrace café and had tea and a pastry. You can see Tia is wearing part of hers," she said with a laugh.

Mademoiselle was a wonderful companion for Lara and the children. She was always cheery, with something fun to say. Her humor was a blessing during these difficult times with the family and the upcoming move to New York. Mademoiselle had decided not to return to the States. She had gone everywhere with them when Tia was a baby. She preferred to remain in Europe, feeling old and wanting to retire.

Four days later Lara and the children crammed into Gregory's Mercedes with little time to say good-bye to Mademoiselle and the housekeeper, who stood on the steps of *La Maison Rose*, tears streaming down their cheeks as they waved good bye. Lara, too, in quiet tears, waved her hand out the window as the car turned onto the street and headed for the airport.

Chapter Thirty-one

The flight home went well except for Alex's crying. His ears hurt during take off even though he was sucking on his bottle. He was now six months old, a chubby, active baby, and it took hours of cuddling and walking up and down the aisle to get him to sleep. The company had given Lara a first class ticket home and Air France was generous and gave her two seats so Tia could have her own space. Alex was put to sleep on the floor. Later Tia would join him for her nap and Lara was able to get a short nap, too.

Lara's mother was there to meet them on arrival. Lara zipped through customs with the children, whom she left with her mother while picking up the bags. Since she was moving home with only personal belongings she went right along and breathed a sigh of relief as she closed the car door and they were on their way home. Oak Hill would always be her home. She and Peter had invariably said to family and friends that they could be found through Tori in Oak Hill and this is how it still was going to be. With all the moving in their lives "Still Pond, no more moving," was home away from home and always would be.

Arriving back in the States was an exhausting task for Lara. The new nanny, chosen and offered by Ida, needed a visa to travel to the U.S.A. and the consulate usually took their time — at least two weeks even for a tourist visa for which she had asked. Thank goodness Tori had a French-speaking couple, Derek and Susie, who took the children in hand, bathed and put them down for a nap. Lara did the same. She was back in her old room, thankful to be there, to be able to let go of the past months of tension and to start her own time of mourning. How long that would last she could not know: she could take the time — she needed the time and knew that one day she would have to get on with her life, not only for herself, but especially for the children. Right now she would sleep and cry, walk alone along the beach when no one else was around, sit in the woods and listen to nature. Little did she know her mother had other plans for her. The plans would have to wait. Lara's blood pressure dropped very low. Every time she stood up her head would spin and she'd have to sit down again, take several deep breaths and again try to stand up. She was constantly tired and in tears. The children were a burden instead of a joy — an annoyance, an intrusion, a reminder of Peter and his death — and a reminder of her responsibility for their well-being. Term Oil had told her Peter's life insurance was not valid. He had let it lapse. Lara felt cheated. Cheated by circumstances beyond her control. She knew it wasn't true. How could a happy father of two very young children let his life insurance lapse? She wondered who had the means and the power to make it disappear? What had happened to the $300,000 she would never know. Of course, if the life insurance company had decided to look into Peter's death they might have come across something that could prove it was murder rather than an accident and those responsible for the crime would be taken to court and a big international scandal would probably ensue. Those responsible could not afford to see that happen. Again Lara wondered if Peter knew he was going to die. The cremation did away with any evidence of wrongdoing and that was what he had asked for.

And so the company "found" a $10,000 insurance policy on Peter's life and Lara decided to open a bank account for each child so that they would inherit something from their father. It might grow into something worthwhile by the time they were eighteen. It would be something their father had left them. Lara had a few thousand dollars she had made on the stock market and a few from Peter's account with the same broker. She would have to rent an apartment in New York, find a school for Tia and a job for herself. All of that would be taken care of by the end of the summer if she could get her health back. In the meantime, her hair was falling out, her muscles going flabby from weight loss, her looks and good humor disappeared very fast.

Peter's urn had been taken to Saint John's Church to await burial and Tori was trying to help Lara organize the service. She felt Lara was putting off the difficult time not having the courage for the final gesture.

"Lara, can we talk?" she asked one very hot afternoon in June when

Lara returned from a walk in the woods with the children.

"Can I leave the children with Susie?"

"Of course."

"I'll be right back." She took Alex in her arms, put him on one hip and took Tia's hand. "Come on, dear, we're going to find Susie. I'll be right back."

With the children in safe hands Lara turned to her mother.

"What is it?" she asked. "You look so serious."

"I'm sorry, I know you're exhausted, but you really need to make a date for Peter's memorial service," Tori said taking her hand and leading her to sit down next to her on the huge living room couch. "A Saturday morning would probably be the best — everyone gets married on Saturday afternoon in June and you'll have more chance to get the church in the morning."

"Mom, I'm not ready yet. Why can't it wait?"

"Making a date will help you move along. It's already going to be two months." She paused and pulled out a calendar. "Would you like it on June 22nd?"

"Oh, no Mom. That's too hard for me. The same day of the month — Unh, unh. Can we put it off until, at least, the next Saturday?"

"May I go and call the church?"

"Now? Right away now?"

"Yes, Lara, now's a good time. It leaves enough time to announce it in the papers. So many people have been asking me." She rose to go to the phone.

"Mom," Lara called after her. "It's the same church we were married in not even six years ago," and she burst into tears saying to herself, *It began there, it ends there, how am I going to get through this?*

Her mother returned saying the church was available for an eleven o'clock service and she and Allen would receive for lunch at home afterwards.

The church was packed again, filled with family, friends and flowers. The family went directly to the cemetery where Peter's ashes were buried next to Lara's grandparents; next to Grandpa, whom he loved so much. They returned to Still Pond and found the only place to park was in front of the door.

The house overflowed with people and music. Someone had hired a jazz band. Lara had a smile on her face as she walked in. Someone had remembered Peter's love for jazz and his love for life. She found solace in the music and the celebration of Peter's life.

As the summer went by Tori found a young student who needed tutoring in French, then there was another and a third. All three came from split homes, had just finished their first year of boarding school and needed someone to listen to them much more than the French lessons Lara was to give them. Suddenly she found herself caring about her charges and thinking less about herself and more about how she could help them. She started loving her children again and found that spending time playing with them at the beach, walking in the woods pointing out the flowers, animals and birds, were really great moments of joy. The French lessons turned into counseling and playtime for the students with her children. Since Tia only understood French, the teenagers would exchange vocabulary with her and she with them. Even their pronunciation improved with much joking, laughter and repetition and Lara regretted the end of the tutoring because her students were going for the other half of their vacation to the other parent. She wondered how she would fill her summer, what would help her think of something other than her mourning, future job and move to New York and her responsibility to her children.

Uncle Elliot took care of that. Peter's uncle was a lawyer. He was working on a copyright case for a client whose music had been used in a song written by another person. Documents concerning the case needed to be translated from French to English. The case was going to court in the U.S. in November and Uncle Elliot needed the documents as soon as possible. Lara spent hours, days and even weeks trying to translate the complicated legal phrases into coherent English and finally in tears on the phone with Uncle Elliot had to admit she was unable to do the job for him. It wasn't as bad as it might have been. Uncle Elliot had been to school in France, was fluent in the language and could take care of finishing the translation with plenty of time to spare. After all, he was tri-lingual. German was his mother tongue, he had worked at the Nuremberg trials after the second World War so this was a piece of cake for him. What it proved to Lara was that she would be unable to apply for a job at the United Nations with any chance of success. Her French was wonderful for social events, was good enough for the UN Indian supply platoon in Leopoldville, but not good enough for UN headquarters in New York.

So in August Lara started taking the train to New York looking for an apartment and a job. The apartment was easy enough — 780 East 86th St. was perfect, with Gracie Square Park just down the street.

The job was something else. She had forgotten how hot the streets of

New York could be in August and walking from one interview to another the hot air burned her throat and lungs. It was so hot she would stop in an air conditioned building every few minutes to cool off. She really didn't get along well in the heat. The heat of Africa had left its scar and the heat of New York was even worse. She was still wearing only black, *chic for the city, hot for the sun, at least the sweat didn't show,* she thought as she entered for her next interview. Sometimes she would have up to five interviews a day. It was an exhausting process with the train ride home at night. Finally she decided to move into the city as soon as possible and find a job later. Peter's and her friends had been wonderful lining up interviews. The disappointment was that no one took Lara seriously. They would see this beautiful socialite who could speak French, had worked for the UN in Africa, had worked and studied interior design. 'Why don't you return to that field,' they would ask. The answer, 'I'd like to do something different.' Her thought being since everybody like her — good family, money, connections—went into interior design; that would be the best place for her. Not having finished college, she even thought of going to night school if she had to.

Chapter Thirty-two

Derek usually picked Lara up when the train got in around six forty-five. Tonight Tori was standing on the platform waving to her.

"What are you doing here? Where's Derek?" She saw the worried look on her mother's face. "Are you all right? You don't look too hot."

"Aunt Lorli wants to talk to you. I thought I'd drop you there for a drink. You can walk across the field for supper before eight, okay?" Tori said as they got into the car.

"I'd like to see the children before they go to bed. Can't I go see her after supper?"

"She needs to see you now. Please." They were silent all the way to Aunt Lorli's.

"Something's wrong. Can't you tell me?" Lara said as she got out of the car and put her head through the window so Tori couldn't drive away.

"She has to tell you, Dear. I wasn't there. We'll be waiting for you and," she paused, "maybe the children will still be up."

Bewildered, Lara rang the doorbell and walked in. The house was cool and smelled wonderful. A bouquet of tuber roses on the hall table mixed with the smell of curried lamb and Lara wished she was staying for dinner. "Aunt Lorli," she called. "Where are you?"

A voice from upstairs answered, "I'll be right down. We'll sit in the living room, it's still cooler than outside." Lara found the bar, poured herself a tonic, put in a slice of lemon and lots of ice cubes and went to wait for her aunt, who appeared in her gardening clothes, her hand bandaged.

"What happened?" Lara asked.

"Oh, it's nothing. I was pruning and cut myself instead of the branch.

I need to talk to you. It's very difficult. I've told your mother and she said it would be better if I told you — since I was the one who saw it."

"Yes, tell me, please."

"Well," she had poured herself a drink and came to sit down next to Lara. "I went to find your mother this afternoon. She wasn't home. Susie and Derek were out. There was just the nurse, Catherine, with the children and since I heard Alex crying, I went upstairs to see what was going on. She was slapping him. This little baby was crying and she was hitting him trying to make him shut up." Lara could tell she was shocked. "You have to get rid of her," Aunt Lorli said, after a brief sip. "You can't keep someone who beats a baby. Your mother agrees."

It was a fight getting rid of Catherine. Lara had to hire a lawyer to intercede with Immigration because Catherine wanted a green card—and of course, two months salary.

Lara called Ida and a new nurse, Sylvia, arrived from Portugal two weeks later. This time Ida had picked a winner. They moved into the city at the beginning of September. Tia started school and their life took on a pattern of its own. After about forty interviews, Lara had a job working for Cointreau at the food fair in the Coliseum on West 59th Street. It lasted two weeks. There she had met and was hired by the new director of I.C.C. of France — a French computer company just opening its office in the U.S. They paid her tuition at night school to learn secretarial skills and accounting. Shorthand was a breeze, accounting, too. Typing was a disaster. She was dyslexic, couldn't spell and spent hours looking up words in the English-French dictionary and then with a piece of corrector tape would white out the misspelled word and redo it correctly. Then she would have to correct the copies, too. Needless to say, she would never make a good secretary. She had helped her boss decorate the office and his apartment, had dinner with him, and chose not to notice the advances he made.

One day he poked his head into her office and said, "Lara, please come into my office." He held a letter she had just finished typing. "I need to talk to you." She stopped what she was doing and followed him into his office. He closed the door behind her, went and sat behind his desk. "Please come here. I went over your letter. There are still several mistakes." He looked up at her as she bent over to see what had gone wrong. Their heads were close together, he reached up, put his hand around the back of her neck and kissed her. She was taken by surprise and then he said, "I can keep you if you'll be my mistress otherwise, I'll have to let you go." She pulled away, unable to believe what she had heard.

"You'll keep me if I'm your mistress?" she hesitated. "Otherwise you'll fire me?"

"You are not meant to be a secretary." This she knew. "You spend half the day with a dictionary correcting what you've typed. You're very beautiful. I'd like you to be my mistress, not my secretary."

Lara thought to herself, *I need to work, I need the money but not like this.*

"I think you're right about my typing. I'll get my things together and leave. If you owe me anything, please put a check in the mail." Remaining extremely calm, she turned and walked back to her office.

A few minutes later, he was at her door with a sizable check in his hand, "I'm sorry about this. I'd like to keep seeing you. I'll give you a call next week."

"I don't think so," she said with a cold glare and walked past him out of the office.

"The nerve of that man!" she said out loud to herself as she got on the elevator. She opened the envelope to look at what she had to live on until she found another job. One month's salary, *at least he's been generous,* she thought sarcastically. Two weeks' severance pay was what she had expected. Two extra weeks was a help.

Lara's decision was to take the first job offered. She could always change if something better came along. So she went to work as a store manager for a Thrift Shop — The Bargain Box — on Third and 88th Street, a short walk from her apartment. There she learned about shoplifting and when you could or could not accuse someone of stealing. She learned how to be diplomatic with volunteers and staff, and her slight knowledge of accounting came in handy. Working so close to home gave her more time with the children. Every evening she would spend at least an hour with them, playing or reading stories. She even had an answering service so she wouldn't be disturbed during their time by telephone calls.

Once people started to notice that she was serious about working, she had three job offers — one with a financial newspaper, another with an environmental group and the third with the public relations department for the New York Hilton, which was to open in June. She took the latter and loved it.

One October morning she left the children wondering if she would ever see them again. The news of the blockade of Russian ships carrying nuclear warheads that could be launched from Cuba terrified her and the country. The office was a disaster when she got there.

"Did you hear the news this morning? The Russians are sending more nuclear missiles to Cuba and we've put up a blockade," said Jenny, her boss. Jenny was a very matter-of-fact woman even in the way she dressed. Her dark hair was neatly folded into a French twist, her make-up just enough to draw attention to her large brown eyes and beautifully formed red lips. Lara admired her cool and was thankful she was in control. The news was constant, no matter what station they turned to. No one was feeling well and even though the group tried to settle down to the job not much was accomplished. The phones were all busy. She couldn't get a line out of the Warwick Hotel where Hilton had taken office space until they could move into the new hotel. Total havoc. On Friday, October 26th, 1962, half the ships had turned around. The others stayed in place. That weekend Lara spent every second she could with the children. They went to Tori's, leaving the city behind, yet knowing that if a missile hit New York they would all die anyway.

Indian Summer passed and winter took over with its cold wind and gray skies. Lara's depression faded. The cold air was invigorating, she loved her job and met many new people and made new friends. She found it hard to understand the fact that their old friends, couples, had cut her out of their lives. They had all come to her parties, but never gave her a return invitation. She did not flirt with married men. She tried to avoid them, and if they insisted on taking her to lunch, or dinner, she always let their wives know. That way they all knew where she stood. At first she had a hard time dating. She left parties early, leaving her date behind. If they didn't understand it didn't matter. She wouldn't see them again. A year had gone by since Peter had died, she was still in mourning wearing black, white, gray and some mauve. She was always well-dressed, as Peter had taught her. She'd recovered her sense of humor, but not the twinkle in her eyes.

Tia was enjoying her bilingual school and taking violin lessons and painting. It always amazed Lara how well Tia had adapted to life in New York: school, activities, birthday parties, meeting friends in the park, and being a good sister to her little brother. She would embarrass her mother when a man came by three or four times because she would ask him if he was going to be her new Papa. He'd be embarrassed, too.

Lara was successful in her new job. The Hilton's name was often in print thanks to her press releases. She made friends with many journalists and TV newscasters who came to cover events at the hotel. Harvey Richards, a correspondent for the *New York Times*, was well-traveled and knew a lot of famous people. He fascinated Lara, who loved watching him work someone for a story. An attractive man, a few years older than she was, he had short curly gray hair, a round face, and he wore glasses which

Lara would remove when they were alone so she could see the expression of his blue eyes. After they had been to a concert at Carnegie Hall, Rostropovich, who had performed a cello solo, joined them for dinner with a few friends. It was a fabulous evening. Harvey took Lara back to his apartment. He had been courting her for a while and hoped to get her between his sheets. He had a talent for kissing, which Lara enjoyed, until he started to undress her.

"Harvey, what are you doing?" She knew very well but wanted to hear his answer.

"You know I'm mad about you," he spoke softly into her ear sending shivers through her. "Marry me." He moved slightly away from her still holding her against him. "Marry me," he repeated, "You and the children would be a perfect cover for me. They're sending me to South America. Will you come with me?"

Careful, Lara thought. *It sounds like something I've already done.*

"I don't know, Harvey." She moved out of his arms and climbed onto his big bed, sitting against a bunch of pillows. She pulled one in front of her for protection. "You certainly know how to surprise a woman." It sounded like a repeat performance and she was scared. Had someone told him to ask her just to see what the reaction would be? "Wow. I think I need to go home to think about it."

"Please stay."

"No, Harvey," she said, as she got up. "I need to think about this — you. It would have been more fun to sleep with you if you hadn't asked me to marry you."

"I leave in four days. We can get married in Rio. Don't say anything now." He got up, put his arms around her, gave her a loving kiss. "I'll drive you home." Lara was off the hook. She knew her answer would be "no," and she'd give it only after he had left for Rio.

The next interesting incident was with Jake Johnson, a newscaster with ABC-TV. He was often at the Hilton with a TV crew covering events. The crew had come to know Lara quite well and thought she would do well as a newscaster. ABC was looking for an interviewer, a smart yet good-looking woman. They did a mock interview, with Johnson playing the role of a newly appointed ambassador who didn't know his geography. They invited Lara back to the studio to see the interview. She was stunned. It was a big success. They asked her to do another in a sound studio. She was spontaneous, humorous and diplomatic with a very sexy voice. If she took the job she knew she wouldn't have time for her children. She would belong to the public with no more private life. So she thanked them for the compliment and left. Lara's social life was crammed between her friends and the charity balls where she and her cameraman watched for opportunities to publicize the hotel wherever they could. She thought, at that time, had she taken the job with ABC-TV, the CIA would be debriefing her any time she traveled to interview famous people.

Miss Sweden showed up at the Hilton — except she wasn't Miss Sweden. They called from the bar downstairs saying: "We have a celebrity, get the photographer."

Al showed up a few minutes later. Later in life he always reminded her of Columbo, the detective who drove a jalopy and wore a mussed-up raincoat. His hair was dark, wavy and uncontrolled. He had a good eye for people and his pictures were easily accepted by the Press. They went down to the bar together, and in the dim light, saw a good looking blond with two men and another young woman.

"Are you Miss Sweden?"

"Yes," the blond answered.

"What's your name? I'd like to include it with our photo, if you don't mind," Lara said as she signaled the waiter to order a round of drinks. "On the house."

"We just call her Miss Sweden," one of her companions answered.

Lara wondered what this was all about and started speaking Swedish with "the girls." It was obvious they didn't understand a word. She then added, "Al take a couple of pictures, if you want, stick around," and more quietly she added, "see what they're up to." She signed the chit for the round of drinks and returned to her office. The next day Al came by with two photos — one of "Miss Sweden," the other of the group. There was nothing she could do with them except warn the bartender to watch for blondes propositioning hotel guests.

By the spring of 1963 Lara had become the Merry Widow. Oleg Cassini was dressing Jackie Kennedy and Lara. He had sent Lara on many interviews when she was looking for a job and now they were friends. He invited her to go to Washington — to the Shrivers' tenth wedding anniversary dinner dance. There Lara met the Kennedy family. She wondered why Bobby and Ted seemed so interested in her. She never met the President and did become good friends with George Skakel. He would fly her up to Burlington, ski at Mad River Glen, and fly her back to New York for her Sunday with the children. George played indoor polo on Sundays at the New York Armory.

By June of 1964, Lara's work at Hilton was a big success — too big for her boss. Jenny started to turn on her and made her life difficult with long hours — seven a.m. to two a.m. and one event after another. She had a room at the hotel for those nights, but it cut down terribly on her time with the children. Then one quiet day at the office, Willy, a coworker, offered to read her cards. Since Lara didn't know where to turn for advice she said, "Let's try the cards. Jenny's not supposed to be in until three this afternoon. That gives us lots of time." The cards were shuffled and laid out.

Willy had a big smile on her face as she started to tell a story. "Things are going too well for you here."

"That's obvious."

"You will meet a tall, blond man with blue eyes," she hesitated. "He will offer you a job. It looks like you'll take it. If you do, I'll miss you. Promise we'll remain friends," she said, looking up sadly. "I think the only reason Jenny keeps me on is because I go out with Russel." Russel Edwards was Society Editor for the *New York Times.* "It's difficult working with her. I hate changing jobs all the time." She put the cards away, straightened out her fluffy red hair, put on green eye make-up, which matched the color of her eyes. "I have a lunch date with Russel. See you later." She walked out the door leaving Lara to think about another job.

Early in July Lara had an appointment with Walter Hoving, CEO of Tiffany & Co. She thought that Hilton and Tiffany should get some mutual publicity by using Tiffany window displays. Mr. Hoving and her mother had known each other as children — they had played together in Central Park — and this made it easier for her to get her foot in the door. Within twenty minutes he offered Lara a job. She didn't know what to say. He offered her the Executive Training Program, making the proposition more tempting. Then came a question, "What's your salary?"

"A hundred and ten dollars a week," she answered. She would have lied to increase the amount, but she didn't dare in case he checked up on her.

"How about a hundred and twenty? Take it or leave it," he said with a smile.

"When do you want me to start?"

"Right away."

"I need to give two weeks' notice and I need some time, maybe a month, for vacation to take the children to their grandmother in Portugal."

"Two weeks notice is the end of July, two weeks with the children in Portugal. Be here no later than August fifteenth," he said firmly.

Lara thought fast. Two weeks notice and to ask around as to the financial health of Tiffany, two weeks with Ida would be more than enough, but not enough with the children. She did want to move away from Jenny and then she remembered the cards.

"That will be fine, sir. I'll be at work by August fifteenth at the latest. Thank you."

The two weeks in Cascais, Portugal, were very interesting. Antoine Pinay, de Gaulle's ex-minister of finance, came to visit with his mistress. The afternoon of Lara's arrival, after her nap, she walked downstairs to find his mistress waiting for her. She put her arms around Lara and embraced her passionately on the lips. Lara pulled away as fast as she could, embarrassed and shocked.

"I'm not interested in sex with another woman," she turned to walk away. "Please excuse me." And disappeared into the kitchen. Then an attractive Portuguese man began courting her seriously. One evening before dropping her off he started making love to her in his car. Lara enjoyed it all until he was putting his pants back together and said, "I never thought you'd give yourself to me."

"Why is that?" she asked, getting out of the car to put her clothes back on.

"Your mother-in-law asked me to try to seduce you. I'm much older than you are. I didn't think you'd find me attractive."

"Oh, no," Lara moaned. "She's done it again. First it was Pinet's mistress and now you." She got back into the car. "Please take me home and don't come near me again. Particularly if she's around."

"I'm sorry. I never should have said anything."

"That's right, you should not have. Is she paying you or do you come free?" she snarled.

"Come on, Lara, that's below the belt."

"That's right. It's all below the belt, isn't it?"

They drove back in silence. Lara was furious that she'd been had by her mother-in-law. She'd been successfully screwed in more ways than one and had three days to go before returning to New York and her new job. She refused to go to any of the parties for those last few days, saying she wasn't feeling well and wanted to stay with the children. Sylvia, the Portuguese nanny, would return to New York to get married. Pat, a young French woman, had come to take her place and Lara took those days to get to know her better, so that when she left she would know that Pat would take good care of the children. Lara's good-byes to Ida were cold and distant, with just enough of thanks for having found the new nanny and for Ida to know how much she appreciated the gift.

Chapter Thirty-three

Lara returned from Portugal, still hated the summer heat in New York and was glad to spend the day in the air-conditioned store at Tiffany's. She worked in every department except where the gems were kept and new pieces of jewelry were created. She studied books on gems and then studied the gems. Her eye was sharp. She could tell the difference in the quality of a diamond by its color, and other stones by the faults or impurities. She studied books on silver and silver marks and did the same for porcelain. Accounting, shipping, selling, gift-wrapping packages with no scotch tape, purchasing, displays — she covered the works and loved it all.

Mr. Hoving called Lara into his office a few weeks after she had started to work there.

"I hear you were asking around town about the financial situation of Tiffany. Is that so?"

Lara, very embarrassed, answered, "Yes, sir. I hoped that if I did a good job the company would keep me for a long time."

"Well, Lara, it's the first time I've heard of someone asking about our financial situation. What did you hear?" he finished with a big smile on his face.

"Financially sound, sir, very well managed, and that I'd be lucky to work for you."

"If you have any other questions, please feel free to come and ask me, okay?"

By then Lara was bright red. "Yes, sir, thank you." She turned around and walked out of the office like a puppy with its tail between its legs.

During that time there were people who came into her life testing her. Fitzhugh Green, a tall, good-looking divorcé with battle scars around his left eye took her out several times. They had known each other in the Congo. He said he was with USIS —Lara thought he worked for the CIA. He tried to seduce her and invited her to Newport for a weekend of trials for the Americas Cup. He loved to sail, so did Lara. The only problem was he took her out in his 25-foot sloop on the bay when the sea was so rough that there were no other boats out. Even the ferry wasn't running.

"Don't you want to go into the cabin? You're getting soaked," he suggested.

"I'd rather stay top-side." The salty cool air felt good and was helpful against nausea.

"What if you fall in?"

"Don't worry, you won't lose me that easily. I'm a very good swimmer." She turned her back on the next wave that came over the boat. "Are you trying to test my courage?"

"How did you guess? The boat's taking on water. We'd better head in." His tone of voice had changed. He was worried more about his boat than he was about Lara.

"A wise decision. I'm feeling a little seasick."

Fitzhugh spun the wheel, they jibed and with the wind at their backs the waves were easier to maneuver back into port.

"You were crazy to be out in that wind even with your engine running." The man who tied up the boat continued, "No one was supposed to go out today. If we'd seen you we couldn't have let you go. Coast Guard was furious to see you out there." He saw Lara, soaking wet, getting out of the yellow oilskin rain gear. "You were out there with a woman? Man, you're crazy."

"Thanks for tying her up." Embarrassed, Fitzhugh added, "You're right, it was crazy. Sorry, Lara. You looked as if it didn't bother you that much."

"It bothered me, just don't try it again." And he didn't. He did introduce her though to Cord Meyer, who at the time was number three in the CIA. The first time they went out together Cord took her to a private party in a swanky penthouse apartment on the Upper East Side, left her on her own, and didn't introduce her to anyone. So, she left. He called a few days later, apologized and asked her out to dinner. That night, he told her that his wife had been murdered, how he had lost the sight of one eye, and that his body was badly scared from bullet wounds and fighting in Vietnam. This man fascinated Lara. To her he was no longer whole and yet very attractive.

Tall, blond, a long thin face and body — even fully clothed she could tell he was in good shape. She wondered why they had been introduced. She knew it was on purpose and that she would have to be careful not to get romantically involved.

He called again. His next trip to New York was to meet with some editors from the New York Times. There was a story the CIA did not want to have in print. He invited her to dinner at the Ryans' home, the son of a newly named ambassador to Spain. When he picked her up she had the courage to ask, "What's this all about?"

He turned to her with a quizzical look thinking that she was starting to take the bait — getting interested in the workings of the CIA, perhaps even working for them. But Lara knew what she was doing, and led him on.

"We need to know some of the family history. Where the Ambassador has his strengths and where and what are his weaknesses." She sat looking at him as if enthralled by what he was saying.

"Can I be of help?"

"Just sit and listen carefully, be beautiful, act dumb, and help my memory later in case I miss something. Oh, also women pick upon things men don't." He took her arm to cross the street, she moved as close as she could get to him thinking, *Look out, buddy, here I come.* She was playing a dangerous game and needed to come out the winner.

"What do you mean?" she asked.

"Your intuition is better than mine. At least it should be. You know about body language?" She nodded. "Watch David and his wife when I ask a question." He turned again and stopped a few yards from their destination. "And for God's sake, don't stare — even if you find him attractive," he finished with a smile.

Lara had a good time playing a role she thought she had never played before. Then she realized that playing dumb is something all children do when they're caught being naughty. It was something she had become a pro at in her youth. She was being naughty again and the part was easy to follow except when her sense of humor kicked in and her repartee was sharp and to the point. She saw how adept Cord was in learning what he needed to know. Watching his game, she learned how to play hers.

The next week she was working on the ground floor at Tiffany in the watch department. A man in a black suit, white shirt, black tie and carrying a chauffeur's cap approached her and asked if she was free.

"Yes, what can I do for you?" she asked, thinking, *this is strange.*

"I'm Ambassador Ryan's chauffeur. He asked me to stop by and pick out a gift for his wife." He tried to look embarrassed and didn't succeed. Now she knew why he had chosen to speak with her. How was she supposed to know who Ambassador Ryan was? "They've had a fight. He wants to make an apology, clear things up before they leave for Madrid. What can you suggest?"

Lara was smiling to herself as she looked around the store for an idea. "Approximately how much does the Ambassador want to put into his gift?"

"Oh," taken by surprise, the chauffeur did not know exactly what to answer. "What does a nice watch go for?" he said pointing to a gold and diamond watch in the showcase.

Lara opened the case, took out the watch and laid it on a leather display mat where the chauffeur could pick it up and look at it. "This costs over five thousand dollars," he exclaimed. Lara looked at the price tag and then at him.

"Too much?" She wondered how low the price would drop by the time he made up his mind. He started looking in another section of the store. Her eyes followed, "Please come with me." She led the way to a counter with silver objects, pens, bookmarks and things more in a modest price range. "Here's a silver necklace by Schlumberger. What do you think?"

"How much?" he asked taking it in his hands. It was wide and very supple and flowed through his palms like a snake.

"It's a thousand, three hundred. A lovely piece and remember, if she doesn't like it she can always exchange it." She took it from him and spread it on a velvet display mat.

"I don't think it's appropriate." He looked further down the case and spotted a silver case holding a note pad. "What about a pen and a note pad holder? What would that cost? It's my boss's money. I don't want to go overboard, you know what I mean?"

"The two together cost about seven hundred," she said pulling them out of the case so he could get a good look.

"Sounds good. Could you gift wrap them?"

"Do you mind if I pass the sale to a colleague? I'm not on commission," she said, calling a friend over to take the sale.

"No, I want you to take the sale," he said, coldly dismissing the other saleslady.

"Certainly, sir," Lara replied. "I'll be right back. Charge card, cash or check, how would you like to pay? And whose name should I make out the sales slip to?" as she started writing everything else she needed.

"Ambassador T. Ryan, please," he said curtly and turned his back to her as she wrote out the slip. Turning back, he added, "It's a cash sale."

"Thank you, sir. May I have your name, please?"

"That won't be necessary. It's all for Ambassador Ryan. You don't need my name."

Lara thought the player didn't know how to act very well. She was sure everything would be returned within two weeks. She did check in the return book and, sure enough, there it was — just two weeks later. No sale, no fight, just another way to check out her discretion. It was two and a half years since Peter had died. Why were they still bothering her?

She decided to have a "working lunch" with her friend from the Hilton. She wanted the cards to help her understand where she was going and why. With the CIA still interested in her she knew she had to be careful. Willy, through the cards, might have an idea.

Lara bundled up in her Dior sheepskin coat and headed out of the office warning her associate she might be late getting back. There was nothing in particular that needed to be done. For once, she would take her time. It was a cold, windy fall day and very invigorating for Lara. They met in the warmth of a small restaurant on West 55th Street where they had reserved a booth in the back and they wouldn't be disturbed. It was a noisy place. The waiters stacked the dirty dishes and walked quickly by in both directions with no time to notice them. With a glass of wine and their order given, Willy pulled out her regular deck of cards and shuffled. "So, what do you want to ask? My Dear, are you in trouble?"

"Don't know if it's trouble. I'm annoyed. I feel harassed by all these games people are trying to play with me because of Peter. Maybe he worked for the CIA. If he did, I never knew. I have nothing to tell them." She paused and thought about a question. "I can't think of how to word a question. I just want them to stop bothering me." Then she smiled and added. "I've become 'The Merry Widow' and I like that, but this stuff is having too much of an effect on me." The waiter brought their plates. The cheese omelets smelled wonderful and Lara's mouth began to water. They ate and chatted until they were finished, sopping up the last runny part of the eggs with a piece of baguette.

"Why don't we ask a general question of the cards, like, what's in your immediate future?" Willy suggested. Lara took the cards, shuffled three times, cut them and gave them back to Willy, who had pushed the dishes away to make room for the cards. She started laying them out in her usual pattern and in her wonderfully melodic voice started to tell their story: "I see a man coming from abroad. He is shorter than you are, but not much, just a little. If he holds his head high, he's about the same size." She moved two cards and scrutinized the new pattern. "He has wavy, dark brown hair — and brown eyes." She paused to look at Lara. "You're not going to like this. You'll be engaged or married by the end of the year." She burst into laughter. Lara wasn't laughing. "Don't you see? If you get married, they won't think of you anymore. You'll be home free!"

"I don't want to get married. I'm having too much fun the way things are. And the kids are fine — though Tia keeps asking whatever man is around, 'Are you going to be my new father?' I think she really wants a father."

They sat in silence until the waiter cleared the table. Of course, he asked to have his cards read and knew it would never happen. He brought them lemon meringue pie and coffee, "Anything else, ladies?"

"No thanks. Sorry about the cards. We have to get back to the office. Maybe next time."

"Sure, you bet," and he disappeared.

"I hate it when you tell me things like this," Lara said. "Every time you've read my cards it comes true. Now what do I do?"

All Willy could do was smile at her. "Stop that silly grin. I just had to tell Grant not to fall in love with me. He's been such fun and a great lover, but I know I'll never marry him."

Finally Lara smiled. "I'll have to get rid of several men in my life. Don't want to hurt any of them or give them a chance to ask me to marry them. Thanks for the warning and by the way, lunch is on me." She signaled for the bill and on their way out the door said, "You're good at what you do. I hope, for once, you're not right." They had a big hug. "Thanks, it may be a way of getting rid of the CIA after all."

By mid-December Lara was going out with only her old buddies and felt secure in her widowhood. Then Sophie, a longtime childhood friend, called to invite her to a dinner party. It was December 19. It had snowed all day. Lara had to walk home from work and couldn't get a taxi to take her to dinner. She was in a foul mood when she showed up at Sophie's apartment cold and wet. A Frenchman opened the door to welcome her. Sophie was in the kitchen. He helped her with her coat and looked at her very intently.

"Where is everybody?" Lara asked. "I'm sorry I'm so late. I had to walk home from work. Hello." She turned to the Frenchman. "I'm Lara."

"Philip," he answered.

"Hello, Philip. As you can tell I'm in a foul mood. Sophie," she called out.

"Hi. Come on in. You've met Philip de Gary. No one else was able

255

to come so there's just the three of us. Fix yourself a drink. I'll be right there." Kitchen noises continued and Philip went into the kitchen to help Sophie while Lara got herself a drink.

"You're right," he said to Sophie. "She's the one I'm going to marry." Sophie turned to look at him holding hard onto the frying pan in hopes of not losing dinner. She didn't know what to say. She finally got out, "Take it easy. You just met." She thought of how her mother had hoped Philip would take to her daughter. And although Sophie was interested, it didn't go beyond that. She felt she might have just become a matchmaker and she felt good. The evening was a success. Philip walked Lara home. She dismissed him at the door to 780 East 86th st. and went up to bed, not thinking about Willy and the cards.

Lara took the children and Pat, the new nanny, out to Oak Hill for their Christmas vacation. She had to work until Christmas Eve and was happy to have some time to herself for Christmas shopping. Tiffany was not a toy store. One evening the telephone rang.

"Hello, Lara?"

"Yes, hello Philip."

"How do you know my voice?"

"You have a lovely French accent," she said, imitating him slightly. "How are things going? Is it a busy time for your business now or do you have time to play?"

"Actually, I have two tickets to the Stanley Cup tomorrow evening. Would you like to go?"

"How did you know I liked ice hockey? Sure, I'd love to go."

"Great," he exclaimed, trying not to sound too enthusiastic. "I'll pick you up at six thirty. We can have a hot dog and a beer at the Garden, if that's okay with you."

"Sounds good. I'll be downstairs at six thirty."

That's strange, she thought afterward. *I'm looking forward to seeing him.* And then she remembered the cards. "Careful, girl," she said out loud to herself as she went off to organize her life for the next day.

They had a great time at the game. She loudly encouraged her New York team. He was rooting for the French Canadian Maple Leafs and, as he was the only one, drew quite a lot of attention. They didn't care and by the end of the evening neither had much of a voice left, so he took her dancing at "Interdit" — a new nightclub. There were hardly any people there and not much of an atmosphere, so he took her home. Again, to play it safe, she kissed him on both cheeks, French style, and left him at the door

"What are you doing tomorrow night?" he hurriedly called out.

"Going shopping for the children's Christmas."

"Where?" he asked.

"Bloomingdales." And she couldn't help herself. "You want to join me?" She was standing beside him back out in the cold.

"May I?" He moved in close again. She turned her head so all he got was her cheek.

"Sure. Six thirty at the information desk?"

"Fine, I'll see you there." He got the picture, turned and walked away even before she had gone back into her building.

Their shopping was finished by the time Bloomingdales closed at nine and Lara invited him in for an omelet as a thank you for his help. The omelet was a flop, but it gave him the time to offer her a ride out to the country with her packages. She accepted.

It was December 23rd and everyone would be on the road for Christmas. They had a snack at a local coffee shop and started out after seven in the evening, hoping the traffic would be lighter.

The roads were wet with snow and the reflection from the headlights coming toward them made it difficult to see. It was cold and damp, with patchy fog and slow going. The bright red sports car was jammed with gifts and Lara was excited about Christmas with her family and thankful for the ride home. She wondered what Philip was doing for his Christmas so far from home. She didn't dare ask, for she felt she couldn't invite a stranger to join their family festivities. Later she learned he had driven back to town, had a Christmas dinner alone in one of his favorite French restaurants, which was open on Christmas day and was back at work on Monday. This was no way to treat a friend, far from home and in a foreign country.

They went out twice the week between Christmas and New Years — once to La Caravelle restaurant and then dancing, the other to the movies. Philip had succeeded in kissing her and Lara, remembering the cards, was trying to keep her distance all the while feeling that she might be falling in love again. The men she had known as lovers during her widowhood had been wonderful, but this time it felt different. To her, Philip had potential and she didn't want to get married. It — he — made her squirm. In any case, he wouldn't have the opportunity to propose before New Year's. Lara had refused two dates for parties on the 31st with men whom she knew were interested in her. She would spend the evening at her mother's house with the children and she was happy to do so.

Her sister walked in dressed to the nines, ready to leave for their New Year's Eve party, "Lara, we're not going to leave you home alone for the evening. Go get changed, you're coming with us."

"You know I don't want to go out tonight, and besides I don't have anything to wear," Lara answered. "Really I want to stay with the kids," she was trying to read them a story and wasn't about to change her mind.

"Susie said she'd watch the children," and insisting, "you can borrow something out of Mum's closet. Come on." At that moment Jimmy walked in. Jimmy was Josie's fiancé, a tall blue-eyed, blonde-haired wonderful looking man.

"Don't worry, Lara, there won't be anyone there to propose to you." He turned towards the children, "You don't mind if we borrow your Mom for the evening. She needs to go to a party with us." Both children were sitting on her lap. They turned towards her with a questioning look. It seemed as if everyone wanted her to go. She found what she needed in her mother's closet and, not making any particular effort to impress anyone, was ready in ten minutes and, after kissing the children good night and thanking Susie with wishes for a Happy New Year, was out the door.

A crowd of young people had gathered at Sophie's parents and to her surprise Philip was among the guests. The party went well until a few minutes before midnight when Philip took her by the hand and led her into an empty library where a fire inside a tiled chimney was the only light. It gave out warmth and held her eyes even though he was still holding her hand. He gave a gentle tug to draw her attention to him. She turned and melted into his arms giving into his tender kiss. When she came to he was talking to her. "Will you marry me?" he asked with love in his eyes. She was shocked, it wasn't midnight yet and he had proposed. The cards had come true again. One moment she was annoyed, another perplexed, another in love and she knew she never should have come to the party.

"I don't know," she moved out of his arms. He pulled a small package out of his pocket and handed it to her. She didn't want to take it.

"Please," he took her hand and put the package in it. "It's okay. It's not an engagement ring. Open it." Reluctantly she undid the red ribbon and flipped the top open. There was a little jade cat with ruby eyes and a gold mustache and ears. It was a charming little pin, a gift she could accept if there wasn't the question of marriage attached to it. He saw her hesitate. "Please, accept it. Take your time — I don't want an answer tonight. I didn't even know if you were going to be here." He put an arm around her waist. "Come on, let's go back to the party." They walked out of the quiet of the library leaving the crackling fire behind and into the noise of the

New Year.

Josie and Jimmy drove her home in silence. She wasn't about to tell them what happened. In any case they probably had guessed and were feeling guilty. Philip and Lara went out once the next week and then he took off for the Caribbean for a week's vacation. It was too difficult for him to wait around New York for an answer and she had promised to give him an answer by mid January. His gifts to the children had made a big hit — a dollhouse he put together with Tia and a large truck Alex could ride on. He had met and played with the children and Tia had asked her usual question.

"Are you going to be my new Papa?" and he answered, "I hope so," which won him an affectionate hug from both children. Lara thought, *it looks like the children have decided for me. I still need some time. Getting married to a Frenchman means moving again; living in Paris; French schools for the children; adapting to another country and its culture now that I feel comfortably at home here. My head says maybe, my heart says yes!*

A few days after Philip's departure Lara called Grant and asked if he'd have lunch with her. She needed someone to talk to. Although they had been lovers she had warned him not to fall in love for she didn't want to hurt him and she felt that with him knowing her so well and caring about her happiness, he could give her good advice. She left Tiffany's telling her colleague she wouldn't be back before three and headed for a small Italian restaurant a few blocks away. It was a bitter cold day, which helped to clear her head. Her thoughts started to fall into place one minute and then fell into confusion the next. She saw him sitting at the back of the restaurant, a table against the wall, no one around to hear what they would be saying. He stood to greet her. A tall slim man, his suit and tie elegant, with slightly graying hair at the temples. He was very attractive with glasses that framed his large brown eyes, and arms in which she still felt comfortable. They sat and ordered and once the waiter had left them alone Lara's hand reached for his. "You're an angel to be here for me." She hesitated not having figured out how to tell him she was thinking about getting married and not to him. "You know I've been going out with a Frenchman." He nodded wondering what was coming next. "Grant, this is difficult for me."

"It's OK. Tell me what's going on."

"You've meant so much to me."

"You know we'll always be friends. Some day you'll get married, so will I. It just won't be with each other," he said with a sigh.

"I feel terrible. Remember Willy and the cards? Well, she was right. Philip proposed to me New Year's Eve, just before midnight. I was furious — perplexed." She paused, remembering the scene in the library and the comfortable warmth that had surrounded her before he popped the question, "And now I feel like a fish — at the end of a line — hooked and being pulled in. And I don't know what to do."

"You hardly know the guy, what did you say? You met him December 19th — how many times have you been out with him anyway?" Grant tried to keep his voice down and to hide his emotions — it wasn't working. Lara took a while to answer.

"Let's see, eleven days to New Year's — once for dinner and dancing, again shopping, a ride out Christmas, once between Christmas and New Year's. Once since he proposed. That makes five times — oh and a hockey game." She looked hard at Grant thinking the whole thing was crazy. "You're right, I don't know him at all, and I'm supposed to give him an answer when he gets back next week."

"Sweetheart, I'm afraid I can't help you on this one. You're going to have to decide on your own. And just because the kids say they want a father isn't a reason for you to say yes. It's your life." He squeezed her hand hard. "If you're not ready by the time he gets back here — that's OK too." Then he had an idea. "Is the CIA still bothering you?"

"Unfortunately, they're still inquisitive, keeping an eye on me even at work. Why?"

"Well, maybe, if you were engaged, occupied by another man, well," he paused, "just maybe you'd be safe. They wouldn't feel you were a danger to them — you'd lost interest in the past. Not that that would be a reason to get married. Well, it's something to think about."

Lara did a lot of thinking over the next ten days and decided she needed to have an affair before making up her mind, so when Philip returned she was prepared. He obliged.

The evening before she was to take the children skiing at Mad River Glen they had dinner. He pulled his family ring off his finger and put it on her finger. It would be her engagement ring until she came to Paris to meet his family. The weekend with Tori, the children and Pat skiing was perfect. There she started to tell her stories about her CIA encounters — at a cocktail party. The host's frown told her to shut up. Her answer: "Tell the CIA to leave me alone and I'll stop talking!"

That was in January. They were married six months later, having to wait because Lara's little sister was to get married first. Their mother had two weddings within ten days of each other, a feat for any mother. Josie and Jimmy's for seven hundred people; Lara and Philip's for a hundred and fifty.

By now Lara was a pro at moving. The apartment had been cleared out before the wedding. The children and Lara stayed at Still Pond until the apartment in Paris was ready for them. She had already had four major moves of her own — not counting all the ones she'd had with her parents before and after their divorce. The move for the family was relatively easy since they all were bilingual, yet not so easy for the children when they left Still Pond and all the people there who had loved and cared for them during the past three years.

Nine months later Philip's first child was born — Edgar, a son to carry the family name. Four years after that they had a daughter — and during that time they moved back to New York so that Philip could manage and expand the family company in the U.S.A. They returned to Paris in 1968 to protect their patrimony during the student "manifo". Riots were nothing new to Lara and seemed not at all as dangerous as the ones she'd lived through in the Congo. After that, their life became peaceful and comfortable, a house in the country, friends and a successful social life. Business was another matter. Feuds in the family company and the death of his uncle encouraged Philip to move back to the States for his business in 1976. They returned again to Paris in 1978 (thirteen tons of baggage both times) because the French Company was floundering. The family dispute ended in court, was thrown out of court by the judge, and again they moved back to New York — for good. He became an American citizen much to the distress of his parents.

Chapter Thirty-four

During all those years the CIA no longer bothered Lara. She did continue to have difficulties with her health over Easter and April 22nd every year. Philip was a dear, understanding that until she knew the truth about what had happened to Peter she would never be at ease during that time of the year. In 1993 he encouraged her to hire a lawyer to try, through the Freedom of Information Act, to discover the truth and reason for Peter's death.

She engaged a lawyer in Washington, DC, a partner in a large law firm — the same firm that had handled all of Philip's court cases in New York during the family feud. John Helms and his assistant sounded interested in helping her, and although they never met with Lara, they were enthusiastic. They sent letters to some twenty-five departments of the U.S. Government. All replies came back with the equivalent "unknown to this department" except for the letter from the CIA stating she could make further inquiries if she wished. Her lawyer told her a further inquiry wouldn't produce any results and suggested she drop the whole matter. But that wasn't possible now. Lara had noticed strange things happening on her phone line. She would dial a number and sometimes have to redial it three or four times to have it go through. Sometimes she'd hear a click on the line and sometimes someone would call and not say anything — as if they were checking to see if they were home or if the house was empty. Some of these times she could hear noise in the background, but nobody spoke to her. She wondered if her line was being tapped, then went looking for a machine that would tell her if someone had hooked on to the line. Another idea was a machine which caused static to the unwanted listener. She had made friends with a salesman at a local electronics shop and finally asked him to come by to check her phone. Once he was there she started asking questions.

"Herb, I've been by the store so often you must have guessed why you're here." She studied his long oval face — eyes wide apart, not much of a forehead, which was covered by curls that looked as if they hadn't been combed in days. His lips were tight, his nostrils small — signs for her that he wasn't getting much out of life. He was seriously checking out a phone, taking it apart to check for a microphone.

"Well, it's kind of obvious. There's no microphone here, which means probably not on any of the phones. The phone's fine — dialing, connection, no problem." He turned his attention to her. "You think your line might be tapped?"

"Yup. I'm getting all kinds of weird sounds on the line. How can you tell if you have a tap on your line anyway?"

"There are several ways. For instance, if there is a wire coiled around your line, it might be tapped."

"That's funny, I saw the phone company working on the lines down at the bottom of the driveway a couple of weeks ago. Would you mind? Let's go see." They walked out in the drizzle of a warm winter day down the wet driveway. They both saw a coil, looked at each other. Herb seemed to think it was possible.

"What makes them interested in you?" he asked. "It's the first time I've seen this in the Northern Valley."

"I haven't the faintest idea." Her thoughts flew by: *is it because Philip is in court in Washington for dumping (selling goods at a cheaper price than in France)? Was he in court because I've started to ask questions and court would be a distraction? Or was it because, finally after thirty years of waiting, I'm making an official inquiry? I'd better use someone else's phone from now on.* She was angry.

"They can't do that without a court order. I've asked the phone company if the line was tapped. I even asked the man working on the line the day he was here." She felt out of breath walking back to the house and stopped midway. "You know what he said to me?" She turned to look at Herb. "'Honey, if your line is tapped and I knew it, I wouldn't be able to tell you anyway.' The guy went back to work and said, 'Anyway, I'm here because you're complaining about the company's service and the problems you're having on the line. I'm trying to fix it, OK?' I went back to the house, kept an eye on him until he left and went to see if anything had changed."

"And?"

"I didn't notice any difference. In any case, I'm careful with what I say on the phone and don't have anything to hide."

Lara made further inquiries and learned that if there was a permit to tap the line — after three or four minutes of conversation, which was of a personal nature, they were supposed to click off the line. Also, it was possible for anyone to hook up and listen to a phone conversation anywhere between the phone and the central. Cell phones were more difficult to tap and a computer on line could be searched by anyone who knew how. Orwell's *1984* was becoming a reality and she was annoyed. Why would they bother with her and what were their risks if she ever learned what happened to Peter? There must be something there.

The next thing she noticed was a series of letters from the IRS, several saying she owed more money in back taxes; or there was a miscalculation; or asking for more information on gifts; did they pay social security and unemployment for their housekeeper? All of these were sent on to their accountant, who also was a lawyer, in New York. He had warned them to be careful because of the future sale of Philip's company and the amounts of money involved. The letters were distracting, nothing more, and two years later they stopped. During that time Lara learned the government could freeze her bank account. She thought of moving her capital "offshore." A specialist told her, if she was a U.S. citizen, residing in the U.S., the government could legally oblige her to return her capital to the States and confiscate it while they took her to court. Not a solution. The house was only half hers; the other belonged to Philip — difficult for the government to do something there. And his money was totally separate from hers. This fact softened her dilemma. The only thing they could take was her money.

The next thing she tried to learn about was listening devices. Bugs and cannons. The bugs were relatively easy. You bought an instrument, which could pick out a hidden bug within a few meters. The cannon was something that could focus in on sound from a long distance — undetectable. The solution was loud music or radio — even whispers could be picked up — writing was a possibility too, but that had to be destroyed. Was she, were they, becoming paranoid? Then a phone call came through from Washington, her lawyer.

"Hello John, what's up?"

"Lara, we've been working on this for over a year now. What's your limit?"

"What do you mean, my limit?"

"What — how much you're willing to spend. Your legal fees."

"But I asked you to bill me regularly. You've never sent a bill."

"Actually, I put one in the mail yesterday. You should have it tomorrow. I should have asked you earlier what your limit was."

"I don't have a limit," she was starting to feel the tension in his voice and in her shoulders. It was creeping up her neck and had hit the base of her skull.

"I need a limit," he said firmly. "Just give me a limit." She was getting on his nerves and she knew it.

"I have to give you a limit?" *Why* she thought and didn't dare to ask.

"Yes, a limit."

"Ok," she thought for a moment. "Ten thousand dollars. Is that a good limit?"

"It will do, thank you," he hung up. One month later the second bill arrived. Ten thousand dollars had been reached with no reason at all. Lara knew their lawyer had been told to close down the case. He wanted out of the picture.

Around that time Lara went to Washington to meet with one of the major negotiators on arms control with Russia (she wondered if they had ever used the Jungian theory of shadowing). She stayed with Alex's godfather, Ambassador Robinson McIlvaine, whom they had known in the Congo and needed to speak with him one more time about Peter. Bob had sent her a letter a while back saying the reason Peter had been sent out on reconnaissance with the United Nations Team was because he was the one who knew the country best — it had been his suggestion. The letter also stated that he had spoken to the Chief of Station at the time and that Peter was not working for the CIA. The evening of her arrival they talked about Joe Rosenburg, a Jungian analyst, and her meeting with Paul Nitze, top U.S. negotiator with Russia, the next day. She finally got around to Peter. "You know I hired a lawyer to find out about Peter." Bob's head spun around to look her squarely in the eye.

"I thought you gave up on that."

"Bob, you know I can't. I need to know — my body still goes into spasm every Spring around Easter — not knowing is still too difficult for me, and, you know, the children also need to know."

"Lara, it would be wise to try to move on in your life," he said kindly. "I've asked around — where I could. Please, let it drop."

"If Lara needs to know — it's normal that she keeps trying." Lois, Bob's wife, broke in. "Lara, you know I worked for the CIA for several years. The problem is, the files from about 1954 through '65 are still a blank page in the history of the CIA. It will be a long time before they're open to the public." Bob gave Lois a dirty look as if to say: 'Stay out of this and for God's sake don't encourage her to continue.'

"You know, Lara, it could be dangerous to push too hard. If they don't want you, or anyone for that matter, to know something, they can cause a lot of problems," Bob insisted.

"Thanks for the warning," she said, thinking *they've already started the harassment.* She felt the conversation wasn't going to go any farther and bid them good night. On her way down the stairs to her room she stopped to listen to their quiet conversation.

"Lois, please don't get mixed up in this. Don't offer to help. Lawrence Devlin told me, 'if she's your friend, warn her it could be dangerous — not to go on with her inquiries would be the best for her. The Agency isn't talking.' So what can I do?" he sighed. "Obviously something went wrong. He was killed. By whom and why I'll never know either." She heard the end of the conversation, went to bed and cried herself to sleep.

The meeting the next day with Nitze was a total disaster, a lesson in humility and her trip to Washington a waste of time. She contested the ten thousand dollar bill from her lawyers, paid only half and let things drop for the time being.

They moved from New York to New Hampshire and a few years later Philip had a heart attack and died suddenly. Lara was devastated. The four children came to her rescue as much as they could and when she was finally feeling well enough they encouraged her to look for another lawyer. One who couldn't be scared away. Both Tia and Alex had read up on the short time span of their parents' life together. They passed their research on to Lara, who started taking notes of her own. Again she made inquiries about finding another lawyer. Philip's cousin, Michael, taught at Vermont Law School and she met with him several times. She gave him her documents and waited to hear from him.

Michael Kelly was meticulous — he read every document — pointed out to Lara the sloppiness of the previous lawyer's letters to the different government agencies and said it would be wise to start again. He would ask a colleague who was used to working with government agencies. The months that followed were fascinating for Lara.

She drove up to South Royalton and the Law School, surrounded by mist and melting snow. She was excited and anxious, needed a lot of help and wanted the meeting to go well. She quickly got out of the car, slammed the door, which caught her scarf. *Slow down, girl,* she thought, her heart pounding with apprehension. Michael came to greet her.

"Hi, you're right on time!" His large dark eyes showed affection, as did his bear hug when he enfolded her in his warmth. "Lousy weather. How were my directions?"

"Perfect. Thanks." She looked at him inquisitively. He was dressed in a black, wide-cabled turtleneck and tweed sports jacket, rumpled gray flannel pants and LL Bean boots. His salt and pepper hair and beard matched the jacket. No coat and tie for professors in South Royalton. Life was relaxed here and it was rubbing off on Lara.

"We have a few minutes before Jeremy joins us — want to have a look around?" She looked at the buildings of the Law School. They looked like expanded homes; most of them white clapboard, many of them facing the town green. It was a beautiful setting even in the fog and reflected cloudy light. *A perfect setting for a murder mystery,* she thought.

"Sure, I'd love a look around. It's a typical New England town — the square, a church, a railroad station?"

"That's a restaurant now, we'll have lunch there later." They walked through several buildings before reaching their meeting place. Jeremy was waiting for them. Greetings were brief as they sat down and got right to the core of Lara's request.

Jeremy started, "I need to know how serious you are about your search." Lara understood his tone of voice. He didn't want to waste his time nor that of his associates.

"It's been over thirty years. My children and I need to be able to put closure on Peter Landon's death — we can't do that without knowing the truth." She looked away. "Every year I relive the same story, Michael." She turned back to Michael, "You've told Jeremy the story, haven't you?" He nodded.

"Yes, but Jeremy might like to know more detail on particular moments; details of why you think Peter was killed rather than an accident, who you've seen," Michael said.

"Have you showed him the file?"

"Not yet — I thought we could take the file to lunch with us. He can flip through it very fast. It's here in the shopping bag." He lifted the white and black bag — papers going in all directions.

She ran through the facts as fast as she could without omission. A few facts were added. The doctor had said he had suffocated — if he had suffocated he would have lost his stools. This did not happen. He was under less than one meter of snow. Stanislas, the other skier who had been caught in the avalanche was under three meters. Peter's face was so

267

traumatized it took the doctor over two hours to push it back into place for Lara to view it. Stanislas's face went undamaged — all the more reason to think Peter had been badly beaten. She spoke about the people who had questioned her; about the incidents following Peter's death; the lapsed life insurance; the ten thousand dollars, which appeared from the company. It took under an hour — she had managed to remain unemotional — sticking to the facts and she was proud of herself. Lunch stayed very matter-of-fact. Jeremy was surprised by the sloppy work of her previous lawyer. "You know, Michael's right. You should start again." He looked at his watch. "I have to get to class — Michael, I'll be in touch. I have a couple of ideas." He rose to leave.

"Jeremy, thanks for your help. Let Michael know what I owe you for your time. I'll let you know if anything changes," Lara said with gratitude.

"Don't worry, this one is on me. They get away with too much — my pleasure to help." He walked out. Michael and Lara continued to talk about another idea. Michael had a friend, Henry Parker, who was being transferred by his newspaper to Moscow. His wife had gotten into the files of the KGB to gather information for a documentary on Ho Chi Minh. Perhaps Lara could get together with them. They could check the KGB files for her. Plans for the trip to Washington were made from a pay phone in town. The flight via New York turned into a nightmare. A snowstorm forced her plane to Atlanta, and she had to change terminals in both New York and Atlanta to get to National Airport in Washington. Thank goodness she only had carry-on baggage, so she played it to the hilt. She checked to see if she was being followed, tried to put peoples' faces to memory. Then, realizing the huge size of the crowd in Atlanta made this impossible; she looked at the way people moved, at what they were wearing. She could duck out of sight if she felt the need — run with the crowd, not against it, blend in, become a no one, nothingness. Still, her name was on her plane ticket, her hotel room on her credit card. It would have been easy just to pick her up once she had gotten to where she was going. She was trying to play Peter's game — or was she paranoid?

Her meeting in Washington was interesting. Both Henry and his wife were intrigued by her story. However, once in Moscow he called Michael and told him he was unable to help. It would jeopardize his job. Another dead end.

Since 1993 Lara had collected stories and newspaper articles about the CIA. She wrote to friends who might have known about Peter's involvement with the Agency. The only thing that came to light was that many of them thought he had worked for the CIA but no one "knew." She and the children asked former classmates what kind of a friend he had been; what kind of stories people could share about this man who they didn't have time to get to know. Few had stories — even his ushers from their wedding had little to say. He had been a very private man.

A few years later Lara met Ben — one of Peter's best buddies. They had gone on job interviews together during their last year at Yale. They had been interviewed by the CIA. Ben knew Peter had been asked back for another interview, and then went to Washington. That was probably when Peter would have been asked to be a covert agent. Lara had come across a CV stating he had been in Army intelligence — his training must have been given, at least part of it, during his military service.

Things were beginning to add up. The new lawyer in Washington didn't get anywhere. Peter's State Department file had disappeared, except for his death certificate. She needed something in writing to go to court for the files, and they had nothing. Then one evening at a dinner party in New York — the ninetieth birthday of the Dean of an Episcopal Church who had helped both Lara and Larry Alden after the deaths of their loved ones, Larry walked over and greeted Lara.

"Hi. You look smashing," Larry said.

"Thanks, you're looking pretty good yourself," Lara answered. "Where's that beautiful wife of yours?"

"You know she teaches autistic children, she couldn't get away in time to make it up here. It's good to see you. It's been a long time. Why don't you come to Washington more often?"

"It seems I'm always on the go. I've been down a couple of times since Philip died. I still spend lots of time in France. Peter's children live there. Tia in the South, Alex in Paris with his two kids. Never seems there's time enough for everything."

The usual peck on the cheek, his light blue eyes looking deeply into hers as he asked, "Where are you in your search?"

"Nowhere," she felt shocked by the question and hoped it didn't show on her face. "The stone wall is still up." *And why do you ask now? Is it because I just hired a new lawyer and they — the CIA — want to know what I know,* she thought rapidly. *Play it cool, girl, no emotion — don't let it show.* "Why?" That was what her son told her to say when she was in a tight spot, 'Why do you ask?'

"You know, I was also an undercover agent when I first joined the government." She thought *and your cover was the State Department.* He continued, "My first post was as a student at the University of Madrid."

You were probably keeping an eye on the political situation shortly after Franco had been named dictator and regent of Spain for life. The Second World War was over and life was slowly returning to normal all over Europe except, of course, for the Iron Curtain. We had to keep our friends in line, Lara thought. *Peter's cover was the oil companies.*

He continued, "I was an American student at the University of Madrid for a short period, then I joined the State Department." Lara thought: *Once in intelligence, always in intelligence.*

"Then you were stationed all over, Africa, Paris and became Ambassador?" she asked. Lara later learned that his specialty was terrorism. He was touring the world instructing people of other countries about terrorism and working out agreements with other governments with mutual interests. The conversation ended there when dinner was announced. Lara's heart was beating hard. Someone she knew well had just told her Peter had been a secret agent for the CIA, or was it some other government department. It was now verbally confirmed. She wanted to know more and knew she would have to wait until she could see Larry again — privately.

Several months went by. Lara decided to call Larry about their brief conversation in New York. It was perfect timing — she needed to be in Baltimore for the christening of a grandson — she called and asked.

"Hi Larry, it's Lara, how does it feel to be back in your own home after living abroad so many years? And how's retirement?"

"Great! We're so glad we kept the house. It's needed a lot of work," he laughed. "I think I'm in better shape today than I've been in years, cleaning the place up," he paused, "By any chance are you coming to Washington?"

"I was thinking of it. Remember what you said about working for the CIA when we saw each other at the Dean's birthday party?" She took a deep breath praying she would say the right thing and not scare him off. "I'd like to talk to you about Peter — since you were just across the river from us in Africa. Actually, I could use your help."

"Did you ever think Peter was with the CIA?" he asked, remembering what he had told her at the Dean's party.

"Probably. He never told me anything. You knew that, and now — well, could we have lunch? I'll tell you the story when I see you."

"Let me ask Kate. Where can I reach you?"

The visit took place on a cold early spring morning in Chevy Chase. Larry listened carefully and decided he would try to find out what he could from friends still working for the Agency. It would take some time.

It took six months — a letter arrived. It said if Peter was "deep cover" she'd never get his file. The file was probably put away someplace in West Virginia where no one could get to it — not even past or present members of the CIA. She later heard a friend say, "deep cover, that means if you're caught, the government will not admit you were working for them." Then dead or alive, it was the same thing. They would never admit to Lara that Peter had worked for the CIA.

Chapter Thirty-five

It was eight fifteen in the morning. Sobeké put down his morning paper, got up and walked to the window that looked out over the Alexandria harbor. This had been his office for many years, ever since he'd left Aswân in 1971 after the inauguration of the dam. While reading today's newspaper he noticed an article about a single-engine aircraft that had been discovered by Bedouins near the Kharga oasis. Winds had swept sand away from the propellers and a wing tip. The Bedouins had completely uncovered the plane. There was a small picture of the Max Holste Broussard and an enlarged picture of the three bullet holes which Sobeké remembered taping up.

It was a short article — one that brought back many memories. As he stood watching the excavation of old Alexandria — three cities, one on top of the other — his mind returned to the past. The work he had done for so many governments. That nice American, Peter Landon and his lovely wife. Peter's death had saved him from his own, put him on guard and made him aware of his own disposability. He hoped that his work with the pharmaceutical companies and research labs had helped preserve mankind. But, now it was time to go look for Felix. Sobeké had seen Felix wandering the building site at Aswân, and had even spoken to him since, by then Sobeké was supervising a work crew. But Sobeké had lost a lot of weight, grown a full mustache and beard, and his hair had turned gray — even white in places. Felix hadn't recognized him.

One evening Sobeké followed him to his hotel and had snuck in at night to leave Felix a note under his door.

I am alive and well. One day I will find you, we will talk, then I will kill you. — Sobeké.

For the next three days Felix hunted for Sobeké. He returned to the dam site. He spoke to many of Sobeké's employers: in personnel, accounting. Felix spoke to Sobeké again without recognizing him. He was carrying a gun for self-defense. Sobeké had his knife, but it was too early. He wanted Felix to feel as tormented as he had when he flew back to Egypt after delivering the doctor. Twenty years had gone by. Now that the plane had been found, Felix would know that Sobeké was looking for him.

At Aswân Sobeké spoke only Arabic: he had moved into the import-export business and he was able to use his fluency in several languages — French, English, German and Russian — which he had picked up working for them at the dam. He had contacts all over the world, and now he would put them to work. Sobeké's passport read Khrim Laika, born 8 September 1928 in Alexandria. It made him a few years older — he looked older from all the outdoor work he had done, and his hair had turned completely white with a yellow tinge. His dark brown eyes were bloodshot and constantly moving. His sixth sense was at its most acute as it had been since he became Khrim. While at Aswân and during his time off at the dam he helped the archeologists with their digs, saving what he could hide for himself, which he sold several years later at a huge profit, and handing over the less valuable objects. He had maintained his contact with the archeologists, thinking they could be a help to him in the future. His first call was to one of them.

"Hello Ted, Khrim here. How's it going up North with your beautiful English weather?"

"How'd you know where to find me, old pal? You still digging down your way?" The crisp British accent replied.

"Once in the loop, always in the loop. I have a few new pieces to show you." His eye wandering around his office already choosing the few pieces he would take to tempt his friend. "Thought I might hop on a flight for London tomorrow."

"What's your hurry, Khrim? You in trouble?"

"No, I feel like getting out of the sun and dust. They're tearing up this place, you know. A few days of fog never hurt me." He was watching some children emerge from a new and unexplored area and he planned to visit it that evening. Perhaps he could find a few new objects to bring with him. "I'll get a room at my usual hotel, give you a call when I get in," he paused, "you will be there on Saturday, right?"

Ted checked his agenda, "Fine, old pal. I'll keep Saturday free for you."

Sobeké told his assistant and secretary that he was leaving for a few weeks. He gave no reason and told them he would not be available. They would have to manage without him. It wasn't the first time, in fact it occurred quite often. That night Sobeké slithered into the narrow hole from which the children had emerged. He was still wiry and supple and knew exactly what he was doing. The cavern was small — he had to crawl on his belly, a flashlight attached to his head. He entered a chamber, was able to stand, saw where the children had come from and continued, discreetly marking his path in case he had to return the same way. He had lost his way once before and it had taken him two days to emerge. He spent a few hours exploring, saw nothing worth while to add to this collection, found a different exit and decided he had what he needed and went home.

Before he left London he changed the color of his hair, obtained a new passport and a few new clothes. It hadn't taken him long to find Felix, even though Felix had been given a new identity with a new name. He had become a reputable banker with a facelift, so as to look younger for his young wife. He was living in a university town where archeology was an important subject, the university known for its research and participation at new archeological sites — where a local banker was asked regularly to teach a class or to confer on a new acquisition. Felix's love for the past had given him away.

Sobeké arrived in Cincinnati by car, one he had bought under his new identity. He took a room in the Hyatt Regency Hotel, one of the nicest his travel agent had suggested, but he also took a room at a small motel out of town on the way to the International airport. Since he had murder on his mind he needed a safe getaway. Canada was too far to drive, there were planes for Toronto and even direct to London. He knew he could disappear easily.

That afternoon he sat in his car outside the Credit Uppsa Bank, hoping to see Felix leave his office. He watched the people come and go, then realized Felix would probably drive home, so he walked around the block to see if there was a garage. He noticed the security cameras and decided not to go look for a car he didn't know, went back to his car and waited.

The sun had disappeared behind the city and it was getting cold. Sobeké got out of his car, put on his raincoat and a scarf and was turning to get back into the car when he saw a tall figure emerge from the closed office building. *That could be Felix,* he thought. He locked his car and followed the tall figure to a bar a block and a half away.

It was hot and stuffy in the bar, conversation loud and animated. Cocktail hour. He hoped to go unnoticed — his dark skin, dark hair and good looks drew attention, particularly from the single women sitting at the bar. He turned his head away from a foursome where he thought Felix was sitting. He saw that it was Felix, two men and a stunning woman in her late thirties — shiny black hair, light clear skin and very dark eyes. He took an empty seat at the bar as close to the foursome as possible between two ladies with long legs and mini skirts, plunging décolletés, showing as much of their breasts as was allowed in American public places.

"Hello, Sweetie, new in town?" one asked. Sobeké turned to look at her. She had puffed lips, probably full of silicone, as were her tits, which he took his time looking at. He wasn't interested.

"Whiskey soda, please." He asked the bartender. "No sweetie, just stopped by for a drink" and still looking her in the eye, "I'm not interested — gay, can't you tell?"

"You came to the wrong bar," the woman on the other side chipped in. "My name's Mila."

"Hi, Mila. I have what I need, thanks," he turned to his left and continued, "are you here often? The tall guy — behind me — do you know him? Good looking guy." She turned to look at the group.

"Which one? They're all good looking to me."

Sobeké turned and took a quick look at the group memorizing all he could about each one. "The one sitting next to the good looking woman, caressing her arm." He turned back to the bar, "guess he's not interested in men, right?"

"Oh, he's a banker, works not far from here," she sighed. "He only goes for the upper class chicks; wouldn't take a second look at Paula and me."

"Can I offer you both a drink?" Sobeké asked.

"Sure, thanks," they said in unison. Paula continued, "You'll have better luck a couple of blocks away. Turn left and left again on Gilbert Avenue. More fun for you there."

He paid for their drinks and left. He then waited, hidden in shadows, until Felix and his group appeared and split up. Sobeké followed Felix and the women to his garage. *What next?* He thought. He ran to his car, moved it to where he could see Felix pull out of the garage. He waited for over half an hour and then he saw the woman walk out. The car followed a few minutes later. "They must have done it in the car," he said out loud to himself, "and he doesn't even take her back home. Or maybe she's going for her next client."

He followed Felix home to the same address he had been given by Ted and returned to his hotel for the night. The next day he would call the archeology department at the University, stop off with his letter of introduction and then check out the wife. It would be a full day.

He met Eleanore, Felix's wife, in the parking lot of a supermarket. He had followed her around the store, caught her attention, smiled at her and openly followed her out to her car. She was flattered by the attention of this good-looking man.

"Can I help you with your groceries?", he said picking up a paper bag stuffed with vegetables.

"Do I have a choice? You're already holding my bag, or," she hesitated, "are you about to walk off with it?"

Sobeké gave her as wide a smile as he could showing a beautiful set of clean white teeth and put the bag back in the cart. "May I start again? Can I help you with your groceries?"

"Why, thank you. Yes, please," she opened the trunk of the car and, embarrassed by the mess, closed the tailgate. "Just put it in the back seat. Are you new in town? Your accent sounds very British, and very charming."

"Yes, I came a few days ago, will be working at the University," he said as he put the last bags in the car and closed the door. "Can I offer you a cup of coffee somewhere?", looking deep into her pale green eyes. She was a plump plain woman, a little dowdy, and definitely not very sexy. A woman whose husband would not have to worry about her going off with another man.

"Oh," she was taken by surprise. "I don't know. I should get home."

"A quick cup of coffee somewhere — do they have a cup of coffee in the supermarket?"

"There's a coffee shop over there," she smiled and nodded in the direction behind Sobeké. "My name's Eleanore," putting out a hand. "What's yours?"

"Sobeké," he answered shaking the offered hand and holding it longer than usual. They walked to the coffee shop chatting easily. He could feel her sexual energy flowing freely; her eyes twinkled when she looked at him. She was flirting with him and he was showing how delightful he found her. He asked when he could see her again.

"You know I'm married," she showed her wedding band.

"Shall we have lunch tomorrow? You tell me where and what time is convenient." He insisted, "somewhere I can take a married woman where we can enjoy ourselves."

"May I call you?" she asked. "Do you have a car?"

"Yes, my car is out in the parking lot. May I pick you up?"

I don't want the neighbors seeing me go off with a stranger, she thought. "I'll call you and let you know. Where can I reach you?"

"The Hyatt Regency, room 333. If I'm not in maybe you can leave a message. I have nothing planned tomorrow until four o'clock."

"I really have to go," she said getting up.

"Please wait, I'll pay and walk you to your car."

"You don't have to do that."

"I'd like to," he said, leaving enough cash to cover the bill and taking her arm. They walked in silence to the car. She got in and opened her window to say good-bye. He put his head in the window and said, "You have beautiful green eyes," and kissed her gently on the lips before letting her go.

"Bye," he said as she pulled away. The rest of the day he explored the city, checked on Felix's activities, found a private eye willing to take pictures of adultery for a decent price and returned to his hotel to wait for the phone call. There was no need to wait. He picked up her message at the desk. 'Eleven thirty at the supermarket parking lot' was all it said. He went out in search of the poorer part of town, looking for a homeless man who would enjoy a night in jail. Supper in the 'Ten Minute Diner' provided him with what he wanted. The man was clean and had shaved within the last twenty-four hours, his clothes as neat as they could be for someone who lived in them constantly, and he resembled Sobeké in size although not in looks. They worked out a deal: two nights, if they didn't get caught the first night. They walked back to the car and drove out to the suburbs, leaving the car a few blocks from Felix's house.

"You're just a peeping Tom, nothing more. Your wife left you destitute. You like to see people doing it. So you were checking out this house. The bus stop is a few blocks away. Do you ever get to ride free?" Sobeké asked.

"I hitch a ride at night in town — never been out here before. Where'd you say the bus stops out here?" Joe asked. He looked around at the quiet street lined with comfortable houses, some with light shining from the windows, some black with just a light at the front door.

"Come on, I'll show you."

"Didn't you say you'd pay me before we do anything?" Joe sounded worried. He never had spent a night in jail and although it was getting cold out he didn't like the idea. This was all new to him.

"Yes, I'll pay before we get near the house." Then Sobeké added, "Where will you hide the money in case the police check your pockets? You don't want any questions about a lot of money."

"Come on man — fifty bucks isn't a lot of money," Joe said with a sneer. "and it's fifty again tomorrow, right?" He pulled out his shirt, lowered the waistline of his pants and pointed to an inside patch on his underpants. "I have to hide any money I have or they steal it in your sleep."

"There's the bus. See where it stops?"

"Yeah. Oh, I can find it."

"You'll take it back tonight. Tomorrow you need to be seen and the police need to see you too. Come on, we need to catch them before they go to bed and turn the light out."

"I thought you said we'd see them screwing."

"I have a feeling that's wishful thinking."

The streets were empty except for a car full of neighbors pulling into their garage. They were two men out for a walk, nothing more. As they approached the house they saw a man and woman in heated discussion. They ducked behind some bushes next to the house, snuck up to a window and looked in.

"You're coming home later and later. We never get to bed together — you're always too tired." She started to cry. "You don't love me any more." She sobbed, "I bet you're out screwing another woman. What if I hired a private detective and had you followed," she turned and walked out of the living room and slammed the door behind her. They could not see her running up the stairs and realized they'd never know if she got screwed or not.

"Honey," they heard him call after her. Then he mumbled to himself, "Shit, it's been months and all of a sudden she's interested in sex again. I wonder what happened."

Sobeké gave Joe a nudge and they moved away. "We'll have to get here earlier tomorrow."

Sobeké picked up Eleanore at eleven thirty as planned. "Where to?" he asked.

"Alexandria, it's just a few miles south of here in Kentucky, a discreet restaurant. Tell me about yourself." He took a quick glance at her, keeping his eyes on the road.

"It's funny," he said slowly weighing his words. "Have you ever been to Alexandria in Egypt?"

"No, have you?"

"Yes, it's a beautiful city." How much did he want her to know? He planned to return to his work there, had not given his current name — if he was sought for murder — that would ruin it all. And Felix would know where to look for him if things didn't work out. "I come from Beirut, Lebanon," and he continued his story until they found the cozy restaurant. From the restaurant they went to a motel and from the motel back to the parking lot. They had been followed all the way, photographed kissing as they entered their motel room, photographed in bed. The detective was even able to get a photograph of her nude in the shower and was pleased with his work. He was curious and wanted to know the what and why, but knew better than to ask any questions.

That evening he photographed a man screwing a whore in the back of a car in an underground garage. Unfortunately, this time the woman saw him and he had to make a dash. He was roaring with laughter as he ducked into an alley and into the back door of a bar he had never been to before. He had at least fifteen pictures of the scene, dressed and partially undressed, the woman naked except for her stockings. He made an easy getaway since they couldn't run after him half naked. He was sitting chatting with the girls at the bar when he saw the prostitute walk in. He quickly turned, paid his drink, hid his camera under his jacket and walked out, hoping she hadn't noticed him. He rendezvoused with Sobeké an hour later.

"I think you'll like what I got for you today," the photographer smirked as he handed over two envelopes. They were standing under a lamppost in the commercial part of town where most offices were empty and so were the streets. Sobeké pulled out the first set — very clear images — he'd have to eliminate the ones where he could be recognized. "Good, very good," he said with a smile. "And the others?" He pulled out the series of quick shots. "You couldn't catch him getting dressed with the girl in the picture?"

"She saw me. I had to run," he sniffed. "They hadn't finished. I could see he was off her and would come after me so I split. I know where she hangs out if you want me to get more pictures. Maybe with someone else?"

"No, I have enough with these, thanks. Where are the negatives?"

"That wasn't part of the deal. That will cost you another five hundred."

Sobeké was furious. "What do you mean, not part of the deal. If you want five more you'd better hand them over fast."

"I don't have them with me." Sobeké grabbed the man's collar.

"Well, let's go get them right now." He started pushing the photographer against the wall. "This is not the smartest move you've made," pulling the photographer's arm behind his back. They started to walk down the street,

"Where's your lab?"

"We're going the wrong way," the photographer cringed.

"We need to hurry. I have another appointment and can't be late." They turned and ran the few blocks to the photography shop. Sobeké checked the two rolls of film. They were his — then he went through the whole store and lab looking for a set of extra prints. If this guy wanted more money, he'd be ready to play the blackmail game and Sobeké couldn't afford that. He needed to find the extra prints.

"I didn't make extra prints," the man cried as he saw his lab and shop ransacked.

"Sorry, Buddy, I can't believe you." There was only one file cabinet for photos. Sobeké flipped through them fast, found what he was looking for. "So, you didn't make extra prints? What are these?"

"My lab tech must have made the extra copies," he babbled.

"You don't have a 'lab tech', do you?"

"OK," he said, "Forget the extra five hundred. I'll forget I ever did any work for you. And while you're still here, can you untie me?"

"Sorry, Buddy, I'll be back when I've finished my work. Or, if you're lucky, maybe your 'lab tech' will be in one day and untie you." Sobeké took the keys and locked the door behind him after turning out all the lights and stuffing a cloth in the photographer's mouth.

He found Joe pacing by the bus stop. "Sorry I'm late," he called out the open window. "Hop in, I want to drive around a few blocks." They circled as if lost and finally came to a stop where they had parked the night before. They had driven past the house twice — the first time it looked as if no one was home, the second time the lights were on only downstairs. They walked in silence, ducked behind the bushes and watched a scene of violence. They were yelling at each other and it was hard to catch a word. Sobeké talked into Joe's ear. "It's time they had a glimpse of you — are you ready?" Joe nodded.

"I'll see you tomorrow evening at the "Ten Minute Diner" if you're out — otherwise the next day. They never keep people like you very long."

His thoughts were running as he moved away to watch from a distance. Joe kept his head and shoulders visible for quite a while before Felix saw him and dashed to the window. Joe played dumb to the growl coming through the window at him and finally turned to walk away. Suddenly he heard the police siren. He tried to run but his legs wouldn't move. They were on him. He was caught, his heart pounding, his face showing terror. Sobeké hoped he'd regain his calm, stick to his story. They put him in the police car, spoke a few words to Felix, "Will you press charges?"

"Yes, of course. We can't have this kind of thing in our neighborhood."

"I'll expect you down at the station within the hour then."

"Yes, of course. Just give me a few minutes to calm the wife and I'll be over." Felix slammed the door behind him and went to find Eleanore sitting numbed in her large comfortable chair.

"There's something going on here, isn't there?" He said, pouring a whiskey. "You want one?"

"No thanks. And what do you mean, 'Something going on'?"

"Do you know that man?" Eleanore thought he looked like Sobeké and would never say so.

"Of course not. I never saw that face before. You're crazy. He's a peeping Tom, that's all." She cringed. "I don't like the idea of strangers watching us, though," she paused, "if you had hit me I'd ask him to be a witness." She got up and headed for the stairs. "I'm going to take a bath. You'd better get going to the station."

"Tart," Felix said under his breath as he walked out the door, got into his car and drove away.

Sobeké walked into the house and called, "Eleanore, are you there?"

"Sobeké, is that you? What are you doing here?" She was startled, half undressed with the water running.

"I saw what happened. Are you all right?" He walked up the stairs and took her in his arms. "Everything's going to be all right." He walked her back into the bathroom, finished undressing her, caressing her as he went and put her in the bath to calm her down.

"Can I rub your back," he asked as he pulled up a stool to sit beside her.

"No, thanks. I just want to soak."

"How long will your husband be away?"

"Don't know, at least an hour I think," she looked at him longingly.

"Would you consider spending the night with me? I'm sure we could find a motel somewhere," he said as he reached for her hand. "Has your man been giving you a hard time?" Her look was perplexed. She wondered how he knew she was alone. He must have been watching from outside somewhere. The police had taken off one man. He looked like Sobeké, but Sobeké was here beside her — holding her hand.

"How did you know I was alone?"

"I was out driving around, heard the police sirens and came to see what was going on." He smiled. "I saw you sitting in a big chair and wanted to

281

be with you. I saw a man walk out the door and drive away. The rest is evident," he leaned forward to kiss her, she moved to meet his lips. She ducked completely under the water and came up saying,

"I'll be right with you, if you'll let me get dressed first."

Eleanore packed a few things in a small case hoping she'd be away a long time and left a note for her husband:

Have gone to spend the night with a friend — will call and did not bother to sign it.

They left the house and went looking for a motel.

Felix returned to an empty house, read Eleanor's note and thought to himself, *good riddance*. He found the bathtub still full of water, wondered why and went to bed.

The next morning there was an envelope on his desk at the office marked "Personal and confidential." He hadn't given another thought to his wife until he saw the pictures. It had been a long time since he had felt fear. It grabbed at his belly, he looked inside the envelope, saw a small piece of paper, "Affectionately, Sobeké." Now it was more than fear that overcame him because there was one picture of him with the prostitute in the package and he knew his reputation could be ruined. What would his colleagues think, and worse, what about his children? Then he thought about the University staff. There wouldn't be a single place he would still be accepted. And if he lived — if Sobeké didn't get him — he'd have to change his name again, his looks, his residence — everything. He had a terrible feeling of doom, wanted to run before Sobeké could catch him, and he didn't know where to go. He had a perfect life — didn't want to lose it. Maybe he'd find Sobeké first and kill him. His troubles could be over if he could create the perfect crime and get rid of the body. His mind wandered on until the phone rang. He jumped to answer.

"Yes."

"Mr. Sob-" his secretary hesitated.

"Sobeké?"

"Mr. Sobeké is here to see you. He said you have an appointment with him."

"I don't know a Mr. Sobeké, and as you can tell, there's no appointment on my calendar." Felix said as he looked at his watch. *8:47, how'd he get in so early?*

"I'm sorry sir, Mr. Sobeké insists on seeing you." She sounded frightened.

She didn't like the dark bearded man whose long black hair covered his ears and was pulled back in a ponytail and wanted him out of the office as soon as possible. He had a strange spicy smell about him that made her feel even sicker than she had when she saw him walk in the door.

"What did you say his name is?" Felix asked, "and what does he look like?"

" Sobeké, sir. He's tall and dark."

It sounded like Sobeké when he was young. It also sounded as if he was trapped. "Please have him come in." Felix stood so as not to be intimidated by his visitor, his desk drawer was slightly open. He could reach for the gun.

"I'm not going to take much of your time this morning," was Sobeké's greeting. The secretary closed the door. They were alone.

"How did you find me?"

"Everyone seems to be asking the same question these days. The point is, I did find you." And Sobeké didn't leave a second for Felix to speak. "You thought you had killed me, right? Well, when I read about Peter Landon and his so-called accidental death, I knew you'd come after me. It seemed like part of the clean-up process. And I didn't take any chances. You spoke to me twice at Aswân. You didn't recognize me." Sobeké laughed. They stood facing each other. "So I dropped you a note, remember?" Felix felt fear at the memory. "I could have killed you then, even with you carrying a gun. My knife would have been faster."

"What do you want?" Felix interrupted.

"Why did you have Peter killed?"

"He knew too much, wanted out. We couldn't let him go." Felix, on his guard slowly sat down behind his desk, ready to reach for his gun. "You've been smart, kept your mouth shut. Nobody is going to bother you."

"You're right because nobody knows I'm alive — even you don't know." Sobeké moved quickly around the desk, slammed the desk drawer closed as he pushed Felix away in his chair. "We're going for a walk." He opened the drawer of the desk, took the gun, concealed it in the palm of his hand partially covered by his jacket sleeve and pulled Felix out of his chair, shoving him toward the door. "Leave quietly or you'll regret it. Tell your secretary your wife isn't well — we're going to pick her up." He opened the door and giving the impression that he was helping Felix along they left the building, then turned and walked around to the underground garage.

Felix was unable to get control of himself, unable to fight back. He hoped for a moment of distraction, which never came. They drove out to the country. He knew he was going to die. He thought of the men and women who were dead because of his instructions and felt the reality of what they had felt. He had never killed anyone himself, but that didn't help his conscience.

Two days later an article appeared in the local paper. "Well known banker and anthropologist commits suicide." It stated that pictures of the banker with a prostitute could — was probably the reason for his death. His wife could not be found for questioning.

Sobeké had returned to untie the detective, warned him again to be discreet and had helped Eleanore leave town before taking his flight out of the country.

Chapter Thirty-six

Peter's mother died suddenly. With her died a part of her past — a part Lara would never know. She lived in a world she had created. Her desires, inspirations, whatever she wanted to be; all of these she had created. There was little reality or truth in her world, so what could Lara have known about her? And when Lara asked about her past — it, too, was what she had created for herself in her mind, what she wanted to be. Lara never really knew Ida and she never really knew her son — and yet they were married. Thirty years later the desire to know kept coming back — waking her at four in the morning.

Ida died with so many questions unanswered. If Lara could piece it together she might come up with the story of Peter's life.

Peter was born in Wiesbaden in 1930. His mother, Ida Hazen, was born in Frankfurt in 1908, his father; Mark Steinberg was born in Neustadt, Germany in 1893. They were married in Frankfurt in January 1930, two months after his divorce. People who knew them said it was a tumultuous marriage. Ida loved parties and spent a lot of money on clothes and on her pleasurable distractions. She was beautiful, vivacious, fascinating and had that wonderful quality of attracting friends. Blond hair, blue eyes that sparkled, twinkled, teased and a petite figure always well dressed in a classic style that one could only compliment. About Mark, Lara knew little. It is said he was handsome, and so he must have been, for their son was a handsome, charming young man when she met him and remained so until he died. Mark was a banker and an officer in the German Army. Was this possible? Hitler was in power. Would he have had a Jewish Army officer?

"Society" at the time did not accept Jews who were forced to live amongst themselves and who created a reputation of being smarter than most, making money hand over fist, and provoking jealousy for those who were not so clever.

As for Ida, she learned what men liked, wanted, desired, and used it to advance in her life. She used sex when she was to pass her *Abitur* and her math scores were not going to help.

Lara was told that one rainy evening she made sure to leave school just when her math teacher usually headed home. They walked out together; Ida seduced him. Needless to say, she passed her math exams and with some extra tutoring passed the *Abitur*.

One pleasant Sunday afternoon in June at a church fair to benefit the poor, Ida was standing behind a counter selling champagne. Men ogled her, their wives pulling them away once they had bought a bottle or two. At mid-afternoon she noticed a tall elegant man watching her. He seemed different from the others, slightly tan, deep blue eyes, she guessed he must be in his late thirties and he looked very rich. She smiled at him as he walked over and stood silently across the counter. Lara could imagine the conversation.

"Allow me to introduce myself. I am Mark Steinberg and I would be honored by your presence at my table this evening." Ida pretended to be surprised but she had seen so many men approach her and although only nineteen, there was nothing that could inhibit her self-confidence.

"Thank you for your invitation. Unfortunately I have to stay here until the end of the evening to sell our champagne." Both were smiling and flirting, amused with each other's composure.

"The only thing to do in that case is to buy the remainder of your champagne. What do I owe you?" he asked as he pulled out his wallet. "Now you are free to leave. Will you join me for dinner?"

She had no choice. A candle-lit dinner, amusing conversation, seductive music, they fell in love. Unfortunately, Mark was married, yet he still proposed saying he would get a divorce and she should not tell her parents until he was free to marry her. For the next six months they lived a passionate love affair. Ida was in bliss. She had found a man who could give her everything she would ever want. Her marriage was guaranteed as soon as the divorce went through. She had an innate ability to manipulate men and knew Mark would do anything for her. He had become a lovesick adolescent at age thirty-six. The divorce was final in November 1929. They were married in Frankfurt in January 1930.

They moved from Frankfurt to Amsterdam where she found the social life exhilarating. Men were very attentive to her, sensing they might have the opportunity of getting into bed with her. The men usually sent flowers to thank her — she would switch the card so Mark wouldn't know about her lovers. Unfortunately she immediately became pregnant and as her figure changed so did the attitude of her new admirers. Their son Peter was born in November 1930. Mother and child were fine. Ida never liked babies and immediately hired a *schwester* to take care of Peter. After Peter's birth, Mark became aloof, preoccupied. *Probably,* she thought, *because of the business.* Little did she know that the depression of '29 had affected their finances to such an extent that Mark was having a hard time fulfilling his obligations. He had bought a small townhouse in Paris for her. The house in Amsterdam was larger and more comfortable. He was running two businesses besides taking an important place in the direction of one of Holland's largest international banks. One of his greatest problems was the fact that he was a Jew and Hitler was closing down businesses in Germany that belonged to Jews. He had been slighted on his last two trips to Frankfurt and had been told that his bank would be more successful if someone who was not a Jew came to do their business. He could no longer sell his fragrant soaps in Germany, nor toothpaste and other dental products from his own companies, and Germany was one of his major clients. The world financial markets were in a slump with no signs of recuperating. His bank had made loans for the purchase of the two townhouses, his soap business, and Ida's cash withdrawals plus the interest payments were more than he could handle. He was headed for bankruptcy and realized she was unable to understand. She thought the Nazi threat was just a bunch of hoodlums the German government couldn't control and that eventually they would disappear.

He was desperate. He would have to tell his wife even if she didn't want to listen. He asked her to stay home one evening.

"We need to talk. There are things I need to tell you and things we need to discuss."

"You know I have accepted an invitation to Alex van der Kentzen's ball for this evening. My clothes are all laid out and I was on my way upstairs to change."

"Ida, we need to talk now."

"Mark, don't be ridiculous, darling. Why don't you come to the ball with me? It will be good for you to get out, have some fun. All you do is sit and drink all night. The only time I see you happy is when you play with Peter. After he goes to bed you sit in that chair of yours and don't say a word. Please come. All of Amsterdam will be there to see you with the most beautiful woman at the party. We can talk about your serious things tomorrow."

He hadn't heard a word of what she said. "You will sit down with me now," he said as forcefully as he could. "You never stay home, take care of our son, all you want is to go out to parties." At that moment he knew he had lost control of his wife. He couldn't shield her from the truth. He couldn't even get her to listen to him.

She came over to him, kissed him on his forehead and said, "Tomorrow, dear, tomorrow you can tell me what has been bothering you all these months. I'm sure it can wait a few hours." She turned and went upstairs to dress. He disappeared into the kitchen and she did not seek him out to say goodnight, not wanting to be detained from her ball.

Mark felt more alone than ever, yet he didn't feel sad, just tired, very tired. Once he heard the car leave with the chauffeur, he went upstairs to visit with his son to say goodbye. He was unable to give her the few hours she had said he could wait. He was going for a drive from which he would never return.

Mark died in May 1932. He drove the car into a tree and was killed instantly. Ida learned about the financial problems, sold the house in Amsterdam and moved to Paris with Peter, Schwester and the cook in June of that same year. She made a success of herself entering all realms of Paris society. Her child did not limit her encounters with eligible men and women who helped her advance in society. They were very generous in gifts of money or objects she would sell to maintain her lifestyle and in June of 1936 she married a handsome Polish count — a diplomat at the Polish embassy in Paris who was head over heels in love with her and willing to take on her son.

Her life was wonderful until 1939 and the spread of Nazism. The war started and Ida worried about her survival and the survival of her son and so the necessary action was taken and plans made for their departure for the United States. During the time they were married, Peter had told Lara what he remembered of his childhood. Of course Ida played a big part.

Lara learned much more about Peter's life after his mother died because she needed legal papers proving that Ida was Peter's mother, and therefore Tia and Alex's grandmother. It was a matter of French taxes. If the inheritance is in a direct line there would be a 20 percent tax; if indirect or of no family relationship the tax was 60 percent. Since Lara's children had not inherited from their father, it was important to her that the children inherit from their grandmother.

In 1993 Ida had been hospitalized in a coma. The doctor said she probably would never regain consciousness. Philip and Lara returned to Paris twenty-four hours after they had returned home from a long trip. Exhausted, they met up with Tia at the American Hospital. They were relieved — Ida came to. She had no will — had never told her Notary she had grandchildren. No power of attorney either — all was taken care of before she was well enough to return home and died a few months later.

It was then things became complicated. Mr. Pouton, the Notary, informed Tia and Alex that he had emptied out a safety deposit box, produced a power of attorney permitting him to do so and told them the papers had been destroyed as she had requested.

"What was in the box?" Tia asked.

"That's of no concern to you," he answered with a disagreeable smile on his small face. He was a man in his mid-fifties, balding and rather unattractive.

"We need papers to prove Mamy was Papa's mother — were those papers destroyed too?" Alex asked as he started to lose his patience.

"No, of course not."

"Was there any money or gold bars? She said she had left some in a safety deposit box for us," Alex insisted.

"Now listen here, young man," Pouton said, his voice rising, "That's no way for you to talk to me. You need me to probate the will, so if you're not careful," he sneered, "you won't get anything." He stood up to make himself more important, walked around to lean against the front of his desk. "You have six months to prove you're her grandchildren, after that 60 percent goes to the government." He read the will out loud that Tia had succeeded in getting her grandmother to write and dismissed them.

Once out on the street they turned to their mother who had not opened her mouth at the meeting.

"I think we need to find a lawyer. He's not going to be of any help. And don't you think it's strange emptying out Mamy's safe?" Lara said.

The lawyer told them what they had to do — get a birth certificate, documents from the U.S. government, change of name, and just one thing after another.

Inquiries were made to the State Department and before they could process the request Lara met with Charlie Watteson, the American Ambassador to France, a charming friend whom she and Philip had come to know well in the States.

"Is this all on the up and up?" the Ambassador asked.

"Do you think I'd ask you for something that wasn't?" Lara replied. "It's very important for the children." They both turned to watch the conversation Tia and Alex were having with Mattie, the Ambassador's wife.

"Wait here a minute. I'm going to get the consul. He'll take a few notes, write a letter," Charlie smiled at her. "Don't worry, I sign the letter," and he walked off. "Oh, by the way, you know Larry Alden? He's still with the State Department." The ambassador turned and walked back to Lara.

"Yes, why?"

"Get him to write a letter too. That way you'll have a better chance of getting everything in time for the probate. He's living in Washington now."

With all their help, they had everything needed, except Pouton wasn't going forward with the probate and they needed to find another notary.

The papers that arrived from the State Department were full of information. Peter had arrived in New York on the *SS Washington* in May 1940. He was nine years old. Lara remembered Peter telling her about his crossing when they were living in Africa. She knew that Ida and the Count were divorced. She didn't know that Peter had not told her the truth about knowing his true father's name and that he was Jewish. *Why didn't he tell me?* She wondered. *Did he think I wouldn't marry him?* As far as she was concerned none of his friends thought he was any different than they were.

In going through the State Department file she found three different years of birth for Ida. Which one was the right one? And that Ida and Peter had been naturalized in 1945 through the request of the Count, who had received his citizenship in 1944 for services rendered to the U.S. during the War. The Count was a spy for the U.S.A. And why did Peter have to re-apply for citizenship while he was doing his military service if he was already a citizen? The State Department had documents asking for a name change — no signature either by Peter or Ida. Other photocopies were so poor they were unreadable. There was something the government was hiding. The affidavit for his name change did take effect in August 1944.

The children decided to hire a detective to find out about adoption papers for their father. If he had been adopted they had the right to inherit from Peter's stepfather. They felt Pouton was responsible for destroying these papers. They hoped to find records elsewhere. What the detective did find out was about Ida's secret life. When she married Landon the wedding was in London. When they were divorced it was in Arkansas. When she married Gregory it was in London. The detective had an idea. He went to

London to find out more about the elusive life of this woman. Bingo. She had worked for MI5, British Intelligence. He returned to Paris and started checking French Records. Although this was not legal, he found what he wanted — a confirmation she worked for numerous countries. He passed the information on to Lara, Tia, and Alex. "You know I'm not supposed to tell you these things, so please be discreet."

"Of course," Lara answered. *What's another secret,* she said to herself.

"I thought you should know. I went to see the Count. He's a long-standing acquaintance."

"You did what?" Lara was shocked.

"I went to see him to ask about his life with Ida. Thought he might tell me something."

"And?"

"He told me less than I already knew. Strange man, very distant. I think he's worried you might go after his inheritance for the children."

"Did he tell you he invited us for tea the day after Ida's funeral?" Lara asked, annoyed.

"No, why'd he do that?"

"He told us Peter was Jewish. 'So what', we said. He also called Alex's in-laws and told them, too. I think he wanted to cause trouble, but since Alex had already told them and they didn't care, Alex's father-in-law told the Count that he knew and to leave him alone." Lara's tone changed, "You should have asked us first. We are the ones who employ you and you never should have gone to see the Count. Please do not do it again without talking to us first." And she hung up. Lara paid his bill and never heard from him again.

As the years passed Ida's friends became more talkative. They told Lara that her mother-in-law was the mistress of many men, that she enjoyed women too. It helped pay her bills and cover the costs of Peter's boarding school. She was involved in politics and diplomacy, had an intriguing life and was always the life of the party and a true friend.

All this didn't get Lara any closer to the truth about Peter's involvement with the U.S. government. She reviewed her facts. Peter had been badly beaten either by Stanislas and Ellie or by the snow slide. Stanislas's face was unharmed; both of Peter's legs were broken, known to be a technique used by the CIA for assassination; his clothes were dry — if he had been conscious his body heat would have melted the snow around him, corn snow at the end of April, and the avalanche dogs would have found him earlier. If he had been conscious and had suffocated he would have lost his stools. This didn't happen. The mountain guide said a woman skied up to the man who had been found and had told him not to speak, not to say where the other skier could be. For as much as they had tried to make it look like an accident, Lara knew otherwise.

Her next project became an expensive one. She hired a second lawyer who was unable to obtain anything in writing, put the file away and eventually it was destroyed. Lara had two senators and a congressman remaining as well as a few friends who were interested in her story and who had known Peter well, many of them assuming he worked for the Agency. And some asked why she was doing this, so she questioned herself.

Her first answer was a vision — a vision of Peter talking to another man standing next to a sleek black metal object, which looked like the body of a jet fighter without wings. They were having a heated discussion. The man was giving him a choice — he, Peter, had to disappear or die and leave a body to be buried. He was shaking his head in disbelief. The man ordered him to get into the cockpit; he climbed in. The man signaled him to close the window. He slid the dome over his head; it locked. He looked panicked as he turned to watch the man signal him forward just as they do on an aircraft carrier. The bullet of black metal slid into the water. Peter disappeared. Lara was crying her heart out. He had no choice but to die.

The second answer was from the Priest of Lara's church. She had asked to meet with him and had something to show him. Their hour together was an eye opener. Lara had brought a reading by a psychic whom she had met, someone she didn't know very well.

"Jean typed this up for me when she got home. She says she can't see very clearly," Lara handed the page to Father Ken. "I wonder what the rest means if she didn't see except through a cloud." Ken took a few minutes to read it and closed his eyes to think.

"How can you be sure she was talking to Peter? Did she describe him — what he looked like?"

"No, she didn't."

"Did she know you were asking if you should continue your search?"

"Yes, that's where I am today. So many people ask me why and then tell me to get on with my life." Lara stood up and started pacing. She was feeling very troubled. "I was warned it was dangerous to ask too many questions more than once. But I can't seem to get on with my life not knowing why he was killed."

"Have you prayed to God for an answer?"

"Not exactly. I meditated once and had a vision. All it said to me is he had to die." Tears slowly filled her eyes. "I hadn't thought of the answer coming from God." She sat down next to Father Ken. "Thanks. That's what I'll try next."

They prayed together before Lara left for home. She had something new to try. In her next meditation Peter came to her. She could see him. "I'm so sorry for all of this," he said. "I need your help. Seek the truth. They are getting away with too many atrocities." A man appeared next to him, a blond, crewcut, balloon-shaped face with ears that stuck out and a pair of glasses that hid his eyes. "This is the doctor I met with in Berlin. He went to work in a Laboratory in Africa. They blew him up." The two men were standing very close to each other. Then the doctor spoke.

"We need you to see the truth. Do not be discouraged. There are people who will help you and the spirit world will guide you, too."

"Why," Lara started to ask, "were you killed?" But before she got it all out they had disappeared.

This is weird, Lara thought, so her next appointment was with a psychiatrist who told her the more she knew, the easier it would be to deal with the pain she was still feeling so many years later.

Donations went out to her senators and congressman. She was told it might take some time. It would be worth the try. Consequently, approximately one year after sending donations locally, she was invited to a breakfast given by her congressman, Bill Carpo, at a local inn and was able to have a few quiet words with him before sitting down for breakfast. She knew no one in the group of sixteen local residents and found herself sitting next to the congressman — the only unoccupied seat at the table. Her limited experience in diplomacy and business had taught her discretion and the subject of her request was dropped.

After introductions, speeches, and breakfast were over, Lara waited patiently while people said good-bye and asked for whatever they hoped from their congressman upon his return to Washington. Bill Carpo called over one of his aides and asked Lara to give him some information about herself and her request and said that someone in the office would be in touch. Bill was a member of the intelligence committee. Lara had hit gold —or so she thought. For her, the usual procedure began again. Lists of federal government departments contacted by her lawyers, photo copies of several of the answers, birth certificates, death certificate, numbers — Social Security, Army, passport, naturalization papers.

Again she waited. Many answers to Carpo's requests stated, "there will be a delay." The reasons — a limited staff and large volume of inquiries. The State Department finally sent a three-page reply. The first page was black with a white square marked "Declassified." The second, a page from a request for passport renewal; the third his death certificate. The rest of his file was no longer available. Lara had called her contact at the State Department and asked what had happened to the rest of the file. The answer was: "This is all we were able to obtain, I'm sorry."

By the end of the century Lara had made sizeable donations to the Senatorial Trust, a fund-raising organization with the opportunity to meet the senators and was invited to the George W. Bush Inauguration. She and her son decided to attend and while in Washington they called upon Congressman Carpo. It was the first time either of them had visited a Congressman in his office. The building was large and spacious with wide halls and stairwells, gray outside and in. The office was in dark wood paneling with a small reception area prior to entering the Congressman's private office.

"The Congressman is running late," his assistant said. "Would you like a cup of coffee and a doughnut?"

"No thanks," they answered and took a seat to wait. They waited over an hour (typical for Washington) before being escorted in by the man who had taken Lara's information over a year earlier.

"Good morning, Lara. Is this your son, Edgar?" They shook hands. "Please be seated, Lara, you remember Tim. He's been helping me with your inquiries."

"Yes, we spoke outside."

"Since your last letter and because you were coming to Washington I made one last stab at the CIA," he went to sit behind his desk. "Tim and I had two men from the CIA come over and talk to us. They found no records for Peter Landon anywhere — no matter how much I insisted. Everything you gave me about being debriefed, his contacts. They said they had nothing. Said it was too bad he hadn't worked for them — he sounded perfect for the job." He looked at Tim who nodded and chose not to speak. Lara started to insist and Edgar said softly yet firmly, "It's OK, Mom, they don't have the ability to exercise the power to get his file." He turned to Carpo, "You're a member of the Intelligence Committee, aren't you?"

"Yes, unfortunately in your case it hasn't helped."

"Who would you suggest my mother contact?"

"I'm afraid there isn't anyone I can suggest. The CIA said they did an extensive search, between your mother's lawyer and my office, we've covered everything." He stood up as a sign for Lara and Edgar to leave. "I'm really sorry I couldn't be of more help."

"You said you received a brief. Can we see it?" Lara asked, trying not to be obnoxious.

"The men from the Agency took it back with them. I don't have it here."

Lara thought that meant, *You read the brief, were asked not to disclose and to get me off their back.* She stood up to leave. "Thanks for trying." She shook both men's hands and walked out, Edgar silently followed her out. "What a waste of time and money," she said to him when they couldn't be overheard.

The Inauguration was an interesting process to observe and the parties were fun. Lara found out later that the ball they went to was one of the best. Some women in unbelievable ball gowns, others more simply dressed. The band was great and the crowd loved to dance. Of course the new President went on stage and danced with his lovely wife, as did the Vice President and his wife.

Tia had become interested in Lara's project and wanted to help. She went to the United Nations library in Geneva and looked up what was going on in the Belgian Congo when she and her parents lived there. She came across page after page of correspondence, which she photocopied and read later before passing them on to her mother. Lara was surprised her daughter was able to do such a thing. But then, Tia was a smart looking woman now, knew how to dress for any occasion and probably looked the part of someone who belonged there doing what she was supposed to do. Her deep blue eyes didn't miss a trick, her shiny brown hair, shoulder length, kept in place by a leather headband, which matched her belt, shoes, and pocketbook. She had earned several degrees, loved books, research, and people.

"Mom, I wonder if you realized what you were living through — what I lived through as a baby." She produced several of the photocopies — correspondence from Zorin, then Vice Minister of Russian Foreign Affairs, to the General Assembly. "Did you know the lack of information getting out to the world of what was actually happening?"

"I didn't know. Your father knew what was going on all over the country, and for most of Africa, too. He probably thought the world knew."

"Look," Tia said passing more pages to her mother to read. "Correspondence from Mali, Dr. Dayal of India — no legal code, no regulations for the government or people — in-house fighting for power," her nervous energy was mounting. "And look here. How responsible were we, the U.S., for Lumumba's assassination? Did you know Lumumba?"

"I didn't. Your father met him —he met just about everyone. He knew who was under house arrest, who was at the Palais de la Nation. I never realized there was so much confusion and now wonder how I could have kept you and Mademoiselle there through all of that. I'm sorry." Lara's tone of voice changed, she became sad, then angry. "Your father should have sent us home. He needed me. I was part of his cover, so were you." She started to cry, "He used us; our country used us; Papa was paid for his work, we weren't. Sure I knew I was in danger — more than once, in that stupid ambulance, running messages with bullets flying," her resentment climbing. She stopped to read some more, "How could I have, we have, lived through all of that. It was crazy." And again she apologized, getting up and taking Tia in her arms to hug the little girl who was now grown up. "I am so sorry, so sorry. Please forgive me."

One sunny, warm May Lara decided it was time to go to Berlin. She needed moral support and asked Tia to go with her. It had been Peter's last trip and she needed to make it for him — to know where he had gone. Yes, it was thirty or more years later. The city wouldn't be the same. The wall had come down. The two Germanys were united. They made sure to land during daylight. The airport was close enough to get an aerial view before landing and taking a taxi to the Adlon Hotel — highly recommended by cousins and next to the Brandenburg Gate.

"Wow, Mom, this is fabulous," Tia said. Their suite was wood paneled with a kitchen and sitting room, fully equipped for business — computer, fax and a large television which they never had time to use. The bedroom was relatively small, just for sleeping; the bathroom large enough for two at the same time, shower and bath separated. They had both been in fancy hotels before, but nothing like this. And because of their introduction they were paying for a simple room. "Look Mom, you have mail and there must be a telephone message, too." She went to get the message off the phone. Her German was good and she could understand more than her mother. "It's from your cousin, Friedrich; he's flying in from Frankfurt to take us out to dinner and dancing with his son. Says the weather's bad so they'll probably be late." She hung up and turned to her mother, "What's the letter say?"

"It's from Vermont Law School. Michael faxed the telephone number for Katarina. She's Michael's Doctor associate right? She'll take us to the

Stasi." Lara called right away and made an appointment to meet in two days. Ten a.m. she would pick them up at the hotel and drive them there.

The first evening, Friedrich and his son, Wilhelm, picked them up for dinner. They had a leisurely meal in a small, typical, noisy restaurant called Barcherts — no tourists; they hopped into Wilhelm's car and arrived at "90°", the most popular nightclub for the young where they danced late into the night.

The next two days were spent sightseeing, one day with the City Circle bus system where they could get off as many times as they wanted, visit and get back on from ten in the morning until six in the evening. The second day was a difficult day for Lara and subsequently for Tia. They went to visit Checkpoint Charlie and looked for places where Peter could have gone. The museum was the house used for the guards during the Cold War. The Kiosk was in place with sand bags piled high as if there was still need for protection.

"Your father didn't go through here, you know, and I wonder why." The Brandenburg Gate was under construction; they had walked through it several times and seen pictures of it back in the early '60s.

"Why did he go through Brandenburg?" Neither knew the answer.

One evening they went to hear the Berlin Symphony Orchestra, the other they went for dinner to the restaurant on top of the Reichstag. The view was magnificent — 360 degrees of the city dotted with cranes. New buildings going up everywhere. Lara asked the Maitre d'Hotel on their way out, "What did they do with all the rubble?"

"Some of it was used to rebuild but most was carted out of the city and made into a huge hilly park. It was covered with dirt and trees planted. There are trails, picnic grounds, it's a beautiful place where we go to unwind."

"It's going to be a beautiful city — in fact it already is," Tia said.

Chapter Thirty-seven

Lara woke with a migraine. She was nervous and fearful and couldn't get back to sleep. Her past ran through her head and then she was in Berlin with Peter and couldn't digest what she was feeling or seeing. She was able to push these scenes out of her head, which made her headache worse. Her eyes were twitching and her breathing heavy. She got up, took a cold shower and went back to bed. The buzzer rang, "Tia, wake up dear, breakfast is here." She got up to let the waiter in. The day had begun.

They were downstairs waiting for Katarina by nine forty-five. The hotel lobby was busy — some were having coffee during a friendly chat, others were going over papers. The sitting area was fully occupied. They decided to wait outside. The cool air was soothing to Lara's throbbing head. Her medication wasn't working and Tia appeared very nervous. They walked back and forth in silence until they saw a small black car drive up and a young woman get out. Katarina was petite with long dark, wavy hair. She was dressed in a black pants suit and looked very businesslike.

"Hi, Lara, Tia? I'm Katarina. It's nice to meet you." She opened the front and back doors for them to get in. "We have an appointment with Frau Dagen at ten thirty and we have a ways to go." They jerked forward and got caught in traffic, turned right and zigzagged on small streets until they were on a large thoroughfare with few cars. "This was the main avenue in East Berlin," Katarina said proudly as she took a quick glance at Lara. "It's been difficult getting East and West to understand each other. I lived as a child in East Berlin — our schools, education, was different. We have had to learn how to talk to each other again. So many misunderstandings."

It was clear to Tia and Lara that East Berlin was a poorer part of the city. The Allies helped rebuild West Berlin into a beautiful, modern city; East Berlin looked practical, well planned and definitely less interesting. They parked in front of a plain ten-story office building with a small sign saying "Bundesbeauftragte" and a black eagle with wings spread. They went in and were met on the ground floor by a receptionist who called Frau Dagen.

After the usual greetings Frau Dagen told them she had reviewed Lara's previous request and asked if there was something else she should add to the file. Katarina was translating everything for them and wrote out a whole new statement of events including Peter's visit to East Berlin by the Brandenburg Gate.

"You say he went through the Brandenburg Gate; not Checkpoint Charlie?"

"Yes," Lara nodded.

"That would only be possible if he was working for the KGB or East German Police," Frau Dagen looked surprised. "Anyone from the Allied side went through Checkpoint Charlie. Could he have been a double agent?"

"I don't know. I do remember him telling me specifically that he went through the Brandenburg Gate. At the time I didn't know it could be important. Maybe it was his way of telling me something was wrong." Lara felt puzzled and looked to Tia for help.

"If he was a double agent, would the Stasi have a file on him?" Tia asked.

"I would think so. Our records are not yet in order, a lot went to America. We have most of them back but as you can see," she held up a brochure with a picture of the cellar piled high with paper bags. "There are many sacks still to be filed."

"You have nothing more to tell us?" Katarina asked.

"I'm afraid not. We will have more information in two years. You can contact me again when the time comes. I'm sorry not to be more help. We will have more to go on with the new information." She stood up. "Thank you for your visit."

"I never thought it could be so important," Lara said getting into the car. "The fact that he went through the Brandenburg Gate means he could have been a double agent." She turned to Tia. "Remember the letter that Sam Holder wrote me after hearing my story? At first he didn't believe Peter worked for the CIA. He said the fact that the two Czechs didn't flee behind the Iron Curtain made it evident that Peter was a double agent, and maybe influenced by his mother who worked for several countries herself."

Lara sat in silence thinking while Tia and Katarina chatted in front. All of a sudden she realized — if she had gone skiing that Easter Sunday she probably wouldn't be here today.

"You know something," she broke into their conversation, "I think my migraine saved my life."

"What are you talking about?" Tia asked.

"If I had gone skiing with your father, they would have done me in too. What's another life to them?" They all were speechless.

Upon Lara's return to the States she started going through a collection of newspaper and magazine articles she had collected over the years. She also had several books to read looking for the reason Peter had been killed. His name was not mentioned anywhere. She didn't know if he had a code name — none of the stories fit their life. Ted Gup, a freelancer for the *Washington Post,* wrote about CIA agents having stars named after them thirty-two years after they were killed, in recognition for their service to the U.S.A. Lara wondered if Peter had one already or if they still needed to keep his secret. Several articles stated that CIA agents did not always inform their Ambassadors as to what was going on and the CIA didn't always say who was working for them. That would be why the Consul General in Leopoldville didn't know Peter was an undercover agent, nor would Lawrence Devlin, who was chief of station.

President Clinton declassified all documents twenty-five years and older at the end of the century. Larry Alden reported that documents from 1953 to 1965 would never be declassified because of the possible danger it might bring to those still living. That was why her lawyer's requests were rejected. David Wise's book *Molehunt* covered the '60s. If Peter was a double agent he could have been considered a mole, but what if he had been asked to be one by the CIA? Would that still mean he was a mole and should be eliminated? She wasn't getting anywhere.

Chapter Thirty-eight

Lara sought someone who had been taught to do remote viewing. She had heard that the government had taught a group of psychics to see what was going on in the USSR during the Cold War. Paris had a convention twice a year for psychics — over the weekend anyone could go for a reading. Lara went several times, asked if someone did remote viewing, had a reading and left without anything new. Again in the U.S. she was more successful. By the end of two sessions with Terry, a skinny young woman from a flower community and a trained psychic, she had something else to work on. It could all be just someone's imagination. It was worth a try. She had asked the psychic to travel to Berlin. Terry gave a fascinating description of a train ride, a boarding house, the fear Peter felt crossing from West to East Berlin through a large monument, the day and weather. And a meeting with a doctor, a bottle of some sort. Terry stopped, "There's something," she paused. "He's walking on the sidewalk. It's dark out, he's cold, worried. A car stops beside him; he gets pushed in. He feels very uncomfortable." Her eyes tightly closed, she took a deep breath and tried to relax. "They're taking him away for questioning. He's caught in something much bigger than he can handle and he wants out." She opened her eyes wide and asked, "Was he a spy? This makes me feel very uncomfortable. Can we look at something else?"

"I'm sorry," Lara said. "I think he was a spy and was killed because he was caught at something he did not understand. But I don't really know." She thought for a moment — another subject — she could try. "The doctor, can you follow the doctor? See where he's going? What he does?"

"I need to take a break. Would you like a cup of tea?" It was always herbal tea.

"No thanks, I could use a glass of water and a stretch."

Fifteen minutes later Terry was back in a trance. She saw the doctor get on a plane, the desert, a research complex, human guinea pigs, again she felt uncomfortable and cried, "I can't do this anymore; it's too horrible," as she clutched her stomach. Lara had another subject to research.

Again she started collecting newspaper and magazine articles, books, and TV tapes on bio-chemical research using humans for testing. It was amazing how much was available and shocking what had been done. *The New Yorker* Magazine had a fascinating story in January 2001 called "The Poison Keeper" by William Finnegan. It told of "Project Coast" in South Africa. Many countries were involved in chemical and biological research and warfare so when the Truth and Reconciliation Commission started, all eyes were turned in that direction. Multinational chemical and pharmaceutical companies were involved with vaccines to block human fertility, Anthrax, cholera, e-bola, AIDS, and numerous others. Some products would kill crops, others livestock and/or humans. There were laboratories in Porton Down, England; Fort Detrick, Maryland and several other places in the States, Russia and around the world. All were top secret, even to members of Congress, as was "Area 51" located somewhere in the Nevada desert and there no one knows what's going on because the U.S. government doesn't admit that the base exists, or so the History Channel said.

Bio-chemical warfare existed in primitive times with poisoned arrows, World War I used mustard gas — when did testing start on humans without them knowing and without a war? The Pentagon admitted to testing from Alaska to Florida and thousands of civilians in Hawaii and Alaska were sprayed with mild bacteria with no evidence of death as a result. Lara wondered if she could believe that. It was back in the '60s, just when Peter could have been involved. Was it morally unacceptable for him? Did he want out? Was he a risk, going to tell the world? Instead of leading to the truth all the information she had gathered confused her. She saw the name of a psychiatrist she had seen in the '60s for therapy in New York. The article said he was an allergist paid by the CIA to experiment with LSD. *Thank goodness I never needed medication from him,* she thought.

With so many possibilities, Lara wondered which ones could apply to Peter and his work. She became discouraged —how could world leaders permit the testing on huge populations, even encourage mass murder in the Middle East and elsewhere? There was nothing she could do about it.

One more try for her to learn about Peter's fate. She wanted one more try.

She called Ben, Peter's classmate at Yale.

"Hi, I feel I haven't seen you in a long time. How about lunch and a museum?"

"Is there something more to this invitation?" he asked.

"Does it sound so evident?"

"As you said, it's been a long time; and all of a sudden you're on the phone. Have you gotten anywhere with what I told you about Peter?"

"You guessed it — nowhere."

"Come spend the weekend. I'm having dinner with friends Saturday evening. Jim knows Ward Krammer, who used to be head of the CIA a couple of years ago."

"Thanks, I'd love to. Who else will be there?"

"You're always so inquisitive," Ben laughed. "Jim and Peggy Pennelli —he's the one who knows Krammer."

"Isn't Pennelli a well-known journalist?" Lara's heart began to beat faster. She had been looking for an investigative reporter to help her. This dinner could offer her both.

"You're right. Jim's freelance and in print for many newspapers. So, will you come?"

"I'd love to." Lara's mind was already packing her bag.

Dinner did offer her what she was still looking for — a journalist who could publicize her story if necessary and an introduction directly to the CIA. A few weeks later she was back in Washington to meet with Ward Krammer, now a reputable lawyer who agreed to help her. He told her it would take some time — everything took time. This would be her last hope and she was willing to wait. Krammer contacted his friend at the CIA and waited for an answer. He became impatient and six months later made a follow-up call. He was told they were working on it; there were complications. He knew that meant trouble. He called Lara, explained the difficulty and warned her to be careful.

Chapter Thirty-nine

The phone rang. "Hello."

"Mrs. Landon —no, excuse me, Mrs. de Gary?"

"Yes," Lara wondered who would call her by her former name.

"Mrs. de Gary, this is Frank Johnson," he paused.

"Yes."

"Mrs. de Gary, I'm with the FBI. I'd like to meet with you."

"Why?"

"There are a few things we need to discuss with you," again he hesitated, "concerning your previous husband. When can we stop by?"

Lara's heart started to pound. The rate increased so fast and her breathing could no longer control the discomfort she felt. Was it for Philip or was it for Peter? She knew it was for Peter. She had been warned to stop her inquiries and she had given it one last shot with Ward Krammer, ex-head of the CIA. Had he come up with something? Lara's silence began to annoy Mr. Johnson.

"Mrs. de Gary, are you there?"

"Yes, I'm here. I don't know why you want to see me. Can you give me a reason?"

"It concerns your inquiry."

"What inquiry?"

"The one Mr. Krammer is taking care of."

Why didn't he mention Peter's name?

"The one about Peter Landon?"

"Yes, we have a few questions to ask you."

"Ask me over the phone," she replied, trying to sound as forceful and in control as possible.

"We need to see you," he said. "And within the next twenty-four hours."

That meant they were already in the area. Maybe at the end of her driveway. *Shit,* she thought. "Well, can you give me some time to get dressed? I've just finished exercising."

"Yes, of course — one hour."

"Make it an hour and a half, please."

"Okay. We'll be there in an hour and a half." And he hung up.

Lara picked up her phone and walked to the window to see if there was a car at the end of the driveway. No one. It was a clear spring day. The garden was coming to life and it had to be spoiled by this. She knew her phone was tapped, yet she picked it up and dialed Michael at the law school. She was in luck.

"I'll be right over," he said.

Lara got out her tape recorder and started to prepare for the meeting. In the library? No, around the kitchen table. That way everything would be picked up on the recorder. She went and changed her clothes, noticed her hands were shaking. Her nerves were on edge. How was she going to manage this one? The tension started to climb up her shoulders, along the back of her neck, her jaw tightened. *This will never do,* she said to herself. She sat down, did her deep breathing, and finally got her heartbeat to slow. Then she realized that she would have to disappear within the next twenty-four hours to protect her children and other family members. She went downstairs, took out her gun hidden deep in a kitchen drawer, loaded it and slipped it in her waistband behind her back. She drew it out a couple of times to make sure that if she needed it, it was handy. Then she took her cash and gold pieces, put them in her travel pouch and locked them up in her safe place. Her mind had shifted from defense to survival. She had thought it all out before. She already had arranged her password with a friend, so the tapped line wasn't a problem. She'd arranged a pick-up place in case they kept an eye on her house. She had more than enough money to get where she was going. No credit card, no traveler's checks to reveal her whereabouts. If she was going to hide, no one was to know where.

The doorbell rang. She still had a half hour before the FBI was to arrive. She hoped it was Michael. She heard his voice.

"Lara, I'm here. Where are you?"

"I'll be right down." She finished packing her backpack and satchel, threw them into the darkness of her closet, and walked downstairs feeling the calm before the storm.

305

"Hi, thanks for coming so fast! Did you see a car waiting with people in it?"

"Yup. It's at the foot of the driveway. They aren't going to like the fact that I'm here as your lawyer and a witness."

"That's their tough luck." She put a finger up to her lips indicating there might be listening devices in the house. She whispered in his ear, "I'm leaving tonight. My story's in your safety deposit box in that sealed envelope in case something happens to me or any of the children. Please try to find some way to tell just the children — no one else. They know what to do. Your phone will be tapped as soon as our meeting is over. I'm sorry." She gave him a hug and then said out loud, "There's the tape recorder. Should I put it on the table or will you?"

"You know they are going to want the conversation off the record."

"That's their problem," she said out loud. "We'll make two copies, one for you, or I'll hide it here in the house," she whispered. "The other I'll take with me."

The front doorbell rang. It stuck. Lara went to open the door. There were three of them — two men and a woman.

"Mrs. Landon? I'm Frank Johnson. This is John Jones, and Priscilla Smith."

"I'm Mrs. de Gary — no longer Mrs. Landon." She thought they were all using fake names and had the guts to add, "Could I see some form of identification, please?" They were shocked and caught off guard. Frank Johnson pulled out his driver's license — lousy photo, she wondered if it was really his. The others didn't budge. Lara turned to them.

"We're sorry," John Jones said. "I left mine at the hotel, I think I saw yours there too before we left," he said to Ms. Smith. She nodded.

"I really shouldn't receive anyone without identification," Lara said trying to leave the other two outside.

"Come on, Mrs. de Gary," Mr. Johnson started when Michael walked up.

"Hello, Mr. Johnson. I'm Michael Kelly, Lara's lawyer. What can we do for you?"

"Nice to meet you, Mr. Kelly. If you don't mind, we'll be meeting Mrs. de Gary alone."

"I'm sorry, that won't be possible," Michael turned back into the house, nudging Lara to follow. "Please come in," he indicated the direction to the kitchen. The kitchen was warm from the morning sun. The men removed their jackets in silence and put them over the backs of their chairs. Lara invited Ms. Smith to do the same. She declined. Lara thought the woman

306

must be wired and was glad that she would roast in the sunny room. Michael pulled out the small tape recorder, placed it in the center of the kitchen table, and turned it on.

"That won't be necessary," Frank Johnson said, as he turned it off.

"Then perhaps Ms. Smith can take her jacket off and leave it in the front hall," Lara added. All three turned to look at her. Michael was smiling as he turned the recorder back on.

The questions started slowly, then picked up in speed, one person after the other asking in turn, trying to catch Lara off balance. She took her time. She had been questioned for eight hours in Paris at the police station. A *Garde à Vue*, by the French police, only to have the complaint thrown out of court. She still had no information as to what Peter was doing in the early sixties. She didn't want to make trouble for anyone, particularly for herself and her family. She wasn't after the government for money. She and the children just wanted to know what had happened and why. She looked at her watch; hours had gone by. She was tired. She had answered almost all the questions, which had been repeated several times. Michael put his foot down when they were too personal — the others she answered.

"Gentlemen, the session is over," he said as he stood up to show them out. "Do you want a copy of the tape?"

"We haven't finished," Ms. Smith said, "and, no, we don't need a copy of your tape. We have a few more questions, Mrs. Landon, if you don't mind."

"Michael, it's all right." She turned to Ms. Smith. "I do mind. You can't even call me by my right name and all I'm doing is repeating myself, answering the same questions you ask in different ways." She felt she'd had enough and wasn't going to say another word. Reluctantly they got up to leave. Ms. Smith put her hand out to pick up the tape recorder, but Michael got there first, turned it off, held on to it tightly, and walked them to the door. When he came back into the kitchen he heard Lara on the phone. "I'm sorry I can't make the movies tonight. I'm exhausted."

"What did you do that exhausted you on such a beautiful day? I thought you'd be out in the garden." Mary answered. "Garden" meant that she understood. Mary was her means of transporation to safety.

"I had some cleaning up to do. Why don't we meet for lunch tomorrow — around twelve-forty-five?" This was the code for the time they were to meet that night.

"See you at the Inn at twelve-forty-five," her friend answered. "Get a good night's sleep."

"See you tomorrow." Lara hung up.

"Who was that?" Michael asked.

"I was supposed to go to the movies with a friend this evening. I'm too tired. Thanks so much for being here, Michael. I'll keep you posted." She whispered into his ear, "I don't know when I'll see you again. We haven't worked out an 'all clear'."

Michael gave her a hug and whispered, "Have a safe journey. Have someone call in a couple of months. Ask how the garden is. If there's snow on the ground — no good; if some flowers are in bloom — you can come home. Okay?" She nodded. It was hard to believe she really had to disappear, but it was the safest way.

Lara went upstairs after he left. She had time. She rested for well over an hour, changed into black pants and a black shirt. There would be moonlight tonight, unless there was some cloud cover. She was sure someone would be keeping an eye on the house, but hoped only in front, thinking she would leave by car. The timers on the lights would make it look as if she had gone to bed. The plan was a good one. Now it had to work!

Chapter Forty

Lara was ready by sundown. She looked for the rising moon and saw it slowly appear in the northwest. It was a new moon and the stars seemed dim. She turned on the television set to the Weather Channel. No cloud cover tonight. Her stomach churned and panic was starting to grip her. She knew if she was to make a clean getaway she needed to stay calm and alert. She pulled out her backpack and checked the contents: there was enough for two weeks, until she decided where she would settle in. She knew that leaving the country by plane she would leave some kind of trail, but after that she would disappear. She closed certain curtains so that the agents on guard wouldn't see her movements, checked the timers on the lights, and went downstairs. As she took a last look at her bedroom she wondered if she'd ever see it again. She sat on the top stair and forced herself to relax — it was easier if she started with her feet and moved up. Too many thoughts were scrambling around in her head.

Learn to live with the pain, panic and peril, she said to herself. *It will help you to survive. Trust your intuition. That's what will save you.* She got up, picked up her bag, and took a deep breath.

"Your angels are with you. Listen to them." She said out loud.

She started down the stairs, talking to the angels. "I know you're there. Thanks for taking such good care of me. Why am I afraid? Because it keeps the adrenalin flowing? It's okay."

Am I going crazy? She said to herself. She went to where it was dark in the house and looked down the driveway to where the street lamp shed some light. She saw a car through her binoculars and saw two men sitting inside. They looked as though they were asleep, and she wondered if there was a third agent walking around the property. From the garage doorway she could see three sides, and there was no sign of a third guard. Back in the house, she checked the fourth side — no one. She was to meet Mary at twelve forty-five, but she always left early. Why should this time be different?

She grabbed an apple and a small bottle of water, put them into an outside pocket of her backpack, slipped into her black rain jacket, and headed for the door off the back porch. She closed her eyes tightly and waited until they adjusted to the dark. When she opened them again she saw someone walking around the house. She ducked and waited for what seemed like a long time. When she looked again, he was gone. She ran to the front window, picked up the binoculars, and saw that only one person was in the car. Another was walking toward the car. *Only two. I can go now,* she thought. She had added squats and push-ups to her daily exercise program and knew that she was in good shape, considering that she was over sixty. She crawled out the back porch door on her hands and knees, turned to lock the door behind her and slid down the stairs to the ground on her butt. She ran low to the ground carrying her pack, ducked between the trees, and climbed over the fence. She headed north to her meeting place, twenty minutes away.

The night was cool, the clouds had disappeared, and Lara lay back on the grass behind a shrub, up the hill from her driveway. She picked out the constellations she recognized. She loved to watch the stars move across the sky, to see the different planets close to the moon. From time to time a satellite sped across the sky and out of sight. A star fell suddenly in the darkness. "I wish I didn't have to do this."

The sound of cars passing brought her back to the present. It was time. Mary's car pulled up just past the shrub where Lara sat and doused its lights. Lara looked around. She had left nothing but a mark in the grass where she had been sitting. She ran low to the car, got in, and started to tremble.

"It's okay, Lara. No one knows I'm here. Where are we off to?" She put a hand on Lara's and pressed down firmly to stop the trembling. "Full tank of gas, food and TP for our pit stops."

"You think of everything, Mary. Thanks. Let's head north. We'll take Interstate 89 up past Burlington and before we get to the border we'll take a small road to cross into Canada and on to Montreal. *'Ni vu, ni connu '* I'll get the first flight out of Dorval."

"Where to?"

"That's a no-no. The less you know about me, the better. They'll check my calls and see you're the movie date. You'll have to be back at the Inn by one o'clock. You'll just have time to spit me out and get home for a nap." Lara turned to look at her friend. Her dark, curly hair framed a troubled face, scrubbed clean, without makeup.

"You look tired, too," Lara said. "I'll sleep for an hour and drive the rest of the way to the airport."

"I'm okay," Mary said. She turned her head quickly, checking to see if they were alone. "Put your seat way back, that way anyone who sees us will see only me." She settled in and put the car on cruise control. "The drive is easy at this hour. I can do both ways."

"No way," Lara answered. "If something happens to you, I'll never forgive myself. And besides, you really do have to be at the Inn as close to twelve forty-five as possible or they'll know." She closed her eyes and to her surprise fell fast asleep. The drive was so smooth that she slept for over an hour. Coming back to her senses she looked at Mary, who was relaxed and confident.

"We've been passed several times. No one seemed interested." Her friend hesitated, "I've been doing up to 100 miles per hour, following other cars at that speed. I didn't think I was risking much." She pulled off the road into an empty rest area. "Get out and stretch your legs. I'm going behind a bush."

"Me, too."

Lara drove the rest of the way. At the airport she hopped out, blew a kiss to her friend and disappeared into the dimly lit terminal.

Chapter Forty-one

At twelve fifty-six the next day Mary was at the Inn. She looked fabulous, in a beige slacks suit and rust-colored shawl. Full make-up hid any telltale signs of a busy night. A woman and two men at a nearby table were watching her. She turned to the hostess, "Is Lara de Gary here?" she asked. "I don't see her." She scanned the dining room.

The hostess looked embarrassed and nodded in the direction of the group who had been staring at Mary. "They're waiting for her, too," she said. "Your table is there by the window. Please follow me."

Mary played it easy. She sat down, put the napkin on her lap and turned her back on the six eyes she felt gnawing at her. Suddenly she felt a presence beside her. "Hi. I'm Priscilla Smith. Are you waiting for Lara?" Priscilla hesitated. "So are we. Can I sit down for a minute?" she asked as she pulled out the chair and sat down. She leaned forward. "We went to her house this morning, and no one was there." Again, she paused and put a serious look on her face. "I don't suppose you know where she is?"

"We're supposed to have lunch today," Mary answered flippantly. "She's probably out running errands, although Lara is usually on time. You know she lived in Sweden. There you always have to be right on time." She turned to look out the window and then back at her intruder. "If you don't mind, I'd rather wait for her alone."

Priscilla was annoyed at being dismissed so easily. "If you know where she is, you'd better tell us." She flashed her FBI identity as she got up and walked back to the two men.

Mary called the waitress over and ordered a drink. She had decided to have a leisurely lunch. That might give Lara a little more time to get away.

Chapter Forty-two

And Lara needed time. The only flights to Europe left in the evening. She took the first one she could get, leaving Dorval at eight a.m., heading south to Mexico. She knew she could fly non-stop from Mexico City to Europe. It would be longer and more expensive, but that didn't matter as long as she didn't touch down in the States.

She could have called her friend in the south of France, but that wasn't what she needed right now. Michael met with a friend who was headed for Paris and asked him to call Jerry there and leave the coded message she had given Michael. Jerry was to check two places over the next two days where they were to meet. One was in a supermarket in a small town, Sommières; the other was at a health club near the station in Nîmes. They were places he knew well. He shopped in one and worked out regularly at the other.

After she arrived in France, day one went by, as did day two. Lara had been delayed by public transportation and had missed her pick-up time by ten minutes at the health club. She hoped he'd try again, without her having to call. Discouraged, she found a cheap B&B to spend the night.

Jerry was perplexed. He'd been by both places both days and he wondered if he should try again the next day, just to make sure. Had he mixed up the times? He couldn't be in two places at once, and wondered if he should invert the time. Had he forgotten? Years ago Lara had spoken to him about all this. He had taken notes that now were too vague to help his memory. He felt frustrated and angry with himself. He decided to go to the health club and work out the next morning.

When she arrived at the health club a little before ten the next day, she was hot. Her black clothes absorbed the blazing sun. She saw his van parked in the shade of a tree. *How thoughtful of him.* The door was open, she got in. "I've made it." and she burst into tears of gratitude.

She closed her eyes and fell asleep, exhausted from the tension and long hours of travel. She woke with a start when the door on the driver's side opened. Her head was spinning and she thought she might pass out. *Who was this man getting into the van beside her? Had Jerry sold the van to someone else?* She couldn't speak, her voice was lost to fear and panic.

"Lara, I wondered if you'd remember the van. I'm sorry if I got things mixed up. Are you okay?" He took a deep breath and continued. She looked hard at him and finally recognized the pale blue eyes, which had lost a lot of their color, but not the twinkle. "You look exhausted. Do you want to head right out or spend the night at my place? Are you okay?" he finished.

"Jerry. Dear Jerry. You surprised me. Of course I recognize you and the van." She leaned over to hug him and tears returned to her eyes. The joy and security she felt in his company were overwhelming. "I'd love to go back to your house and rest if you think the call wasn't traced. It's been," and she took the time to count the days on her fingers, "three days. They would have found you by now if they're going to."

Jerry started the van, pulled out of the parking lot, looking right and left for traffic and headed for home. "The person who called said it was made from a pay phone — out of state — by someone totally out of the circuit who didn't understand a thing about it and apologized for disturbing me. I think we're okay. I'll drive by a couple of times. We can have a look. What the hell have you gotten yourself involved in, anyway?" He took a quick glance at his friend.

"You don't want to know. I had a feeling my inquiries about Peter's death might cause trouble. After thirty years everything should be an open book," she sighed. "It must still be something quite important or they wouldn't be doing this. Peter must have known something, and they think he told me. And I don't know diddly-squat. If I did, I'd stop asking questions." She closed her eyes again and tried to stop the thoughts running through her head. She had asked a friend who had just been transferred to Moscow — an investigative reporter and his wife — to get into the KGB files. The wife had gotten into the files because she was writing a biography on some famous Chinese communist. But the files were closed down, and Lara had learned that the KGB would recreate just about anything you wanted for enough money. Lara next had tried the East German Stasi files. She finally had gotten on a plane to Berlin, had a contact drive her to Stasi headquarters and act as an interpreter for her. She was told they had nothing now — but to try again in two years. Of course, the U.S. government had taken the Stasi files and Lara wondered if they all had been returned. And of course, the Stasi needed time to put the files all back in order. Lara didn't have a code name for Peter, and wondered if Peter had been a double agent. Who had asked those two people to kill him in Switzerland?

The van made a sharp turn and came to a stop. A garage door opened and they drove in. "Are we at your place?" she asked. "I must have fallen asleep again." She saw the door close behind them as Jerry turned off the motor.

"Come on. I'm going to feed you and put you to bed." Jerry got out, went around and literally pulled Lara out of the van. She was wobbly on her feet and welcomed his support.

The house hadn't changed in the many years since she had been there. The walls were white stucco covered with Jerry's art, or that of nearby friends with whom he painted. The floor, cold to her feet since she'd left her shoes in the van, were beige polished stone squares, clean and smooth. "Who does your housework?" she asked.

"Who do you think? I've waited three days for you and had time to clean up." They headed for the kitchen where Lara saw a pot of cold soup sitting on the stove.

"Oh, please don't heat the soup, it's so hot out."

She picked up a bowl, helped herself and sat down on a stool at the small kitchen table. "It's like home. Thank you so much." The soup was gone in no time, and Lara went up to her old room. She stripped and fell into bed, "I'll see you in the morning," she called out. "Wake me if you need to."

It was two p.m.

Jerry let her sleep until she could sleep no more. He left the house early the next morning to add some fresh produce to her grocery list and picked up a few pieces of warm clothing that he hoped would fit her. If she was going into hiding for a long time she needed warm clothes. Autumn was only two months away. He already had packed a set of watercolors, lots of paper, and blocks of pads for her writing in case she felt inspired. When he returned after eleven he found her in the kitchen eating eggs and toast with her coffee.

"Good morning!" He went and gave her a peck on the cheek. He smelled her freshly washed hair. "You smell delicious," he said.

"Are you flirting with me?"

"I know it's not the right time," he said. She moved a hand up to his face, gave him a kiss on both cheeks and returned to her eggs. He sat down next to her.

"You know, I've been thinking about this happening for years. That maybe one day you would show up and ask me to take you some place to disappear. The *bergerie* we both chose is cold and damp — no running water. It's out in the middle of nowhere." He got up and started walking around the kitchen table. He seemed worried. "You might need help one day. How will you communicate?"

"Come on, Jerry. We've been through all this before. The man who lives up the mountain with his huge white dog…what's his name? — Pépé. He makes those beautiful knives that cost a fortune. He's still alive, isn't he? Anyway, between now and the fall I thought you'd come up with supplies once. Please," she smiled. "I'll probably end up talking to myself." She didn't like the idea of being alone for months at a time and knew that it was going to be difficult for her. Since Philip had died she hated to be alone and she had kept busy traveling to visit her friends. Many of these friends now had health problems so she had made great efforts to meet younger, healthier friends while still keeping contact with her pals. Here, there would be no one.

"What about if I had a bike? I could ride down to town and give you a call," she continued studying him as he walked by.

"That's an idea, but then the people in town would get to know you."

"What's wrong with that if I wear a disguise?" She laughed at the idea. "My hair will be gray in a few weeks. I could make my wrinkly skin look more wrinkled. Where could we buy a big brownish-black spot to stick on my face like a mole? Maybe two or three with some hair sticking out of one?" she laughed. They both laughed, breaking the tension. "Sorry," she said. "I'm being silly. What do you suggest?"

"Let's get moving. We have at least three hours to drive before we get there." He was thinking about the roads they'd be taking. "We go through Alès, maybe we can find a store there. There's nothing in Sommières, and by the way, I took the liberty of buying you some clothes."

"Oh, Jerry. You think of everything!" She got up and put her arms around him. It was a comfortable hug. She felt his large potbelly separating their bodies. "I do have that duffel I left behind here years ago. Give me twenty minutes to check it out and we can be on our way, okay?"

The road was clogged with tourist traffic, most who didn't know where they were going. In Alès they stopped for a bite to eat, checked out some stores and bought some hair dye and make up. It was late afternoon by the time they got to Florac, the last relatively large town before the mountains of the Cévennes.

"Why don't we stop for the night in Le Pont de Montvert? It's getting late," Jerry said. He was thinking of the last time they were together many years ago with Philip and some friends. "Remember that little *auberge* — what was it called?" They both went back in time — years back. "La Truite Enchantée," Jerry called out enthusiastically. "Will you share a room with me?" He saw the look she gave him. "We can ask for two beds."

"That sounds good to me. You're right, it will be better to go up in the morning."

They took a sharp right and drove along a winding, smoothly flowing river. The winter thaw had flooded the banks and new growth was just coming out. The *auberge* was on the main road through town. They got out and walked up a steep set of stairs to the entrance and found the owner behind the bar talking to a customer. There was still a room available, but it had just one large bed. Before Jerry refused Lara said that would be fine.

They settled into the room and spent some time looking out at the river from their third floor window. Slowly Jerry put his arm around her. She was happy to have it there, stepped closer to him and laid her head on his shoulder. They turned toward each other, their lips barely touching, and Lara pulled back.

"I think we'd better have supper before we go any further," she kissed him tenderly. "I won't be able to get up and get dressed again. I think I'd just like to spend the rest of the night cuddling with you." Then she wondered and asked, "Is this something you want, too?"

"I've always wanted you," he whispered into her ear. "Even when you were married to Philip, I wanted you. You knew that, didn't you?"

"Yes. It embarrassed me. I was a married woman." His lips moved over hers so she couldn't finish her sentence.

They went down for dinner, although neither was particularly hungry. They spent the night in each other's arms — their union had been successful for both of them and they slept the deep sleep of the satisfied, lulled by the rushing sound of the river below.

The next morning they headed out to the *bergerie* on a winding road through hills, which turned into a mountain. The Lozère. The countryside was spotted with young forests and open spaces where sheep and goats grazed. Streams were in every valley between the hillsides and wild flowers grew profusely wherever they could. It was a beautiful sunny day and even though she was anxious, Lara was happy to be alive and with Jerry.

The road was dirt now, rather bumpy, with sharp rocks and they both wondered if the tires would take it. It twisted and turned, climbed and descended, doubling back and forth in hairpin curves until they neared the crest of a hill where it straightened out. There the fields were filled with huge boulders, disintegrating parts of the mountain worn by the wind and rain. The fires that raged through the area when violent lightning storms rolled over this mountain had changed their colors. Lara and Jerry spotted the familiar rock formation that told them they were approaching the hardly visible turn that would take them down to an old farm and the *bergerie*.

After a steep decline and another sharp curve, the old stone buildings appeared on the right. They pulled up in front of what used to be the home of sheep farmers. About fifty years ago the farmer and his wife who lived there were too old to continue working and living in such a cold place. Five months of winter were followed by seasons with violent storms the rest of the year. Friends of one of Lara's children had bought the place to vacation in during the summer with their large family. They loved this savage countryside. They would hike all day and sometimes camp out under the stars in warm sleeping bags around a campfire. Those were the good old days. Then civilization had caught up with them. A law went into effect that there would be no new building anywhere in the area. Sheep and goats came up from the lowlands and grazed in the summer. Those property holders lucky enough to have sheep could keep their homes and land. The rest was to become a national park.

Lara, knowing that the place wasn't used much after the family's grandfather died, had asked permission to use the house. She hoped no one would be there and no one would come while she was there. If they did, she knew they would be smart enough to keep their mouths shut. And besides, Jerry was to let the owner know that she was there on a spiritual retreat of several months and, if possible, preferred not to be disturbed.

"Looks like I'm lucky," Lara said. "No one is home." She walked up two worn stone steps, pulled out a loose stone, and reached in for a large, heavy key. "It must be as old as the house," she said, looking at it. "How old is this place anyway, you who know your architecture?"

"I'd say between three and four hundred years. Even some of the wood looks that old." He helped her open the door. "We'll pick up some oil for

318

the hinges when we go back into town. And I forgot a chamber pot. We'll get that, too." Lara didn't think she was going back into town.

"What are you talking about? You're leaving me here."

"I need another night with you," he said, taking her empty hand and moving next to her. "I reserved our room for tonight, too, in case I could get you to come back with me.

"Jerry," she kissed him on the nose, "all of a sudden, you're irresistible. It will be more comfortable at the *auberge* than spending the night here."

"Maybe I'll do that, too, tomorrow?" He paused. "It was a question. Don't answer now. We'll see when the time comes."

They unloaded the car and checked out the spring water — cold and clear — and the outhouse.

"If you're here after the snow, you can bring the outhouse into the sheep shed. I'll dig you a hole tomorrow."

The farm was built for harsh weather: all the buildings were attached to the house. Cows and cattle had been housed to the right, *basse cour* were to the left, and then an L-shaped room for the sheep with birthing pens in the middle. She wouldn't have to walk through two or three feet of snow to get to the outhouse when she had to. The glass on all the farm building windows was gone. Perhaps she would move into a city for the winter, a city where she could get lost in the crowd.

The sun was still high that evening at seven o'clock. They were both exhausted and decided to lock up and get down to the *auberge* for a shower and supper before night fell. Lara studied the winding, bumpy road down to the village. "Do you think I can ride down this on a bike?" It would be difficult to maneuver between protruding rocks and potholes at any decent speed and she'd probably have to walk most of the way back up.

"I think you can forget about the bike, don't you?" Jerry said as he braked hard to miss an oncoming car and avoid the gully on the other side. "Isn't that Pépé?" He blew his horn hard, came to a stop and jumped out trying to get Pépé to stop. "Oof. Come on Lara," he called as he started to walk back up the hill to greet his friend.

Pépé stepped out of his new four-by-four jeep and said, "*Salut, mon ami.* And is that Lara?" He squeezed his eyes in surprise. "What brings you here?" He was a large man, well built, with dark, long, curly hair that was turning gray around his ears. His well-kept beard was still pitch black as were his eyes. He was wearing a fishing jacket over a khaki shirt and jeans — had just spent the day fishing, and smelled like fish. He embraced Jerry with a powerful hug and a slap on the back and Lara with a tenderness she hadn't expected.

319

"Come on, Pépé, she's with me," Jerry said.

"Not if I can help it. Lara, you want to be a hermit? What's he talking about?" Pépé stood back and looked at one then the other.

"Actually, I'm moving into the *bergerie* down the mountain from you," she sighed. "For quite a while."

"What's quite a while?"

"I don't know. I'm getting lost and don't want to be found. Mustn't be found."

"She's trying to stay out of trouble," Jerry interjected. "If anybody comes looking for her — you don't know where she is. If she needs you," and a pleading look crossed Jerry's face, "can you be there for her?"

Pépé saw that both of them were tired and worried. The sun was putting on a spectacular show, and he put an arm around each of them turning them toward the sunset.

"Why don't you come home with me for supper, for fresh fish — once this show is over." They stood silently until the last spot of red disappeared behind the mountains.

"We're on our way back to town tonight," Jerry said. Looking at Lara, he asked, "What about tomorrow night?"

"The fish will be smoked by then," Pépé said with an understanding smile. "That's fine with me. How about you, Lara? You can finish your story then." The wind had picked up and it was getting cold. He could feel Lara trembling. "On your way." He gave her fanny a pat and started back to his car. "Can you bring up some fresh bread and a dessert?" he turned and said. "I have everything else."

"What about wine?"

"Oh, you can bring lots of that, too! Thanks. Rosé would be great! See you around seven?"

"We'll be there." Jerry called back.

They returned to La Truite Enchantée and a hot shower, a delicious dinner and bed. Too tired for more than cuddling in each other's arms, they fell asleep.

Lara woke the next morning to the sensation of a loving hand exploring her body. Her dreams had taken her far away to a time when Peter had taught her to discover her own body and what was pleasing to her. She had a hard time coming back to the present. She was afraid to open her eyes to the man who was next to her, yet she knew she had to. He had just covered every intimate part of her, telling her he was ready. Slowly she opened her sleepy eyes and looked at a man who was yearning for her and her body reacted. He felt the moisture between her legs, rolled her over on top of him, moving in such a way that soon they were coupled and moving in harmony. He kept the rhythm slow and Lara asked, "are you playing with me?" and she let out a groan.

"Do you like it?"

"What do you think? It's like electricity shooting through me."

"Let me know when you're about to hit 220 volts."

"I'm almost there." No longer being able to contain herself, the 220 volts shot through her body and she wanted to scream, but was able to hold it to a soft sound that came from deep within. She realized he still had a need and again their movement took on a rhythm, which accelerated until they both hit the 220 volts together.

"This is a moment I'll never forget," Lara said as she slid off and snuggled up next to him.

They fell asleep and were awakened by a knock on the door and heard a voice: "Do you want breakfast?"

"Yes, please. I guess we overslept. We'll be right down. Thank you."

They had a quick breakfast, went back to Florac for the things they still needed and took six bottles of vin rosé for Pépé, and six for Lara. "A bottle opener?" Jerry asked.

"Actually, I could use a Swiss Army knife with a corkscrew. I had to leave mine at home because of all the airline security."

They spent the day settling Lara into the *bergerie*. They brought in wood for an evening fire. Jerry dug a deep hole in the sheep pen, fixed a few boards to make it as comfortable as possible, boarded up a few windows and helped her clean up a few rooms for her long stay. They had lunch in the sun and napped on her future bed. The afternoon passed quickly and they climbed the mountain to Pépé's for supper. Her story was the same for Pépé as it was for anyone else. She didn't know a thing about Peter's work. All she wanted was to know the truth, why he was killed so young. Who had ordered his death? For whom had he been working? She didn't want any money; she didn't want to make any trouble for anyone. She just wanted the truth.

Pépé's home was warm. They enjoyed a copious dinner and two bottles of wine for the three of them. Lara was light-headed.

"I'll drive with you down to the *bergerie*. It's been a fascinating evening. I'm looking forward to knowing you better, Lara."

As Jerry walked out the door Pépé pulled him aside and said in a soft voice: "Fair game? I don't think so. She's mad for you." He looked at Jerry, "I've lost before I begin."

"Let us out at the fork, we'll walk down to the *bergerie*. We need some fresh air after all that wine." Jerry put his hand on Pépé's shoulder. "You smoke a mean fish. Thanks for all you'll be doing for Lara. She's got plenty to keep her busy," he hesitated.

Pépé dropped them off at the fork and watched them walk down the road hand-in-hand.

Jerry left early the next morning. He didn't want to say goody-bye. He was up before sunrise, wrote a note for Lara which he left on the kitchen table and closed the door quietly behind him. Tears filled his eyes as he drove down the mountain. "She'll be fine," he said aloud to himself. "She has everything she needs for months. Pépé will take care of her if she needs help." He took a deep breath. "I can use this time to get back in shape. What's that saying? 'Absence makes the heart grow fonder'?" He put the car into gear and headed home.

Lara found the house comfortable. The luxuries of home were put aside, and she proved to herself how adaptable she could be. In fact, she loved it. For how long was another matter. She had a book she wanted to write and after thirty years she finally had time to paint. Food took on less importance unless she felt sad. If the weather was good, she went for a walk. And then again, she had to be careful. One of the most terrifying things that had ever happened to her had been when she had been out during a fast drop in temperature. A cloud pushed by the wind of an electrical storm darkened the sky and within minutes she couldn't see more than a few feet around her. She wasn't properly dressed and ran as fast as she could but she could not out-run the storm. Lightning started to hit the ground around her, starting small fires, which burned the shrubs on the mountain. If she remained standing she was sure she would be hit and burned also. And nobody would find her. She found a group of boulders and huddled as best she could beneath them. She was trembling from the wet and cold. *I have to stay awake,* she thought, but she was exhausted and slowly fell asleep.

Pépé saw the cloud roll in and wondered how Lara was doing. He waited until the lightning had passed and headed out with his dog. They followed the road in the rain and fog. His dog knew the way. They never got lost when they went to check the farm buildings to make sure nothing had caught fire after the lightning. Even in the worst snowstorms, the dog knew what to do. After walking at a good pace they found the fork and half slid down the incline because of the rushing water. The dog led him right to the door and scratched hard. Pépé knocked loudly. "Lara, is everything all right?" he called. "No answer," he said to the dog and tried the doorknob. The door was locked. He removed the stone, took the key, opened the door and walked in. Everything was in order, and again he called out only to be answered a clap of thunder. He rushed upstairs — she wasn't there. He checked the buildings. She was nowhere to be found. He went back into the house, saw the basket of dirty laundry. "Shipshape, come boy," he said and put the dirty laundry under the dog's nose. "Smell it. Come on, we've got to find her." Shipshape pulled a dirty sock from his master's hand and headed for the door. Shipshape was a farm dog, not a bloodhound, but he seemed to understand what was needed of him.

Pépé locked the door and they were on their way.

It was difficult for the dog to follow a scent with all the rain, so instead of following with his nose to the wet ground, Pépé saw him sniffing the air — up the incline and off to the right. "I hope she hasn't gone too far. Come on, boy, pick up the pace." It was extraordinary that the dog could smell anything except the odor of burned shrubs sizzling in the rain. They ran along the road at a slow pace for about fifteen minutes and the dog suddenly headed up hill pulling hard on his master's arm. It was rough terrain with puddles of rain, jutting rocks, and slippery soil. Shipshape began to growl. He couldn't bark with the clothing in his mouth, and he wasn't going to lose that piece of laundry. He was standing by Lara licking her face when Pépé found them between the boulders. "Good boy, Shipshape, good boy," he said, patting the dog with force. "Now we have to get her home."

He tried to revive Lara. She was a large woman — about 70 kilos — and totally limp. He rubbed her hands, her legs, then her face and head. He rubbed harder and slapped her face. It was getting dark. The light drizzle around them seemed like a claustrophobic shell closing in on them. Visibility: zero. She came to; he tried to lift her, she started to stumble. "We'll never get home." He shifted her weight around and with his arm around her waist felt relatively comfortable, stood up. "Come on, boy. Show us the way home." They headed what seemed to be cross-country, found a road they followed for a while and before Pépé realized they were walking up the slope of the garden in front of his house. He put his wet package in a wooden chair, took off his warm jacket and laid it over her until he had a fire going, could get her undressed and wrapped in a warm blanket.

Shipshape lay on her feet.

The fire was lit, a pot of water was heating on the stove, and Pépé gave Lara a clean shirt, warm sweater, a couple of towels.

When she had changed into the clothes she returned to the room. Pépé had made coffee and handed her a warmed bowl.

She took a sip of the hot, sweet coffee and milk and thought: *Thank you, Lord. And thank you Pépé.*

Shipshape bounded over to Lara. She put her arms around him and snuggled him with thanks. "Come on Shipshape. Down, boy."

Pépé and his dog kept Lara for another twenty-four hours to make sure she was well enough to go home. He was about to give her some advice about going out for a walk when she said, "I know. Always be prepared: jacket, matches, compass and food. What else will I forget?" He didn't answer. She had understood.

"Let me know when Jerry arrives," he said, giving her a big hug. "No need to tell him about this, okay?"

"I'm glad I'm alive and can thank you — and that hound of yours." She turned and walked down to the *bergerie* — happy to be home.

Summer turned to autumn. The days were still warm. The nights were cold. She lit a fire in the chimney only when there was fog and needed to dry out the house; she read by the light of an oil lamp; the batteries had gone dead in the radio. She was living like a hermit now and decided that this life was not for her. She waited impatiently for Jerry to return. He would call twice a month to the States to see if Lara could return to civilization. Obviously it wasn't time.

After nearly three months Lara heard a car pull up onto the grass in front of the door. She ran up the stairs two by two to the attic, removed a slate shingle quietly, and slowly looked at the car. Jerry, it's Jerry, she was ready to yell, but thought twice. Was he alone or had he been forced to bring someone here. Jerry got out of the car, walked around to the other side, and opened the door. A white ball of fur jumped out. It was a junior Shipshape. Jerry had brought company for Lara.

"Lara, are you there?" he called as he removed the stone, found the key, and opened the door. "Lara, it's Jerry and a friend. Where the hell are you? Out for a walk?"

She walked quietly down the stairs. The puppy came to greet her and she sat down to caress it.

"I should have known better. He gets all the attention and I don't get any," Jerry said.

"Who are you?" she asked.

"Come on, Lara."

"You're not the Jerry who left me in July." She put the puppy down, got up and circled him. "My, how you've changed." She put her arms around him and held him tight to her. "Where'd you leave the pillow you used to wear? You look good enough to eat." She nibbled his ear. The electricity was back. Their embrace was tender, their hands adventurous as they walked upstairs. They were together again.

That evening, once the car was unpacked and they had enjoyed a dinner of escalope de veau aux morilles, haricots vert and a delicious, light Beaujolais, Jerry took her hand and said he needed to talk seriously with her. He had several messages from the States. It wouldn't be safe for Lara to surface for a long time. The journalists she had talked to before going into hiding had done a good job. Her story had hit the media and several investigators had embarrassed the government. The public was appalled by reports of the use of human guinea pigs for bio-chemical research without their permission. Peter had been disposable — at least that was what Lara had thought.

Lara sat in shock after hearing the news. Never be herself again? Never see her children or grandchildren?

"Jerry, what have I done? Is this the price I have to pay to learn the truth?" She could feel the tension crawling up her back again. Her shoulders grew stiff and even though she tried deep breathing and relaxation exercises, her neck stiffened and a pounding migraine took hold.

"One of the reasons I didn't come back earlier was to take some time to think of solutions to all this." Jerry said.

He walked behind her and started massaging the knots in her neck. "Next winter we can go to the place where Alexander and Tia take their children to ski. In the summer we'll go to the beach where Maria is with her kids. I haven't figured out a way to see Edgar, but something will come up. We will be replacement grandparents. They'll probably recognize you," he hoped. "Maybe we will even be invited to visit later and all this, of course means," he hesitated, came around in front of her, and took her hands. "You know I don't want to get married again. That's never worked for me." He looked deeply into her sad eyes. "Will you come live with me when it's time? I don't have much to offer you. We've gotten along well when we've been together." He pulled her up into his arms, "I love you — think I always have. Do you think we can work something out?"

Lara was numb. She felt the warmth of his body, knew he loved her, and was unable to answer. They stood together for several minutes and then she pulled away. She didn't want to cry. How many emotions could she feel at one time? Deprived of her identity she felt lonely, abandoned. No more family. No more friends. People who had been part of her life for forty or fifty years. All of that replaced by intrigue and danger. Someone had once said to her, "Do you think that with everything else that's going on they'd spend a fortune looking for you? They have so many more important matters to think about." But the FBI had threatened her in her own kitchen and she had fled to protect her family, who now seemed to be secure.

She knew the man standing in front of her loved her and would protect her. Now she needed time to think about the future, a future so different from the one she had planned on. Staring at him the words came slowly into her mind, but not to her mouth.

"It's so much to think about, let's try to get some sleep. We can talk all day tomorrow and you don't need to decide anything for a while." Jerry took her hand and led her to a chair. "Have a seat. I'll get you a glass of hot milk and honey." He hoped it would soothe her.

They spent the next two days talking and walking. They returned to the Auberge de la Truite Enchantée and by then Lara had decided that it would be wise to continue alone for another few weeks before joining Jerry as his companion. That would give him time to tell his neighbors and friends that a woman was moving in with him. Lara needed to develop a disguise that was easy to maintain. During her last days alone at the *bergerie*, she thought about what she had been through these last months. She took a long walk with her puppy every day — even in the fog. But now she went prepared, properly dressed with food and water. She had learned to recognize the witches' claws of burnt shrubs along the road, and when they ventured into the countryside, she'd tie a long piece of string to one of them. When the string ran out they'd head for home. She had grown to love this safe haven. She would miss it and knew she would return — not to hide, but to live a full life. Her children and grandchildren would come some summer. They would all be together again. And Jerry? He'd probably be a part of her life from now on. She really didn't want to live alone. And she thought she could love him.

She wrote her dreams into her journal and took the time to analyze them. Dreams of her past, of her life's journey, the childhood she felt she had never had. She dreamt of her adventures as a young woman and mother, of her two husbands and her children — the ones she had lost and the four she had had. She dreamt about her search for the truth, the walls and doors.

Camus said something to the effect that every wall has a door. The wall between Lara and the truth was too high to climb. She had found the door. In her dreams it was an old one — very old — made of heavy, hard wood, too dense to penetrate. It was of a dark hue, with huge rusty hinges and enormous nails dating back to prehistoric times. The thick wood was carved with overlaid and interlocking symbols: circles, triangles, eyes, crosses of different shapes, sun, moon, and stars. The lock was old and rusted, the keyhole large and had a complicated shape that no one could look through to see the other side. Probably no key had ever been made to fit the lock. It was the door of secrets, secrets of the past that only the initiated would be able to open.

La Fin
?

Acknowledgments

I would like to thank Cleopatra Mathis for permitting me to attend her creative writing class; Robin Dutcher for teaching me how to write a novel; Jodi Kehoe for typing and correcting the manuscript; Ambassadors Walter Curley, Allen Lukens and Robinson McIlvaine for their research; Jean-Marie Daillet for his editing and correcting foreign languages; Dr. Lea Ceria for her insights; My readers: Ethel Woolverton, Deming Holleran, William H. Woolverton III, Nicola Smith and Elene de Saint Phalle; and most of all, Oliver Goodenough for his continued encouragement and advice and Thomas Dunham for his memory of life in Africa and his constant help on a computer with his editing skills; and of course, my children for their support.

With discretion, I have not named many others who have helped with research.

This novel is a fictional story rooted in history. In some places I have utilized the names of historical people who play a real part in the story. While their depictions are based on their characters and their place in history, this is a novel and no implication or conclusion of any kind should be drawn from it about real events in which they, or any other person might have participated.